It begins in Laos, when a brash young American journalist witnesses a hideous murder, and is bold enough and foolish enough to start following a story which ends up following him...

"SOMETHING NEW IN THE DANGEROUS ADVENTURE LINE... ENOUGH ACTION FOR SEVERAL BOOKS!"
—*San Francisco Chronicle*

"RICH VARIETY OF VILLAINS... FROM MARTIN BORMANN AND SPIRO AGNEW TO WATERGATE AND OPEC!"
—*New York Times*

ONYXX

TONY CHIU

BERKLEY BOOKS, NEW YORK

Epigraph and lines on p. 340 from THE COCKTAIL PARTY, copyright © 1950 by T.S. Eliot; renewed 1978 by Esme Valerie Eliot. Reprinted by permission of Harcourt Brace Jovanovich, Inc., and Faber and Faber Ltd.

Previously published as PORT ARTHUR CHICKEN

This Berkley book contains the complete
text of the original hardcover edition.
It has been completely reset in a type face
designed for easy reading, and was printed
from new film.

ONYXX

A Berkley Book / published by arrangement with
William Morrow and Company, Inc.

PRINTING HISTORY
William Morrow edition published 1979
Berkley edition / August 1981

All rights reserved.
Copyright © 1979 by Tony Chiu.
This book may not be reproduced in whole or in part,
by mimeograph or any other means, without permission.
For information address: William Morrow and Company, Inc.
105 Madison Avenue, New York, New York 10016.

ISBN: 0-425-05004-1

A BERKLEY BOOK ® TM 757,375
Berkley Books are published by Berkley Publishing Corporation,
200 Madison Avenue, New York, New York 10016.
PRINTED IN THE UNITED STATES OF AMERICA

Acknowledgments

For their help in the writing of this book, I thank:
Carole Abel, Kathryn Alvarez, Richard Blystone, Claudia Dowling, Kashiyo Enokido, Max Geltman, Rae Geltman, Harry Johnston, Alexandra Mezey, Alan Parter, Rick Spreyer, Martha Sternberg, Norman Snyder, and Frank Wohl.

TOBY AND
HSI-CHIH,
WITH LOVE

But let me tell you, that to approach the stranger
Is to invite the unexpected, release a new force,
Or let the genie out of the bottle.
It is to start a train of events
Beyond your control.

—T. S. Eliot, *The Cocktail Party*

Introduction

I know that on November 26, 1975, a Red Flag limousine left a government building off T'ien An Men Square in Peking and sped through the morning chill to Capital Airport. At the terminal the Chairman's personal secretary stepped from the vehicle. Awaiting him was a diplomatic courier. The courier quickly unlocked the pouch chained to his left wrist; the secretary deposited an envelope bearing the *t'u chang*, or personal seal, of the Chairman, watched the courier lock the pouch, and then accepted the key.

The courier boarded an Iran Air flight to Tokyo and, after a three-hour layover, continued on Air Canada to Ottawa. There he was driven from the airport to the People's Republic Embassy on St. Andrew Street. The ambassador himself unlocked the pouch, removed the single item from within, and handed the Chairman's letter to a low-level aide in the agricultural mission. This aide was in fact an intelligence officer.

On November 28, 1975, the intelligence officer signed out a grey Ford from the Embassy motor pool. As he headed toward the center of Ottawa he watched in his rearview with some amusement as an inexperienced Mountie in a black Plymouth tried to shadow him inconspicuously. Thirty minutes later he pulled into an underground car park. On the third level he spotted a space next to a wall and jockeyed his Ford into it so its right side was exactly three feet from the wall. A brief call by public telephone to a youth hostel, and finally the intelligence officer embarked on a leisurely ramble through the downtown stores.

At 11:15 A.M., forty minutes after receiving the call, a female Chinese-American architectural student from New York entered the car park. She descended three levels and located the grey Ford. Hidden from view by car and wall, she knelt by the right front wheel and pried off the hubcap: taped inside, and thoughtfully wrapped in a Glad Bag, was the envelope bearing the Chairman's *t'u chang*.

On November 30, 1975, the student flew back to New York. That afternoon she left her apartment near Columbia University and subwayed to the Canal Street station, from which she pressed, through Chinatown's clot of Sunday shoppers, to a restaurant on the west side of Doyers Street. On the second floor there were five private banquet rooms. She entered the second-from-last room, grasped a wall-mounted lighting fixture near the door, and turned it ninety degrees counterclockwise.

A section of the far wall slid silently to the right.

The student stepped through and into a private banquet room of a restaurant fronting on Mott Street. The man waiting for the envelope was an attaché to the People's Republic delegation to the United Nations. He was also the Chinese Chief of Intelligence/North America.

An hour later, at the People's Republic mission on West Sixty-seventh Street, the Intelligence Chief unlocked the door of a windowless room on the fifth floor. The walls of this "safe room" were reinforced with concrete and lead, as were ceiling and floor. The Intelligence Chief relocked the door, seated himself at a large, square ebony table and opened the envelope. The two notes inside, one in Chinese and the other in English, also bore the Chairman's *t'u chang*. As the Intelligence Chief began to read his pulse quickened: back in Peking his mentor's course of action had obviously won the day. But that victory must be vulnerable to factional sabotage, for the notes had come by way of an unorthodox network of sympathetic hands rather than by direct diplomatic pouch. Finally the Intelligence Chief reharnessed his concentration; he memorized his instructions and then carried out the first order by feeding notes and envelope into the safe room's shredder.

On January 13, 1976, the unlisted telephone in a San Clemente, California, den began to ring. A male aide answered. The caller identified himself as "Mr. Patton"; within one minute Mr. Patton's party was on the line.

"Uh, hello?"

"Morning, Searchlight. This is Yangtze."

There was a sharp intake of breath—how did the caller know his Secret Service code name?

"You recording this?" the caller asked.

Still silence.

The caller chuckled. "Have it your way. Listen: 'The second crop of one hundred flowers has been hit by an unseasonable hailstorm. You will of course wish to personally inspect the damage, so we have arranged transportation.' Be ready February twentieth, okay?"

"Shit!" But the expletive might as well have been deleted for the caller had hung up. When Searchlight slammed down his receiver sweat streaked the talc on his fresh-shaven jowls.

On February 6, 1976, it was announced that the man from San Clemente had accepted an invitation relayed by his younger daughter and her husband and would shortly be the personal guest of the Chairman. The White House was not amused; at the start of an election year, surely the trip would be a red flag in front of those who'd never pardoned the pardon.

On February 20, 1976, Searchlight was chauffered the fifty miles from his Elba-on-the-Pacific to Los Angeles International Airport. The Chinese jet liner dispatched for him made refueling stopovers in Anchorage and Tokyo before landing Capital Airport in Peking.

The day was cold and misty. Searchlight scowled when he saw the disappointing crowd, a cadre of 350 bused to the airport on the Chairman's orders. Noticeably absent, were the honor guard and military band and greeting line of high dignitaries that had made his last visit, just four years to the day earlier, such a pompous circumstance. Slowly Searchlight picked his way down the metal steps. He was almost inside the idling Red Flag limousine when he remembered to smile thinly at the press contingent.

On February 22, 1976, three hours before the banquet in his honor at the Great Hall on T'ien An Men Square, Searchlight was in his lakeside guesthouse refining his ad libs when he heard a gentle knock. The messenger carried a note politely commanding the American to an audience with the Chairman in thirty minutes.

Searchlight was apprehensive when he arrived outside the reception room in another part of the complex. Waiting there was the young, American-schooled woman who was the Chairman's personal interpreter. "Good afternoon, Mr. President! You look marvelously well. I trust your journey was not too taxing?"

"Why, thank you, Miss, uh, Miss Tang. I, uh..." When Searchlight grinned, he bared his teeth. "I thought the Chairman's and me's—uh, my session was scheduled for tomorrow."

"This is so. But the Chairman also has business of, shall we say, a more discreet nature that he wishes to conduct with you. He does not feel such affairs should be known by others. Please." The interpreter opened the door and stood back. "Unfortunately, Mr. President, I will not have the honor of translating for you and the Chairman. However, the other gentleman in the room, Comrade Tsu, has an impeccable command of the English language. Of course, I will have the privilege of seeing you at the banquet tonight." She smiled, waited until he entered, and then closed the door.

Searchlight looked about quickly. As usual there were several high-backed armchairs facing away from where he stood. As usual a cluster of darkened klieg lights loomed in front of the armchairs and, in the midst of the lights, a tripod-mounted Sony videotape camera. Somehow, though, the reception room seemed smaller than he remembered.

A slim Chinese man in his early thirties was adjusting the Sony. He looked up, saw Searchlight, and promptly strode over. "An honor, sir. I am Franklin Tsu."

"Your English is indeed impeccable," Searchlight blurted.

Just then a muffled cough. Searchlight thought it came from behind the new maroon drapery along the far wall, but Comrade

Tsu seemed not to have heard the sound, for he said, "Thank you. I was graduated from the University of the Pacific, just up the coast from your alma mater." Then he put a hand to the visitor's elbow and guided him into the room.

When the American saw the Chairman already seated in one of the armchairs, he automatically beamed and thrust his right hand up in awkward salutation. The Chairman—heavily drugged on L-dopa in an attempt to arrest the ravages of Parkinson's disease—gazed back vacantly; slowly, a gob of drool slid out of the left corner of his mouth and down his chin. Searchlight was undeterred. Cranking up his smile another notch and striding toward his host, he boomed, in his best stump bass, "My good Chairman!"

The Chairman deliberately closed his palsied eyelids and rasped out a single word: *"Pu!"*

Confused, Searchlight stopped and looked back to Comrade Tsu.

"In general it means 'no,' in this context it means 'no further.'" As Comrade Tsu continued to talk Searchlight, growing pale as a fresh lichee's flesh, protested profanely. The Chinese replied, "But you have no alternative . . . sir," and calmly finished presenting the meeting's agenda.

"Why?" Searchlight's voice was a hoarse whisper. "Why this?"

"You know of Voitinskii?"

"Uh, uh . . ."

"Voitinskii was a Comintern lackey sent by Moscow in the nineteen-twenties to 'instruct' our Chinese comrades. He was nothing but a corrupt revisionist jackal. Furthermore, he forced many of our comrades to submit as you shall shortly submit. He claimed it would bind them to the international brotherhood." Comrade Tsu glanced at the Chairman. "Our Great Helmsman thinks it appropriate that such barbarism be revisited on a barbarian."

With that Comrade Tsu walked to the far wall and pulled back the new maroon drape.

Searchlight began to quiver. The reception room had seemed smaller because the drape was actually a partition that had concealed a large platform, and on the platform stood an operating table and a medical team dressed for surgery.

Now Comrade Tsu was at the kliegs. He flipped them on and activated the Sony; then he started to give stage directions.

Searchlight had lapsed into a daze as profound as the Chairman's but the orders penetrated, for he slowly walked to the seated figure. From up close the Chairman looked, if possible, even worse: only eye whites showed through half parted lids, and beneath his gaping mouth the meaty chin was aglisten with spittle. The American drew himself to attention and performed three stiff kowtows.

Then, as Comrade Tsu panned the camera, Searchlight made his way to the platform and mounted it. He hesitated. Comrade Tsu spoke again. With one last plaintive look at the camera, Searchlight wrestled off trousers and drawers and climbed onto the operating table. Comrade Tsu hoisted the Sony from its tripod onto his right shoulder and approached to within six feet.

Now a young male doctor stepped to the operating table. As soon as Searchlight saw the five-inch-long needle, he shut his eyes. When he dared look some forty-five seconds later, he couldn't believe that the acupuncture needle, which was rigged by wires to a small grey box that hummed, had already been positioned deep in his groin.

Now the kliegs were glinting off the scalpel in the hand of the surgeon. Searchlight shut his eyes again and began to pant. The surgeon, a female, lightly pricked the operative area. No reaction: it was fully numbed, so she grasped the foreskin, stretched it free of the limp erectile tissues, and began delicately to slice it away.

Halfway through the circumcision Searchlight looked. He shouldn't have.

Just then Comrade Tsu pivoted with the Sony and zoomed back to the Chairman's face. Even without floodlights in his eyes, the Chairman's vision had so deteriorated he could barely see past his own hands. His hearing, though, was unimpaired, and as he heard Searchlight's harsh, primitive, labored grunts, his moist lips came together and curled slightly upward at the corners.

Ten minutes later the surgeon knotted the last suture. Two assistants hurried forward to cleanse Searchlight's thighs. Next the injection of 100 mg of morphine into the patient's right buttock; Searchlight winced, for it was the first pain he had felt. When the anesthesiologist was sure the morphine had taken effect he gently removed the acupuncture needle from the American's groin. Then the surgical team stepped from the platform and in single file left the reception room.

No matter how often Searchlight wiped his face the sweat returned. Finally he eased himself off the operating table and, averting his eyes from the bloodstained dressing, struggled gingerly back into drawers and trousers.

Now Comrade Tsu spoke again.

Searchlight stepped from the platform and, with the Chinese still operating the Sony in tow, wobbled to a nearby desk on which were a sheet of paper, an envelope, a pen, and a red ink pad. He picked up the sheet and started to read. Ten seconds later he was clutching the desk for support. Then the moment passed; Searchlight skimmed the rest of the page, wiped his mouth with the back of a hand, and picked up the pen. When he finished his task, he held the envelope up to the camera. On the back his signature, and across the sealed flap, like a poor man's *t'u chang*, his thumbprint in red ink; on the front his signature again, beneath a brief passage typed in English:

> For behaving dishonorably toward all the comrades of the People's Republic of China, I have of my own free will consented to the token act of contrition witnessed on this videotape, and to sign the document within this envelope.

Now Comrade Tsu pulled back for one more pan—past Searchlight, who stared glassily into the camera, to the Chairman, still slumped in his armchair—before returning the Sony to its tripod and switching off the kliegs. Then he pressed a buzzer.

Instantly two female attendants entered the reception room. One prepared tea on the low table between the armchairs, the other set down a tray containing hot face towels and a vial of pills.

Comrade Tsu coaxed Searchlight into an empty armchair and gently wiped the American's face and ink-stained thumb. Next he forced him to take a few sips of tea brewed from the finest Yunnanese leaves. Finally Comrade Tsu picked up the vial. "These are morphine tablets. You shall feel discomfort for about a week, or until the dressing is removed."

Searchlight nodded. Slowly his color returned. And then he was sobbing uncontrollably; dropping the teacup onto his lap, he clutched his face and toppled, almost in slow motion, out of the armchair, and now he was rolling around on the superb sixteenth-century Tibetan rug, and now, with tears coursing down his cheeks, he was nestling into a fetal position, and now he was rhythmically smashing his fist into the tightly woven wool: "Noooo . . . why . . . how could this . . . how could this happen to me . . . oh my God noooo . . ."

Comrade Tsu knelt and gently shook Searchlight's shoulders. "Sir, perhaps it is time for you to refresh yourself. The banquet commences in less than ninety minutes."

I know of these events because I have in my possession:

* A report describing the above, written in Chinese by a high CCP cabinet official who survived the post-Mao "Gang of Four" purge;

* Several hundred feet of electronic videotape, including the segment recorded in the Peking reception room on February 22, 1976;

* And most important, three envelopes, including the one that Searchlight signed and sealed in the Peking reception room on February 22, 1976.

These were given me last month by a representative of the People's Republic of China.

Why?

First, it's Peking's way of thanking me for my role in unearthing a plot that might well have crippled China's economic development. My involvement was inadvertent, but it has thus far led to two attempts on my life; this new information, along with documents and artifacts I'd previously collected, should preclude a third.

Second, those who passed me the precious evidence knew its possession would enable me to write this book. The People's Republic hardly emerges as a heroic force in the global machinations that follow, but then the regime that participated in many of the events has, like the Great Helmsman himself, passed on. I must therefore conclude that Peking has more to gain than to lose by full exposure of an intrigue that began in 1966 and took a decade to halt.

To reconstruct my part in this intrigue I will rely on my collected data, my diary, my notes, and, of course, my memory. Certain names, addresses, and telephone numbers—both personal and corporate—will be altered; the degree of anonymity I provide will depend on my residual goodwill toward the real-life individuals. The conversations in the book will be based partly on transcripts of tape-recorded interviews and partly re-created. In the latter case the dialogue will be at least eighty percent accurate in specifics, ninety percent accurate in tone and spirit, and a hundred percent accurate in substance.

It is now a sunny Thursday afternoon. From my window I can see a hard breeze whipping miniature whitecaps out on the Bosporus; a ferry is bucking up the strait while a Turkish oil tanker cruises down from the Black Sea. Such sights will be my main touchstones to the outside world until I can complete my manuscript and thus not only guarantee two lives but more important, liberate two souls.

RAYMOND HUANG

Vanikoy, Turkey
March 1977

Book I

16 February 1972: Vientiane

From the balcony of the Hotel Constellation the vaporous glow of the scattered streetlights on the avenue below made the city look like London on a foggy night. But it was the dry season, so it was dust scuffed up during the day and not mist hanging over the capital of Laos. I stepped back into my room. My travel alarm clock read 9:30, which meant I'd napped three hours since my return from up-country. The sleep had not refreshed.

Downstairs, the proprietor of the Constellation manned the front desk. It was because of Maurice that I had booked here. His reputation throughout Southeast Asia—considerable, even among travelers like me—had little to do with his admittedly mingy establishment; there were far nicer beds in town. Rather, it stemmed from the fact that if in those years Vietnam was Big Muddy, then Laos was one of its soggy banks, on which gingerly trod newsmen and intelligence agents of all nations. In this cloak-and-dagger atmosphere, the Constellation had evolved into the capital's leading atelier for rumor addicts, with Maurice its guiding patron.

Back in the States I would never have sat at a bar and eavesdropped. At the Constellation it was not only unavoidable—the juicier the morsel the louder the stage whisper—but downright fun. In fact there were times I longed for my trench coat, even in this saunalike climate, or one of those boldly tailored, telegenic-blue bush suits that made correspondents like Morley Safer look so damned in-the-know.

Tonight the bar was empty. But then it was early yet.

"Good evening, Maurice," I said. "Where can I get a bite at this hour?"

He glanced across the lobby to where his cook and three waiters were deep in a poker game, discarded the notion as preposterous, and sighed. "This is Wednesday, no? Yes, they will all be at the Café de la Paix tonight." Maurice gave me directions to the restaurant and then asked if I'd had a successful trip to the North.

Very, I replied, thinking about my visits to the splendid *vats*, or Buddhist temples, of Luang Prabang and to a "school" where elephants were trained to haul cut logs out of the dense teak forests. I'd recorded more than enough on paper and on film for two solid articles. "By the way," I said, "I think I spotted some Pathet Lao—don't they dress like garbage collectors?"

Maurice's eyes flicked nervously about the room, giving me the sinking feeling that comes with finding a foot—your own—in your mouth, for the Pathet Lao was no joking matter; these grim young insurgents were slowly winning their battle to turn their officially neutral homeland Red. Then the moment passed. Seeing no one had overheard my gaffe, Maurice relaxed and said, *"Bon appétit, monsieur."*

Four days in the country had taught me that Godot would sooner cruise by than a cab so I began walking to the restaurant. It was warm and muggy, like an August night in New York. And dark, except for the inverted yellow cones that shone down from the occasional streetlight. The silence was so deep the air hummed.

I was on Rue Sam Sen Thai when I picked up low voices chitchatting up ahead. Beneath the next streetlight a cluster of men in neatly pressed khakis and natty maroon berets; these were troops of the Royalist government. As I passed, several gave me curious once-overs. Understandably so: though my dress and walk were those of a Westerner, my face looked an awful lot like theirs.

I remember being chagrined that after five weeks in the Orient I was still so self-conscious. For though born of Chinese parents, I had grown up American. To be more precise, the kind of advantaged American cushioned suburbs produce. Had my parents been less intelligent, less cosmopolitan, I'd probably have appreciated the "old ways" more. But in their desire for me to integrate they had indulged me: baseball before Chinese lessons, Saturday afternoons at the movies instead of at the feet of visiting elders, hamburgers rather than pepper steak. When I was a teen-ager they had even courted the ire of Westchester County's small but tightly knit Chinese community by not requiring me to date another family's eligible but desperately ugly daughter.

To be sure, assimilation had not been entirely painless. My father, an engineer, had wanted me to take up a "serious" profession. Such as his, or medicine or the law or accounting or even bookmaking, which, if not serious, was at least profitable. But they'd been too lenient with me. When I took stock of my talents—I was a quick study and reasonably glib—I chose to become a writer.

My father's opposition had waned when after college I latched onto a staff job with a newsmagazine, but flared anew when I quit to go off on my own. I defended my decision by saying I wanted out of the squirrel cage, that my satisfaction came from seeing through to a good conclusion projects more fulfilling than condensing seven days' news into 850 words. His answer—entirely in Chinese, a tactic he saved for when he was livid with me—was that I lacked perserverance. The phrase he used, "lazy turtle," is very high up on our list of terminal insults.

Be that as it may, I had built a decent practice in New York hammering out magazine pieces, industrial film narrations, and book rewrites from my West Village apartment. Along the way I'd even taught myself to take publishable photographs to illustrate my articles, though few big-league magazines would be so foolish as to commission my camera alone. The fact that I was by then earning in the high teens and low twenties didn't appease my parents, though. Slick 1,500-word essays on a movie star's psyche or dragonfly reproduction cycles or laser technology weren't "serious," and photography—well, that's only good for filling up the family album. Or so my father had volunteered recently when he and my mother returned East for what was to have been a pleasant celebration of my thirty-first birthday.

That blowup was one of the pressures that had driven me to take the trip I was on. Another was my increasingly sedentary stream of assignments; I used to get out of New York at least a couple of times a year to do pieces, but hadn't in the past eighteen months. If as Fitzgerald wrote action is character, then I was turning into an ass, because that's what I sat on as I researched and wrote. There was still a third reason I needed to quit the city for a while: within the preceding eight months I'd fallen for a lady whose only drawback, in my subjective eyes, was her husband.

In the end my accountant sparked my journey. We were lunching to assess my indebtedness to the IRS when he ventured that if I could bag just a few assignments, I'd be able to deduct most of any trip I took. Having no desire to do Europe again, especially in wintertime, I decided on the Orient. I fired off a barrage of queries; within the month I had four firm assignments and five written expressions of interest. So shortly after a New Year's Eve I did not spend with Martha—she had separated from Tim but was committed to attending a party with him—I jetted out of Kennedy for Tokyo.

Though my impressions of the Far East had been based on such movies as *Blood Alley* and *The Ugly American*, it had taken me less than a week to become an instant Asia Hand. How? By haunting the foreign press hangouts in each country. In those years the Far East was inundated by hotshot journalists who chased wars as some lawyers chase ambulances. Not only did I soon know who was probably doing what to whom, but cultivating the Fourth Estate had paid off in practical terms: I was passed, like a relay-race baton, from one set of correspondents to the next. If the cynicism along the young boys' network could get wearisome, at least I'd been guided through six countries with an expertise that Baedeker might have envied. For instance, I had been rightly steered to the Constellation in Vientiane. And in Hong Kong, where I'd be on the morrow after a two-hour layover in Bangkok, I'd again check into the Fortuna on Nathan Road while I completed my last assignment. Then, home.

I was coming up on another streetlight and another group of Royalist soldiers. Several of them scrutinized me and again I felt the flush of acute self-awareness. Because I had never experienced that sensation in the States or while touring Europe, I'd taken to wrestling with my problem, for that was what I judged it. I'd finally got a handle on it three weeks ago. I was in predominantly Chinese Singapore when a bunch of German tourists stopped me for directions. My first impulse had been to answer, "How the hell would I know—I'm an American." So what it was, was an identity crisis. How ironic that it should strike me on my ancestral side of the world.

Suddenly off to my right a series of sharp reports.

Several Royalists flung themselves to the ground. One soldier nervously raised his rifle. After a split-second hesitation their leader, though flinching, made himself edge forward and peer into the darkness. He was greeted by the high-pitched laughs of the youngsters who'd set off the firecrackers.

I let out my breath, shaken by the unexpected reminder that sleepy Vientiane was in fact a war zone, with the dreaded Pathet Lao encamped around its outskirts. I remembered one pundit at the Constellation expounding on why the Communists had yet to take the city, which they could have with ease: "They can quote Chairman Mao all right, but the Little Red Book doesn't teach you how to patch up a sewage system." In other words, civil administration wasn't a Pathet Lao forte.

Fifteen yards past the regrouping troops I cut across one of Vientiane's parched parks to Rue du Boun. Two blocks up on the right shafts of light and noise spilled from a building and ricocheted through the hushed night: the Café de la Paix was still serving. As I entered, a party of well-to-do Laotians was leaving, having consumed its French meal of the week. Save for the waiters I was now the only Oriental in the room.

"Ray... Ray, over here." A hand was waving from behind a potted palm so I walked over to it. It belonged to David Thurston, an ex-Peace Corpsman I'd met at the Constellation's bar the night before I headed up-country. "Come on, join us," David said. "Allman never showed." With him were Jubilee, an Australian bird he'd hooked up with in Singapore, and a squat, swarthy man I'd not seen before. "You know Jubilee, and this is Ivan Arkadian. Ivan, Ray Huang, an American journalist."

Ivan nodded and filled my tumbler from the bottle by his

side. "Vodka," he grunted. I thanked him. "You write?" When I nodded he said, "You hear maybe of William Saroyan?"

"Of course."

"He Armenian too." Ivan broke out in a huge smile, sat back, and tossed down what remained in his tumbler.

"Ivan's the Soviet cultural attaché to Laos," David explained.

Ivan smiled at me.

I smiled back, then turned to Jubilee. "How come you're not at your restaurant tonight?" I asked, for I knew that after meeting David, she had talked him out of going home to Dallas and into becoming a wire-service stringer in Vientiane while she founded the country's first Korean soul-food shop, a place called Seoul Chitlins.

"Look around, luv." She gestured at the crowd. "In this town them's as can afford eating out do it in a group, and the group prefer a different place each night. So it's the old French Army Commissary on Mondays, Tan Dao Vien on Tuesdays and so on." She sighed. "Friday's my place." Then she brightened. "You going to be around for some ribs and *kimchee*?"

"Afraid not, luv."

A waiter came by for my order.

"What's good here, Jubilee?"

"Escargots."

"Here?"

"They use land snails."

I settled for *bifteck* and wine.

"How was Luang Prabang?" David asked.

"Worth the trip. But God am I tired—your contact got me up before dawn every day, and he must have felt for the money he owed me entertainment at night, too, because he kept dragging me to whorehouses and opium dens."

The waiter returned with my wine. It was nothing the French vintner who synthesized it would drink, but then Laos was just a far-off ex-colony, emphasis on the ex. Anyway it was wet, it cost all of 700 kip, or about eighty cents, and it was a welcome change from quaffing local beer or Coke with your meal. Around us journalists were interviewing each other—a visiting *Newsweek* nabob was pontificating on what Senator Ed Muskie's Polish policy would be if he gained the presidency he sought—and spies were swapping white lies and embassy staffers were discussing what could be bought cheap, and where.

Suddenly Ivan bolted to his feet and hoisted his refilled tumbler. "A toast on that greatest U.S. of A. writer, William Saroyan!" The babble in the room stopped for two beats. Ivan sat down. Slowly conversations resumed.

"What did you get up at Luang Prabang?" Jubilee asked.

"About five rolls on the *vats*. Caught them at sunset, like you suggested. And I did manage to get up to the elephant school."

"Elephant school?" Ivan asked. "What teach?"

"Oh, a little Hegelian dialectic. The smart ones learn to hum the 'Internationale.'"

It was the funniest thing Ivan had ever heard, or a liter of vodka had softened him up for an elephant joke. Either way he giggled himself right onto the floor. This time he went unnoticed; in Vientiane heads turned for a toast on Saroyan but not for a drunk hitting the deck.

I was halfway through my meal and two-thirds of the way through my bottle of wine when I glanced up at the door, looked away, and then did the biggest double take of my life. Once, like every New York photographer, I'd shot a photo essay on Bowery bums. But that was three years ago and twelve thousand miles away—what was this refugee from the Lower East Side doing here?

He was tall—about six feet three—gaunt, and old. His white hair flowed down onto his shoulders. His black suit was shiny from age and a full two sizes too large; the jacket was buttoned high but couldn't conceal the fact that he wore no shirt. His bare feet were jammed into high-cut black sneakers. And to complete the picture, he carried a brown paper bag that obviously concealed a bottle.

As I stared, the man entered the Café de la Paix and thereby changed my life.

"What do you say, Ray?" It was David.

"What?"

"I said it's almost time for the ten-thirty show at Lulu's, and then we're going over to Simone's for a couple of hits."

That seemed to be the evening's game plan, for all around us people were requesting checks. I'd been to Lulu's Rendezvous des Amis once and seen the rather gross strippers. I'd not visited Simone's, having no desire to develop an opium addiction. Neither now appealed so I said, "I can't, David. I'm on the morning flight, and I've got a lot of paperwork to catch up on."

"Oh, come on, luv," Jubilee said. "Lulu found a fab sheila up in the hills who does smoke rings out her you-know-what."

"I was going to order dessert until just now," I said, wincing.

By this time the white-haired man had taken a table less than ten feet from ours and was sitting with his eyes closed in apparent meditation.

I turned to David and whispered, "Any idea who that guy is?"

"Nope. I've seen him around once or twice—probably some Pentagon biggie who predicted the boys would be home by Sixty-seven."

Jubilee leaned over and said, "No, he's a defrocked minister. You know, got caught boffing the female parishioners or some such."

Just then a waiter approached the man and, addressing him as *"monsieur le professeur,"* apologized in French for taking so long. Without opening his eyes the man ordered. "The fish if it's fresh," he said in a midwestern American accent, "and string beans. And a bowl of ice." As the waiter passed our table David asked him to tab their bill. I hesitated, then ordered another bottle of wine.

"You're going to stake out Judge Crater," David said, laughing. As I smiled sheepishly my three companions rose; we wished each other well and then they staggered toward the door.

As they left, two surly Laotians incongruously sporting dark glasses loomed out of the blackness. In any country their function would have been obvious: muscle. They scanned the room, spotted the white-haired man, and then headed for a table near the door. The owner of the restaurant approached them and pointed to another table. The thinner thug removed his dark glasses; whatever he sneered sent the owner into a bowing and scraping retreat.

The old man's eyes were still closed. For the sake of appearances I took out my little spiral notebook and began to scribble sweet nothings. I was feeling rather silly sitting there, and was toying with the idea of canceling the wine and settling my bill, when the waiter swung by and deposited the fresh bottle on my table.

Then he set a bowl of ice before my mystery man, who thereupon opened his eyes and shed fifteen years—his pupils were cerulean marbles set in the whitest whites this side of a Visine commercial. The man reached a large, meticulously manicured hand into his paper bag. The sixteen-ounce amber bottle, which once held one of the region's favorite beverages, 33 Beer, sweated heavy condensation. He removed its cork, poured two inches of a pale, unbeerlike fluid into his tumbler, and screwed the bottle into the ice cubes. Now he sipped his drink and allowed himself a smile.

I was starting to get hooked.

The man dipped into a side pocket for a pair of gold-rimmed aviation glasses. Next he extracted from his right breast pocket a gold Mark Cross ball-point and a neat sheaf of papers, from which he pulled a prefolded aerogram. Opening the sheet and smoothing it out, he began to write. The man worked slowly, as if precision mattered. At one point he raised his left hand to gently massage his temple. That's when I glimpsed his watch: the band was a cheap strip of clear plastic but the instrument itself was unmistakably a gold Patek Philippe.

I was hooked.

When the waiter brought his meal the man put aside his letter. Now I could feel my string of eighteen-hour workdays and the vodka and wine of the evening catching up. Yet that very same languid semi-sobriety, coupled with the wonderful flush that accompanies voyeurism, rooted me to my seat; I refilled my tumbler.

The man finished his meal and resumed writing. It went much faster this time; he must have been composing as he ate. He was sealing the flaps of the aerogram when the waiter arrived to clear the dishes. The man asked for a *café filtre*, then stood and headed for the john in the rear. By now there were only two other tables of diners in the café, plus the muscle boys by the door. On his return the man poured himself a demitasse, unfolded a second aerogram, and began writing again.

Suddenly, a soft burring sound. The man automatically reached to his left wrist and touched his watch. The burring ceased. Then he peered at his Patek Philippe, angling it up to catch the light. I could see the face clearly: 4:11.

I sneaked a glance at my own watch. It was 11:11, at least in Vientiane.

The man hurriedly removed his glasses, gathered up his papers, and threw some kips on the table. The two surly Laotians were already on their feet, the thinner one ducking out of the café and turning left. When the white-haired man reached the door the other thug signaled him to wait. Then a light whistle floated down the silent street; the Laotian waved my man on and fifteen seconds later followed him through the door.

I sighed and motioned for my bill. As I awaited my change I noted that the 33 Beer bottle had been left behind, and that it still held a half inch of liquid. Unable to resist, I went over, picked it up, and sniffed the mouth. It smelled like wine. I took a swig. Now, I know very little about wines, or I should say wines retailing for more than $3.99 a bottle, but I recognized this one: a Pouilly Fumé, quite possibly vintage. It figures, I thought, a strange end to a strange evening.

I was setting the bottle down when I spotted something blue on the floor. It was an aerogram, most probably knocked under the table when the waiter cleared the dishes. I bent down, picked it up, and was almost out the door when I heard the waiter calling. I signaled him to keep the change and started jogging along Rue du Boun in pursuit of the old man.

Suddenly a block ahead the heavier Laotian, who faced away from me, darted out of the shadows and across the street. I pulled up fast—even from that distance, in the dimness, I could see the gun in his hand. Now what? After a moment's hesitation I found myself continuing to edge forward along the darkened storefronts.

Now the Laotian sprinted for the small park I'd traversed on my way to the restaurant. He pulled up behind a large tree, paused several counts, and then stalked out into the park, gun at the ready. I made my way to the last building on the street and slowly peered around the corner. The dust of the day was finally settling so I could see, with remarkable clarity:

The heavier Laotian in the middle of the park, some fifteen yards ahead of me, still in an anticipatory stoop;

My gaunt, black-garbed man some thirty yards in front of his rear guard, passing under a streetlight as he started across Rue Sam Sen Thai;

And the thinner Laotian already across Sam Sen Thai and turning past a high wall onto a side street.

As my man strolled toward the same side street I had time to notice that the Royalist troops who had been bivouacked on Sam Sen Thai earlier were now all gone.

The man disappeared behind the high wall.

Now a *pop* that sounded like backfire, then the whine of a car being started.

The older Laotian began sprinting forward.

A squeal—tires under sudden acceleration—and then a sickening *whummpp*, like a fifty-pound sack of meal hitting the floor.

The American's body came arcing back past the high wall. As it somersaulted lazily some five feet off the ground objects spun out of pockets and the metal and glass among them described their own glittering orbits beneath the streetlight. The body landed in the middle of the street, bouncing hard enough to throw off one sneaker.

Another squeal of tires and a black Mercedes 280SE with its lights dimmed skidded out of the side street and onto Sam Sen Thai. The heavier Laotian opened fire. From the Mercedes' left rear window an automatic weapon stuttered. The Laotian spun like a rag doll, the front of his body suddenly crimson. Still the weapon roared. Several rounds spanked off the building I cowered behind; others glanced off the walls across Rue du Boun; still others sang into the dark night. The Mercedes hopped the curb, drove directly through the small park—passing some six feet from my prone body—and raced toward the Mekong River.

Even as I lost my dinner I was memorizing the license-plate number of the car. It was of Thai registry.

A hush fell again over Vientiane. I began to shiver. Not a light had gone on, not a door had opened, not a soul had ventured out to investigate. Then I heard scuffling noises back on Sam Sen Thai.

A cadre of young men dressed in what looked to be hand-me-down garbage collector's suits had gathered over the dead American's body. What the hell were the Pathet Lao doing within the city limits? Their leader pointed to the corpse in the park and four men hurried toward it. Now a three-wheeled scooter truck putt-putted out of the dark side street; within a minute both bodies had been tossed aboard.

Just then six Royalist troops emerged from the gloom. I braced for more action.

Instead, the Royalist commander strode swiftly to the Pathet Lao leader. The two talked animatedly for a minute, then parted. The Royalists assumed relaxed positions under the streetlight while a second group of Pathet Lao, some carrying buckets, appeared. This cadre carefully retrieved the items that had spilled from the old man's pockets and sloshed away all traces of blood on Sam Sen Thai and in the park. Then both Pathet Lao detachments and the scooter truck evaporated down the side street, leaving only the Royalists.

I made myself consume two cigarettes before pulling myself up and heading for the Constellation. I suppose my staggers could have been interpreted as the drunks or an opium high for as I passed the Royalists their leader stepped forward. "*Bonsoir, monsieur*," he said, eyeing me solicitously and saluting. As unsteady as I was he had obviously picked up my loose-limbed gait, and now up close he could see my Western clothing; he added it up correctly for despite my Oriental face he asked, "You are *americain*, no?" I nodded. "Too bad, you miss just now, how do you say, *le fireworks*?" He began to giggle. Then, saluting again, he sauntered back to his men.

At the hotel I told the boy at the desk to send up coffee. He looked at me disbelievingly—most of what I'd seen of the Constellation's clientele slept with either a whore or a bottle or both—but promised it within five minutes. Upstairs I rinsed out my mouth and splashed cold water on my face. The thermos of coffee arrived. Naturally it was Nescafé instant, but I made myself drink it until I'd completed my journey to sobriety.

I knew I should go to the authorities, for I had witnessed murder. But if I belatedly came forward I would surely be detained as a material witness—and in that part of the world investigations tended to stretch out. If, that is, there even was an investigation: I suspected the crime might never grace a police blotter thanks to the mysterious appearance of the Pathet Lao in beautiful downtown Vientiane. Were these ruminations self-serving or pragmatic? I didn't know.

I dug out the aerogram from my pocket. There was no address on it. I turned it over. No return address either. Then it struck me that the pale-blue envelope had a fresh stamp, issued by the Crown Colony of Hong Kong, affixed to it. Aerograms don't require stamps. I opened my kit bag, flipped out a fresh razor blade, and carefully slid it through the mucilage binding the stamp. The aerogram had been printed by the Democratic Republic of Vietnam—or, as that country's late leader Chi-minh might have said, Ho-Ho-Ho. I pondered my next move for all of three seconds, though because of the thinness of the paper it took the better part of a half hour to free the three flaps sealing the aerogram.

I refilled my coffee cup and began to read:

2-16-72

Darling Pat,
Tonight is the one hundred and fourth consecutive night that I have been absent from your side, and I do, as ever, miss you. The days since I wrote you last have been really too, too ghastly to recount. Suffice to say I shan't soon Jeep out over spine-crunching ox-paths in search of 50 gpt+ shale. Instead, I shall be returning to Sweet Civilization tomorrow. That is when I deliver my oral preliminary report. Then, promises my (our) benefactor, I shall complete my survey in an Edenic retreat. I hope to be finished by the Ides of March, so—beware! More seriously, my dear Pat, during the past week an omnipresent if intangible sense of doom has visited me. It has been felt by others; I have been assigned two bodyguards, churlish brutes who dog my every step. And they've made me don the most outlandish getup; oh that you could see me now, for I must resemble no less than a model for Robert Hall. Still, we have discussed the possibility of harm coming to me. I now believe that if I go, so may you. So I bequeath to you the following: 4/1/2/1/10. You'll find it a challenge, but stay any *ad homonym* attack until you consult our arbiter. Gamester that you are, I know the answer will pop into your head by the time I can again apostrophize thy virtues from the harbor of your arms.

All my love,
HARRY

I stared at the letter feeling like a total shit for having breached this poignant—and prophetic—communication. But then I made myself reread it in search of a clue to Pat's identity, for she had to be warned. Nothing.

I looked at my watch. It was just after one. My body was beat to hell but my mind was sprinting, albeit on a treadmill, so I made myself pack. As I checked my camera gear I noticed there were four frames remaining on a roll of Tri-X I'd started at the elephant school. I flipped on the fluorescent overheads and unscrewed the shade from the night-table light. Then, spreading out the aerogram, I exposed two frames each of the front and back panels. I removed the roll from the camera and finished stowing my equipment. By now my mind had slowed to a jog so I ordered a wake-up call for 7:30 A.M. and went to bed.

17 February 1972: Vientiane/Bangkok/Hong Kong

It was the chill preceding the sun's arrival and not the wake-up call that roused me from my shallow sleep, but by the time I had showered and dressed the streets of Vientiane were surging with activity and the temperature had already climbed into the mid-seventies. It would be another scorching day.

The aerogram still lay open on the night table. I read it again. Sleep had not sharpened my powers of perception—or, more correctly, detection. I refolded it, tucked it into the envelope I was using for receipts, then carried my luggage downstairs.

I wasn't due at the airport for almost two hours so I took breakfast in the cool lobby. I was fretting on a croissant when Maurice came in. The proprietor asked if he might join me; I was glad for the company. Since little in Vientiane escaped Maurice's attention, I decided to ask obliquely about the previous night. "Something odd happened when I was returning from dinner."

"Yes?"

"I passed some soldiers, and they said I just missed some fireworks. Do you know anything about it?"

"No, *monsieur*. The city was most quiet last night. Perhaps one of the men celebrates his birthday."

I considered telling Maurice what I'd seen, but concluded that his penchant for gossip might land me in a sticky situation with the locals. I decided there was only one person I could trust in Laos—David Thurston—so on finishing breakfast I went out into the heat. He and Jubilee lived in the back of her restaurant over by the Mekong. On my way there I took a slight detour to the scene of the crime.

My first surprise came at the park at the foot of Rue du Boun. When the Mercedes cut through it the night before it had wiped out a row of scraggly bushes. These had been replaced; I was now staring at probably the only verdant shrubbery in all Vientiane. I continued over to Rue du Boun and my second surprise: the bullet gouges in the building I had hidden behind and in the buildings across the street had all been filled. Not only that, but those structures sparkled in the early-morning sun under fresh coats of whitewash. I touched one wall. It was still damp.

When I finally reached the Seoul Chitlins I banged on the front door. After about a minute a muffled voice—Jubilee's— yelled to go around to the back. She met me wearing only a T-shirt, virtually transparent with perspiration, that ended above her naval. But she was as arousing as a bowl of gruel; her blond hair was a tangled snarl, her blue eyes were glazed and her face puffy. I remembered David's telling me the two of them got by on thirty-five dollars U.S. per month. Looking at Jubilee I realized that if they stayed out of opium dens like Simone's they could probably make it on twenty.

"Hi," I said. "Sorry to wake you, but I've got to talk to David."

She blinked a few times and snuffled. "Come on in, luv."

I followed her down a hallway into the single room they called home. It was musty and hot. There was a desk on which David's typewriter sat, and a mattress, and that was it for furniture, the floor serving as seating, bookshelf, and file cabinet.

Jubilee looked around. "Shit, I forgot... Davey went upcountry before dawn." She flopped onto the mattress. "Simone's just wastes me, know what I mean?" She yawned and idly scratched her crotch, but the sweat I now wiped from my upper lip hadn't sprung from lust; I had far more urgent matters in mind than banging a spaced-out broad. "Any message? Or you want to wait?"

"When'll he be back?"

"Sundayish."

"No, I've got to leave this morning. And no message."

Her pale lashes fluttered. "Stay awhile, I get so ho..."

I didn't have to answer because Jubilee was asleep. I let myself out and went back to the Constellation, where Maurice had taken up his station at the front desk. As I settled my bill

I remarked on the renaissance of Rue du Boun.

"They say it is to honor the new German ambassador." Then he laughed. "Now if the Germans will only send an ambassador."

The temperature was in the nineties by the time I reached the modern little airport that had been financed by a Soviet "loan." Naturally, there was a delay. The DC-6 that was most probably the flagship of the Royal Air Lao fleet was leaking oil from a port engine; a team of sweating mechanics was up on the shimmering wing hammering at the offending nacelle.

"Hey . . . writer."

I turned. It was Ivan Arkadian, who did not look well. "Comrade Ivan," I said. "When did you get to bed?"

"No bed," he grunted. In the relentless morning light his complexion was like a slug's. Ivan tapped his watch and said, "Red Chinee come. I make report." With that he led me by the arm to the observation patio, where he spotted an elegant black man dressed in a Brooks Brothers seersucker standing in the shade. Ivan steered me over and said, "Gordon, this is American writer."

The black man turned.

"Hi. I'm Ray Huang, a free-lancer from New York."

"Gordon Hailey, Ray. Civilian adviser on an irrigation project."

"Gordon spy like me," Ivan said. Hailey grinned. Ivan scanned the apron and then pointed to a sleek Lear executive jet. "Gordon, who plane that?"

"Charter out of Hong Kong, heading for Bangkok when he lost pressure in one engine. They tried to put down in Hué, but the runways there got chewed up in an attack last week. Got in here about three."

"You believe?"

"Sure. Why not? They're all over at the Settha Palace now, sleeping."

I turned to Hailey. The events of the past twelve hours had me all knotted up, and I had to know if he was really CIA, so I asked, "Are you really with the Company?"

He looked at me, then Ivan, and then back to me. He started to smile as he said, "Do I look like a spook?"

Just then the drone of a prop-driven plane; we squinted upward toward a C-47-type cargo liner painted olive except for the bright-red stars on its wings and tail. The Chinese

Communist craft landed and taxied to the parking position farthest from the terminal. Its rear doors opened. A ramp was lowered onto the tarmac. A dozen men descended from the plane's cavernous belly and hunkered in the shadow of one wing.

Ivan scowled. "No cargo."

"How often do they fly here?" I asked Hailey.

"Not very—that's why Ivan and I came. They land Luang Prabang about twice a week, here once every two weeks."

"What for?"

"To off-load goodies like mortars, Type 56 assault rifles, and ammo for their buddies the Pathet Lao."

"They allow that here?" I asked incredulously.

"See any Royalists out there trying to shut down the Ho Chi-minh Trail?"

My flight to Bangkok was called; the mechanics up on the wing must have found the hole through which oil had been leaking and pounded it shut.

"But they're not unloading this trip," I said to Hailey.

"That's why Ivan and I might be around a long time today."

"You know a lot for an irrigation adviser."

He regarded me for several seconds. "A lot, but never enough." Then he smiled and extended a hand. "Have a good flight, Ray."

An hour later I was crossing the sun-softened tarmac at Don Muang in Bangkok. On clearing Customs I immediately called the Associated Press office and asked for George Dibley, the New Zealander who headed it. I'd done some drinking with him on my stay the previous week; now I was going to repay his hospitality with a story. His secretary told me he was expected back by noon so I went to the Lufthansa counter, canceled my seat on their midday plane to Hong Kong, and rebooked on a late-afternoon Singapore Airlines flight. Then I left the air-conditioned sanctuary of the terminal and hopped a minibus for the Patpong district.

Vientiane had been hot; this felt hotter. Though the downtown was steamy enough to wilt a plum pudding, the whores of Patpong were busy strutting the streets advising GIs on R & R they were available to bang koks. I crossed Silom and went up to the AP office.

Dibley wasn't back yet so I went over to the ticker, which was chattering out a summary of the day's international stories:

WASH. D.C.—U.S. PRESIDENT RICHARD M. NIXON DEPARTS TODAY ON THE FIRST LEG OF HIS HISTORIC "JOURNEY FOR PEACE" TO THE PEOPLE'S REPUBLIC OF CHINA. HE WILL FLY ABOARD AIR FORCE I TO HAWAII FOR TWO DAYS OF PREPARATION. FOLLOWING ADDITIONAL REFUELING STOPOVERS IN GUAM AND SHANGHAI, MR. NIXON IS SCHEDULED TO LAND IN PEKING ON MONDAY, FEB. 21.

* * *

LONDON—BY A VOTE OF 309 TO 301, BRITAIN'S HOUSE OF COMMONS APPROVED LEGISLATION THAT WILL ENABLE THE NATION TO ENTER THE EUROPEAN COMMON MARKET. CONSERVATIVE PRIME MINISTER EDWARD HEATH HAD THREATENED TO RESIGN IF THE MEASURE DID NOT PASS.

* * *

JAKARTA—THE INDONESIAN AIR MINISTRY ANNOUNCED A LIGHT AIRCRAFT HAS CRASHED IN A REMOTE PART OF WEST IRIAN IN WESTERN NEW GUINEA. SEARCH PARTIES ARE SCOUTING FOR THE PLANE, BELIEVED TO BE CARRYING PETROLEUM EXPERTS TO A NEW OIL FIELD JOINTLY OWNED BY PERTAMINA, THE INDONESIAN COMPANY, AND THE AMERICAN FIRM ONYXX.

* * *

MANAGUA, NICARAGUA—NICARAGUAN PRESIDENT ANASTASIO SOMOZA ANNOUNCED THAT AMERICAN BILLIONAIRE HOWARD R. HUGHES HAS ARRIVED IN MANAGUA. THE RECLUSIVE TYCOON, WHO HAS SPENT THE PAST 14 MONTHS IN THE BAHAMAS, RECENTLY HELD A RARE PRESS CONFERENCE BY TELEPHONE TO BRAND CLIFFORD IRVING'S PURPORTED BIOGRAPHY OF HIM AS A HOAX.

Just then Dibley's secretary told me that instead of returning to the office George was headed for lunch at the Foreign Correspondents' Club. I was to join him there. I got directions, went down to Silom, bargained a cabby down to ten bahts, and squeezed into his oven-on-wheels.

The Oriental Hotel, in which the club was headquartered, sat on the banks of the Chao Phraya River. Most bodies of water exert a cooling effect, even in weather such as this. Not the muddy Chao Phraya; at midday it glistened like a sheet of beaten brass, its claustrophobic calm broken only by the throaty passage of klong boats, those uniquely Thai craft powered by automotive V-8s.

Dibley was seated on the veranda overlooking the river. "Didn't expect to see you again so soon, mate." To conserve energy he didn't bother to rise. I grunted as I sat down and waited for the overhead fans to begin drying my shirt. Dibley was a large, amiable man about my age, prematurely pudgy from too many ales. He ordered a dark rum and tonic for me and another Foster's for himself. Then he looked at me more closely and pushed across a saltshaker.

"Think so?"

He nodded. I poured some salt onto my hand and licked it. It tasted pretty good, so I did it again. Then I looked up and said, "I saw a man murdered last night, an American I'm pretty sure, and I think it's being covered up."

Instantly Dibley seemed less a basset than an Airedale. Starting with my first sight of Harry at the restaurant, I quickly told him the entire story—except for the aerogram. I suppose I was still too guilt-ridden about my prying; I remember rationalizing it at the time by thinking he could surely solve the mystery without the meager clues, the names Pat and Harry, I possessed. When I finished Dibley put away his notebook, sat back, and gazed at the river. Then he hand-signaled for another round and said, "Want lunch, mate?"

The heat, coupled with the sheer physical relief of having got my story out, had dampened my appetite, so, breaking a cardinal rule of equatorial survival—eat, eat, eat—I shook my head.

"Well then," he said as he drained his glass, "since you have a few hours to kill, let me tell you 'bout the time me and Skip and Blye were nipping around the Central Highlands after Montagnard women..."

Two hours later I'd paid dearly for so stupidly waiving the meal and then drinking on an empty stomach: George's driver had to pour me onto the airplane, and it took two stewardesses to slap me awake in Hong Kong.

20 February 1972: Hong Kong

The problems I was having on my last assignment in Asia had one salutary effect: they were blotting out Vientiane and the letter I carried. Or so I kept telling myself.

I was in town to profile kung fu movie star Bruce Lee for *Show*. Perhaps it was too many years of breaking boards with his head, but Lee was such a bum interview he made Charles Bronson sound like Noël Coward. Luckily he was shooting yet another chop-socky epic, which at least afforded me splendid photo opportunities—that very day I'd snapped him in a midair posture that reminded me instantly of Harry on his final flight.

Harry. Should I have gone to the police that night? Or to the American Consulate?

I sighed and looked up. The studio limousine bringing me back from the New Territories had arrived at my hotel. I got out and went up to my tacky room. It was 6:30 P.M., and I wanted nothing more than a fast drink, dinner, a hot tub, and bed, for I had another day to spend with Bruce. But this was not to be an early night, for I'd bowed to family pressure and agreed to dine with a "cousin."

Among the Chinese this term is often used casually, though not as promiscuously as the phrases "brother" and "sister" by which some blacks have taken to addressing each other. We tend to be clannish, especially the *hoa chiao*, or overseas Chinese; thus, granting cousinhood to a non-blood acquaintance has the reassuring effect of expanding the family. I'd never met K. H. Tsao, a Hong Kong entrepreneur. But he was a "cousin" because, I believe, his paternal and my maternal grandmothers had attended the same elementary school in Hangchow.

His wife had booked a bridge party at their house so he and I were meeting at the Foreign Correspondents' Club for a drink and then grabbing a bite out. We would probably pass the evening making ever-so-polite small talk about family trees, the price of copra, and the vicissitudes of journalism. I prayed the food would be good.

I cleaned myself up and hopped a double-decker bus down Nathan Road toward the ferry. There was something enormously pleasing about Hong Kong, especially after traveling through cities built of First World materials by Third World minds. To be sure, such capitals as Taipei and Manila and Jakarta have a certain inimitable air, but then so does a brain surgeon who drools; here, many of the appurtenances were old, but they worked. At the pier I paid my nickle and rode the Star Ferry across the wide bay from Kowloon to the glittering island that is Hong Kong.

The club was shoulder to shoulder with self-styled China Hands trying to cover Nixon's trip to the Mainland from afar; I chalked off some of the bitter comments to the fact that these journalists hadn't the clout to win visas from Peking. As I stood by the elevator mapping a route through the bodies and the smoke the manager brought K. H. over.

He was in his early forties. He wore a faded denim suit over a cotton golf shirt. His loafers were by Gucci. His hair was razor-cut and free of the sticky substances every barbershop in Asia insists on dispensing. Some of my reservations about the evening were disappearing.

"Come on," K. H. said, "let us get the hell out of here." When we reached his car the last of my misgivings evaporated: it was a Ferrari-red Ferrari. "What shall it be," he said, "Chinese or Western?"

"How about a nice rare piece of meat that's too big for chopsticks?"

We piled into the Ferrari, slithered through the central-city traffic, and then whipped up the serpentine road to Victoria Peak. On the elevator up to the restaurant K. H. said, "Drinks here rate ninety-five, the food seventy-two, and the view a hundred and eight."

He was right, especially about the view; from our table atop Hong Kong's highest elevation we could see the entire harbor still atwinkle with the lights of night-running craft. My host began a story in the Mandarin dialect. I was pleasantly surprised that I could follow him, for my Mandarin was not only rudimentary but rusty. My plans for practicing it on the trip had been thwarted by the fact that in Hong Kong and the *hoa chiao* communities throughout Southeast Asia, Cantonese and Fukienese—as alien to my ears as Finnish—were the predominant dialects. But language is like sex in that you never forget how, and soon I grew confident enough to reciprocate in Mandarin, so long as the subject matter remained simple. When it grew more complex, though, I reverted to English, as when K. H., a keen follower of American politics, asked about Muskie, McGovern, and other Democrats who would be president.

We were over brandy when my gaze fell again on what was left of the liner *Queen Elizabeth*, which had been gutted by a mysterious fire some six weeks before. Though we sat some 1,800 feet above the harbor I could make out the warning lights encircling the wreckage. "The *Queen*," I said. "Everywhere

I've gone, the local papers have had stories on it. They all say arson. True?"

"Yes, I think so. A marine court of inquiry is investigating. Their report will not be out until summer, but my sources say it is probably sabotage."

"By who?"

"There has been talk the owner planned it himself. For the insurance."

"What do you think she was insured for?"

"About eight and a quarter million U.S.," he said. "And the claim is good—it will be paid. But Tung did not do it. It was eight agents provocateurs from an electrical union run by the Communists."

"Peking ordered her torched?"

K. H. nodded.

"Because Tung's a prominent Nationalist?"

"You are being naïve, Raymond. The two governments hate each other, they even lob artillery at each other. But it is all a game. The shells that strike Kinmen and Matsu contain propaganda leaflets, not explosives. And the Communists do not thwart the monthly Nationalist commando raid on the Mainland, just as the Kuomintang has never smashed the Communist intelligence network on Taiwan." K. H. snipped another Havana, lit it, and continued. "No one will confirm this, but both sides have been meeting secretly, my guess is in Albania, to prepare for when Mao and Gimo die. Peking wants to annex Taiwan peacefully. That is preferable to a war that would destroy most of Taiwan's industry, as well as perhaps trigger American intervention."

"What do you mean, 'perhaps'?"

"I assure you Nixon is not meeting Mao only to accept a pair of pandas."

I looked down at the harbor. "But then why burn the *Queen*?"

"As a warning to Tung."

"That's one hell of an expensive warning."

"For Lloyd's of London yes," he replied, "for Tung no. You see, the arsonists very carefully left signs of their work. Had they not, Lloyd's might well have argued negligence, and the subsequent settlement would have left Tung poor."

"What was Tung being warned about?"

"Several months ago I heard that several Chinese ship-owners, of whom Tung is the most prominent, were discussing merger. They planned to pool their resources to build supertankers. Not the two-hundred-thousand-tonners in service today, but superships in the four-hundred-thousand-ton range."

K. H. paused; now he too was looking at the *Queen*. "Ten days after she went down, the Japanese shipyards in Kure and Nagasaki, which had been booked through 1977, suddenly began soliciting orders. Commencing in 1974–75."

"Which means?"

"Raymond," K. H. said, laughing, "for that answer there are parties in Hong Kong willing to pay one million dollars. That's one million U.S."

25 February 1972: New York

No matter how long you've been traveling and no matter how many hotel rooms you've awakened in, you're never disoriented—not even for an instant—when you open your eyes that first time again back in your own bedroom.

It was midafternoon, which meant I'd slept nearly sixteen hours. I swung my feet to the floor and gasped; the bare wood was cold. Through the bedroom window I could see greying mounds of frozen slush in the air shaft between buildings. I'd blanked out the dispiriting meanness of a New York winter during my five weeks in the tropics but stepping from the International Arrivals Building at Kennedy the previous night had been like getting goosed by Nanook. I padded into the kitchen. Martha had cleaned away the debris of my welcome-home dinner. I started the burner under the coffee she'd left, then called her at her magazine.

"Well well, Sleeping Beauty himself," she said.

"Nice of you to just steal away this morning."

"What do you mean—I roused you at eight."

"You did? Did I get up?"

"Just barely." She laughed.

Though of course she couldn't see it, I smiled. Of her attributes, the one that first drew me to her, and the one I'd missed most during my trip, was her laugh. In New York most sharp, attractive women always hold back a little when they laugh; you can tell by their eyes. Martha suffered no such self-consciousness.

"Are we on for tonight?" I asked.

"Can't, Ray, there's a cover-story crisis. It feels like a brutal closer." Which meant the magazine wouldn't be put to bed much before dawn.

"How about tomorrow night?"

"I told you I have a date."

"Oh, come on. With who?"

"Whom. A guy from my pottery class."

"Shit. All he'll want to do is examine your toby jugs." She laughed again so I decided to press my luck. "Can't you cancel? Or give him a rain check?"

"No," she said, suddenly brusque. "Look, Peter wanted me to go to some party in northern Connecticut. I knew you'd be back so I told him I couldn't stay overnight, because I want to spend Sunday with you. Really, Ray, I don't need this hassle. We've been through this enough."

I thought of a wisecrack but decided to keep it to myself.

"Anyway," she continued in a lighter tone, "you need the time to make a dent in all your assignments." Martha was referring to our accord of the previous evening, during which she'd understandably badgered me for a play-by-play of my trip. I'd demurred, claiming I needed to keep my impressions fresh for my articles. That was only part of the truth—frankly, I still hadn't figured out how to justify my lack of action that night in Vientiane. Finally she'd agreed not to press if I promised to write my way out of the self-imposed quarantine quickly.

I cleared my throat. "Well..."

"Damn it, my other phone—don't go away." When she returned to the line Martha said, "California calling. Listen, stock up your pantry and I'll be over for brunch Sunday. Eleven o'clock, okay? Bye-bye."

I hung up the phone and went back to the kitchen. The coffee was barely tepid but I poured myself a cup and wandered back into the living room, where I slumped on the couch and brooded about Martha.

Martha. How can you rationally describe someone who has on occasions the rare quality of being closer to you than a suntan? Right from the first, before we'd experienced enough together to develop the private shorthand each couple acquires, there'd been the oblique references that never needed explanation. Some men—including her husband Tim—obviously found Martha too acerbic and headstrong; I happened to enjoy those very qualities. Perhaps, as she once suggested, my Chinese side is conditioned to accept matriarchal strength. Or perhaps, heritage aside, I'm just plain passive. Whatever, I rarely felt threatened by her independence, for she never marinated her bra in kerosene or subjected me to any vaginal politics. And that occasional dinner at the Palm or the Russian Tea Room or the Algonquin after the theater is that much more affordable if the lady insists on paying her own way.

We seemed in short a good mesh—except for one thing. She wanted to retain the right to date other men—"To make sure I don't make another mistake like Tim"—while at the same time remaining possessive about my social life. "You've been on the market all your life," Martha had said, "but I've been out of circulation for six years. Surely you understand." All I understood was that it was evidently all right for her to go out with potters and tinkers, but I was damned if I saw an old flame for dinner. All of which had led to several ominously quiet evenings and, ultimately, contributed to my leaving for Asia.

Now I was back, and nothing seemed changed. To stop the self-pity, I got up and went to a side table on which Martha had neatly separated my back mail into letters, bills, junk mail, and magazines. I opened the personal letters. One announced my tenth college reunion. Another was from Freddie, a friend living on the West Coast, informing me he was taking a leave from his law firm to work for the Democratic party through the elections; he'd be coming East to Washington in late February.

Next I went to my desk. Martha had left a note saying my checks had arrived and she'd banked them; attached were the deposit slips. Before my trip I'd solved a cash-flow problem by hitting up my best friend for a loan. Though Alan, being a Park Avenue shrink, was in no hurry for repayment, I conscientiously made out a check for a thousand dollars. With more than half the money Martha had deposited now gone, I decided to ignore the rest of my creditors for the moment.

Instead I unpacked my camera case and separated the color film I would send out from the black-and-white rolls I'd develop myself. Then I took the cameras and lenses to my secret hiding place. In my three years in the apartment I'd been ripped off twice. But neither time had the junkies found my real valuables: photo equipment, documents, savings passbook, a few pieces of jewelry, and a gold heirloom pocket watch passed down from my grandfather. That's because they were in a compartment under the bookcase I'd knocked together myself. The case had a false bottom, and I had deepened my cache by ripping out the floorboards beneath; to protect against fire I had lined my "safe" with half-inch metal sheets. Entry to the hiding place was gained by removing all the books on the bottom shelf, lifting the board, and sliding it toward me.

After stashing my gear I opened my suitcase and dumped its contents into the hamper. And then I was out of procrastinating chores. Should I start to transcribe my notes, or, more realistically, go to the launderette or satisfy a six-week craving for pizza? My problem was solved when a lethargy compounded of residual jet lag and depression over Martha struck. I plucked a magazine off the stack and plopped back into bed. I was asleep again within ten minutes.

27 February 1972: New York

I was in the shower when Martha let herself in. "Hi," I said, giving her a quick peck on the forehead as I headed for the bedroom to dress. "I'm fresh as a daisy—how's about some good clean sex?"

She grunted and continued to read the Sunday *Times*.

When we first started dating the previous summer, we inevitably and speedily wound up in bed. But since she'd moved out on Tim our sex life had become erratic. It wasn't that the illicit bloom was fading, Martha had said. It was just that she felt herself becoming too dependent on me—not until we were pretty heavily involved had she finally seen a lawyer, and that bothered her. A lot.

I'd just drawn on my pants when I heard her behind me. I turned.

"I'm sorry," she said as she gave me a hug, nuzzled my neck, and provoked an erection. "I didn't mean to be so cool."

"You might have warmed up a few seconds earlier."

"No," she replied, gently touching my throbbing member, "this is much safer behind two layers of cloth." I let out a mock groan. Her eyes became suddenly serious. "Don't you ever get angry?"

"No."

"Never?" Martha moved away and sat on the edge of the bed.

"I seem to remember a tantrum when I was eleven," I said as I pulled on a shirt. "And last fall some slob of an editor kept fucking with my copy. Finally, I told the oaf to his face that he was an illiterate asshole. Quote unquote."

"Did that make you feel better?"

"Yup."

"How about the girl you used to live with—did you fight?"

"You mean fight fight? No. I mean, we had our differences, or we'd still be together, but when it came time to split we split. Amicably. Why the third degree?"

Martha looked around, found a pack of my cigarettes, and lit one. "I thought about us a lot when you were gone," she said. "Mostly about why I'm attracted to you. I decided it's because you're so easy to be with. Almost too easy."

I sat on the window ledge to pull on my socks and shoes.

"Is there anything you care—really care about, Ray?"

"Sure. You. My work."

"Your work." She studied the filter tip. "And what do you want to be when you grow up?"

"A better class of whore." I smiled. "It's kind of late for me to stop being a writer, and my kind of writer writes for bread. Maybe if I can get ahead someday I'll try a novel, a big book set in nineteenth-century China." Surprised at myself for confiding this secret, I stood and turned to the window.

"I thought novelists had to understand things like character and motivation," she said softly. I resisted the temptation to face her. "When you were gone," Martha continued, "I found myself wondering if you're even-tempered or if you're just not there. I mean you let me yell at you, but you never yell back, even when you should—like right now."

"I thought you had enough yelling to last a lifetime," I said, thinking about the violent quarrels she had had during six years with Tim.

"What do you think I am, a goddamn masochist?" Her voice demanded I turn so I turned. "This is important, Ray—it's coming up on make-it-or-break-it time for us, and I've got to know why you're always so controlled."

"Emotions, or I should say carryings-on, were frowned upon in my family."

"You also didn't become an engineer," she said tartly.

"WELL SHIT, IF IT'S SHOUTING YOU WANT, IT'S SHOUTING YOU'LL GET!" Despite herself, she giggled. "I don't know, Martha. I mean, it's not easy to articulate the way you are. Some people like to let it hang out. Me, I feel comfortable keeping it in. But just because I don't think anger's worth showing doesn't mean I don't care or feel."

"Do you feel?"

I nodded solemnly. "If you must know, right now I feel... hungry as hell."

For a heartbeat Martha's face remained pensive; but then a laugh that was like a surrender. "Damn it, you bastard, one day I'm not going to let you joke your way off the hook."

"Warning noted," I replied as I headed for the kitchen. I returned to the living room with a chopping board stacked with bagels, lox, and cream cheese, then sat on the couch and picked up the first section of the paper. On Sundays the *Times* fills its few columns not devoted to White Sales ads with dreary national and international snippets that are printed because they fit:

> ITALY IS AROUSED BY RISE IN CRIME
> UN STUDY FAVORS MARIJUANA CURBS
> FRANCE WILL GIVE NEWLYWEDS BOOKS

Normally I preferred to gawk at the lingerie ads, but I was still tracking some stories from the Far East that had broken while I was out there. I'd leafed my way to page 37 when I saw:

> U.S. GEOLOGIST VICTIM
> OF INDONESIAN AIR CRASH

JAKARTA, Feb. 26 (AP)—The Indonesian Air Ministry announced today that a U.S. geologist and an Indonesian pilot were killed when their light aircraft crashed on Feb. 16 in a remote area of West Irian on the island of New Guinea.

The American has been identified as Harry Helmsley, 62, of New York, N.Y.

A spokesman for the Air Force, which recovered the bodies, attributed the accident to engine failure. The plane was on charter to Pertamina, this country's nationalized petroleum company.

A Pertamina spokesman confirmed that Mr. Helmsley, who was completing a four-month survey for the company, had been flying to a newly opened oil reserve along the coast of West Irian.

I had been in Bangkok waiting for Dibley, of course, when the crash had first been announced. I started to turn the page. Then I stopped; something was at the back of my mind, like a snatch of a long-forgotten tune.

"Hey," Martha said, "if we're going to make the early show we'd better hurry."

I gobbled down the rest of my bagel and grabbed my parka.

28 February 1972: New York

Upon returning from Martha's apartment to mine shortly after 9 A.M., I headed directly for the Sunday paper, which was still spread out on the coffee table. I quickly reread the brief item on the geologist. What was there about those four paragraphs?

Indonesia. American geologist. Killed. Harry Helmsley. Age 62. Four months.

I had seen an elderly American, most likely named Harry, killed—but not in Indonesia.

I dug out the aerogram from my receipts file. My Harry, the letter writer, had been away 104 days. Geologist Helmsley had been on a four-month survey. I went to the dictionary and looked up "shale," for which my Harry had been searching. It is a fissile rock. But my Harry had been run down on a Wednesday night while geologist Helmsley had crashed on what must have been Thursday morning latest, since I'd read the first bulletin in Bangkok. To prove to myself that I was crazy, that it was all coincidence, I took out a ruler and went to my atlas. Vientiane and West Irian were thirteen inches, or 2,600 miles, apart—an overnight passage that would tax even SPECTRE's Stavros Blofeld.

Still, I phoned the *Times*. After a fifteen-minute wait I was told there'd been no further information in the original dispatch; that though there was a New York realtor by the same name, geologist Helmsley had not merited a folder in the paper's bio morgue, where past stories are clipped and filed; and no, they weren't planning a follow-up obit.

Next I called Martha, catching her just as she was leaving for work. I asked her to run geologist Helmsley through the Time Inc. morgue, which cast a wider dragnet for data: stored on the twenty-sixth floor are not only clippings gleaned for major newspapers and magazines but also raw reports from correspondents that are retooled by the in-building writers.

While I waited for her to reach the office, I pulled out the Manhattan telephone directory. The only Harry Helmsley listed was the real estate man. I dailed Information and asked for a check of the other four boroughs. Nothing, I looked up Pertamina. The company had a New York office so I called and got put through to Public Relations. The man I spoke with knew little; Jakarta had merely telexed to advise that the body had been recovered and already interred in West Irian. There had been no mention of surviving relatives or a New York home address. I'd just about convinced myself I was behaving like a twit who'd read too many Eric Amblers when Martha called.

"Ray? I checked Edit Ref—you trying for a better apartment?"

"You found the real estate guy, hunh? But no geologist or scientist?"

"Nope. Want me to have the librarians run a full-scale search?"

"No, I guess not. Thanks. See you about seven, right?"

After we rang off it suddenly occurred to me that if geologist Harry Helmsley had been of sufficient professional stature to conduct a survey for a firm the size of Pertamina, he might well have been either the subject or the author of articles in trade journals. A long shot, but I bundled myself up and took a subway uptown to New York's best general research library, the Mid-Manhattan. In the fourth-floor reference room I sat at a table holding the *Reader's Guide to Periodical Literature*, which indexes more than 150 magazines, and began digging. I'd worked my way back to the 1964 volume when I found:

HELMSLEY, HARRY. *Rifle, Colorado, Reconsidered*. Symposium on synthetic liquid fuels; Jerrold Dodson, Ed. Sci Am, Mar 64, 88+.

A little extra adrenaline began to trickle through my body.

I retrieved the bound volume of *Scientific American* containing the March 1964 issue and turned to page 88. Helmsley had been one of six geologists discussing federal experiments conducted near Rifle, Colorado, during the years 1916–29 and 1944–54. Those experiments were to determine the economic feasibility of extracting oil and other liquid fuels from . . . *shale*. According to a footnote, Helmsley had written a paper on the subject in the October 1963 issue of the *Society of Petroleum Engineers Journal*.

I hurried across the reference room to the notebook listing the periodicals subscribed to by the Mid-Manhattan. The *Journal* was among them. A research librarian directed me to the stacks containing technical publications.

I found the issue. By now my palms were sweaty. The table of contents on the *Journal*'s front cover listed Helmsley's article—as well as, on page 2, a column titled "About Our Authors." I turned to page 2. Each engineer contributing to the issue was afforded a small bio blurb. And a photograph.

It was him.

My Harry was, or had been, Harry Helmsley.

I could hear my heartbeat. I slowly lowered myself into a squatting position. Nine years ago he had worn his hair much shorter. And that hair had not yet turned pure white. And his glasses then were enclosed by horned, not aviator's, rims. But it was undeniably him. As I stared at the snapshot my body turned terribly cold despite the library's heating. Then I read the blurb below the photograph:

> Harry Helmsley, Ph.D., the author of "Three Methods of Increasing the Efficiency of the Pumpherston Retort," has long specialized in the technological problems of extracting petroleum equivalents from shale. Dr. Helmsley participated for four years in the pilot shale liquefaction project at Anvil Points, Colo. He has also been a consultant to Union Oil Co., and during IGY analyzed shale formations in Indo-China. Dr. Helmsley (B.S., U. Minn., '32; Ph.D., U. Mich., '35) was from 1938 to 1961 a member of the faculty of the U. of Michigan. The author of two books (*The Economics of Synthesizing Liquid Fuels; Shale: The Neglected Alternative*) and numerous articles, he is presently a private consultant based in Tulsa, Okla.

Finally I stood, located a Xerox machine, dropped in a dime, and copied the page. Then I went out into the preternaturally gloomy winter's day.

It was only 2:30 P.M. when I got home but I mixed myself a drink. It didn't make sense, I thought. Twenty-six hundred miles overnight. Unless... I examined the *Times* article again. Unless the airplane crash, assuming there'd been one, hadn't occurred on the sixteenth.

But I'd read about it in Bangkok on the seventeenth. I knew inexplicable events were commonplace in strong man Suharto's Indonesia, where he and his cronies controlled the press, Pertamina, and of course the air force, which had handled the search mission. Before the Indonesians could plant Harry's body, though, they had to obtain it. Therein lay the rub— Suharto, who'd overthrown Sukarno in the mid-1960s to set up an *anti*-Communist dictatorship, wasn't the sort to cooperate with the radically Red Pathet Lao. Thus the problem became: who in that part of the world had the leverage to pry these strange bedfellows onto the same mattress?

I drained my drink, thought once, thought twice, and made another. Then I phoned the central switchboard of the University of Michigan and asked for the geology department. A secretary answered.

"Good afternoon, my name's Ray Huang, and I'm calling from New York. I just heard about what happened to Ha... to Dr. Helmsley."

"Oh yes," she said, "wasn't that a dreadful tragedy?"

"It certainly was."

"Why, I remember the good professor as vividly as if he had just been in my office."

"So do I—I mean, I had the privilege of taking several courses with him, and those lectures are still fresh in my memory. In fact, that's why I'm calling. Professor Helmsley meant a great deal to me during my years at, uh, Ann Arbor, and I want to send condolences to his wife. But I've misplaced their address."

"His wife?"

"Yes—Pat."

"Oh. I see. Well, I'm sure I have his address somewhere. I know he still receives our department newsletter."

"After all these years?"

"Why certainly," she said, a little snappishly. "Lifelong friends are lifelong friends, and the professor likes to keep up with them. He doesn't blame *them* for that unpleasantness, you know." She put me on hold for several minutes. "Here we are now. Professor Helmsley lives... lived at Fifteen East Sixty-ninth Street, New York. Would you like the telephone number too?"

"Yes, ma'am."

"That would be area 212, 880–0347."

"Thank you very, very much."

"Not at all," she said. "You know, I do believe I remember you. Aren't you about five feet five, and you always wore glasses?"

"That's me," I lied.

Quickly I dialed Harry's number.

"Oh-three-four-seven." The voice was male and mechanical; I'd got a machine. "There is nobody here to take your call right now. But at the beep please leave your name and number and, if you wish, a brief message. Your call will be returned. Please wait for the beep. Thank you."

I returned the receiver to its cradle. I'd expected a woman's voice—had I been given the correct number? Or could Pat still be using a tape Harry had made? I decided to wait. Then I began wondering why I hadn't found the number in the Manhattan directory. I dialed Information again and was told it was unlisted, which added to my puzzlement until I remembered I'd previously asked the telephone company for a check of non-Manhattan listings.

I made myself wait until 5:30 P.M. before trying again. Again the machine answered. To fight off my fidgets I went into the kitchen to start dinner.

At 7:45 P.M., shortly before Martha and I sat down to Chicken à la Shake 'n Bake, I dialed the number once more, and once more hung up as soon as the tape started.

Later, while we were watching TV, I worked out a message to leave on the machine. Just before 11 P.M., during a commercial break in some awful George Peppard flick, I called again. At the beep I said, "I've just returned from Asia, and a man I met there asked me to call this number and speak to Pat. If this isn't Pat's number, I apologize. If it is, please call QU8–3062."

By the time I dozed off during the late news watching Nixon assure the nation he'd cut "no secret deals of any kind" with Peking during his just concluded "journey for peace," my phone hadn't rung.

29 February 1972: New York

At 9:30 A.M. of Leap Year Day, as I was having a second cup of coffee by myself, I found something besides the calendar was going to jump: me.

My phone rang. It wasn't Pat. But it was the editor of a credit-card magazine who had assigned me the story on the elephant school, a piece due at the end of April for inclusion in the September issue. However, Herb explained, the writer assigned the July cover on alpine backpacking had suddenly freaked out because his wife had left him for a theater critic. So could I ram my article through?

"Gee, Herb, I'd love to help you, but..."

"Well of course it'd be the cover, so we'd want to go through your color takes and give you first crack." I'd taken several rolls and there were some nice shots; if he agreed, that meant an unexpected five hundred dollars. "Plus of course we'd want to expand the story," Herb continued. "We talked it as a four-pager—as cover, it'd have to go six. But you won't have to write that much more if your black-and-whites are up to their usual standard." That meant he was willing to fill the extra spread with photographs, and photo page rates were much better than the pay for words.

"What's the catch, Herb?"

"Well, we have to lock in the cover by Friday. And the absolute deadline on the inside stuff's March tenth, a week from Friday."

Not bad, I thought, but I said, "I'd love to do it, Herb. Trouble is, I've promised another book a piece due at the same time. Let me try to put them off, and I'll get back to you in, say, an hour, okay?"

"Right. And thanks, Ray."

Why the lie? Seven years of self-employment had taught me if you don't inflate your own coinage, ain't nobody else going to. Besides, this way Herb wouldn't go away thinking he'd done me a favor by giving me what was shaping up as an eight-hundred-dollar windfall; instead, he'd feel I had done him the good turn.

I put my undeveloped Laotian takes into my pouch and rushed out. It was chilly on the street but I was warmed by smug self-satisfaction. At the lab that processes my color I handed over the Ektachrome and specified "Rush." Then I went up to my pal Duke's.

Duke was a studio photographer unsurpassed at the surprisingly difficult task of making gems look like gems, whiskey like whiskey, and food like food. This proficiency earned him an annual income well into six figures, mostly from Madison Avenue, which in turn allowed him to maintain a staff of four, accept whimsical assignments, and indulge his taste for Savile Row tailors in an age when most young photographers flaunted ripped denims as a badge of rebellion. We'd met years ago when Duke, bitten by the movie bug, commissioned me to script an experimental short subject. We ended up collaborating on three films. But his grandiose ambitions for Michelle Films, Ltd., a subsidiary named after one of his daughters, waned when his accountant pointed out that tax write-offs were only useful up to a certain point. Duke and I had remained friends, though, and I'd become one of the regulars who used his splendid darkroom.

When I got to the studio his chief assistant, Mario, told me Duke was in South Africa making diamonds look like diamonds. I headed for a phone, called Herb, and said I'd do it. Then I tried Pat again.

Busy—which meant someone was home.

I smoked a cigarette to kill time before dialing again. Still busy. Reluctantly I went to the bin where I kept my materials, withdrew some supplies, and went into the darkroom. As soon as the developed negatives were in for their thirty-minute rinse I placed another call.

"Hello?" The voice was male.

"I'd like to speak to Pat, please."

"Yes?"

When I become confused I usually tend to babble. Not this time. After five seconds of silence Pat said, with a touch of edginess, "Hello, who's there?"

"Uh, I called yesterday."

"You left the message? Been trying your number all morning." Suddenly his voice relaxed. "Who asked you to call—Harry?"

"Yes." My relief was enormous; when I left the message on the machine I'd deliberately avoided using Harry's name. "I apologize for my hesitation just now," I said, "but I expected you to be a woman."

Pat chuckled. "You didn't know Harry well."

"No. Listen, I hate to sound so melodramatic, but it's very vital that we meet, and as soon as possible."

"Can you tell me why?"

"I'd rather not over the phone."

"I see." He was silent for several seconds. "Be glad to come to you, Mr.—ah..."

"Huang, Ray Huang." I was about to give him the studio's address when I remembered that not only was the aerogram at my apartment but that I'd never resealed it. "I'm afraid I'm tied up for the rest of the morning. Would it be okay if I came to your apartment at, say, one?"

After a slight pause Pat said, "Fine. Know the address?"

I told him I did, hung up, and returned to the darkroom. As I waited for the rinse cycle to end I ruefully decided I must be a closet sexist for automatically assuming, on the basis of the aerogram, that Harry was getting his rocks off on a member of the opposite sex. I also now understood the geology department secretary's polite surprise when I'd mentioned Harry's "wife." The timer sounded. I wanted nothing more than to hang up the dripping rolls and take off for my place, but my methodical habits made me take the extra twenty minutes to squeegee the negatives, clip them to a line to fully dry, and then clean up the darkroom.

Which was why I ran into the mailman in the lobby of my building just as he started to sort the letters. I said hello to Sal—as a free-lancer working out of his home I saw him more days than not—and went into my apartment. I dug out a bottle of LePage's and carefully glued the three flaps of the aerogram, as well as the stamp, back into place. When the mucilage was dry I ducked back outside. Sal saw me coming, reached into my mailbox, and handed me a few letters. I stuffed them into a pocket of my parka and headed toward Sixth Avenue.

My cab uptown got caught in a traffic jam so I retrieved the letters and shuffled through them. One had been airmailed from Hong Kong. I opened it; it was typed on the stationery of the Associated Press, Bangkok office:

24/2/72

Raymond my boy,

You've no idea the Pandoran box you opened with your tale of hugger-mugger in Vientiane. You'll note I had this letter posted from HK, since our friends the Thais have been known to peek at outward-bound missives from *farangs* stationed here. Why the precaution? Because if you got the license plate correct, the car belongs to one Field Marshal K., of the junta-that-rules-Thailand fame. You'll find this interesting; I found it positively fascinating, so much so I made a special trip to Laos. Only to be advised by even trusted contacts that no, absolutely nothing untowards had occurred—but why didn't I be a good lad and get my nose out of it anyway? Then yesterday at the Oriental I heard murmurs that your CIA has been all atwitter around here of late. Now since everyone more than suspects your covert boys of propping up Field Marshal K. and his playmates, it seems you caught the start or the end of some intelligence gambit. I dare say I'm letting Pandora lay in her box for now. Strongly urge you copy.

Cheers,
GEO. DIBLEY

P.S.: Upon unraveling more I shall of course communicate. But I shan't share the Pulitzer, though I'll stand a round of Foster's.

I put the letter away and pondered how much of it I should reveal to Pat.

The cab pulled up on 69th Street just west of Madison. The town house bearing the number 15 was one of those immaculate four-story structures that had survived the onslaught of developers and land packagers and, by its very presence, almost—but not quite—brought the neighboring high-rises down to a human scale. I pushed through the massive varnished oak door into the vestibule. The building had obviously been partitioned kindly for there were only three mailboxes. I drew a deep breath and pressed the button beneath the one marked "Helmsley."

The intercom squawked to life. "Yes?"

"Ray Huang."

"Third floor." A metallic click and then the inner door was buzzed open.

I started up the stairs, which were as elegant as the building's exterior. On the first landing an exquisite console bore a vase of fresh lilies. On the next landing the nameplate read "Harry Helmsley." I rang the bell.

The door was opened by a hearty-looking man in his early forties. He had sandy hair and a roundish face that looked as if it smiled a lot. His closely tailored three-piece suit subtly trimmed a body tending toward portly. He extended his hand. "Hi. Pat Ritchie. Good of you to come—please."

I stepped into the grandest living room I'd ever seen outside of a decorating magazine. Half the floor above had been removed to create a two-story ceiling, and a skylight had been carved out of the roof. To my left was a massive two-tiered bank of windows. The long wall across the room featured an oversize hearth in which a fire roared; on both sides of the fireplace hung a dazzling collection of paintings. In the center of the room stood a sectional conversation pit that opened toward the fireplace.

"Sorry I'm a little early," I said as I handed Pat my parka.

"No problem. A drink, Ray? Some sherry?"

"That'd be fine. Mind if I look at the paintings?"

"Help yourself." He laid my parka next to his overcoat on a long, low lacquered table next to the door. "You like the genre?"

"Yes, very much. In fact, I've written on it."

As I crossed the room he went to a lowboy and opened one of its two doors. He looked inside for a second before reaching a hand in. There were several clicking noises and a screech and then the brisk strains of a Vivaldi concerto flooded the room. Now Pat opened the other door and peered in before kneeling to rummage through the bottles.

The canvases in the room were of such quality that even a good-sized museum would covet them—if, that is, it were into Pop Art. On one side of the fireplace were three Jasper Johns, a small Rauschenberg, and an early Warhol.

"Damn," Pat said. "Looks like we're out of sherry. Something else?"

"Brandy if you have it," I replied, rubbing my hands against the slight chill.

Pat fished out several bottles and went into the kitchen. I

walked past the fireplace and studied two more Warhols, a Lichtenstein, an early D'Arcangelo, and a Wesselmann nude. The collection virtually encompassed the entire Pop movement. The juxtaposition of pieces wasn't particularly tasteful, but it sure got the message across: if you've got it, flaunt it.

Pat returned with a snifter for me and a Rob Roy for himself. When we'd seated ourselves in the conversation pit he said, "You said it was vital we meet."

I nodded. "The papers said Harry died in a plane crash in New Guinea. He didn't."

Pat leaned forward.

"I saw him run over by a car in Laos. In Vientiane."

His eyes dilated ever so slightly and his jaw muscles knotted. "Is..." He cleared his throat. "Is that where he asked you to call me?"

My voice tends to rise when I tell someone a lie to his face so I just nodded. "Actually," I said, "I have a note for you." I got up, walked to my parka, and dug out the aerogram. Pat had followed me across the room. As I gave him the aerogram I noticed a fresh smudge on it. My hand was grimy; evidently I'd brushed it through the film of dust on the lacquered table.

Pat gazed at the blue envelope for several seconds before reaching into a vest pocket for a tiny Swiss army knife. He unfolded the blade and began to slice open the flaps. He seemed oblivious to my presence so I turned to browse around again.

Near the tall bank of windows stood a handsome game table flanked by two Breuer chairs. I inspected the tabletop closely, never having seen an inlaid Scrabble board before. Pat was still rooted across the room with the open letter in his hand so I strolled to the fireplace and gazed at the flames. Some kindling at the bottom must have burned through just then, for the logs shifted with a *thunk* and a shower of sparks that sent me back a step.

Finally Pat cleared his throat. "Sorry for my rudeness, Ray," he said as he walked back toward me. "It's just that this letter... I imagine it was Harry's last." I remember thinking that whatever business Pat was in, he must have been a hard case, for he'd managed to keep his composure even after reading the awful prophecies in the aerogram. We sat down again. "You'll never know how much I appreciate getting this," he said. "Now tell me about Harry's death."

After inventing a meeting between Harry and me at the Café

de la Paix, and a reason for following him out of the restaurant—to recheck Pat's phone number—I told the truth. When I reached the part about seeing the Mercedes' license plate I added that the vehicle was registered to one of the heads of the Thai junta.

"Why do you think that?"

I'd decided I didn't want Dibley's name to come up so I said, "I made some discreet inquiries."

Pat started to pose another question, but instead asked me to continue.

I went on to describe the removal of Harry's corpse by the Pathet Lao, and how on my return to the States I'd learned that the body had turned up in West Irian. "Why was he run down?" I concluded. "And why would the Communists take the body away and then turn it over to the Indonesians?"

Pat gazed down at his glass, then finished off his drink. "Another?" he said, pointing to my empty snifter. I shook my head. He pursed his lips and asked, "How well did you know Harry?"

"We've talked a longer time than I spoke with him."

"Who else knows what you saw?"

"One person."

"The person you had check out the license plate?"

I nodded.

"You didn't tell your wife?"

"I'm single," I said, baffled by his questions.

Pat turned and stared at the fire, as if he were weighing something. Finally he turned back to me. "What I'm going to tell you must remain in the strictest confidence. Promise?"

I nodded again. I could feel my palms moistening.

"In the summer of 1961," Pat began, "Harry was a tenured professor at the University of Michigan. He was a geologist specializing in extracting oil from shale, which is a type of rock. That August a man representing a foreign nation visited Harry with a business proposition. Harry reported the offer to our government. Two days later he was flown to Washington." Pat's body had relaxed and the clipped cadence of his speech had turned leisurely, almost dreamy; he seemed lost in memory as he recounted what sounded like an oft-told tale.

"That winter there was a homosexual scandal at the school. Now it was no secret on campus that Harry was gay—he and I had been living together openly for several years. But when the shit hit the fan, none of it fell on us. Harry went to Washington again during this period. On his return he submitted his resignation, though he'd remained unsmeared. It was an excruciating decision." Pat looked into the fire. "The hardest one of his life, and that's what it ultimately cost him.

"As soon as he was off the faculty, he contacted the foreign agent and accepted the engagement. When he drafted his report, of course, he cut a copy for our side. In the ten years since, Harry averaged at least one engagement a year, ostensibly for foreign powers. As you can see"—Pat gestured around the living room—"it paid very, very handsomely, since there were two 'clients' each time.

"But the threat of violence always hung over our relationship. We... we could see the skull beneath the skin." He paused and picked up the aerogram. "In here Harry said he feared for his life. And for mine. He was right, at least about himself."

I sat there stunned. Without a word Pat stood, picked up our glasses, and went back to the kitchen. While he was gone it all started to come together: the "unpleasantness" the secretary out in Ann Arbor had referred to, Harry's cloak-and-dagger death, Dibley's intimations of CIA involvement, the posh apartment I sat in. There didn't seem to be any missing links thanks to Pat's candor—he'd even confided some of the contents of the aerogram.

When he returned with fresh drinks I said, "How did you feel about Harry getting into all this?"

"Absolutely against it. I threatened to leave him when he left Ann Arbor."

"Why didn't you?"

Pat looked me square in the eyes. "I loved him."

I shifted uncomfortably. That had been a remarkably stupid question, or at least an insensitive one, but his unflappability pleased me for it reinforced my growing appreciation of his classiness. I said, "Are you in intelligence too?"

"No, insurance. The Company checked me and found, surprise surprise, that fags can be discreet. I'm tolerated."

"Did you know about Vientiane?"

"The day after it happened. And that Harry's body would be found thousands of miles away, though of course not why."

"Then why were you startled when I brought it up?"

His chuckle surprised me. "One day I'll control that slight

flaring of my eyes," he said. "Bad habit. Usually the Company is very, very good at covering up...but this time they overlooked something, eh?" I must have looked puzzled because he added, "You."

Suddenly the hairs on my nape bristled. "What would they have done if they'd known about me?"

Pat laughed again. "You read those paranoiac thrillers? Thought so. They would've fed you a story just as believable, but not nearly as accurate, as mine. In fact I should've let them debrief you. Any objections if one of their men calls?"

"You'll be reporting this meeting to them?"

He nodded.

"No, no objections. Listen, I've got one last question for you—you said that Harry warned you about danger."

"I'll discuss it with the Company, but I've never known the details of Harry's engagements, so no one has cause to harm me. Of course"—he smiled—"if anything happens to me, call them...they're in the White Pages."

I looked at my watch. It felt as if our talk had consumed the entire afternoon but in fact it wasn't even two yet. "Well," I said, "at least I'll be able to get some sleep tonight, for the first time in about two weeks."

"Sorry we didn't meet earlier. Must've been a hell of a mystery to carry in your head—and," Pat added, pointing to the aerogram, "in your hands." He walked me to my parka, picked it up, and helped me into it. "Perhaps we'll meet again, Ray."

I extended my hand. "I'm sorry again about Harry's death."

"Thank you. The Company told me he was dead before he hit the ground—I find that of comfort." Pat cleared his throat and dabbed one eye. "He...my Harry was the music while the music lasted." Now Pat blushed. "Sorry, Eliot's a passion, and ought not be misquoted." I was too moved to share his embarrassment.

At the door I reassured him that I'd not repeat our conversation. When I got outside I just didn't have the heart to trudge through the cold back to Duke's to finish working on the negatives so I went home.

I was, and still am, a compulsive collector of anything that might someday be recycled into an article or even a good paragraph within a piece. Martha called it anal retentiveness; I claimed it was the basic pack-rat nature of writers. In any event, I automatically gathered the papers related to Harry—the *Times* article, the Xeroxed author's page, and Dibley's letter—and placed them in a fresh file folder. Then I turned on Mike Douglas and waited for Martha.

2 March 1972: New York

There was a topical joke at the time about Henry Kissinger: an hour after a heady banquet at the Great Hall in Peking, he was hungry for power again. I was also suffering from a kind of Chinese restaurant syndrome; that is, having the mystery of Harry's death explained was proving strangely unsatisfying. Normally when I'm agitated I talk it out with various friends, but because of my promise to Pat I couldn't even ask Martha to serve as a sounding board. To keep myself from phoning Pat—for there was so much I still wanted to know—I made myself start on the text of my Laotian article.

First, though, the chicken scratches in my notebook needed deciphering, so I'd spent the previous day in my apartment transcribing. It hadn't gone well; I'd wasted half the day on the phone. There were several business calls, and I had to cope with a slurry-voiced asshole who rang every two hours asking for "Chuck."

To be honest, I also chatted with friends like Freddie, who'd just arrived in Washington to serve as a campaign volunteer with the Democratic National Committee. "I didn't know you had a Don Quixote complex," I'd chided. "Now that Teddy's burned his bridge behind him, what Democrat's going to knock off Tricky Dick? Hubert? Clean Gene?"

"You never know," Freddie mumbled. Then, brightening, he said, "Anyway, the DNC offices are nice. Behind enemy lines, so to speak—I see people like Mitchell and Dragon Lady Chennault every day."

"Where the fuck are you, Burning Tree?"

He laughed. "No, a new high-rise complex. Posh but tacky... the Watergate."

Because I hadn't seen Freddie since he went West I'd even made a date to visit when the cherry trees were blossoming: "The last weekend in April, then? Good, I'm jotting it on my wall calendar right now—'FW at Watergate re GOP.'"

I looked at the wall calendar and chuckled as I sipped my

coffee. Then I looked at my watch. It was after 9 A.M., and I had a ten-o'clock with Herb and his art director, so I hustled to my lab, collected the Ektachrome slides on the elephant school, and went uptown. When I knew for sure I'd sold them a cover—they had narrowed it down to two shots—I subwayed to Duke's studio to finish up the black-and-whites for the article.

My negatives still hung in the darkroom. I was snipping the rolls into six-frame strips when I came to the four frames I'd exposed of Harry's aerogram. I started to ditch them, for they were of no further use, but then I wondered if they had come out in the Constellation's wretched lighting. I printed them on a separate contact sheet and after the sheets dried put a loupe to the one containing these four frames. The images were clear and legible: bless Tri-X. I allowed myself to reread the letter. Just about everything now made sense, except for the numbers "4/1/2/1/10." Considering the swank apartment, I reflected, it was probably the combination to some hidden wall safe.

I was aware my mind was again drifting back to Vientiane and to Pat so with a sigh I gathered up the contact sheets and edited them. Then I spent the afternoon at the Mid-Manhattan reading up on the characteristics of pachyderms.

That night Martha and I met at a nearby restaurant, McBell's, where we drank and ate well and cheaply. I was even emboldened to snipe at the guy from her pottery class. "When're you going out again with the clayboy of the Western world?"

She started to get angry, then giggled. "Tuesday. And his name's Peter. Jealous?"

"Who, me?"

I walked her back to her apartment. A moment of hesitation before she asked me in; a brief kiss and then she broke away. "Wine, wine, too much wine," she muttered as she began unbuttoning her blouse.

"What's that supposed to mean?"

"Wine lowers my inhibitions."

"In other words, you've got to get drunk to fuck?"

Martha glared at me. "With you, sometimes, yes." As I went to the closet for my parka she said, "Ray. I'm sorry. Please stay."

"I'm not staying to fight."

"No, no fighting."

Later, as we were drowsing off, I turned to her and said, "I'm going to write a novel about him."

"Who?"

"Your potter friend. It'll be a *roman à clay*."

Martha didn't even open her eyes as she murmured "Prick" and snuggled closer.

3 March 1972: New York

I got out of bed in time to share coffee with Martha, then stopped at a supermarket on the way home to pick up some easy-to-grill meats, frozen vegetables, and other staples of a bachelor's pantry. I was lugging the groceries up the stoop of my building when I saw Mrs. Morabito, who lived in the ground-floor front apartment across the hall from mine, waving to me. *La signora* was something of a neighborhood fixture, for she sat for hours on end at her window reading or sewing or gossiping or writing letters to kin back in her native Tuscan village. From her perch, not much escaped Mrs. Morabito's notice.

I let myself through the glass lobby door and went to hers.

"Raymond dear, I think you check apartment, see if okay."

Suddenly I had that sinking feeling—had I been ripped off a third time? I stepped across the hall and gingerly tried my door. It was locked, which made me feel better; I'd installed a pickproof Medeco cylinder, and since Martha and I had the only two keys, any thieves leaving this way couldn't have secured the door after them. I put down my package and unlocked the door. For no good reason—I certainly wasn't expecting anyone inside—I inched the door open and slowly stuck my head in. I spotted my TV and stereo, which meant I hadn't been trespassed on by junkies again. I let out my breath and looked back at Mrs. Morabito, who was wide-eyed and wringing her hands. I laughed, picked up my groceries, and invited her inside. She hesitated until she'd made peace with her sense of propriety, then entered.

"Why did you think something was wrong?" I asked.

"Well, yesterday afternoon I shop. I come home, see very strange man in lobby, he looking in your mailbox."

In the Village oddballs were always hanging around lobbies to keep warm or give themselves a fix or rip off Social Security checks; I'd even caught one guy trying to pee in semi-privacy. "What did he look like?" I asked.

"Very strange. Thin fella, not too young, he wear a mop."

I chuckled. "You mean wig."

"No, no wig. Mop. Mop like doll—you know, Rackety-Ann."

"And then?"

"I say, 'What you want?' He run away *pronto* so I say, 'Flora, lotta crazy people, mind your own business.' But later I go to window and see him in car, and he looking at your windows. Then other man I not know leave here, get in car, they go away."

"What did this other guy look like?"

"Big." Mrs. Morabito flexed a bicep to show she meant muscular. "And big mustache, very nice mustache."

I told her they were probably visiting the rather unsociable tenants who'd recently moved in upstairs—I privately suspected they were scoring out of 4-E—and thanked her for her concern. After she left I examined my special bookcase safe. The layer of soot on the bottom shelf lay undisturbed. Then I inspected the windows. After the last burglary I'd drilled holes in the sashes and inserted tenpenny nails; these were also in place. Finally I checked my closets and file cabinet. My lesser valuables were all there.

Well, I thought as I unpacked my groceries, for once I'd been spared.

10 March 1972: New York

I spent the morning putting my elephant-school story through the typewriter one last time; the fact that it had gone well was just another sign my life was getting back to normal. Now I only thought about Harry and Pat two or three times, rather than two or three hours, a day. And I'd been called out of the blue by a producer of industrial films and commissioned to write a short but lucrative script. Best of all, Martha had decided to drop "Clay." The previous week he'd indeed grabbed at her toby jugs, which was understandable, but he might have waited until the concert at Lincoln Center was over. In short, it looked to be a great spring.

I dropped off the story with Herb in the late afternoon.

Then, since Martha had another bad closing—Muskie had beaten McGovern in the New Hampshire primary—I went to my psychiatrist friend Alan's athletic club.

I was already on the basketball court when he arrived. We immediately joined a three-on-three game, won, and continued to play. Though I was still in pretty good shape thanks to the trip, I was grateful when my pal and I were finally beaten and had to surrender the court.

"Sorry I had to cancel lunch Monday," he said when we'd regained our breath.

"No problem, I had more than enough to do. I figured you were probably trying to coax some neurotic lovely into a little lay analysis."

"Why do all you laymen... Shit." He laughed. "Why do all you shmucks think that all we do is screw our patients?"

"Who's saying all shrinks do? But we go back too far—I know you went into psychiatry just to meet your type of girl... pretty isn't enough, she's got to have nails nibbled down to the quick."

Alan grinned, but when he turned back to watch the action on the court the smile was gone. "Actually, it's been one brutal week. My office was broken into last weekend, and it's got me baffled."

"Why? What did they take?"

"That's just it—they ignored everything of value. Like money, which I'd foolishly left in an unlocked drawer, or drugs, which would have been about as easy to get at. Or even potential blackmail material."

"Sorry, I don't follow. About the blackmail, I mean."

"It's every psychiatrist's fear. Our patients are often people of means. They come to us to confess. That can be an explosive combination. For instance, I'm treating a lesbian whose career would be jeopardized if it got out, and a financier whose 'hobbies' would stun even Wall Street. Plus, several of my patients are going through messy divorces—their secrets would be damaging if their files fell into the wrong hands."

"So nothing was out of place?"

"I didn't say that. They did go through one set of files. I never would have known except I was suspicious enough to call in a locksmith, who stripped every cylinder in the office and found pick marks on two—my office door and the lock on one file cabinet. Oddly enough, those files are my most pedestrian. Still, I was obligated to contact each patient whose record might have been read." Alan looked down at the floor. "It took me most of the week, and it was not pleasant."

"Any idea who did it?"

He nodded. "Last Saturday, a crew wearing telephone-company uniforms showed up at the buidling saying there was a problem in a main switching relay. They spent about forty-five minutes inside. When we checked with New York Tel on Monday, we found no crew had been sent."

"Anyone get a description?"

"Sure. Four middle-aged Hispanics. Helpful, hunh?"

Out on the court someone nailed a twenty-two-foot jumper and the other players relaxed, their game over. Dickie, our third, called us; we were up again. As Alan and I loosened up with a couple of shots he turned and said, "Funny, but if you were one of my patients, I'd've kept our lunch date."

"How's that?"

"The files they went through were in my 'H-I-J' cabinet."

"I may be crazy, Alan, but never enough to give you any of my hard-earned bucks." I missed a jumper. "Not when I can get your advice free."

30 March 1972: New York

Two pieces of news today, one annoying and the other very bad.

The first came in the morning mail by way of a letter from the People's Republic of China's delegation to the United Nations. Earlier in the month the Communists had purchased, for a tidy $4.85 million, the 260-room Lincoln Square Motor Inn on West 66th Street to house their mission and staff. Though it was a long shot, I'd applied for permission to photograph inside once they moved in—and they had just moved in the day before.

I tore open the letter. It was from a press attaché:

Mr. Raymond T. Huang:
    In reply to your communication of 18 March we cannot allow you to make photographs within the Mission.
                                                                 KUO YU-TANG

I'd got politer rejections in my career, I thought, but nothing ventured... Then it struck me: very few people knew my middle initial, not even Martha, for the simple reason that I never used it. Someone must have run one damned thorough check. I got pretty pissed, even though I was sure the fact that my family had been, before fleeing the Mainland, "running dogs" and "capitalist lackeys" had nothing to do with the Communists' refusal; I doubted if any outsider would have been allowed to breach their notorious privacy.

I was about to throw the note away when I noticed the white-on-white embossing at its top. The seal consisted of one big star, four smaller stars in a semicircle under it, and a building that looked to be the Great Hall on T'ien An Men Square in Peking. Beneath the seal was a row of raised ideograms; of the fifteen characters I recognized the two which comprised *Chung-kuo*, or China. Pretty ritzy for a government that eschews ostentatious materialism, I thought, so I filed it as a souvenir.

The bad news came late in the afternoon by way of a call from Martha: "Ray? Didn't you meet an AP writer named Dibley on your trip?"

"Yeah, in Bangkok. Why?"

"A file just came in from Saigon. The North Vietnamese and the Cong seem to be launching their biggest attack since Tet—what caught my eye was that Dibley was up on the DMZ, and when the Reds broke through... well, our wire lists him as missing in action."

"Jesus. George put in his time in Nam—I wonder why the hell he was sent back."

"I thought you'd want to know."

"Yeah. Thanks."

"Oh, and you'll be at Grand Central before five, right?"

"Right." It was Passover, and after giving it a lot of thought Martha had invited me to a Seder at her parents' home. According to Jewish tradition on this night, which is different from all other nights, strangers are always welcome at the table. Still, I felt honored, as well as more than a little encouraged about the progress of our relationship. "I'll save you a seat in the last smoking car," I said.

I looked at my watch. There was time, so I dialed the AP office in Rockefeller Center and asked for the friend who'd originally put me on to Dibley.

"Merry? It's Ray. I just heard about George—anything new?"

"Yeah." Her voice was ominously flat. "It... it just came over the wire a couple of minutes ago. They've found his body."

"Oh my God." Only a month ago I'd been bending elbows with him. "What was he doing back there? He put in his time, and then some."

"That's what's so awful." I could hear her fighting for control. "Last week, one of the men in our Saigon bureau had a freak accident—some shithead on a moped hit-and-ran him and broke his leg. We needed a backup, Thailand's been quiet, so... God, Ray, George was only supposed to cover until we could fly some eager beaver out from Stateside." Now Merry began to sob.

When we finally rang off I found myself pondering the luck my friends and I shared. We had all been graduated from college when the only Americans in Southeast Asia had worn green berets and by the time LBJ decided to show the world our balls were bigger than theirs we were safe behind the middle-class shield of graduate school deferments. So the war had never become personal—until now.

I don't know whether it was proper or not, but that night at Seder I said a silent *kaddish* for George.

13 May 1972: New York

Martha had accepted the invitation with great reluctance for it had been tendered by a colleague of Tim's, and her estranged husband would surely be present. But Davis was still her friend as well—indeed, he'd helped her decide to separate—and the party was in honor of his engagement. I was equally apprehensive. Before Martha moved out I'd met Tim several times; having your flesh pressed by the guy you're cuckolding is never pleasant. Since the split we'd made it a point to traffic different circles, a practice I'd just as soon have continued, but I knew Martha needed me at that party.

To gird ourselves we splurged at La Petite Ferme. The food was brilliant. Our conversation wasn't.

"Fuck it," I finally said, "this is silly. After all..." I broke into a grin. "After all, we're adults."

"Are we?" She smiled. "Did I tell you about the time they tried to bump Tim and me off an overbooked flight to Rome?"

"No."

Something in the way I said that one word stopped her. She looked closely at me. "Do you want to hear about it?"

"Sure."

"No you don't."

"Aw, come on, Martha."

"No, you really don't. It's not because it might make you jealous, is it?"

"Of course not. I accept your past, just like I presume you accept mine."

"Accept." She rolled the word around much as a lexicographer might. "You know, that's the key. You never ask me about my past because... because you accept it?"

"Right."

"Well I don't necessarily accept your past, or at least your version of it. But when I ask you questions you turn them aside, usually with a joke."

"Because, to quote Flip Wilson, 'What you see is what you get.'"

"See? You just did it again."

"But I'm not joking," I protested. "I believe it. Whatever's happened to us in the past, we are what we are. Right now."

"That sounds like Chinese fatalism."

"Bullshit. We can—we do—change. All the time."

"And if I'm different a month from now?"

"Then you'll be what you are at that moment." Martha shook her head and sipped her wine. "Look," I continued, "of course the past is important. But we all tend to be very subjective when we describe it. And all I've ever heard about Tim is the bad side—the bickering, the wounds inflicted."

"That's only human," she snapped.

"Well, if it helps you, fine, but I don't see how it helps me understand you any better."

I'd hurt her enough to make her glare. Only when I finally looked away did she say, in a dangerously low voice, "Sometimes I think your so-called rationality is just a cover-up, that deep down you're nothing but a selfish shit."

With mock solemnity I touched my napkin to my mouth, then poured the last of the wine. "Well," I said mournfully, "I guess that means no sex tonight."

She couldn't suppress a snort.

"And that means there won't even be a chance of spawning a little Chew tonight."

"A what?"

"Chew. Cross between a Chinese and a Jew."

Martha laughed. "Don't you have anything better to do with your time?" I shook my head. "Damn it, Ray, I hate you for being able to do this to me."

"Do what?"

"You know exactly what I mean—getting out of something serious with a funny."

"Take my serious lover...please."

"Enough enough enough," she said, but she didn't mean it.

We finally arrived at the party late but in good spirits. Our cheer, however, lasted only until we'd congratulated Davis and his fiancée.

Martha and I were at the bar when a tall, dark, handsome man who was no stranger sauntered over, his free arm around the waist of a young and very pretty blond. "Hello, babes," Tim said to Martha; as he nodded in my direction I automatically straightened my spine and squared my shoulders. "Tina, this is my wife, Martha, and this is her boyfriend, Ray Huang. Guys, Tina." With that he lowered his hand and gave Tina a possessive pat on the rump. Tina's smile was weak; she didn't know whom to be embarrassed for. But then Tim surprised us all, for having acted out his macho shtik, he became civil. Too civil. We were casting about for bon mots when a burly, red-faced man our age swaggered up.

"Hey Tim ole buddy," he drawled. "Hey, Tina, whatta ya say?"

"Donny," Tim acknowledged, a bit nervously.

"And you gotta be Martha...heard a lot about ya." Now Donny, teetering a little in his size thirteens, zeroed me in his bloodshot eyes. "And you gotta be the Chink that's puttin' away Tim's wife."

"Donny!" Tim said sharply.

Without taking my eyes off Donny I set my glass on a table.

"You gonna fight, Chinky? Nah—killed too many of you slopes in Nam, never one of ya fought."

"God damn it, Donny." Tim gripped Donny's shoulder

hard. Donny shrugged off the hand and pushed Tim back several steps.

In the nervous silence growing around us Donny's words sounded like a bellow. "Ya know why? Know why Chinkies don't fight? Cause they got little dicks. Real little." He turned and leered at Martha. "Way too little for white cunt."

With a roar Tim went for Donny. I'd seen it coming so I took one quick intercepting step, ducked under Tim's roundhouse, and grabbed him by the waist. "No," I said insistently as I wrestled him backward, "no, it's not worth it."

"Shit, you can't take that crap from him! What the hell kind of..."

"Shut up!" I hissed. "Shut up, Tim!" He glared at me; his lips were twisted and his eyeballs pulsed. "This isn't your fight," I said.

"Goodness me, looks like Donny's gonna git hisself another gook tonight."

I turned to face the taunting voice.

"Break it up...break it up, right now!" It was Davis, our host, hurrying out from the kitchen.

"Come on, ya yella piece of shit," Donny sneered.

"Cain't fight ya, Donny, it be a sin to whup a good ole boy stoned on whiskey an..."

Donny snarled and lunged. I pivoted out of his path. His momentum carried him into a table piled with hors d'oeuvres but the sound of breaking plates was covered by the screams and shouts erupting around the room.

At that moment Davis, having pushed his way through the crowd, tried to throw a hammerlock on Donny. Donny punched out wildly; Davis staggered backward, blood seeping from a nick high on his forehead. Now Donny spun full circle, ready to charge as soon as he could target me.

"Over here, good buddy," I mocked from five yards away. "Hey, good buddy, ever tell ya 'bout the time I slipped it to your sister?" Donny began to shake with rage. "Yeah, in a Chevy by the levee . . . had to keep my eyes shut, though . . . boy is her pussy ugg-lyyy..."

His eyes the color of coral, Donny lowered his head and charged. He never saw the wall he rammed at full speed; he dropped like a poleaxed steer.

In the three beats of silence before the room dissolved into babel I staggered to a chair and collapsed. Martha rushed up. "Sorry I couldn't make him apologize," I gasped, but the quip was quivery and empty. She tomboyishly ruffled my hair. Around us people scurried for their coats. Tim and Tina came over. When he offered his hand I took it and our eyes locked for a second; then he looked at Martha, started to speak, didn't, and led Tina away.

"Drink?" Martha asked.

I nodded.

"Think you can stand?"

I nodded again.

When we reached the bar she said, "That was brave but silly."

"Nah. He was very drunk, and I knew I was much quicker." I'd bolstered my nonchalance with half a tall Jack Daniels when Davis made his way to us.

"Sorry, Ray—and thanks."

"You okay?" I said, looking at his forehead.

"Sure, it's just a shallow cut." He poured himself a stiff one. "I'm just pissed as hell that no one else tried to help out."

"Come on, I didn't expect it. Look at us—the original effete Eastern establishment. We're not fighters... negotiators maybe, but fighters, lord no."

Davis's wry grin slowly dissolved into a grimace. "Shit, nobody loves a loser, do they?" He pointed past me to the supine Donny, all of whose pals had long departed.

By the time Martha and I caught a cab downtown my metabolism had finally stabilized. She looked over and said, "Ray, I've got to know something. Why didn't you use your fists, or a bottle, or trip him or something?"

"I bruise easy."

"Seriously."

"I once killed a man in the ring."

"Seriously."

"Seriously? Because when I'm scared shitless I run much better than I attack. It makes me feel more... more in control if I can provoke the other guy into something stupid." I closed my eyes. "Which makes me yellow, I guess." She giggled. "Yella with a teeny-weeny dick." She guffawed; the cabby choked. I opened my eyes and looked into hers. "Like I said a long time ago, Martha, I don't fight. Rally. Can you abide that?"

"You don't—but can you?"

"Maybe someday."

"Well," she said, leaning her head on my shoulder, "I'll just have to abide until that someday, won't I?"

19 June 1972: New York

It was a year to the day since our first date, and Martha and I were dining out to celebrate.

I arrived at her office shortly after 6 P.M. to find a note saying to come to the conference room on the twenty-fifth floor. When I got there an office party was under way. I fixed myself a drink and began looking for her.

She was in the midst of a small knot of writers and researchers from the Nation section and she was being harangued by a pompous baldpate who looked like a young Melvin Laird: "If the press secretary says it's a 'third-rate burglary,' then it's a third-rate burglary."

"Ziegler's a third-rate asshole and so are you," Martha shot back. "What were those Cubans doing in there—trying to cop Dictaphones?"

"All you goddamn liberals are alike. When are you going to give the guy a break?"

"Listen, Gurney, I'm not the genius who invented the phrase 'the New Nixon,' I just have to check it . . . and that ain't easy."

The writer scowled. "If you don't like working for this section, just tell me, and I'll pass the word along."

Martha's eyes narrowed. "You're such a twit you would. But if I'm not happy here I'll tell Henry myself." Just then she saw me and stalked away from Gurney.

"Is that a happy face I see?"

"Oh shut up," Martha said, flashing me her Cheshire-cat smile; I decided to back off unless I wanted the evening to end in calamity. Still muttering to herself, she threw ice cubes into a tall plastic glass and slopped vodka to its rim. The glass was almost at her lips when she suddenly looked up. "Remember how we met?"

I nodded. June 19, 1971, a twilight bash in the Hamptons; I'd been on the verge of leaving when Martha arrived by herself. At first I thought her pliancy was due to my charm. In truth, she'd had another violent quarrel with Tim and drained the pitcher of Harvey Wallbangers she'd found in the refrigerator of their shared summer home, a fact brought home later that evening when she squirmed out of bed in midstroke to throw up.

Now a sad smile played across Martha's face; she remembered, too. Slowly she set the untouched drink on a table. "Come on, Ray, let's go eat."

I was digging into the Coach House's justly famed choclate cake when she said, most casually, "I just learned that the girl I'm subletting from's coming back to New York earlier than she thought."

I carefully finished chewing and swallowed. "Really? When?"

"First of July."

Damn it, I thought, I'm supposed to be a gentleman and make the offer, but why couldn't I? Because I didn't want her to move in with me? Of course not. Because of the fear of rejection? The sociologists were right—the male of the species was getting more and more passive. To stall I said, "What are your plans?"

"Oh, I don't know." Martha tilted her head back so she could look down her nose at her nails.

"You're not moving back in with Tim, are you?"

She flashed another Cheshire-cat grin.

"Doesn't he care? Or wouldn't it make a difference?"

"Wouldn't what make a difference?" Da Vinci would have recognized her smile.

"Oh, I don't know, something like, um, moving in with me?"

Martha giggled. "Oh Ray—I thought you'd never ask."

4 September 1972: Block Island

It had been the best summer of my life. Shortly after our anniversary dinner Martha left her place for mine, which we spruced up with some new furniture, including a spiffy sofa, and an extension phone in the kitchen, for she liked to cook. Ours was a paradigmatic urban relationship: by day we each had our own careers, and at night we had each other. In addition, many of the inevitable traumas suffered by two willful beings adjusting to close quarters were eased by several work-enforced separations. In early July her magazine sent her down to Miami Beach as part of its task force to the Democratic Convention that nominated McGovern; later that month I flew to the Coast to hold the hand of the director of the industrial film I'd scripted; and finally in August Martha went back to Florida for the GOP's reanointment of Nixon.

She'd been given the pre-Labor Day week off to recuperate, and my next deadline was three weeks away, so we joined Duke and his family at their vacation retreat on Block Island. Martha and I had the shack they euphemistically called a guest bungalow to ourselves until the Labor Day weekend. That's when dormitory conditions—women in the house, men in the bungalow, and kids in outdoor pup tents—were imposed to accommodate the hordes that ferreid over for Duke's annual end-of-summer clambake.

The feast out on Scotch Beach began when the sun was crimson. We were totally without manners as we pawed through the platters of lobster and clams and chicken and corn and potatoes and babbled with full mouths about the great autumn we'd all have. Duke, spying two young lovers walking barefoot on the packed sand near water's edge, gave a great yell and lobbed a couple of ears of corn to the startled boy. They ended up staying for dinner. So did an Irish setter and a yellow mutt, though the food the kids fed them must have constipated the dogs for a week.

Back at the house much later, Martha and I were still too revved up to sleep.

"Hey," I said, "how about some good outdoor screwing? We could go down by the pond."

Martha chastely cupped her breasts with her hands. "That's all you want me for—my supple body."

"It's certainly not your mind I lust after. Come on, I'll whip your ass another way tonight," I said, pointing to a half-played Scrabble game by the fireplace. She whooped derisively, for it was a fact that, much to my consternation, I was lucky to beat her more than one game in five.

Half an hour later we were down to the short strokes. I led by two points, with one tile left, but it was her turn. Martha scanned the board and used her last tile, a U, to form UDO. "That's game," she said, laughing.

"Horseshit. That was a Richard Widmark character—I challenge."

With a smirk Martha fetched a dictionary. We looked it up:

udo (ōō dō), n. (Japan.), a Japanese plant with blanched, edible roots resembling celery.

"Poor Ray," she murmured as she kissed me. "So sweet, so lovable, so dumb."

I tweaked her tit. She kept nuzzling me so I tweaked her other tit.

"You two still awake?" It was Duke's wife, up for a snack.

Martha gave me another peck and broke away from our hug. "Yeah," she said, "but I'll join you for a goodie and then bed. I'll let Ray do his pushups by himself."

Duke's wife laughed. I flashed them my martyr's look and started to slide the tiles back into the box.

Something—an almost visceral sense of cognition—stopped me. I sat and looked over the board. Five minutes later I still hadn't figured out what mental threshold I'd crossed so I laboriously restudied each of the words that had been spelt. None jogged any dim memory. This is futile, I thought, and yet I finished off my brandy and went into the kitchen in search of leftover coffee. There wasn't any. But when Duke had fancied up the house he had installed an instant boiling-water tap in the sink. I dug out a jar of freeze-dried, made myself a cup, and returned to the living room.

I took a sip. God, how I loathed instant coffee.

And suddenly the memory returned. The taste was that of the Nescafé which that night in Vientiane, when I read Harry's letter, the bellhop had brought me.

I hadn't consciously thought about the aerogram since printing it on a contact sheet shortly after meeting Pat, but no doubt because I'd pondered it so many times with such intensity, snatches now came back with crystal clarity:

Gamester. A challenge. Consult our arbiter. 4/1/2/1/10.

I had "challenged" Martha while we played Scrabble, and we'd consulted an arbiter—the dictionary. Someone at 15 East 69th Street had enjoyed the game enough to have spent several hundred dollars on a special inlaid table. Could those cryptic numbers derive from Scrabble?

Quickly I separated out the tiles with values of 4, 1, 2, and 10 points. Then I arranged the letters in five groups:

4 pts.	1 pt.	2 pts.	1 pt.	10 pts.
F	A O	D	A O	Q
H	E R	G	E R	Z
V	I S		I S	
W	L T		L T	
Y	N U		N U	

When I finished, my enthusiam had just about vanished—I was enough of a Scrabble and crossword maven to know that very few English words end in either Q or Z. Furthermore, the consonant/vowel patterns looked decidedly unpromising. Still, I made myself try mental combinations for fifteen minutes. Then I put the game away, turned off the lights, and crossed over to the bungalow.

5 September 1972: Block Island/New York

I hadn't seen so much confusion since the Mamaroneck cops raided our high school beer blast—cum—skinny-dip. Starting at sunrise, men, women, and children drifted between the house and bungalow packing, trying to get into one of the bathrooms, unpacking, queuing at the kitchen door, repacking, squabbling over possession of the new *Spider Man* comic, and all at a decibel count dangerous to your health.

I squeezed my way into the kitchen and poured myself coffee from one of two big pots on the stove. Duke offered me a couple of pancakes. I shook my head—the lobsters and clams of the previous evening were discoing in my stomach—so he tossed them onto a seven-year-old's plate. Faster than you can say "Cookie Monster" they were drowned in butter and syrup and devoured.

At 7:15 A.M. Duke rounded up his brother, two other men, Martha and me and drove us to the Block Island airstrip. The morning mist lifted off on schedule and so did our chartered plane; forty-five minutes later we'd crossed Long Island Sound and were touching down at Flushing Airport. When we got out of the cab in midtown Martha headed for her office. I had planned to stop at the Mid-Manhattan to research an esoteric science article due two weeks thence.

I didn't.

Six months had passed since I'd solved to my own satisfaction what the trouble with Harry had been. That solution must have been eroded by my dreams of the previous night, for I had awakened with a malaise unrelated to faulty digestion; it was at five thousand feet over the Sound that I'd decided to see whether I needed to have my head examined by my psychiatrist friend Alan.

Back at the apartment, as I pulled out the folder in which I'd filed the contacts of Harry's aerogram, I was conscious of the fact that my adrenal glands were pumping, that I was recapturing the gut-twisting excitement I'd experienced during my search for Pat. The numbers were as I'd remembered. I pulled out our Scrabble set and again laid out the five groups.

The phone broke my concentration. "Ray?" Martha sounded shaky. "Have your heard?"

"No—what?"

"Munich. Some Arab goons hit the Olympics. They're holding a bunch of Israeli athletes as hostages."

"Jesus."

"It's on TV . . . Oh God, Ray . . ." Her voice broke and she began taking deep breaths. "What's happening to the world? Are we all mad? Are we . . ." She started to cry.

"Hey, hey," I soothed. "Look, I'll come up and we'll have lunch. Or drinks."

"No," she said, pulling herself together. "When this broke, Henry scrambled the magazine. The story I'm researching's been scrubbed. I'll be home early."

I flicked on the television: it was late afternoon in Munich. I remember having no thoughts at all as I watched, no morbid curiosity, no horror, just numbness.

Martha came home in the early afternoon; though she'd built up a healthy tan the past week she looked terribly, terribly pale. She sat down on the sofa an arm's length away. After a half hour she finally spoke. "That shit Brundage wants the Games to go on. Says politics can't intrude—that the athletes have sacrificed too much to get here." With that she stood and began to methodically clean the apartment.

And so the day passed, with Jim McKay, primed to bring us the thrill of victory, now trying to prepare us for the agony of death. And it was all live, folks, another demonstration of the marvels of technology. No more tear-stained Walter Cronkite confined to a New York studio passing along teletype reports of how two thousand miles away Kennedy had reached

Parkland Hospital; since Watts, mobile units could bring it all right into your living room. I hated it but I wouldn't—couldn't—turn it off.

It was nighttime in Munich and late afternoon in New York when the terrorists and their victims were bused from Olympic Village to an airport. I wandered into the kitchen and found a bag of potato chips. They were stale but Martha and I consumed them silently, mechanically, never taking our eyes from the screen.

And then the reports of a shoot-out.

And then the first body count.

And then the anguished announcement that all nine Israelis had been butchered.

And then we went to bed. Without a word. What was there to say?

6 September 1972: New York

I woke up in a sweat that had nothing to do with the heat. It was midmorning. By now the street outside my front window should have been throbbing with traffic but it wasn't. I called Martha; she confirmed that on her way to work the city had seemed shell-shocked on this black September day.

I puttered aimlessly around the apartment, trying to sort out why I felt such despair. From afar, after all, what were nine deaths? A two-car collision in Nebraska, a tick of the clock in India, a fire in a Rio slum. But of course this was different: equally senseless, yes, but equally random, no. Munich had been premeditated, as all terrorism is premeditated. And if such savagery could be planned so could a lot of other things, and not just by punks—looking at the headlines, you had to wonder about the captains of business and government on whose orders dreadful mischief was being perpetrated. Was there such a prevalence of moral rot in high places in days gone by? Of course. But this was the 1970s and presumably we should have learned.

Admittedly my thinking was paranoid: the villains were Them. But I'd grown up in mid-twentieth-century America, in which They have worn so many masks. The Axis. The Russky Devils. Red-neck sheriffs or the Warren Court, you pick it. Lee Harvey Oswald. LBJ's War Machine or Jane

Fonda, you pick it. Orwell, with his propaganda *enemy du jour*, may not have been right but he wasn't wrong, either. And as I shunted down these dark mental corridors I found the root of my despair: the sinking realization that the average person, the Good Guy if you will, is still a serf, still helpless before the machinations of the power elite—which is not what's taught in Citizenship Education classes.

To snap out of it I picked up the morning paper, and just as quickly threw it aside. I punched on the tube; babbling idiots in bunny suits trying to make a deal, as if nothing had happened. I turned it off and started to clean the apartment before remembering Martha had done it the day before. Then I noticed the Scrabble tiles. Just the right touch of absurdity, I thought bleakly—Harry was just another victim, dead, and buried, so why bother? But I made myself regard the letters, which might just as well have been bits from a jigsaw or a model-car kit, for I intuitively knew any abstract challenge would be soothing. The tiles read:

F	A O	D	A O	Q
H	E R	G	E R	Z
V	I S	—	I S	
W	L T		L T	
Y	N U		N U	

To calculate the number of five-letter words possible with the tiles I multiplied the number of letters in each group: 5 × 10 × 2 × 10 × 2 = 2,000. But the unlikely assortment of letters suggested that most combinations would yield gobbledygook. I reread the last part of Harry's aerogram:

> You'll find it a challenge, but stay any *ad homonym* attack until you consult our arbiter. Gamester that you are, I know the answer will pop into your head by the time I can again apostrophize thy virtues from the harbor of your arms.

If the numbers did in fact refer to Scrabble tiles, then the "arbiter" was a dictionary. That rules out nonsense words. At the same time, because the solution would be a "challenge," the solution was either a proper name or a recognized acronym.

ONYXX

I studied the five groups again. Any of the two thousand possibilities could be an acronym, but to achieve a proper name, Groups 2 and 4 would almost have to be vowels, since Group 3 contained only consonants. I weeded the board and recalculated; now there were five hundred combinations. I decided to start with this more wieldy assortment, for by now I was appreciating the therapeutic effects of the puzzle.

I rolled two sheets of paper into my typewriter, told myself it was only time, and began tapping in five-letter bursts. Soon I felt like one of those computers that spits out non-words for manufacturers needing to name new products. Du Pont is famous for this practice, as witness such appellations as "nylon" and "Mylar." And of course one oil giant spent tens of millions to re-educate the public once its board approved the computer-generated name Onyxx, though no one had been brave enough to kill off the cartoon animal that allegedly crept into your tank with every refill of gasoline.

At the end of seventy-five minutes I was finished:

```
FADAQ  FADEQ  FADIQ  FADOQ  FADUQ  FADAZ  FADEZ  FADIZ  FADOZ  FADUZ
HADAQ  HADEQ  HADIQ  HADOQ  HADUQ  HADAZ  HADEZ  HADIZ  HADOZ  HADUZ
VADAQ  VADEQ  VADIQ  VADOQ  VADUQ  VADAZ  VADEZ  VADIZ  VADOZ  VADUZ
WADAQ  WADEQ  WADIQ  WADOQ  WADUQ  WADAZ  WADEZ  WADIZ  WADOZ  WADUZ
YADAQ  YADEQ  YADIQ  YADOQ  YADUQ  YADAZ  YADEZ  YADIZ  YADOZ  YADUZ

FEDAQ  FEDEQ  FEDIQ  FEDOQ  FEDUQ  FEDAZ  FEDEZ  FEDIZ  FEDOZ  FEDUZ
HEDAQ  HEDEQ  HEDIQ  HEDOQ  HEDUQ  HEDAZ  HEDEZ  HEDIZ  HEDOZ  HEDUZ
VEDAQ  VEDEQ  VEDIQ  VEDOQ  VEDUQ  VEDAZ  VEDEZ  VEDIZ  VEDOZ  VEDUZ
WEDAQ  WEDEQ  WEDIQ  WEDOQ  WEDUQ  WEDAZ  WEDEZ  WEDIZ  WEDOZ  WEDUZ
YEDAQ  YEDEQ  YEDIQ  YEDOQ  YEDUQ  YEDAZ  YEDEZ  YEDIZ  YEDOZ  YEDUZ

FIDAQ  FIDEQ  FIDIQ  FIDOQ  FIDUQ  FIDAZ  FIDEZ  FIDIZ  FIDOZ  FIDUZ
HIDAQ  HIDEQ  HIDIQ  HIDOQ  HIDUQ  HIDAZ  HIDEZ  HIDIZ  HIDOZ  HIDUZ
VIDAQ  VIDEQ  VIDIQ  VIDOQ  VIDUQ  VIDAZ  VIDEZ  VIDIZ  VIDOZ  VIDUZ
WIDAQ  WIDEQ  WIDIQ  WIDOQ  WIDUQ  WIDAZ  WIDEZ  WIDIZ  WIDOZ  WIDUZ
YIDAQ  YIDEQ  YIDIQ  YIDOQ  YIDUQ  YIDAZ  YIDEZ  YIDIZ  YIDOZ  YIDUZ

FODAQ  FODEQ  FODIQ  FODOQ  FODUQ  FODAZ  FODEZ  FODIZ  FODOZ  FODUZ
HODAQ  HODEQ  HODIQ  HODOQ  HODUQ  HODAZ  HODEZ  HODIZ  HODOZ  HODUZ
VODAQ  VODEQ  VODIQ  VODOQ  VODUQ  VODAZ  VODEZ  VODIZ  VODOZ  VODUZ
WODAQ  WODEQ  WODIQ  WODOQ  WODUQ  WODAZ  WODEZ  WODIZ  WODOZ  WODUZ
YODAQ  YODEQ  YODIQ  YODOQ  YODUQ  YODAZ  YODEZ  YODIZ  YODOZ  YODUZ

FUDAZ  FUDEQ  FUDIQ  FUDOQ  FUDUQ  FUDAZ  FUDEZ  FUDIZ  FUDOZ  FUDUZ
HUDAQ  HUDEQ  HUDIQ  HUDOQ  HUDUQ  HUDAZ  HUDEZ  HUDIZ  HUDOZ  HUDUZ
VUDAQ  VUDEQ  VUDIQ  VUDOQ  VUDUQ  VUDAZ  VUDEZ  VUDIZ  VUDOZ  VUDUZ
WUDAQ  WUDEQ  WUDIQ  WUDOQ  WUDUQ  WUDAZ  WUDEZ  WUDIZ  WUDOZ  WUDUZ
YUDAQ  YUDEQ  YUDIQ  YUDOQ  YUDUQ  YUDAZ  YUDEZ  YUDIZ  YUDOZ  YUDUZ
```

FAGAQ	FAGEQ	FAGIQ	FAGOQ	FAGUQ	FAGAZ	FAGEZ	FAGIZ	FAGOZ	FAGUZ
HAGAQ	HAGEQ	HAGIQ	HAGOQ	HAGUQ	HAGAZ	HAGEZ	HAGIZ	HAGOZ	HAGUZ
VAGAQ	VAGEQ	VAGIQ	VAGOQ	VAGUQ	VAGAZ	VAGEZ	VAGIZ	VAGOZ	VAGUZ
WAGAQ	WAGEQ	WAGIQ	WAGOQ	WAGUQ	WAGAZ	WAGEZ	WAGIZ	WAGOZ	WAGUZ
YAGAQ	YAGEQ	YAGIQ	YAGOQ	YAGUQ	YAGAZ	YAGEZ	YAGIZ	YAGOZ	YAGUZ
FEGAQ	FEGEQ	FEGIQ	FEGOQ	FEGUQ	FEGAZ	FEGEZ	FEGIZ	FEGOZ	FEGUZ
HEGAQ	HEGEQ	HEGIQ	HEGOQ	HEGUQ	HEGAZ	HEGEZ	HEGIZ	HEGOZ	HEGUZ
VEGAQ	VEGEQ	VEGIQ	VEGOQ	VEGUQ	VEGAZ	VEGEZ	VEGIZ	VEGOZ	VEGUZ
WEGAQ	WEGEQ	WEGIQ	WEGOQ	WEGUQ	WEGAZ	WEGEZ	WEGIZ	WEGOZ	WEGUZ
YEGAQ	YEGEQ	YEGIQ	YEGOQ	YEGUQ	YEGAZ	YEGEZ	YEGIZ	YEGOZ	YEGUZ
FIGAQ	FIGEQ	FIGIQ	FIGOQ	FIGUQ	FIGAZ	FIGEZ	FIGIZ	FIGOZ	FIGUZ
HIGAQ	HIGEQ	HIGIQ	HIGOQ	HIGUQ	HIGAZ	HIGEZ	HIGIZ	HIGOZ	HIGUZ
VIGAQ	VIGEQ	VIGIQ	VIGOQ	VIGUQ	VIGAZ	VIGEZ	VIGIZ	VIGOZ	VIGUZ
WIGAQ	WIGEQ	WIGIQ	WIGOQ	WIGUQ	WIGAZ	WIGEZ	WIGIZ	WIGOZ	WIGUZ
YIGAQ	YIGEQ	YIGIQ	YIGOQ	YIGUQ	YIGAZ	YIGEZ	YIGIZ	YIGOZ	YIGUZ
FOGAQ	FOGEQ	FOGIQ	FOGOQ	FOGUQ	FOGAZ	FOGEZ	FOGIZ	FOGOZ	FOGUZ
HOGAQ	HOGEQ	HOGIQ	HOGOQ	HOGUQ	HOGAZ	HOGEZ	HOGIZ	HOGOZ	HOGUZ
VOGAQ	VOGEQ	VOGIQ	VOGOQ	VOGUQ	VOGAZ	VOGEZ	VOGIZ	VOGOZ	VOGUZ
WOGAQ	WOGEQ	WOGIQ	WOGOQ	WOGUQ	WOGAZ	WOGEZ	WOGIZ	WOGOZ	WOGUZ
YOGAQ	YOGEQ	YOGIQ	YOGOQ	YOGUQ	YOGAZ	YOGEZ	YOGIZ	YOGOZ	YOGUZ
FUGAQ	FUGEQ	FUGIQ	FUGOQ	FUGUQ	FUGAZ	FUGEZ	FUGIZ	FUGOZ	FUGUZ
HUGAQ	HUGEQ	HUGIQ	HUGOQ	HUGUQ	HUGAZ	HUGEZ	HUGIZ	HUGOZ	HUGUZ
VUGAQ	VUGEQ	VUGIQ	VUGOQ	VUGUQ	VUGAZ	VUGEZ	VUGIZ	VUGOZ	VUGUZ
WUGAQ	WUGEQ	WUGIQ	WUGOQ	WUGUQ	WUGAZ	WUGEZ	WUGIZ	WUGOZ	WUGUZ

The list looked like a crib sheet for an Esperanto teacher or a UN bureaucrat picking an agency to funnel money through. Still, I cracked my dictionary and began to check each of the five hundred combinations to see if any was a word. An hour later I knew four hundred ninety-nine of them weren't. But one was; it appeared in the extreme right-hand column, third line from the top.

Though I'd always considered myself reasonably knowledgeable, not until that morning did I learn that Vaduz is the capital of Liechtenstein. According to my *World Almanac* this principality, which is "slightly smaller than the District of Columbia," is known not only for its stamps but for its false-teeth industry and as a corporate tax haven. Wonderful, I thought, Harry left Pat a valuable stamp collection or diamond-inlaid choppers. Or perhaps he'd incorporated himself.

My stomach was growling so I bought a sandwich and repaired to a bench under a shady tree in Washington Square. The park was crowded with tykes splashing in the fountain and minstrels and Frisbeers and addicts nodding off. What mourning there'd been for Munich seemed over, including mine—but then perhaps our ability to get on with it is the most valuable of all human traits.

When I returned to my apartment I was glumly resigned to typing out and checking the remaining 1,500 five-letter possibilities, for therapy had become obsession. To delay the chore, I again read the last part of Harry's aerogram:

> You'll find it a challenge, but stay any *ad homonym* attack until you consult our arbiter. Gamester that you are...

I guess it had always bothered me that in such a precise letter, written in a meticulous hand, Harry had misspelled one word. And given the fact that he had been an academic, it seemed ironic that the one word should be part of the common Latin phrase *ad hominem*. Homonym, after all, meant...

A word that sounds like another word.

Vaduz. I tried it both the way I would naturally say it, *Va-dooz*, and by its proper pronunciation, *Va*-doots. Nothing.

Liechtenstein.

> ...that you are, I know the answer will pop into your head by the time...

Pop. Liechtenstein...homonym: Lichtenstein—Pop artist Roy Lichtenstein, one of whose canvases hung in the living room on East 69th Street.

No, it couldn't be, I thought even as I scrambled madly through the folder on Harry for Pat's telephone number. As I dialed I realized I'd be revealing my knowledge of the aerogram's contents but I was frankly too excited to care—I'd wing it.

The phone was answered on the third ring by a machine. Not, however, Pat's machine. "The number you have reached," intoned a metallic feminine voice, "880–0347, has been changed. The new number is 718–2600. Please make a note of it: 880–0347 has been changed to 718–2600. If you need..."

I hung up and dialed the new number.

"Cruickshank and Robeck, good afternoon," a woman answered. It was a law firm. When I explained my call she checked her files and put me through to one of the partners.

"Mr. Thatcher, my name is Ray Huang. I'm trying to reach Pat Ritchie."

"I'm afraid that would be rather difficult, because, you see, Mr. Ritchie is deceased."

"Oh my God," I blurted, remembering instantly the warning in the aerogram. "How did it happen?"

"A heart attack, I believe. Wait one moment... yes, that's right, he suffered a heart attack last winter while vacationing in California."

"There was nothing, uh, unusual about Pat's death?"

"No," Thatcher said, surprise creeping into his plummy voice. "It is my understanding that Mr. Ritchie suffered from a cardiovascular problem, though of course I see your point—he did seem rather young, didn't he?"

I remember thinking rather crossly that the mid-forties wasn't all that young for us non-patricians. "Uh, Mr. Thatcher, I gather you aren't Pat's attorney?"

"Good heavens no. I am the New York representative for the late Dr. Helmsley's estate. May I ask to what this call is in reference?"

"Well, shortly after Dr. Helmsley's death, I expressed to Pat my interest in some of the art in their apartment."

"You must be mistaken, sir."

"About what?"

"You couldn't have spoken to Mr. Ritchie after Dr. Helmsley's death," he corrected like a smug schoolteacher. "Mr. Ritchie died *before* Dr. Helmsley. In early February."

"But, but..."

"In addition, Mr. Huang, the art in Dr. Helmsley's apartment belonged to Dr. Helmsley; there was no joint ownership."

"I see," I said, trying desperately to regroup. Who the hell had I met in the apartment? And why was Thatcher pussyfooting about ownership? "Of course you're right, sir—I must have mixed up my dates. Uh, what happened to the paintings?"

"They were bequeathed to Dr. Helmsley's brother." He allowed himself a chuckle. "Mr. Victor Helmsley happens to be quite conservative in his tastes. I suppose they are in fact important works..." Thatcher never uttered the next word, which would have been "but." Instead an old-boy shrewdness entered his voice. "May I ask if you have an interest in purchasing any of the works?"

Suddenly I understood the shift in the lawyer's attitude: he was charged with liquidating the collection, and there must still be canvases unsold. That meant he probably understood how the art world works, so I replied cautiously, "I'm afraid not. But I am advising a client who's seeking to develop the finest Pop grouping in the Orient."

"I see," he said, working manfully—and vainly—at suppressing his excitement; it was no secret that several Japanese collectors were paying asininical sums for Pop works. "I believe two of the pieces have been sold. But the others are on exhibit at the Castellano Gallery—you know it, of course?"

"Of course," I lied.

"If you'll permit me, Mr. Huang, I shall take the liberty of personally phoning Mr. Castellano to relay your interest."

I knew I couldn't stop him so to prevent the gallery employees from groveling before the first Oriental to set foot in the place I said, "I'm afraid I can't get over there until next week—could you tell him I'll ring for an appointment?" That seemed to clinch it for Thatcher because he became positively ebullient, so much so I decided to try to sneak one past. "By the way, sir, I'm still rather stunned by Pat's death. Do you know how old he was when he, uh..."

"I wouldn't know exactly, but... wait a minute. Yes, here it is in the file. According to the death certificate, Mr. Ritchie was, let me see now, twenty-nine. Yes, twenty-nine."

When I got off the phone I was so jittery I had to go take a leak. I thought back to the meeting at Harry's apartment and began to remember little things: the dust on the table, the hesitation at the lowboy when "Pat" went for liquor and found the tape deck, the chilliness in the room and the fire so fresh the kindling hadn't yet burned. And of course "Pat" had seemed more agitated by my mention of Vientiane than the threat contained in the aerogram—or, for that matter, the code. Still, the impersonator had not only known a lot, he'd carried it off convincingly. But was any of what I'd been told true?

According to the telephone directory the Castellano Gallery was on East 57th Street. Thatcher must surely have called in the good news by now so I donned a paint-specked work shirt. Then I found my old book bag, which I plumped out with a notebook and some newspapers, and into which I stuffed the contact sheet of Harry's aerogram. Satisfied that I now looked like a grubby student rather than a wealthy collector's point man, I headed for the subway.

The gallery was a long, wide room at street level. Clusters of portable partitions had been erected to increase the wall space. Toward the center of the room was a grouping of sculptures; even from a distance I recognized two Oldenburgs and several Segal plaster figures. At the back, near a door that most likely led to the executive offices, stood the receptionist's desk.

The place was deserted except for the receptionist. This young lady, who was watering a planter near the front door, seemed the archetypal snooty gallery go-fer: lank, frosted hair, a freckled face attractive in an equine way, and a rangy body draped in Peck & Peck. She looked me over, sniffed mentally, and turned on the twenty-five-watt smile. Then she treated me to a demonstration of classic Long Island lockjaw; her lower face never moved as she honked, "May we help you?"

"I'm doing a term paper on Pop Art."

She compressed her lips for an instant, nodded, and went back to her gardening.

Had I really been studying Pop Art I would have come to the right place, for the Castellano Gallery specialized in it; the oldest piece of canvas there had probably been stretched no later than 1957. Slowly I browsed my way through the alcoves, making a show of taking notes to allay the Junior Leaguer's wary gaze. Now I began to recognize several of the works I'd seen up at Harry's. As I neared the back, though, my nervousness increased. Thatcher had said two of the paintings had been sold. Which two? Then I reached the alcove directly across from the receptionist's desk.

Sob, Sister, as it was titled, was executed in 1963. Lichtenstein was then spoofing cartoonists; the work before me was one of his satires on the true-romance genre. Its subject was a young blond lady, wearing a pink cashmere sweater, pleated blue skirt, and saddle shoes, who was slumped on the arm of a sofa. In the background a night wind ominously billowed the gauzy white drapery. A single tear slid down the girl's cheek. The caption within the balloon read:

> I . . . I'M
> JUST SO
> CONFUSED . . .

Why had Harry wanted to draw Pat's attention to this canvas? It couldn't be just its value, for although I suspected the Lichtenstein could fetch almost fifty thousand dollars, I knew other works in Harry's collection were worth even more.

I started doubting myself again. Perhaps I'd interpreted the clues incorrectly, or perhaps what I'd interpreted weren't even clues; after all, those numbers could refer to a lot of things besides Scrabble tiles. But my waffling was quickly replaced by conviction: I had to be on the right track, for the events leading me to this spot were too well meshed to be mere coincidence.

If it wasn't the painting itself, I decided, it must be something hidden on it. I toyed with pulling the canvas from the wall to look at its back but I knew I was under scrutiny, and anything secreted there would have been discovered when the painting had been moved to the gallery.

I pawed through my book bag for the contact sheet. As I peered through the loupe, one word suddenly leapt off the glossy: APOSTROPHIZE.

Sure enough, there was an apostrophe within the caption balloon.

I'd been standing some five feet from the canvas. Now I stepped forward and planted my face less than five inches from it. The black paint of the apostrophe seemed fractionally lighter than that of the surrounding characters and lines. There was a strong light source to my left so I edged slightly to my right, turned my head toward the light and moved still closer until my right cheek almost touched the canvas. The receptionist, who'd returned to her desk, let out a very nervous "Ahem."

I stepped back immediately. I'd seen enough.

Most Pop works have a deliberately flat texture as opposed to, say, the tactile impasto of an Impressionist painting. Because of this I could clearly observe, when I'd squinted at the backlit canvas, the fabric's warp and woof. It was regular— except for where the apostrophe was. This small area seemed to be covered by a smooth patch that bridged several rows of woven canvas. I wasn't sure what the patch was but I'd never be able to approach it while the receptionist sat there, so I made myself continue to the next alcove, which was also the last before the offices.

I was feigning interest in one of the Warhols from Harry's apartment when a competent-looking woman in her fifties emerged from the executive suite and crossed to the receptionist. "Amanda," she said, handing over a file folder, "Mr. Castellano will be returning from Osaka on Friday. He'll need these verified by then."

"Yes Mrs. Post." As soon as Mrs. Post returned to the back Amanda savagely chucked the folder into one of her desk drawers.

I put away my notebook and headed back outside. The early

rush hour had started so rather than fight the subways I trudged down to Paley Park, one of several vest-pocket oases in midtown, and sat by the artificial waterfall. The mist felt good.

By now I'd decided unless Harry was pulling some cosmic prank, the smooth-surfaced patch held a message. The body of the apostrophe was about three-quarters of an inch long by one-quarter of an inch wide: ample space for a safe combination or the number of a secret savings account.

What I was having trouble figuring out was what the damned thing was made of. It was very thin—I'd spotted it not because it rose above the canvas but because it had covered the weaving—and it had to be able to take a coat of paint, as well as withstand paint remover. Wait a minute, I thought, that couldn't be right: if the message were on the outer surface, you'd erase it when you scrubbed off the paint. That meant the message faced the canvas. This in turn meant Harry must have used an easy-to-dissolve adhesive, for if you had to scrape off the glue you'd run a strong risk of damaging the message, too—not to mention that no one in his right mind would want to chance defacing such an expensive painting. I finally narrowed it down to two possibilities. The material could be Scotch tape. Or it could be a thin slice of glass, plastic, or metal, or a piece of film, secured by something no stronger than rubber cement.

It was almost 6 P.M. so I swung by Martha's office. She took one look at my grotty outfit and started to say something.

"Let's have our drink at the Roadhouse," I interjected; at that bar near Sheridan Square they couldn't care less if you showed up in a jockstrap.

"You have an answer for everything, don't you?"

"What do you mean?" I protested. "I didn't even hear a question." But secretly I wished she was right—that I did have an answer for, if not everything, at least the suddenly reborn mystery of Harry and Pat.

7 September 1972: New York

Because I'd never told Martha about my adventures stemming from that night in Vientiane I waited until she left before I performed my two experiments.

First I took down the only painting on canvas in the apartment. I wrote my name on the sticky side of a piece of Scotch tape, pressed it to the back of the canvas, and then peeled it off. The tape was clean but my name was on the canvas, backward. I was puzzled until I realized I'd used a felt-tipped pen; when I repeated the procedure with a ball-point the ink held to the tape.

Second, I took out a scrap black-and-white negative, since of the other materials I'd narrowed the apostrophe down to, film was the most fragile. I applied a light coat of rubber cement to the emulsion side, pressed it to the canvas, and, after it had fully dried, tugged it off. The film was gummy. I squirted rubber cement thinner on it and then whiped off the residue with a clean cloth. When I put the loupe to the negative I saw a few light nicks, but no more than those left by a mediocre commercial lab; removing the apostrophe without damage, then, should pose no real problem.

But that receptionist would. That's when I realized that thin as she was, surely Amanda lunched. It was almost 11 A.M. so I quickly showered and dressed. In my suit pocket I placed a small plastic envelope designed to protect color transparencies, an X-Acto knife and a pair of tweezers.

I was on East 57th Street by 11:40 A.M. I strolled by the gallery and pretended to inspect the Lindner in the window. Despite the glare off the plate glass I could see Amanda sitting coolly at her desk. I walked to a nearby bus stop, leaned against the closest building, and opened my *Times*. Soon I longed to move under some shade, but I didn't dare give up an ideal vantage point so I stayed put. And perspired. And tried to read. I was skimming a piece on the secret GOP slush fund whose existence presidential fund raiser Maurice Stans had just admitted when Amanda finally emerged on the arm of a dapper young Mad Ave type. Lucky man, I thought darkly as I hastened back to the gallery window.

Mrs. Post now sat at the receptionist's desk reading a book. She seemed to be alone.

I calculated I'd need about a minute, then figured out a plan to give myself twice that time, then hurried to a pay phone. "Martha? Hi, it's me. Listen, I need a favor that's got to be done exactly like I tell you. What time do you have?"

"Twelve-oh-six. Why? What's..."

"Not now. I want you to look up the phone number of the Castellano Gallery—it's on Fifty-seventh. Call them at exactly twelve-thirteen. Tell them you're an associate of Jay Wong—that's J-a-y W-o-n-g. You want to make an appointment with Castellano himself for sometime next week. When..."

"Ray, what's this all about?"

"I said later. When his secretary's got his calendar, stall her—make a date, change it, that kind of thing, okay? Promise I'll fill you in tonight. Bye."

Mrs. Post looked up as I entered the gallery but when I headed right for a Jasper Johns near the front she resumed reading.

At 12:11 P.M. I walked back to her desk and said, "Would you have a..." Then I pretended to notice the painting in the alcove across from her. "Oh, you do. Sorry to trouble you."

"Not at all." She smiled and returned to *The Female Eunuch*.

I started to peer at the Lichtenstein.

At 12:13 P.M. the phone rang.

I reached into the pocket containing the X-Acto knife and gripped it.

"Castellano Gallery, good afternoon," Mrs. Post answered. "Oh yes, Mr. Castellano is expecting your call. Would Mr. Huang like... Oh, I beg your pardon." She picked up a pen. "W-o-n-g. I'm so sorry. Would Mr. Wong like to come in... Wednesday? Let me check Mr. Castellano's calendar. May I put you on hold? Fine." She got up and went into the back offices.

A quick scan of the room: no one had entered the gallery after me.

I pulled out the knife. My hand trembled so I took a deep breath, fixed my eyes on the apostrophe, and guided the blade to its rim. The edge of the material worked free without much resistance; I'd guessed right on the adhesive. Quickly I flicked the raised edge with a finger. Nothing. I flicked again. Still no purchase. The tweezers, dummy—I fumbled them out and clamped them to the edge and tugged and the apostrophe peeled right off and I began to breathe again. I whipped out the plastic envelope, blew it open, and dropped in my haul; only now did I permit myself to wipe away the beads of sweat that had formed on my upper lip. The operation had seemed interminable but in fact it took all of twenty seconds.

I inspected the painting: there were a few snot-like gobs of rubber cement dangling from the original apostrophe but no damage.

Then I made myself walk slowly and without a backward glance out of the gallery. Once I hit the sidewalk, though, I broke into a fair approximation of a jog. Two blocks away I stopped to examine the contents of the plastic envelope. The "apostrophe" was a sliver of film.

Back at the apartment I used a loupe to study the emulsion side of the sliver; it was extremely fine-grained stock. I squirted thinner on the cement and gently wiped off the gunky residue. There were four tiny images on the film. Before I could view them, though, I had to remove the paint from the shiny side.

I collected several Q-tips, a can of turpentine, and the scrap negative I'd experimented on earlier. I placed the apostrophe emulsion side down on a piece of felt, wet a Q-tip with saliva, and vigorously twirled the damp cotton against the paint. None came off, which meant it was oil- rather than latex-based. Next I dipped another Q-tip in turpentine and rubbed it briskly on the scrap negative's shiny surface. When the film was dry I checked it with the loupe: the solvent had not damaged the stock. Now I began to gently dab the turp on the apostrophe. Harry hadn't needed much paint because the film itself was black; it took only three swab sticks to clean it off.

I was about to run up to Duke's studio to use his enlarger when I realized I could view my microfilm just as easily at home. I trotted to the camera store around the corner and bought a box of thin glass mounts, which are designed to protect color slides that are handled frequently. Back at my desk I positioned the sliver of film between two thin sheets of glass and crimped the plastic frame into place. Then I set up my Carousel and screen.

I took a deep breath and flicked on the projector.

The images were those of four upside-down sheets of paper. I fumbled the slide over. The first sheet was jammed with typewritten words, the second and third pages seemed to be a report on letterhead stationery, and the final sheet bore just a few paragraphs typed in a style similar to the first sheet.

I began to read:

[Sheet 1]

Sept. 14, 1971

Dearest Pat,
Unbeknownst to you, I have left such a communication before each of my *expeditions noirs*—and destroyed it upon

my safe return. So now I repeat an introduction honed from having been written six times previously: In all probability, this letter comes to you from my grave. May it be profitable.

In our six years together, we've never discussed my missions. But I am certain you've sensed they are, shall we say, extralegal. Some, like falsifying and forging surveys so my clients among the Seven Sisters could obtain more favorable lease terms, have been inoffensive. Others have not. Once I seduced a high Filipino oil official for the purpose of blackmail. Another time I helped analyze which Venezuelan petrochemical expert was most indispensable to his nation's technological growth. Five weeks after I "fingered" the man, he met with a fatal "accident."

Thus, mine is not a record of which to be proud. But perhaps a stigmatized academic should not fret about such niceties as conscience; I can clearly remember the Dutch gentleman who gave me my first commission sneering, with infuriating *patroon* propriety, "But Professor, is this worse than blowing a farm boy in a toilet? At least with us you shall not be caught." And of course I have never balked at accepting my clients' largesse. After all, who else would pay a man like me such sums?

Of course it is a bit silly—and a bit late—for me to justify, even to myself, my last decade. So on to my present and your future.

Within the month I depart for the Far East. In one sense seven is my lucky number; that is, on my seventh assignment I will for the first time be working in my field of expertise, shale.

I have been retained by Mr. George Blair of the consulting firm of Irwin D. Small, Inc. of Cambridge, Mass.

I am to survey the Annamese Cordillera. This is a range that snakes out of southern China through the Vietnams, Laos, and parts of Cambodia and Thailand. I am to determine whether the native shale can be economically refined into petroleum synthetics.

For this I will be paid, by Small, Inc., the sum of $36,000. There is a signed contract in our safe-deposit box, along with a term life-insurance policy for the amount of $100,000 premiums paid by Small, Inc.; you and Victor are co-beneficiaries.

But I said this will be an *expedition noir*, and so it is to be. No matter what my findings, I am to draft my final report to show a convertibility factor of at teast 50 gpt, sufficient to justify the construction of an advanced refinery. To guarantee this analysis, I have been promised an extra $114,000. Though Small, Inc. is not famed for clean hands, I doubt if they are behind this stipend; Mr. Blair himself deposited in Account No. H4–982, at Leclair & Cie, a private bank in Geneva, an advance of $57,000. The balance is due on completion, though since you are reading this, the mission was most probably aborted. There is also in that account approximately $27,000 remaining from previous *expeditions*.

Only two people can withdraw this money. I am one; you are the other. To liquidate the assets, write Herr Adolf Zeiss of that bank. Your identificatory codes are your Social Security number and your signature, both of which I have furnished him.

In my previous communications, I have ended with the above instructions and my adieus. But this time I must continue.

When Mr. Blair gave me the coordinates I am to explore, I ascertained that my search would take me not only into Communist China and North Vietnam, but territories now held by the Pathet Lao, the Viet Cong, and the Khmer Rouge. When I pointed this out to him he replied that I need not worry. I did worry, given the instability of Southeast Asia. In fact, I was on the verge of declining the mission when I decided to have a check run on Mr. Blair. For a fee which eventually totaled almost $13,000, the investigative firm of Datatec produced the report on the succeeding two pages (the originals are in a safe-deposit box at Leclair & Cie; you may retrieve them using the same procedure).

[End of Sheet 1]

[Sheet 2, on Datatec stationery]
DATATEC for Dr. Harry Helmsley/Page 1 of 2
RE: BLAIR, GEORGE FREDERICK
    34 College Lane,
    Wellesley, Mass.
DOB: 8/13/29; St. Louis, Mo. HT: 6'1" WT: 170 lbs.
HAIR: Lt. br. EYES: Br. IDENT SCARS: None.
FAMILY: m. Deborah Winger Cranston (12/31/58); s. Thomas
    S. E. (b. 2/17/60); d. Julia C. (b. 10/7/64).
POL AFFIL: Republican.
ACTIVITIES: Congregational Church, Wellesley; Rotary Club,

Wellesley; Country Club, Brookline, Mass.; Eastward Ho C.C., Chatham, Mass.; coach, Wellesley Little League.

EDUCATION: St. Louis (Mo.) Country Day; B.A., U. Missouri, '50 (Pol Sci); MBA, Harvard, '53.

MILITARY: 2nd Lt., U.S. Army (Intelligence), '53–'55 (18 mos. Athens, Greece).

PROFESSIONAL EXPERIENCE:

1955–57: Chase Manhattan Bank (mgmt. trn./N.Y.; asst. mgr./Paris, France).

1957– : Irwin D. Small, Inc., Cambridge, Mass. (currently ltd partner).

Among his many engagements for Small, Inc., colleagues cite several as being of particular interest:

Petrochemical by-product development, Saudi Arabia, '64.

Analyzing crude oil shipping, Greece, '64–'65.

Feasibility of non-petroleum powered utilities, Macao, '66.

Offshore oil exploration, Gulf of Siam, '68–'70.

FINANCES: 1970 salary: $41,500. 1970 bonus: $3,900. Assets include home, assessed value $130,000 (2nd mortgage due $78,000); savings (Shawmut Bank), $6,400 as of 7/71; investments (Merill Lynch), $27,500 as of 7/71; two cars (1970 Ford station wagon, 1968 Porsche).

[End of Sheet2]

[Sheet 3, on Datatec stationery]

DATATEC for Dr. Harry Helmsley/Page 2 of 2/RE: BLAIR, GEORGE FREDERICK

It has been learned that MR. BLAIR maintains a second savings account, under the name GEORGE FRIEDRICH, at Leclair & Cie of Geneva, Switz. The balance as of 12/70 was $225,000 U.S. It has been learned that this is not a Small, Inc., slush fund. Rather, at least one recent large deposit to the account was paid by Entrepays, a Swiss company that conducts limited trade with the People's Republic of China (1970 Ex-Im volume: $0.82 million U.S.). Entrepays was chartered in 1966. Its chairman is PRINCE JEAN DE BROUILLY, a French politician/entrepreneur.

It has also been learned that since 1969 (when his passport was last renewed), MR. BLAIR has visited Switzerland four times, though his colleagues at Small, Inc. can remember no engagements that might have taken him to that country.

Finally, a copy of a Xerox of an interesting letter:

7/18

J:
Encouraging news. Frew saw The Man Monday and outlined our alternatives. The Man rejected assassination ("We could do it for sure, but it would be wrong—we can stonewall one, but not four"), subornation and laissez-faire. That leaves aiding the insurgents ("Risky, make no mistake about that. But we're propping up some pretty goddamn unstable people, and if the whole thing blows it's a war the Democrats dragged us into. I like it"). Which means we stand a good chance of subcontracting arms through our pipelines. See you next month.
G.

[End of Sheet 3]

[Sheet 4]

It was on the basis of this report, my dear Pat, that I decided to accept the mission.

It is obvious to any reader of newspapers that "The Man" in Mr. Blair's letter occupies the White House, and that he was referring to Southeast Asia, most probably the nations I shall visit.

But what the agents of Datatec—as well as most other people—can't know are these facts:

* "Frew" is the nickname, used only by intimates, of Franklin Renfrew Fanning, chairman of Onyxx;

* In 1968, Onyxx illegally contributed several hundred thousand dollars to the Republican party, and will most assuredly match that sum next year, no matter how the new campaign finance laws are enforced;

* Late last year, Onyxx covertly retained Small, Inc., to investigate long-range trade feasibility with Communist China.

It is my surmise that the President may talk about more than normalizing diplomatic relations when he visits Chairman Mao next spring; he may be acting as an agent of Onyxx as well. Where Mr. Blair and Small, Inc., fit into this puzzle I do not yet know, and certainly Entrepays bears investigation.

I hope that by participating on this survey I may uncover facts that ultimately will buy us total financial security for the rest of our lives. If you read this letter, I shall not have been successful in avoiding the mission's obvious perils. But I urge you to make use of the above information and monies.

I love you now as I have always loved you, Pat.
Goodbye.
HARRY

[End of Sheet 4]

I flicked off the projector.

Slowly I became aware that my arms were crisscrossed tightly across my chest and my hands were jammed under my armpits; though it must have been over eighty degrees in the un-air-conditioned room I felt as if I were freezing. Finally I stood. I removed the slide from the machine and added it to the file folder I'd started on Harry. I took the folder to my bookshelf and deposited it in my secret cache.

Then I ventured out into the afternoon heat. When the streetlights blinked on at twilight I found myself in the northeast corner of Central Park, eight miles from my apartment, staring at the southern edge of Spanish Harlem.

I still don't remember how I got there.

Book II

8 September 1972: New York

Martha was sprawled on the sofa watching the window turn from the black of night to the purple-grey of false dawn. I was slumped in an armchair across from her, calculating how many more cigarette butts we could squeeze into the ashtray before it overflowed. The exhilaration of airing my mystery had passed hours ago; now the silence was suffocating, all the more so because neither of us would breach it.

I cleared my throat and shattered the stillness.

She turned to me. "Well?"

"You're right—but you're wrong." As her eyes flared I ducked mine. "Of course I can't keep this under wraps. But who the hell do I tell? The cops? They're only going to care that I messed up a painting. Justice or the FBI? You think Kleindienst or Gray'll order an investigation leading to their sugar daddy? With the elections just two months off?"

"I told you, Ray, go public. This has to come out before November. Write it yourself. Or see Sandy at *Life* or Sheehan at the *Times*, or how about those two hotshots down at the Washington *Post*, the ones working on the Watergate thing?"

I shook my head.

"Well then why did you ask me for advice? You seem to..."

"Shit, we're talking about a career story," I said vehemently. "I'm not about to give it to somebody else, not if I can pull it off myself. And I will pull it off, but it's going to take time." I picked up my clipboard from the coffee table. "No editor, including yours, would print what I've got so far. I mean, we know there was a Harry Helmsley, and that I saw him killed. And that he was a geologist who was probably canned by Michigan for sodomy. And that he had money, lots of it. And that there's a detective agency named Datatec, which the phone book says has offices at 666 Fifth Avenue. But hell, maybe Harry took his severance and plunged it in some oil stock that came home. Maybe the blackest expedition of his life was cruising 125th Street."

"And Vientiane," Martha interjected sarcastically. "I suppose he was there for the same reason? With two muscle boys to pimp for him?"

I ignored her and continued with my checklist: "Maybe Harry had an irrational grudge against Onyxx and wanted to embarrass them. Maybe there is no Fanning, no Blair. Maybe..."

"Maybe maybe maybe! Jesus Christ, just listen to yourself. Maybe Helmsley's corpse moved itself to Indonesia and maybe that was the janitor who entertained you up in his apartment." She shook her head. "Why are you trying so hard to play devil's advocate?"

"Because it's got to be nailed down before I go public."

"Or?"

I sighed. "Have you forgotten..."

"Or you'll lose face?"

"It's not face."

"Oh no, you're too much of an American to have face, you have an ego. No wonder you're always right—you never try, you never gamble unless it's wired beforehand." Martha moved to the edge of the sofa, holding my gaze with hers. "What's going to happen when you finally blow one? Are you going to be able to admit it? If things go bad between us, will you have the guts to kick me out... or am I going to have to make the decision?"

"Stick to the topic."

"This is the topic."

"What..."

"Because life's not a game, Ray. You never talk about your childhood much, but I look at you now and I can see it all. You're so Americanized that you must have wanted it very badly, the joy of beating the natives on their home field. You write better in a second tongue than most people can in their first. You're always pleasant and charming, even to schmucks. But don't you see those are also games, just like softball and basketball? Rules, they all have rules that allow a second chance—you screw up and you can redeem yourself the next inning or the next party or the next assignment. Of course that makes you very can-do, very optimistic, and I like that. But what's not a game? Are we? I've just finished a six-year game with Tim and I'm not up for a doubleheader, thank you."

I was speechless because I was confused and annoyed. Annoyed because her complex digression, for that was what I thought it, was shunting my concentration from the problem at hand. And confused, much like a butterfly that awakens from an ether funk to find its wings pinned and the lepidopterist's eye near: though I rejected Martha's analysis, I felt skewered on its very precision. How could I have known her so long without knowing how she viewed me?

"What I'm trying to get at, Ray, is that this thing"—she gestured at my notes and the scraps of film and paper on the coffee table—"this thing isn't just a harmless little game. You solved the first part, and knowing you, you had a damn good time doing it. But you're an amateur who got lucky... and if any of this is true, then it's the big leagues. So get some help, okay?"

I nodded wearily. "Listen, I know I might not pull it off alone—but if I do go to some magazine or newspaper, I've got to have things like Fanning and Blair red-checked. I started to ask you earlier if you remember the trouble the old *Saturday Evening Post* got into over the Bear Bryant—Wally Butts thing. And *Look* over Mayor Alioto? I can't afford that—my merchandise has to be kosher."

Martha stubbed out her cigarette, folded her arms, and sank back into the sofa. I got up from the armchair and sat next to her. Why did I feel so clumsy, even oddly formal, with her? I started to put my arm around her but she resisted. Then she leaned back into me.

Down the street a garbage truck compactor began to whine.

"I'm not sorry for what I said," she whispered.

"You shouldn't be."

"You've got to take a chance—you've got to trust somebody besides yourself."

"I trust you."

"I'm not enough." Martha yawned. "Anyway, I got you to fight."

I didn't respond.

"Well, almost got you to fight."

"Yes, almost."

She pushed harder now until I toppled onto my side, and after snuggling against me she cleared her throat softly, her eyelids fluttered, and her breathing became rhythmic. But for me sleep held no appeal; I knew it would be no sanctuary from the malevolent revelations of the past day. In my fatigue my tear ducts had dried so to chase the stinging in my eyes I blinked once, then again, and I was out.

Until the phone rang. It was daylight, and I was alone on the sofa.

"Hi," Martha said.

"Mmmmm. What time is it?"

"Almost noon."

"How're you feeling?"

"I've been better. Listen, I've done some homework for you. The chairman of Onyxx is..."

"One Franklin Renfrew Fanning?"

"Correct. Unfortunately, our files don't show any nicknames. I also called Small in Cambridge. They've got a limited partner named George Blair... nothing on him in Edit Ref."

I knew what Martha expected from me, but I felt I still needed evidence less circumstantial. The silence started to stretch so I said, "Hey, thanks for doing all this, it helps a lot. What I need now is a little more time to sort it all out. Be patient?"

"Have I got a choice?" she replied softly.

I poured myself coffee and started to sort. So the principals in the microfilm did exist; but how could I link them to the complex but fuzzy conspiracy outlined by Harry?

If his hypothesis was correct, Fanning called the shots. Motivation couldn't be simpler—the first oil giant to sign with Peking would reap immense profits. What's more, Fanning was in a perfect position to expedite the plot. As head of a multinational his fingers dipped into virtually every country; he had the clout to order Harry's corpse moved, to have Entrepays established, to lard a Swiss account for Blair's use as a slush fund.

That would make the White House not a partner but certainly a willing hired gun. Motives? Public vindication of its Asian policy, in terms of proving that rapprochement with the Mainland would materially benefit Americans, or at least corporate America. And below the table, a healthy kickback for the campaign—or personal—coffers. Suddenly I found myself nervously eyeing the bottom shelf of my homemade bookcase. I had to assume that once I began my probe the targets of it would react immediately. If the White House were hip-deep in the conspiracy, I was sure it wouldn't hesitate to use federal agencies to deflect me. My makeshift safe had withstood junkies but it would be child's play for government-trained operatives: I needed a better cache.

I returned to my cast of characters. Blair was obviously a foot soldier, in it for relatively small gains and perhaps a promotion if he handled himself well.

Finally there was Datatec. The agency seemed to be the only crack in the monolithic plot Harry had outlined, for I doubted the other participants were aware of its tangential involvement—if it had in fact been involved. I surmised that for reasons of confidentiality Datatec would never confirm that it had on Harry's behalf dug into Blair's affairs, but...

That's when I figured out my first step. I phoned Datatec and ascertained its president's name. Then I wrote that man, Emmett Culver Stahl, introducing myself as a writer assigned to profile the investigative industry; did his firm have a press kit? Not only should the company's literature reveal whether it was capable of gumshoeing Blair on two continents, but more important I'd see if Datatec's letterhead matched the one on the report in the microfilm.

As I typed Stahl's name on the envelope the implications of my act suddenly sank in: having long since learned the advantages of addressing myself to the head man, I was again going straight to the top.

I'd been racking my brains for a way into Onyxx. Why not confront Fanning with the prints of Harry's microfilm? Just as quickly I knew this was easier said than done—you don't send material like mine through the mails, and heads of billion-dollar firms don't grant appointments to the likes of me. Still, it behooved me to find a way; any legitimate publication would afford Fanning a rebuttal, and I'd look that much more professional for having already done so.

But first I needed to secure my papers. I decided on a safe-deposit box taken under an alias so investigators—especially Feds—couldn't track and confiscate the documents. Placing my fattening folder on Harry in my pouch, I went out into the muggy afternoon, mailed the letter to Stahl, and proceeded to the bank on Sheridan Square.

"I want to rent a safe-deposit box," I told the man at the service desk.

"Do you have an account here? How about at one of our other branches? Then you'll need primary identification. That's something with your photograph on it, like a passport."

"I don't have one," I lied.

"Then we require several pieces of secondary identification—driver's license, charge cards, documents we can verify your signature with."

"Why the rigmarole?"

"Because we must be sure you're who you say you are," he replied in the tone one takes with a backward child. "What if you gave us a fictitious name? And what if you used the box for illegal or immoral purposes? How could the authorities trace you?"

My gloom lasted into the night. Obtaining forged papers was messy, though I thought I had a source: Carl, a college classmate who between 1965 and 1970 had rented his training as an artist to those seeking to elude General Lewis Hershey's ever-greedier clutches. The alternative was asking someone else to rent a box in his name. The problem there boiled down— as most of life's issues do—to whom I trusted. Why not Martha, who already knew, or Alan and Duke, who could be counted on not to peek at my material? Because anyone investigating me couldn't help but stumble across them. Why not some other acquaintance? Because even if I retained the key to the box, he could always authorize the lock forced.

It was late at night, on my third spin through the Rolodex, that the answer presented itself. I was again studying Duke's card. On it was the notation I'd made on first meeting him: "Michelle Films, Ltd." I knew, though Duke hadn't fondled an Arriflex in three years, that the subsidiary corporation had been kept alive because our short subjects still earned beer money at college film festivals. Were Duke to open a corporate safe-deposit box, I could with his approval cosign under any name I chose.

When I reached him at his vacation house up on Block Island, he was amenable. I then asked advice on printing the microfilm, for there were technical problems in enlarging from so small a negative. A minute later I had the solution. We were signing off when he suddenly said, "If I ask, will you tell me what's going into the box?"

"If you ask, yes."

"And if I don't?"

"What box?"

After five seconds of silence Duke said, "See you Monday, Ray."

9 September 1972: New York

When my eyes popped open Martha was still curled in sleep. The alarm was set for noon, which meant she hadn't returned from her closing until 4 A.M. I showered, left her a note, and set off with the microfilm for Duke's studio.

In the darkroom I went to the workbench on which his enlargers stood. Both were set up for conventional use; that is, each machine's body was on the vertical, so its beam shone downward from the lens to the stand on which printing paper is placed. It is a law of optics that to increase magnification you increase the distance between light source and paper. With the bodies vertical I could only crank the light sources two and a half feet above their stands, which meant a maximum magnification of about twelvefold, but I needed a fortyfold magnification to enlarge each of the microfilm's images so it filled an 8 × 10 sheet of printing paper. That's why Duke had instructed me to use the Beseler 23C, whose body can be swiveled ninety degrees so its beam shines horizontally. This would allow me to position the printing paper not on the stand but on any surface any distance away.

I measured off ten feet from a wall and set up a small utility table there. Next I wrestled the Beseler off the workbench and onto the table, swiveled its body, and inserted the glass mount containing the microfilm. When I flicked on the projector lamp Harry's message sprang onto the wall. Then I taped a scrap 8 × 10 to the wall so Sheet 1 of the microfilm fell on it and adjusted the Beseler until the image filled the sheet and the words were sharp.

As I reread the material I found myself again fantasizing about taking the prints directly to Fanning. And then I began to convince myself it needn't be a fantasy, that it was just the kind of audacious stroke that might cut through a lot of red tape and bullshit. But if the prints I was making were for Fanning's eyes, I should edit from them all mention of Datatec—the detective agency being my potential hole card—so I positioned a large sheet of clear acetate over the 8 × 10; by affixing strips of electrical tape to the acetate, I could block portions of the image from reaching the paper behind it.

On Sheet 1, I masked the passage on Harry's hiring Datatec plus his parenthetical note on where the agency's original report lay. Then I decided Fanning need not know the procedure for liquidating the Swiss bank account so I taped out that paragraph too. I switched off the Beseler, lifted the acetate, and push-pinned a sheet of high-contrast Kodalith printing paper over the scrap 8 × 10. Dropping the acetate back into position, I flicked on the enlarger and made an exposure.

On Sheet 2, I masked the Datatec letterhead and the heading "DATATEC for Dr. Harry Helmsley/Page 1 of 2." On Sheet 3, I masked the letterhead and the heading "DATATEC for Dr. Harry Helmsley/Page 2 of 2/RE: BLAIR, GEORGE FREDERICK." And on Sheet 4, I masked the lone mention, in paragraph 3, of Datatec.

The prints were in the dryer when Martha called. "You sound cheery," she said.

"Not cheery, ecstatic. I'll tell you about it over brunch—I think you'll approve."

11 September 1972: New York

Martha hadn't approved. "It'll give him a chance to cover up," she'd protested of my plans to sock it to Fanning.

"Look, whether I go or it's somebody from your magazine or the *Times*, he'll have the same opportunity."

She'd finally seen it my way—or at least she gave up trying to argue me out of it.

My first stop this Monday morning was the lobby of the Empire State Building, where I met Duke and proceeded with him to the anteroom of his bank's safe-deposit vault. I'd decided to make the needle smaller, or the haystack larger, for anyone searching for a Chinese boxholder by changing my persuasion to Japanese. Thus, I cosigned the application "Ozu Kurosawa" and also imparted a touch of cinematic class to Michelle Films, Ltd. Inside the vault the guard and Duke unlocked his new box, into which I placed a bulky sealed envelope. Then they double-locked the box back into its slot.

Outside the bank Duke flipped me the key.

"Thanks again," I said. "Look, uh..." I shuffled my feet. "If anything strange happens to me, break open that box. Read what's in that envelope. You'll know what to do."

Duke pursed his lips at my melodrama but only said "Say 'hi' to Martha for me" before turning and strolling toward his studio.

I went the opposite direction, toward Sixth Avenue, where I caught an uptown bus. I hopped off several blocks south of the Time-Life Building, crossed the street, and entered the Onyxx Building.

The lobby looked like one of Mussolini's bad dreams, an oversized amalgam of travertine, brushed aluminum, and plate glass. The designers had obviously striven for a light, airy feeling, perhaps to make you forget that Onyxx's success derived from a product that bubbles up hot and black and dirty from the bowels of the earth. What they had achieved was antisepsis: even the live shrubs in the aluminum planters were so lush and immaculately tended they appeared plastic.

But I hadn't come here to review the decor, I'd come to case the building's security. As I suspected, Onyxx used employee and guest passes, a system many midtown corporations had instituted to brake a growing rash of thefts and even armed robberies on their floors. That meant I'd have to obtain a slip to ride up to Fanning's office, or try to get him at his home.

I ducked back outside and walked up to Time-Life; before tackling Fanning, I wanted to study his Edit Ref folders. Martha was away from her cubicle when I arrived but she'd already called the files up so I made space for myself and began to read.

Franklin Renfrew Fanning, it turned out, was the apotheosis of the self-made American. Born in 1910 in a rural Pacific Northwest community, he had put himself through Cal Tech. Degree or no, it was by then the Depression, so he signed on as an oil-field roustabout and thereby backed into the petroleum industry. As soon as the company learned of his engineering background, Fanning was given a refinery to run. He ran it well and soon embarked on a rapid corporate rise.

During World War II he joined the government war office. In Washington he attracted the attention of several of the Seven Sisters; after V-J Day the one that later changed its name to Onyxx won the bidding for his services.

Working for a giant didn't slow Fanning. In the mid-1960s, after convincingly demonstrating his administrative prowess, he was promoted over a bevy of Ivy League biz-school types to the presidency. In 1969 he was named chairman of Onyxx as well.

Though one of the nation's best-paid executives—his 1971 salary and bonuses topped $500,000, and perks included golf-club memberships around the world and the obligatory limousine—Fanning appeared to live modestly. He and his wife had owned the same comfortable but unprincely house in the bedroom suburb of Rye for more than twenty years. In fact, when a *Fortune* reporter followed him around in 1970, she'd bemusedly described the couple's chief luxury, a pleasant but hardly lavish Tuesday-night ritual: dinner at the Oak Room of the Plaza, followed by opera or the ballet.

By the time I'd sifted through the last folder I was quite perplexed. Though it was obvious Fanning was one tough cookie, all the files stressed that he was unswervingly fair, a real straight-shooter. In short, he hardly seemed the bribe-doling Machiavelli Harry would have him. I wrestled with this contradiction for a while before deciding to go through with my plan; if Fanning was indeed aboveboard, so much the better.

I took the prints of Harry's microfilm from their manila envelope. They needed a covering note. Twirling a couple of sheets of paper into Martha's typewriter, I wrote:

Mr. Fanning:

Last February an American geologist named Harry Helmsley was killed in the Far East. The AP reported he died in a plane crash in Indonesia. Not true; I saw him murdered in Laos. When I attempted to reconcile this discrepancy, I met with the deceased's lover, a Mr. Pat Ritchie, who said the death was related to a CIA operation. You can imagine my surprise on recently learning that on the day I saw Ritchie, Helmsley's lover actually lay in a California cemetery. Subsequent to this discovery, I obtained the enclosed, which was intended by Helmsley for the real Ritchie. Your comments, please.

RAYMOND HUANG

By the time I cut a Xerox of my note it was past noon. Martha walked in from her story conference. "Well?"

"I'm going to do it." Her lips compressed but she remained silent. I took a deep breath, called Onyxx, and asked for Fanning. A secretary answered. I identified myself as a golf pro from one of his clubs, calling to set up a lesson.

"I'm sorry, Mr. Harmon, he's in conference. May we get back to you?"

"I'll be on the practice tee most of the afternoon. When's a good time to try again?"

A pause as she checked his schedule and then, "How about two-thirty?"

I was all atingle when I hung up, for I had my quarry; now for the building pass that would allow me to stalk him. I redialed Onyxx and asked for Public Relations. Did they have a press kit on offshore drilling rigs? Of course. I arranged to pick one up shortly before 2:30 P.M.

"Having fun?" There was sarcasm in Martha's voice.

"Fucking right I am."

Despite herself she smiled.

At 2:15 P.M. I presented myself at the security desk in the Onyxx lobby. The guard phoned up to PR, then issued me a pass. I rode to the forty-first floor, picked up the press kit, and promptly ditched it in a men's room. Then I caught another elevator up to the fifty-third floor.

Judging from the lobby and from visits to other corporate headquarters, I'd expected this executive bastion to be bright and chromey, with giant Lucite maps flanked by ceiling-to-floor photographs of smiling hard hats and unpolluted ponds, hard in the shadow of an Onyxx refinery, on which ducks swam. And from hidden speakers, of course, 101 Strings playing "Spanish Eyes."

I couldn't have been more mistaken: Naugahyde would have been as unseemly in this sanctum as double-knit polyester vestments in the Vatican.

The furniture here was Louis XV, the paintings pre-Impressionist landscapes, and the music chamber. I walked across the springy white carpeting to the receptionist seated behind an eighteenth-century *secrétaire*. She was the kind of lady for whom *droit du seigneur* was invented. When I told her I had a hand delivery for Fanning she directed me to the office of his executive secretary, Mrs. Shipley.

I traversed a corridor lined with solid walnut doors, all shut, to a small but well-appointed waiting area. A secretary looked up from her typing. I checked her nameplate; she wasn't Mrs. Shipley.

"Hi. I've got a packet for Mr. Fanning."

She smiled and reached out a hand.

"I'd prefer to give it to him myself."

Her smiled hardened. "What is this in reference to?"

"It's, uh, it's confidential."

She sized me up. I was glad I'd worn a suit. Finally she said "Wait here," stood, and let herself into the office her desk guarded. Thirty seconds later she was back outside and beckoning: "This way. Mrs. Shipley will see you."

The office was as roomy as those assigned to Time Inc.'s brass, but then Mrs. Shipley looked as formidable as any magazine editor I'd ever met. She put down the microphone into which she'd been dictating and regarded me with annoyance. "What seems to be the problem?"

"I . . . my name's Raymond Huang, and I have an envelope that must be hand-delivered to Mr. Fanning."

"From?"

"Me."

She leaned forward and placed her left hand over a button. "How did you get up here?"

"I have a guest pass. It's valid."

"But not for the fifty-third floor."

"No, not for up here. But Mrs. Shipley, it's extremely vital that Mr. Fanning receive my envelope." She still hadn't pressed the button so I plunged on. "I know how irregular this is, and I can guess what's passing through your mind, but look, let me prove that it's just several sheets of paper." I fumbled open the manila envelope and withdrew the covering note and four prints. "If you want to take these in to him, fine, but I've got to know that he sees them. And I'd like to wait, because I'm sure he'll want to speak to me afterward." I slid the sheets back, refastened the clasp, and laid the envelope on her desk.

"You still haven't told me what this is about, Mr. Huang."

"It's highly confidential," I answered lamely.

She kept her finger over the button and her eyes on me until I began to sweat. Then she drew her hand back. "Very well. But if Mr. Fanning chooses not to see you, you'll leave ... quietly. Now take a seat outside." As I passed through the door she added, "No, leave it open."

I walked self-consciously to an armchair and picked up a copy of *Business Week*. Then, despite my resolve, I looked up. Mrs. Shipley's secretary embarrassedly darted her eyes back to her paperwork. Through the open door I could see Mrs. Shipley watching me too, but she didn't bother to look away. I glanced at my watch—could it really be only 2:33 P.M.? I sighed and forced myself to begin a profile of a bauxite company president that seemed written in Urdu.

Then a muted chime in Mrs. Shipley's office and the click of a doorknob being turned.

The sunlight tumbling out of Fanning's office was so strong the three men emerging were but shadows. As my eyes adjusted I spotted a figure standing at one of the far windows; then the door was pulled closed.

The trio of executives, each bearing his slim, leather-bound briefing book like a shield, headed through the waiting area toward the corridor. When they encountered Mrs. Shipley, who was striding toward Fanning's office with my envelope in one hand, they instantly broke into obsequious smiles. She nodded almost imperceptibly in return, continued to her boss's door, and knocked lightly.

As she entered I could again see inside; he still stood by the window. I lit a cigarette and plopped *Business Week* back on the coffee table. A minute later Mrs. Shipley reappeared— empty-handed. Behind her the silhouette was gone.

After what seemed like an hour I allowed myself a peek at my watch. 2:45 P.M. I squirmed into a more comfortable position and lit another cigarette.

2:52 P.M. What the hell was he doing in there? A sixth-grader could have read the stuff by now.

There was a light tap at Mrs. Shipley's door. One of the two men standing there stuck his head in and said, "Is he ready for us, Dorothy?" She checked on her telephone, then told him, "Let's push it back to three-forty-five. And why don't you ring before you come?" As the men left I noticed Mrs. Shipley inspecting me with newfound interest.

At 3:02 P.M. I asked Mrs. Shipley's secretary for directions to the men's room. By now she was as nervous as I.

At 3:08 P.M., as I stubbed out yet another half-smoked cigarette, the soft chime in Mrs. Shipley's office rang again. She picked up the receiver, listened for ten seconds, then punched another line. The call she placed was equally brief.

Four minutes later a tall, elegant gentleman in his early sixties presented himself at Mrs. Shipley's door. She stood, stepped out of my sight for several seconds, and then came out of her office carrying a portable Sony tape recorder and two cassettes. Now she and the man were walking toward me. "Mr. Huang," she said, "Mr. Fanning will see you now." I got to my feet and fell in step with them.

At Fanning's door she knocked and then turned the knob.

The dazzling light made me recoil; the Onyxx chairman's lair faced west and south, and though the afternoon sun spangled harshly off glass and polished wood, the drapes for the picture windows that comprised the outer walls remained undrawn. To my immediate left was a conference table. In the corner where the two windowed walls met sat a couch flanked by a pair of leather wing chairs. Directly ahead was Fanning's desk, behind which he was again standing, his back to us. He was in shirtsleeves.

The patrician gentleman ambled across an Aubusson to the couch in the corner as Mrs. Shipley led me to one of the chairs in front of Fanning's desk. From up close I could see he was a tall, burly man; it wasn't hard to imagine him as a roustabout. I sat. Then I realized that from my vantage point the other two men would be backlit—I'd be talking to haloed smudges. Recognizing this hoary ploy didn't calm my nerves any.

Mrs. Shipley placed the Sony on Fanning's desk next to an identical machine and popped fresh cassettes into both. Then she positioned the omnidirectional microphones equidistant from us three men. The clicks when she depressed the "Record" buttons seemed deafening in the airless silence. Mrs. Shipley gently tapped each microphone with a fingernail as she checked the sound-level needles. "Ready, Mr. Fanning."

"Thank you, Dorothy," he replied, still gazing at the Hudson. His voice was deep but much softer and gentler than I'd expected.

When he heard the door close behind Mrs. Shipley, Fanning finally turned. His eyes were slate, and they were focused on me. I started to rise. Instead of offering his hand he sat. I plopped awkwardly back into my chair.

The silence was unreal, yet Fanning extended it by shaking out a Chesterfield from the pack on his desk, tamping one end, and lighting it. I noticed on his right forehead, above his beetling brows and below his surprisingly long grey hair, a jagged inch-long scar now white with age. He exhaled, then absently flicked a shred of tobacco from his tongue.

I wiped my palms on my pant legs.

"I'm Franklin Fanning," he finally said, "and with me in my office are Mr. Harris Knox, chief counsel for Onyxx, and Mr. Raymond Huang. Do I pronounce your name correctly, sir."

I nodded.

"It is three... three-sixteen P.M. Monday, September eleventh, 1972." His voice was so soft I couldn't resist checking the sound-level needles. They were registering. "This conversation is being simultaneously recorded on two machines. Mr. Huang will be given one tape. I, as chairman of Onyxx, or Mr. Knox will retain the other." Fanning leaned back in his swivel chair and looked at Knox. "Sorry for this hugger-mugger, Harris, but I didn't have time to brief you. About a half hour ago Mr. Huang"—he turned to me—"whom I have not met before, arrived with a most provocative document. The document alleges impropriety on the part of Onyxx, and on the part of me, personally. Is this correct, Mr. Huang."

His openness took me aback. I cleared my throat. "Ye..." I cleared it again. "Yes."

"And you want answers."

"Yes."

Fanning turned back to the lawyer. "Frankly, the material is damned volatile. It's also so complicated I can't respond at this moment." He took another drag on his Chesterfield. "I need an opinion, Harris: I propose to keep this matter confidential until I can fully investigate the charges."

"How confidential?"

"Completely. Until I... until we know more."

"The documents implicate you?"

"Yes."

"Then in my judgment that would be improper."

Fanning nodded calmly. Either this guy's got balls of brass, I thought, or he's innocent. He shifted in his chair and fingered the scar on his forehead. "Suppose, Harris, I Xerox the document in your presence and give you copies in a sealed envelope."

Knox studied the tassels on his shoes for a while. "Possible. It would depend on who conducted the investigation and how long it took."

"Onyxx personnel, you select them." Knox nodded. The two of them were so reasonable, so low-keyed—could this be a giant con? "The timing depends on Mr. Huang," Fanning continued. He swiveled to me. "What's in this for you, sir."

I stiffened. Was he leading up to a bribe, on tape and in front of counsel? My eyes flicked to Knox. He was still studying his loafers. "I'm a writer, Mr. Fanning. If the charges are true, I'll have one damn salable exposé."

"Suppose I prove they're false."

I shrugged. "Then I have nothing."

"I can think of several publications interested in those nothings."

I waited until I knew my tongue would be civil before replying, "So can I, but I don't deal with them. Besides, I doubt an *Enquirer* article would touch off a Senate investigation or send Onyxx stock tumbling."

Knox coughed politely.

Fanning methodically stubbed out his cigarette, then looked up at me. "What might a successful exposé pay."

Knox ahemed, a look of concern on his face. "Frew..."

Within a heartbeat Fanning's eyes and mine locked. Time stopped. I felt light-headed, as if all my blood had rushed to my jugular, which was throbbing. I heard myself reply, "Probably several thousand dollars, plus a book contract."

Fanning cleared his throat. Then he began the ritual of lighting another cigarette. Knox now contemplated his steepled hands. Finally and with great deliberation Fanning said, "I don't begrudge you any monies, sir, but I sincerely hope you'll never collect those thousands." I could sense by Knox's shifting on the couch that the lawyer was relieved that the subject of my possible gains was now behind us. "I realize speed is important to you," Fanning continued. "It is to me, too. Would you agree to answers no later than one week from today."

I nodded, then said "Yes" into the microphones lest there be any ambiguity.

Fanning turned to Knox. "Harris."

"Acceptable, with one provision."

Fanning leaned forward. How did he stay so cool? Or had this all been rehearsed, possibly on the phone while I'd been kept waiting?

"If the charges are true," the lawyer said, "we can depend on Mr. Huang to air them. If, however, you prove to his satisfaction they are false, you and I will place my copy of the documents, along with your report, under seal. We will then present them to the board with the supplication the materials remain *in camera*."

Fanning thought it over, nodded, and turned to me. "Mr. Huang, I have several other questions to put to you. Harris, object if you think any of them improper."

I sat up a little straighter. Knox now looked through his steepled hands at us.

"How did you obtain these documents," Fanning asked. Was there any harm in telling him? "If any illegality was involved," he added, "I would respect your silence."

"There may have been."

"Mr. Huang," Knox interjected, "you need not continue."

Were they double-psyching me? It didn't matter so I said, "The originals are on a microfilm. The film was hidden on a painting on consignment to a gallery. I located the microfilm and removed it."

Fanning frowned and looked to the lawyer. Knox said, "Do you own the painting?"

"No."

"Is the painting owned by the person who hid the microfilm on it?"

"No, that person's dead."

"The painting is now owned by an heir?"

"Yes."

"To the best of your knowledge, Mr. Huang, is the heir aware of the existence of the microfilm?"

"I'm sure he isn't."

"Why?"

"Because the microfilm was intended for someone else, and that person's also dead."

"Finally, did you damage the painting in removing the microfilm?"

"No."

Knox turned to Fanning. "I feel we're clear, Frew. Assuming the microfilm contains neither unpublished copyrighted material nor classified government papers, you'd be hard put to establish actual ownership. Without actual ownership, Mr. Huang's act cannot be construed as even petit larceny. Therefore, it's not criminal for us to receive the microfilm, or copies of it."

Jesus, I thought, these guys are in another league altogether. Then I remembered what Martha had said.

Fanning glanced now at a checklist on his legal-sized note pad. "Can you describe the man you met, the impersonator."

I tried to visualize "Pat." "Fortyish. About six-two and stocky, I'd say two hundred and twenty pounds. Roundish face, sandy hair, he dressed well. No particular accent. Sorry, that's the best I can do—it's been six months."

He nodded. "There are deletions in the material you gave me. You did it."

"Yes."

"Why."

"It's information I can use to double-check your rebuttal."

Fanning glanced at Knox; their eyes met. Fanning stroked his scar again and said, "Who else knows about this matter."

"The lady I live with," I replied, for there was no sense in trying to keep Martha a secret. "She'll treat it as confidential as long as I do. Plus the person safeguarding the actual microfilm. That person hasn't read it yet, but will should anything happen to me."

"Whatever you gave Frew," Knox said, "it sounds urgent. Seems to me if I were a concerned citizen, as you appear to be, I'd share my suspicions with more than just a few friends. There are many government agencies that investigate charges of misconduct by big business... why did you come to us instead of one of them?"

Fanning was studying his desk top, his face carefully neutral. I shifted back to Knox and said, "Because I don't trust any of them."

"But you trust us?"

I shrugged.

Knox's chuckle surprised me. "Frew, we've finally found a bunch held in lower esteem than Big Oil." Fanning grinned—wanly, I thought.

I sensed the meeting was winding down so I said, "Am I correct in assuming that part of your investigation will be directed at me?"

"There'd be nothing illegal in that, Mr. Huang," the lawyer replied.

"Unless your operatives used illegal means."

Neither man rushed to assure me that wouldn't happen. At last Knox said, "In my thirty-seven years here, I've not personally known of this company conducting an illegal investigation. Such an investigation would be contrary to our policies. Should you suspect your privacy has been wrongly invaded, you have recourse under law."

His overly precise circumlocution hung over the room like smog. Finally Fanning leaned forward. "I think we can conclude this meeting. Mr. Huang, I'll give you one tape. Harris, in light of what's transpired, you'd better take the other one." Fanning pushed the "Stop" buttons, ejected the cassettes, and handed me one. Knox uncurled himself from the couch and ambled over to accept the other. "Mr. Huang," Fanning continued, "I'll call you no later than Monday. Harris, will you show our guest out." I stood and started to offer a concluding pleasantry but he was already on his private line to Mrs. Shipley—"Dorothy, I'll see Doug and Frank now"—so I followed Knox across the vast office.

Outside, I realized I hadn't had a cigarette during the entire meeting. I accepted a light from Knox's gold Dunhill and inhaled greedily.

"Mr. Huang, you handled yourself well."

"Thanks," I said, not at all sure I had.

"Coming to Onyxx was a shrewd decision, one you'll be glad you made. Frew's straight."

"You're assuming he's innocent."

"Not necessarily." Knox flashed an enigmatic smile and then stuck out his hand: "Frew forgets the amenities when he's preoccupied."

In the lobby I slumped onto a phone-booth bench. Why did I have the feeling that as hard as I'd run all day, I'd made no headway? The cassette weighed heavily in my pocket but the bank was closed so I dug out a dime and dropped it in the slot. "Hi, it's me. Can you get out now? No, I'll tell you over a drink. The Ground Floor in ten minutes? Okay." Then I drew a deep breath and headed for my rendezvous with Martha and, equally important, a double Gibson.

14 September 1972: New York

The deadline for my article on "black holes" in space neared but the only void I cared about, could concentrate on, was the one Fanning promised to fill. The phone broke my idle reveries. It was Duke's chief assistant, Mario, who was preparing to go off on his own; did I know of any cheap Village loft suitable for a studio? I said I'd keep my eyes open.

I was back at my typewriter fooling with a lead when I remembered that the building across the street, a nondescript commercial structure, had long sported a "Space Available" sign next to its front door. When I went to the window and gazed over, though, the placard was gone. Hadn't I seen it there just the other day? Yes I had. Mario should have called sooner; I shrugged and reluctantly returned to work.

15 September 1972: New York

"One scientist," I typed, "has likened black holes to cosmic whirlpools, into which are sucked not only nearby bits of matter but also passing waves of energy, such as light. And what becomes of the matter and energy entering the black hole?"

Damned if I know, I thought bitterly; I was deep into my typical on-deadline despair, my certainty that the piece stank balanced by the knowledge that somehow, at some bleak post-midnight hour, I'd pull it off. For I always had.

The phone rang. "Mr. Raymond Huang?"

"Yes."

"Mr. Fanning calling. Please hold." My lips felt suddenly dry; it was only Friday, and I hadn't expected to hear from him until the following Monday.

Several seconds later Fanning came on the line. "Mr. Huang, can we meet in an hour."

"Sure."

"There's a building called the Dakota on Central Park W..."

"I know it."

"Very well. Apartment Nine-C at three."

I hung up and called Martha. She was equally baffled by why Fanning wanted me at the Dakota, the classy co-op most famous as the setting of *Rosemary's Baby*, and not the Onyxx Building. "Listen, Ray, be careful."

"What's with the Amanda Blake imitation? He won't pull anything funny—hell, he's the chairman of a billion-dollar corporation."

She met my bravado with silence.

Though I showered and changed I was sweaty again by the time I emerged from the 72nd Street IND subway station and passed through the Dakota's baroque arched entrance. It was 2:58 P.M. The doorman consulted his clipboard, found my name, and pointed me to the elevator.

The nameplate beneath the peephole of Apartment 9-C was blank. I steeled myself and pressed the bell.

Immediately the clack of locks being thrown and then the door opened. "Come in, Mr. Huang." As before, Fanning didn't offer his hand.

I'd been to the Dakota for parties so I knew apartments here tended to be as lavish as their maintenance charges. Not this one. The vinyl and Formica furniture in the vestibule would have looked at home in an airport lobby. A commercial coat rack, the kind on rollers, stood in an alcove. Fanning double-locked the door and without a word led me down a hallway. We passed three rooms containing conference tables; one of the tabletops was strewn with empty coffee containers and overflowing ashtrays. At the end of the hall was the living room. As we entered it, though sunlight streamed in from two exposures, Fanning flipped a switch and the concealed fluorescent banks in the ceiling sizzled on. The same institutional decorator had been at work here: Feininger and Dubuffet reproductions on the wall and enough Naugahyde sofas and armchairs to furnish a golf-course clubhouse. All the seats had been tugged around to face a movie screen which dangled from its ceiling housing.

Fanning picked his way to the window and as he began closing the shutters said, "Would you give me a hand." I walked over. The shutters appeared wooden but they felt chilly to the touch. I tapped one and heard the dull ring of metal. Soon our splendid view of Central Park, which seethed with colorful T-shirts bright in the sun, was gone; now the only light in the room came from the fluorescents.

Fanning dusted his hands with a handkerchief. "Sorry it's so messy here, but our ad agency screened a new campaign this morning, and the staff didn't have time to clean."

"What is this place?"

"Our safe house. Care for a drink, Mr. Huang."

"Will I need one?"

He permitted himself a smile as he walked to a long, low sculptured metal cabinet and raised its top. "Whiskey, soda, Perrier, beer..." I started to ask what he was having, then settled for a beer. He reached down, pulled out two San Miguels, and began to pour them into mugs. "This apartment is soundproofed and swept once a week and before key meetings. Most corporations dealing in sensitive information have a place like this."

"The shutters?"

"Lip-readers. You can see across the Park with a thousand-millimeter lens. Oh, you mean the metal—to guard against parabolic dishes."

"Helluva way to run a business."

"Yes, business was once simpler." Fanning sounded almost wistful. He handed me a mug, pointed to a seat and took an armchair across from me. Then he cleared his throat. Instead of opening his defense, though, he shook out a Chesterfield and embarked on his ritual preparation; that's when I suddenly realized he was nervous as hell.

"Mr. Huang, in answering Dr. Helmsley's charges, I must refer to information Onyxx regards as confidential. I can't prevent you from repeating what we discuss, but I can make sure no one else hears these admissions from my lips."

"You're not taping this session."

"Correct. And I ask you don't either—tapes have a way of coming back to haunt."

"Mind if I take notes?"

"As you wish." He flicked a tobacco shred from his tongue. "Your material is most disturbing, but not for the reasons you suspect. Dr. Helmsley's allegations are based on a few facts he spun into a malicious web of deceit and innuendo. I'd like to be charitable and think he did so out of ignorance, but on two key points he out-and-out lied. We're... Don't look so angry, sir, until you've seen my proof."

I blushed.

"What bothers me," Fanning continued, "is the furor this material would raise if made public. You know as well as I retractions never catch up with accusations, especially in today's climate. That's why I've burned out a lot of good men these last few days to get you fast answers."

He leaned forward and opened a folder on the coffee table separating us. "Harris Knox selected the men. I split them into teams, each operating on a need-to-know basis. All reports came directly to me, with a sealed copy to Mr. Knox. I gave the team led by Harris complete access to my diaries and dictation files pertaining to my July 1971 visit to the White House, to my dealings with Small, and to my role in Onyxx's negotiations with the People's Republic of China." Fanning looked up, noted my surprise, ignored it, and returned to his notes. "Other teams investigated Dr. Helmsley, Mr. George Blair, the banking firm of Leclair, and the firm called Entrepays. I hope you approve of my methodology, Mr. Huang."

I looked at him closely; was he being sarcastic? "Yes, the conception seems meticulous," I finally replied.

Now he peered closely at me before reaching into the folder and passing over a set of sheets. They were Xeroxes of my prints of Harry's material, deletions and all.

"Before we get down to specifics, sir, you should know our industry regards Asia as the potential North Slope or North Sea of the mid-Eighties. Today petroleum's cheap and seemingly limitless. Yet, world reserves are finite, though every time we make this point we're accused of crying wolf. We also have the specter of the crude-producing nations threatening a cartel. It seems totally inconceivable when you consider the political rifts in the Middle East—for example, Gaddafi and Faisal hate each other—but I must confess the more affluent we become at the Third World's expense, the more inevitable a cartel appears.

"That's why each of the Seven Sisters is busy positioning itself for the day we establish diplomatic accord with Peking, and Southeast Asia stabilizes: those people out there have the reserves, but we have the technology. Onyxx has retained Small to help us formulate proposals. Our liaison is through Mr. George Blair of that firm. In fact, last winter..." Fanning consulted the sheet before him. "Last December, Mr. Blair was a member of a Small task force to Peking. Contrary to Dr. Helmsley's hints of secret deals, the trip was reported in several newspapers, including the New York *Times*.

"Now, Dr. Helmsley's charges are pretty convoluted, and I think it best if I answer them in sequence. Any objections."

I shook my head.

"Okay, Sheet One, paragraphs one and two. There've been rumors of a sexually compromised Filipino oil official, and a prominent Venezuelan engineer did die under suspicious circumstances. We can't confirm these were among what Dr. Helmsley so quaintly calls his *'expeditions noirs.'* I am able to say, however, if they were, Onyxx didn't commission them."

I looked up from my sheet. Harry hadn't named his previous employers, so I had no basis for challenging Fanning's assertion of innocence.

"Paragraph three. Yes, Dr. Helmsley was fired by the University of Michigan, in 1962, for his participation in a homosexual ring.

"Paragraphs six, seven, and eight. Yes, Dr. Helmsley was retained by Mr. Blair, on the contractual terms mentioned, to assay shale potential along the Annamese Cordillera. Mr. Blair was aware of Dr. Helmsley's background, but considered him one of the world's foremost shale experts. This judgment is consistent with soundings we've since taken with several Sisters.

"Paragraph nine—we come to the first of Dr. Helmsley's demonstrable lies." Fanning passed me another sheet. "The circled passage is Mr. Blair's instructions to Dr. Helmsley. You'll note it doesn't mention any predetermined convertibility factor."

"But..."

"What's more, had he reported fifty gpt, we would have thought Dr. Helmsley daft and ordered another survey."

"Why?"

"Thirty-five to forty gpt is sufficient to justify a conversion plant. Fifty gpt would represent a bonanza—and would have been detected long ago. Any knowledgeable person cooking a report would never pick such an outrageous figure."

I made a note to double-check Fanning's claim.

"Still in paragraph nine... Mr. Blair denies promising Dr. Helmsley additional monies. He also denies depositing any money in any Swiss account. Yes, I know what you're going to say, but I prefer to discuss Mr. Blair in detail shortly." Fanning sipped his beer. "We come now to Leclair. The Swiss have tough banking laws. We could only confirm the account number Dr. Helmsley gives is consistent with the bank's numbering system, but I'm prepared to stipulate he maintained an account there. The real question, though, is did Mr. Blair contribute to it, and here I must again ask your indulgence."

I nodded.

"Now, sir, will you tell me what you deleted." He referred to the paragraph in which Harry explained how to tap the Leclair account. Fanning had no need to know so I shook my head. He stared at me several seconds before compressing his lips and returning to Sheet 1.

"Finally, the territory Dr. Helmsley was to explore." He dealt me another page from his folder. "The marked passages are from Mr. Blair's instructions. I've plotted out the coordinates myself—they were carefully drawn to keep Dr. Helmsley not only out of Communist-held areas, but well clear of demilitarized zones."

"May I take this with me?"

"I prefer you just copy the coordinates."

When I finished, I looked up. "How do we know Harry wasn't given another set of numbers?"

"We don't. But I should think a man as cautious as Dr. Helmsley would have documented such material in his microfilm."

"Maybe they were passed verbally, or..."

"Mr. Huang." Fanning's voice was steely. "Hypothesize as you choose, but I find my material sufficient."

The chances of proving there had been other coordinates seemed infinitesimal, so I gave him a reluctant nod.

"This next deletion of yours—it masks the name of the agency investigating Mr. Blair. Are you ready to share its name with me."

"No, not yet." I was being less coy than self-protective— suppose Datatec, which had yet to reply to my query, proved to specialize in eye-in-the-keyhole divorce cases.

Fanning's snort surprised me. "If I were they, I'd pay you to forever conceal their identity. The report certainly isn't worth thirteen thousand dollars; any second-rate agency could have furnished the biographical data on Sheet Two for several hundred dollars. No, I think this one tried to justify its fee with the fiction on the next page."

We both turned to Sheet 3.

"The material here is strewn with booby traps, Mr. Huang, so allow me to proceed slowly.

"First, Entrepays. This Swiss firm exports European-made household appliances to China, and imports fine fabrics from the Mainland. It was capitalized on an investment of under one hundred and fifty thousand dollars, and still grosses less than one million dollars U.S. The chairman of Entrepays, Mr. de Brouilly, is frankly a scoundrel—the French have a thick dossier on his financial connivances—but it seems implausible such a marginal firm could contribute substantially to a two-hundred-and-twenty-five-thousand-dollar slush fund . . . if such a fund indeed exists.

"Now we come to Mr. Blair. The case against him rests on three assumptions. One, he travels frequently to Switzerland, where he attends his own account at Leclair, and on at least one occasion transferred money into Dr. Helmsley's account. Two, Mr. Blair is acquainted with Mr. de Brouilly and Entrepays. Three, Mr. Blair is the author of the note addressed to 'J,' who in this context appears to be Mr. de Brouilly.

"I've worked with Mr. Blair for almost ten years, and I respect him greatly. For this investigation, though, I presumed him guilty of the innuendos. Therefore, my team in Cambridge, with Mr. Blair's most begrudging consent, inspected his office files, his home files, his home safe, and his safe-deposit box."

"But that was with Blair's consent . . ."

"He was given no choice, nor the time to hide or destroy evidence. Stan Harmer, the chairman of Small, will attest to that."

"You mean you just barged in and gave him an ultimatum?"

"Something like that." Fanning lit another cigarette and continued. "We examined Mr. Blair's current passport, as well as his previous one. He last visited Switzerland in August, 1965, some seven years ago. I had another team check State. A search of the photo files showed of the George Friedriches in the United States who hold passports, none bears the remotest physical resemblance to Mr. Blair.

"We also combed Mr. Blair's files and address books for any mention of Entrepays and Mr. de Brouilly. Nothing.

"Finally, we determined the note to 'J' was typed on an Adler portable. This machine is fairly uncommon in metropolitan Boston. We lacked the resources and authority to check sales records, but we ascertained none of the stores carrying the brand rents them. Furthermore, there are no Adler portables at Mr. Blair's residence, at Small, or at the clubs he frequents.

"I realize the absence of an incriminating typewriter, and the absence of matter pertaining to Entrepays and Mr. de Brouilly, is not conclusive. But I submit our investigation of Mr. Blair was—how should I put it—as meticulous as its conception. And the results, sir, seem pretty damned compelling."

I looked away both out of embarrassment and because I was feeling increasingly like a passenger on the *Titanic*.

"Now for the note to 'J,'" Fanning said. "Of all the material in Dr. Helmsley's microfilm, this is the most baffling, because your mysterious detective agency seems privy to confidential information."

My eyes flicked back to Fanning and my breathing became more rapid—that note linked Onyxx to the White House.

"Don't get your hopes up, sir: the note's not only a forgery, it's a piece of libelous shit." The vehemence with which he pronounced the uncharacteristic obscenity stunned me. "I was invited to the Oval Office on Monday, July nineteenth, 1971. The meeting was no secret, but the substance of our talk on oil import legislation was supposed to be. During the session the President turned to another matter much on his mind, Southeast Asia. He asked for my thoughts on public reaction to two proposals by the Joint Chiefs."

Fanning inspected the sheets in front of him, then handed

them to me. They were Xeroxes of two pages from a legal-sized pad. Most of the jottings on them had been masked off.

"Those are from my notes of the meeting. One proposal was to helicopter an elite force thirty miles beyond the DMZ to a hamlet where American prisoners of war were being detained. The President had been burned on a similar mission at Sontay, so he ordered extra intelligence. Luckily he did, for Intelligence ferreted out four or five Cong units within two miles of the hamlet. Please look halfway down the first page."

I read, in Fanning's handwriting:

Est. VC strength: 4/5 units @ 10–12

An inch below this I saw:

Could do for sure but not right. (Stonewall) 1? Yes but not 4.

"The President meant our boys could easily stand off one unit, but he couldn't condone the risk against four or five units."

"Why did you circle 'stonewall'?"

"I'd never heard the term before. Seems to be a favorite of those USC boys in the White House—it means to repel or block. Now, the other Joint Chiefs proposal is still under consideration, so I can't discuss it beyond the fact it's highly controversial, even among the President's advisers. But if you'll look near the bottom of the next sheet..."

I found the passage:

Of course risky, make no mistake. But some allies out there pretty g.d. unpopular here. If all blows still war Dems started, lot I like about it.

"You may not admire the man or his politics, sir, but you must admit his assessment is both shrewd and correct."

I felt spent. Fanning's explanations had the ring of truth; and even if he were lying—if he and the President were thick in conspiracy—the White House would by now have altered its records of the meeting to match his.

"The most sinister thing about the note, Mr. Huang, is not

the blatant use of quotes out of context, but the author's access to an off-the-record discussion. I'm checking into the security of my files. The White House is doing the same. You could help us greatly by telling us which agency produced this report."

Why not, I thought, everything seemed to be going down the tubes anyway. "It's..." It's the only straw left to clutch at; shouldn't I keep clutching until I could make my own judgment on Datatec's veracity? I shook my head. "It's going to remain my secret."

Fanning grew ominously calm. Then he snapped, "Sheet Four. You know my nickname is Frew. You know Onyxx's ties with Small are no secret. In 1968, Onyxx as a corporation didn't contribute a penny to the GOP. I as a private individual donated twenty-five hundred dollars, a sum you'll find on both Republican records and my IRS return. As for the current campaign, I was visited in my office last February by Mr. Maurice Stans of the Committee to Re-Elect. He left empty-handed. Mr. Stans is less than proud of his failure, but I assure you he will verify it on a witness stand if need be. Now, if I haven't answered all of Dr. Helmsley's scurrilous allegations, Mr. Huang, please be good enough to tell me."

It took more than a minute for the waves of anger radiating from Fanning to ebb; during that silence I found myself swallowing more than necessary.

When he'd simmered down, though, his voice took on a gentleness that sounded genuine. "I don't really fault you for your reactions to the microfilm. It's very provocative, and you acquired it under extenuating circumstances; perhaps if I tell you what happened in Vientiane, I can clear away the mystery.

"The intelligence forces of Laos and Thailand have long been at odds. Officially, it's over a female suspected of being a double agent. In fact, it concerns opium shipments from the Golden Triangle. Last February sixteenth, four members of the Thai force, driving a black Mercedes registered to Field Marshal Kittikachorn, the head of their government, arrived in Vientiane to eliminate two Laotian counterparts. They accomplished the mission at eleven-twenty P.M., on Rue Sam Sen Thai."

I closed my mouth, which had fallen open. "They were after the two men guarding Harry?"

Fanning nodded.

"He was just an innocent bystander?"

"Yes."

"Jesus." That explained why the gunman in the Mercedes had shredded the Laotian in the park with submachine-gun fire. But there were so many other inexplicable events...

As if reading my mind, Fanning said, "The AP reported Dr. Helmsley's body was recovered in West Irian. It was. We moved it there."

I sank back in my chair, my hands like icicles.

His voice grew even softer now. "It was done for industrial security... we simply didn't want it known we had a shale expert along the Cordillera. Ironically, Dr. Helmsley was to have left Vientiane the same evening by chartered jet for Hong Kong. The Small man aboard the jet cabled us the news. It reached here four hours after we'd learned a plane flying equipment to our Pertamina co-venture had gone down in West Irian. We consulted Pertamina, then flew Dr. Helmsley's remains to Hong Kong. From there it was transferred to West Irian. I can show you our cable traffic if you wish."

I shook my head wearily. Then it struck me he was leaving something out of his neat scenario: the Pathet Lao. Keeping my voice neutral I said, "Who discovered Harry's body?"

"A detachment of Royal Lao troops who..." Just as my adrenaline surged, Fanning coughed. "Pardon me. It was a Royalist detachment disguised in Pathet Lao uniforms—something to do with a patrol of enemy-held territory north of the city."

As much as I hated to admit it, the answer was damnably plausible, for I remembered how the Royalist and Pathet Lao leaders had chatted calmly even as the corpses were being dragged away. And then suddenly my feeling of helplessness burst before my festering frustrations: "Didn't you ever stop to consider the ethics of your cover-up?"

Fanning regarded me levelly. "Our actions injured no one except the intelligence agents employed by our competitors, and then only their professional pride."

"What about the professional pride of the Vientiane police?"

"They knew why the murders occurred, as well as who committed them. They had no objections to the removal of Dr. Helmsley's body."

"How much did you pay them?"

Fanning remained silent.

"How do you justify that bribe to your stockholders?"

"As part of the cost of doing business."

"How convenient. And I suppose to ease your conscience you gave Harry the best damned Indonesian funeral rupiahs can buy."

Fanning sighed. "Dr. Helmsley was himself beyond help. His only surviving beneficiary, Mr. Victor Helmsley, was paid two hundred thousand dollars, the double-indemnity settlement stipulated in the Small contract. The money came from Onyxx funds so there'd be no question of defrauding the carrier."

"Just another business expense, eh? And why not? It certainly wasn't enough to screw up your bottom line... hell no, you had more than enough left over to pay out your almighty dividends, so why should you give a damn about such fine points as morality when..." I stopped myself; Fanning didn't deserve the tirade. "I'm sorry, sir."

He pursed his lips and gave a quick nod. "One last thing, Mr. Huang. I'm afraid we've drawn blanks on the man who impersonated Mr. Ritchie. In terms of defending ourselves against Dr. Helmsley's accusations, this man's identity is immaterial. But like you I find his intrusion into this matter most unsettling—if you can furnish us a more detailed description, I'll have our men continue on it."

I shrugged and shook my head.

Fanning uncrossed his legs and gently slapped both thighs simultaneously. "Then the defense rests, sir."

I tried to read his face but couldn't. I massaged my temples, thinking whether there was anything left unsaid. There wasn't. The silence was growing so I stood.

Fanning cleared his throat. "Should you decide to make the contents of the microfilm public, would you do me the courtesy of informing me." When I nodded he led me back through the apartment to the vestibule, where he paused and reached into a breast pocket. "Mr. Huang, no matter what your decision, we thank you for your time and your good faith."

Inside the envelope was a check, drawn on "Onyxx Account E," for one thousand dollars. Fanning was too sophisticated to think this sum would buy my silence. But how could I... Just then I noticed that the check was made out to "Raymond T. Huang" so I handed the envelope back: "Was it good faith to have me investigated?"

He didn't bat an eye. "Had our report shown you professionally untrustworthy, we wouldn't have had this meeting. Instead, we would have concentrated on ensuring no reputable publication would ever run your piece."

"You mean a smear job."

Fanning broke into a wintry smile as he opened the door. "We're not General Motors, nor do we consider you another Ralph Nader. Thank you for your time, Mr. Huang."

24 September 1972: New York

Martha and I had been invited to a Sunday buffet in the garden of a Brooklyn Brownstone, but I'd spent the afternoon closeted in a bedroom watching an early-season pro football game, emerging only to refill my glass. In the eight days since my meeting with Fanning my mood had remained rotten. I'd always thought Martha the romantic and myself the pragmatist, yet it was she who'd first concluded the Onyxx defense seemed seamless. It took me several more days of poring over Fanning's rebuttal, but I'd also reluctantly agreed. Pat Ritchie's impersonator? It really didn't matter. Onyxx's cavalier shuttling of Harry's corpse? Not nice, but who ever said big business was nice? So why was I still so bitter... why couldn't I let go of it?

Martha finally nagged me outside during the second half. She soon wished she hadn't for I became the compleat churlish lout, guffawing in a voice too loud by half through my repertoire of dirty jokes: "... and so his buddy shouts through the window, 'Turn her over!'" My audience of two smiled politely. "Then there's the one about an army of ants pushing a turd up a hill..." My audience of two excused itself. I looked at my half-empty glass; three seconds later it was empty.

Martha intercepted me on the way to the bar. "I've said our thanks, Ray. Come on." I shrugged, delicately balanced my glass on the arm of an aluminum lawn chair, and followed her. She kept two steps ahead of me on our walk to the subway and on the train she stared fixedly at the "*if u cn rd ths u cn gt a gd jb*" poster; soon I knew how people living below a suspect dam must feel.

Back at the apartment I immediately lowered myself onto the sofa and tried to slow the room's spin by closing my eyes.

When I awoke Martha was standing near the TV. As soon as the weather forecast on the late news was over she flicked the set off, turned, and saw I was up. "You proud of yourself?"

I couldn't meet her eyes.

"If you're still not satisfied with Fanning's answers, it's not too late to talk this out with Mag or Sandy."

"No, it's not that. It's...hell, Martha, maybe it's because I'm a bad loser. I mean, I don't like to lose, but I hate losing this way." Her face was without expression. "Fanning must have known going in that he had it sewn up. But he rubbed my face in Harry's shit, he handled me...he handled me as easily as he would handle a child."

Slowly Martha's face curled into its Cheshire-cat grin: "Gee, I wonder why."

26 September 1972: New York/Boston/New York

All hurts heal, and perhaps it was my masochistically shameful performance at the party that cauterized my wounded ego. I suspected I was recovering because my anxieties were beginning to stem less from the humbling by Fanning than from the fact that I had a lot of queries out but no assignments in.

When I saw Sal the mailman climbing the stoop, I drifted out to the lobby.

"You look like a man waiting for a check."

"Something like that."

He unlocked the boxes and began flipping letters into their slots. Without looking up he dealt me a squarish envelope, the kind invitations come in. I opened it. The card bore a gold-bordered red seal depicting five stars and the Great Hall on T'ien An Men Square. The message inside was in Chinese but there was a translation:

In honour of the
Twenty-third Anniversary of the Founding of

> the People's Republic of China
> the Permanent Representative of the
> People's Republic of China to the United Nations
> Huang Hua
> requests the pleasure of your company
> at a reception
> on Sunday October 1, 1972, at 6:00–8:00 P.M.
>
> R.S.V.P. (regrets only)
> Tel. 787-3838
>
> Please present this card

Why had I been sent this? Sal handed me another letter. It was from *Esquire*, which I'd queried, so I ripped it open: thanks but no thanks. Now he was doling out magazines, advertising circulars, and oversize envelopes. I reread the invitation. It still made no sense—unless the Chinese had changed their minds about letting me photograph within the mission . . . Sal handed me an advertising circular and began locking the boxes. I glanced at the light-blue 9 × 12 envelope, which looked like a solicitation for something pricey, like porcelain snuffboxes, and then did a double take: the return address read Datatec.

I hurried back to my apartment and fumbled out the envelope's contents. My gaze fell immediately on the covering note's distinctive letterhead. It matched that contained in Harry's microfilm. I skimmed the note from Datatec's flack and turned my attention to the enclosed material. Because of its Fifth Avenue address I'd suspected the agency was no fly-by-night outfit; the spiffy Mylar binder confirmed it.

Inside was an 8 × 10 glossy of President Emmett Culver Stahl. Lean, very Ivy Leaguish, and in his forties, Stahl perched casually on his desk, smiling at the camera. On the wall behind him were four photographs: Stahl with family, Stahl with JFK, Stahl with LBJ, and largest of all, Stahl in the embrace of J. Edgar Hoover.

Beneath the glossy was a two-page bio of Stahl: Amherst, Virginia Law, and the FBI before founding Datatec.

Beneath the bio was an eight-page, four-color brochure modestly titled "The Datatec Story: Solving Today's Security Needs with Tomorrow's Technology." Wading through the fulsome copy, I learned Datatec was founded in 1966, had office or affiliates on both coasts and in three European cities, and specialized in electronic intelligence and counterintelligence. Which meant, if I read the euphemisms correctly, they bugged and debugged.

Finally there was a photostat of a laudatory *Wall Street Journal* piece on the firm, near the end of which I found a paragraph mentioning some of Datatec's major corporate clients. Fully half were not only listed on the Big Board but were blue chips to boot—including Onyxx.

So Harry had gone to one of the best. But was my hole card an ace or a deuce? Had Datatec in fact perpetrated such fictions as four Swiss entry stamps in Blair's passport, or had Fanning lied through his teeth? Either way it was time to play my last hand; only this deal, I was cutting Fanning out.

I caught the 12:30 P.M. shuttle to Boston with three minutes to spare. What to say to Blair? I finally decided to tell him I had concrete proof he'd visited Geneva in 1971. It was a lame bluff, but I'd learned that the do-you-still-beat-your-wife question is more valuable for the reaction it elicits on your victim's face than for the answer.

We landed Logan an hour later. At the terminal I looked up the address of Small, Inc. and checked it against a map; the consulting firm's office was far from public transportation, so I rented the cheapest car Avis had left. I drove through the Sumner Tunnel to Boston, crossed the Charles to Cambridge, and then headed north on Massachusetts Avenue past Harvard Square toward Route 2.

The Small, Inc. headquarters in North Cambridge was one of those anonymous modernistic structures remarkable only because it rose in splendid isolation from what used to be someone's North 40. I turned off Route 2 onto the access road cleaving the manicured lawn, followed the signs to the visitors' parking lot, and then walked to the brightly colored lobby, which had the tacky gaiety of an ersatz Mondrian.

"Do you have an appointment, sir?"

"No, I just happen to be in town and thought I'd drop in on George."

As the receptionist dialed Blair's office I rested my hands on her desk to steady them. Then she looked up and flashed a sympathetic smile. "I'm sorry, Mr. Blair's on vacation this week. But his secretary says you might catch him at home—do you have the address?"

I told her I did. Back in the Valiant I slumped into the driver's seat. It was the first time since opening the envelope from Datatec that my tension had abated, and suddenly my presence here seemed, well, silly. But as soon as I finished a cigarette, I started the car and pulled out of the parking lot.

I took Route 2 west to 180 and then sped down Route 180 to Wellesley. Checking my map frequently, I wound my way past the campus. It was so peaceful here—the air fragrant with new-mown grass, young ladies gliding by in madras Bermudas to showcase lean legs still tanned from the suns of summer—that I decided I was enmeshed in the wrong Seven Sisters.

Several turns later I nosed the car onto College Lane. The houses here, sitting on small, well-groomed plots, bespoke affluence. The street was lined with stately shade trees not yet shocked by first frost into the riot of colors that is a New England autumn. In the distance a power mower buzzed. I drove slowly as I inspected the houses in search of No. 34.

Midway up the third block I spotted a Ford station wagon and a yellow Porsche in a driveway to my right. As I touched the brakes I felt my metabolism accelerate. Now I could see past the parked cars. A couple worked in the garden, their backs to the street. She was a rangy woman wearing a T-shirt, khaki shorts, and sneakers; she stood holding a chrysanthemum plant. He was a wiry man dressed in shorts and sneakers; he knelt by the hole he was digging in the flower bed near the house.

I angled the car toward the curb.

Just then she offered him the chrysanthemum plant.

As he turned to receive it the lowering sun played across his profile.

My right leg spasmed but I fought my nerves and my breath under control and ducking my face toward the driver's side window I eased the steering wheel to the left and slowly stepped on the gas.

The man in the garden and I had met before. But he'd been much heavier then, and up at Harry's apartment he'd called himself Pat Ritchie.

I found a phone booth a half mile away and called Fanning long distance. Mrs. Shipley said he was in a meeting. I hightailed it back to Logan and before boarding the 5:30 P.M. shuttle tried him again. He was still in conference so I called Martha, filled her in, and asked her to dredge up his home phone number in Rye.

The cab pulled up to the Time-Life Building at 7:10 P.M. Four minutes later I was in Martha's cubicle dialing the Rye number. No answer. Then I remembered it was Tuesday so I called the Plaza Hotel and asked for the Oak Room. "Good evening, I'd like to speak to Mr. Franklin Fanning."

"Surely, sir. If you'll hold I'll have a phone brought to his table."

I slammed the receiver down and grabbed Martha's hand. "Come on—we're eating out tonight."

It was 7:32 P.M. when we bolted out of the cab in front of the Plaza and hustled across the lobby to the Oak Room; if the Fannings had a curtain to make they'd be finishing their meal. As the maître d' held us at his lectern while he pondered which of two dozen empty tables to give us, I rubbernecked until I spotted the Fannings in a corner. A waiter was serving them coffee. Now the maître d' strolled us to a table, seated Martha, and took our drink orders. As soon as he left I stood and smoothed my collar. "Well, here goes."

Fanning's wife was a slim and stunning blond who could have been any age between thirty-five and fifty-five. He smiled warmly as he talked to her. Then he drew out a pen and signed his bill. When he looked up again I was standing by his table.

He leaned back. For a split second apprehension and anger danced across his eyes, but his face remained amiable and his voice soft. "Chris, this is Mr. Huang, who brought me those documents. Mr. Huang, my wife."

Mrs. Fanning extended her hand.

"I'm sorry for intruding, ma'am." Her touch was as cool as her looks. I turned to Fanning. "I've got to speak with you, sir. It'll only take a couple of minutes."

Fanning glanced at his wife, then sighed as he stood. "I've been accused of being a chauvinist for shielding her from my business life; perhaps I am. Excuse us, Chris."

I looked at Mrs. Fanning. A peculiar mood—amusement?—vivified her face.

We walked across the dining room to the lobby. He stopped there: "I know you phoned me today. Dorothy tried to return your call several times. What is it." Instead of answering I surveyed the several clusters of people seated within earshot.

He followed my gaze. "Mr. Huang, I'm sure anything you have to say can be said here."

"It'll have to do, won't it? I mean, if we go all the way up to the Dakota your coffee'll get cold."

Fanning shot me a glare that, had I been a subordinate, would have instantly driven me to the employment classifieds. He whirled and I trailed in his wake as he marched across the lobby, down a flight of stairs, and through a vestibule into the men's room. As we entered, the attendant hopped off a shoe-shine chair and assumed an eager-to-please smile. There was no one at the urinals. The stall doors all stood open. Fanning withdrew his money clip, peeled off a ten and pressed the bill into the attendant's hand. "This room is out of order for five minutes."

"Yessir!" The attendant pocketed the money and scurried out.

Fanning walked to a washbasin, leaned against it, and crossed his arms. A geologist would have found his slate-colored eyes of interest.

"There were several loose ends from our meeting at your safe house," I said.

"I'm only aware of one."

"Okay, one. The person who impersonated Pat Ritchie."

His nod was barely perceptible.

"I found out who it was."

Fanning didn't move an inch, but somehow his posture seemed to straighten.

"It was the right honorable George F. Blair."

Fanning blinked and then looked at his shoes. Had he known all along? He cleared his throat and reached into a pocket for his Chesterfields. He hadn't known. He patted another pocket, then another. When I offered him my pack Fanning took one, absentmindedly snapped off the filter, and accepted my light. The drag he took was so deep his exhalation sounded like a sigh. "You're sure."

I nodded. "As much as I didn't want to, I accepted your rebuttal. But I hate unfinished puzzles, so when..." I caught myself before I mentioned Datatec. "So when it really got to me I went up to Boston. I recognized him instantly."

"What did he have to say?"

"We didn't speak." But this Fanning did know, for Blair

would have reported contact; no, he was stalling for time.

He took another puff. "You realize this has no bearing on our defense against Dr. Helmsley's accusations." So I'd been wrong: no matter what my hole card, the game was dealer's choice. I looked around; how ironic it should end in the men's room of the Plaza. Then I realized Fanning was still distractedly studying his cigarette. Finally he looked up. "It has no bearing, but I understand your puzzlement, and I share it. Will you be home tomorrow morning. Good—you'll hear from me."

"Thank you. Again, I'm sorry for disturbing your evening."

His eyes narrowed. "Facetiousness doesn't become you, sir."

"But I..."

Now his eyes softened and he gave me another quick nod, which I took as an apology. As we left the room the attendant called after us, "Any time, gentlemen, any time."

27 September 1972: New York/Boston/Washington

At 10:45 A.M. someone rang the apartment from the lobby. I went out into the hallway and looked through the glass door. It was a tall black man in a grey chauffeur's uniform; when he saw me he removed his cap and held up an envelope. I pressed the buzzer. As he pushed the glass door open and strode toward me I noticed he was built like an outside linebacker.

"Mr. Raymond Huang?" When I nodded he handed me the envelope. "Mr. Fanning asked me to wait until you've read it."

"Okay. Come on in."

He hesitated a second, then followed me into the apartment. Inside the envelope were a note on Onyxx stationery embossed with Fanning's name and title, a set of airline tickets, five twenty-dollar bills, and a blank check, drawn on "Onyxx Account E," payable to me. I read the handwritten note:

September 27

Mr. Huang:
    George Blair will meet you at your convenience to ex-

plain his impersonation of Mr. Ritchie. His story will be corroborated by a government official in Washington. Should you wish to travel to Boston today, my driver, Clarence, is at your disposal. The enclosed cash is to cover your incidental expenses. The enclosed check is to compensate you for your time. Please call after your return.

F.

The tickets were made out New York/Boston/Washington/New York, and they were open, which meant I could use them on any flight. I turned to Clarence. "How long to LaGuardia?"

He checked his watch. "We can catch the eleven-thirty."

"I've got to make a call first."

"There's a phone in the car."

After a moment's indecision I collected my wallet, an extra pack of cigarettes, and a madras sports jacket and followed him out. On the street Clarence automatically started to open one of the Mercedes 600's rear doors.

"Mind if I ride in front?"

"Not at all. And don't look so worried—we'll make that flight easy."

Clarence threaded his way deftly up Sixth Avenue and then east on 14th Street; I began to think I'd be on that plane after all. By the time we crossed Second Avenue we were doing forty-five. Just then a delivery boy pedaled his crate out from between two double-parked trucks, saw us bearing down on him, and froze. Before I could even brace my hands on the dashboard Clarence accelerated, flicked left and flicked right; we missed the boy by eight feet.

"Where'd you learn to drive like that?"

"Used to be a state trooper. That, plus a week at Bondurant's school."

"Out in California, where they teach you to drive race cars?"

"They also run special courses for executive chauffeurs—so long as I'm beind the wheel, nobody's putting the snatch on Mr. Fanning."

When we pulled onto the FDR Drive Clarence handed me the mobile telephone. I called Martha to tell her my plans and he called Mrs. Shipley to say I'd be on the 11:30 flight. Then the speedometer needle jerked to the right; we got to LaGuardia in time for me to stroll leisurely to the Eastern boarding gate.

When I deplaned in Boston Blair awaited me. Again he wore a three-piece suit but this time he appeared trim, not pudgy. "Thanks for coming up, Ray."

"I'm always interested in miracle diets."

"Easy. Put the T-shirt and the cheesecloth and the suit cut two sizes too big back in the closet and you get this." He laughed and patted his flat stomach; his voice, too, had changed, taking on a pronounced Boston inflection.

"Looking like a fatted calf helps you in your business?"

He maintained his practiced smile. "Any baggage?" I shook my head so he led me through the terminal to a yellow Porsche Targa sitting brazenly in a No Parking zone in front. The Targa's top was off, making conversation difficult, but Blair tried. I continued to gaze stonily out the windshield. Finally he shrugged and shifted his attention to traffic: "You want to play games, play games."

When we crossed to Boston he wended his way to School Street and pulled up in front of a restaurant named Maison Robert. "Best food in town, Ray."

"I prefer the Union Oyster House."

He was so smooth I almost missed the hesitation before he snicked the Porsche back in gear.

My mood hadn't improved by the time we took a booth at the Oyster House.

"Come on, cheer up, Ray. I understand..."

"Cut the condescension, and while you're at it cut the phony accent."

Blair smiled affably and slipped into his Pat Ritchie voice: "Prefer the way I sounded up at Helmsley's?"

"And cut the smile, it falls heavily among the bric-a-brac."

Now he laughed. "Very good, very good... you read Eliot."

"No, but I own a Bartlett's."

The telltale jaw muscles tensed and his face went blank. "Then you'll surely recognize this quote: 'This is how your mystery ends, not with a bang but a whimper.'"

At that moment the waitress arrived with our drinks. She pulled out her order pad, noticed our faces, and quickly withdrew.

Blair sipped his Rob Roy, then stirred the ice cubes with his finger. When the drink was cold enough he finally looked up. "Want to can the bullshit? Here it is straight. You heard the truth in Helmsley's apartment—you stumbled into a Company engagement."

"Why didn't Harry or Fanning say so?"

"They didn't know."

"I thought you were canning the bullshit."

"The Company operates on a need-to-know principle. Helmsley was a gifted geologist and a total shit who'd do anything for a buck. Thought this was just another cook job...no need to know. Onyxx was perfect cover, they wanted a shale survey and they were getting one...no need to know."

"Onyxx wanted real numbers, not cooked ones."

"They were going to get real numbers."

"Then why the fifty gpt crap?"

Blair picked up his drink and studied it against the light.

"If Fanning didn't know, he must have been thrilled when you told him."

"He'll live."

I leaned back in the booth. "Why did you impersonate Pat Ritchie? And how did you know about my call?"

"The Company had a tap on Helmsley's phone. They knew you'd been in Vientiane the night he bought it..."

"Impossible. First, I didn't leave my name on the..."

"You left a number. They checked a reverse directory and pulled your file."

My jugular began to throb. "They have a file on me?"

Blair nodded. "Not much in it then, but there was a report from an agent named Hailey." Gordon Hailey, I thought, the black "irrigation adviser" at the Vientiane airport. "The Company couldn't tell if you were a casual acquaintance or one of Helmsley's conquests. I knew him best. They shuttled me down to debrief you."

"So you are CIA."

"Nope. Just a friend."

A "friend" with a $225,000 slush fund? And false papers under the name George Friedrich? And was Entrepays a CIA front? The discrepancies between the Datatec report and Fanning's story were starting to jibe, but one big piece of the puzzle was still missing. "What was Harry's mission, Blair?"

He stared at his drink for a long time before speaking. "Half a block below Christopher and West there's a pay phone. The Company keeps a clean line on it."

Why the hell was he talking about a phone booth on the West Village waterfront near my apartment? Five seconds passed and he remained silent. "So?"

"Maybe someday we'll talk on it and I'll fill you in. Shit, Ray, you deserve to know, but I've got orders." He took another sip. "Unless..."

Again I let it dangle until I could stand it no longer. "Unless what?"

Blair shifted uncomfortably and ran a forefinger around the rim of his glass. "The front office wants this job stonewalled." He was still looking down so he didn't see my eyes widen at his use of the unusual verb. "Field op hates loose..."

"Field op?"

"Field operations. They hate loose ends. Knot this package, you get a peek at the goods. Unofficially, of course—anything I say'll be denied."

"What strings do I hold?"

"Two. Helmsley's microfilm and the detective agency's name."

"What value can they be now?"

"The microfilm's led you this far. The Company doesn't want anyone else traipsing down the same path. The agency name because they need to know how close the engagement came to being flushed."

The waitress, who'd been hovering several tables away, took my leaning back as a sign to approach. As we broke off to study the menu, I suddenly put my finger on Blair's ploy: I was the cat, and he was stroking my curiosity. But why? What little information I still held seemed moot at this point and hardly worth swapping for the lowdown on some CIA operation. Perhaps I was wrong, but I wasn't wrong about the fact that Blair was running another game, which meant he was dangling more lies. My drink was still untouched. Now I took a sip to help douse my anger: if that bastard dared go to the well again, I'd match him bucket for bucket.

"All right, the microfilm's in a safe-deposit box under my name at the Seamen's Bank on Fifth Avenue and Forty-fifth Street."

He nodded. "The agency?"

"It's your turn."

He shot me a bemused look. "Fair enough. When the lights

go out in Southeast Asia, the Soviets and the Chicoms'll both be rushing in. It'll be messy. We like that—in fact we want to make it messier. Helmsley was to prepare two reports. The kosher one was for Onyxx."

"And?"

"You're a bright boy."

"Let me guess. The cooked one was for the Company, and the Company would somehow leak its contents to Peking and Moscow."

"Like I said, you're a bright boy. Now the agency."

"Four-fifteen Montgomery Street, San Francisco. Spade and Archer."

Blair nodded, drained his drink, and then choked on the last of the Rob Roy. "What the fuck! You trying to jerk me around?" Heads turned at nearby tables.

"Why not? You've been jerking me around since I first met you."

Now he had his jaw muscles under control. "Have it your way. Only don't expect them to be so easily amused down at Langley."

"Who says I'm going to Langley?"

"You have two choices, mister. I make a call and we wait here until the man with the subpoena comes, or you get your ass down to Washington."

"When?"

"I'll know at three-fifteen."

I stood and turned to leave. "I'll be at the Café Pamplona in Cambridge."

"Huang." I looked back. Blair took out his wallet and sneeringly withdrew two hundred-dollar bills. "Buy yourself some grown-up clothes on the Square."

I made a show of inspecting my madras jacket, chambray shirt, faded Levi's, and Adidas. "If I'd known I was going to the last bastion of democracy, I'd of brought my tux. But I didn't, so I'll just have to wear the bottoms of my trousers rolled." Then I stalked from the restaurant.

At 3:30 P.M., as I chatted with Josefina, the owner of the Pamplona, and sipped my third *cappuccino,* Blair ducked through the door. He scanned the jam-packed whitewashed basement, finally spotted me at the table I'd chosen along the far wall, and began edging his way over. Halfway across the room, a Cliffie must have told him what to do with his cigar because he glanced at his Havana, flushed, and then defiantly jammed it in his mouth.

When he reached our table he looked at Josefina. Josefina looked questioningly at me. I looked from her to Blair: "Yes?"

He took the cigar from his mouth and idly tapped its ash into the ginger parfait in front of me; without even turning I knew Josefina's black Basque eyes had begun to flash. "Your appointment's tomorrow morning. Fanning offers the On..." He looked down at his spit-shined shoes, on which I'd just dropped an inch-long cigarette ash. "Grow up, Huang. Fanning's offering the Onyxx suite at the Madison. Acceptable? Good. Your pickup's at nine-thirty." Then Blair smiled. "Pleasant journey, hear?"

My plane landed National Airport shortly after 7:30 P.M. When I couldn't reach my pal Freddie at his office at Democratic National headquarters or at his apartment I took a cab straight to the Madison. The man at the desk inspected me closely but finally gave me the key. Up in the suite I rang room service because I was starved, and the valet because though my clothes weren't fancy, they needn't be grubby, even for the CIA. Then I chatted long distance with Martha until the waiter arrived. After dinner I switched off the TV and browsed a bookcase filled with Reader's Digest condensations and Books-of-the-Month. I settled on *The Day of the Jackal*, grabbed a fistful of the hotel's complimentary chocolates, and read myself to sleep.

28 September 1972: Washington/New York

The wake-up call came at 8 A.M. sharp. It took me five rings to fight my way out of a dark, druggy sleep.

I sat up in bed and lit a cigarette. This is absurd, I remember thinking, spending the night in a $60,000-a-year-suite so I could meet some good grey Langley bureaucrat who'll tell me men like Blair are making the world safer. Suddenly I felt as significant as a mayfly. To cheer myself up I ordered from room service two newspapers, fresh melon, steak-and-eggs, and a split of Moët. When I came out of the shower the waiter was setting up my breakfast. I ate slowly as I leafed through the Washington *Post* and the New York *Times*: McGovern was flailing about the hustings, probably planning his last supper come Election Eve; the People's Republic and Japan were about to paper over three centuries of enmity with a new treaty; the pennant races were winding down.

I was decked out in my neatly pressed clothes at 9:15 A.M., but the call announcing the driver's arrival didn't come until 9:50. Two can play that game, I thought savagely, so I told the front desk I'd be another fifteen minutes; then I poured myself the last of the coffee and resumed reading *Jackal*.

I finally ambled downstairs at 10:20 A.M. The lady at the desk pointed out the liveried driver, who sat erect but patiently near one of the ornate Oriental cabinets that dot the Madison's lobby. His black Mercury was directly in front and idling. I settled into the back seat, sorry I hadn't filched *Jackal* for the ride out to the Virginia suburbs.

The driver edged onto 15th Street, hung a quick left, and then turned left again. Several blocks later he made another left, and then left once more; these sinister turns had put us back on 15th Street, headed toward the Madison Hotel. Just as I started to tense he swung right onto Pennsylvania Avenue. Maybe this was part of the grand patriotic tour, I thought, as we passed No. 1600. At 17th Street the driver made another left, then pulled into a driveway leading to a funky pile of grey stones in the shape of a mansion. I hadn't known the CIA maintained an office in the Executive Office Building.

At the gate a guard stuck his head in, then waved us through when the chauffeur said my name. The car stopped at what looked to be a side door.

A thin, bespectacled young man in grey flannels with an American-flag lapel pin awaited me: "Adam Fairleigh. Come on, we're late."

I followed him into the building and down a high-ceilinged marble hallway.

"Exactly how do you pronounce your name?"

"Huang, as in . . . as in Hiram Fong."

He laughed. We boarded an elevator at the end of the hall. Then Fairleigh checked his watch and shook his head. "Was there some problem with the car?"

"No, why . . . what time's my appointment?"

"About four minutes ago, at ten-thirty."

"Then why did you send a driver before ten?"

"The Boss is on a very tight schedule."

"Well, so am I."

His eyes suddenly appeared enormous behind his glasses. The elevator doors opened and Farleigh ushered me through a series of antechambers to the desk of a lady who would have been attractive except for her beehive coif. "Barbara, this is Mr. Huang."

She glanced at me and pressed her intercom: "Your ten-thirty's here, sir."

"Very well." The voice emerging from the amplifier sounded oddly familiar. I looked around the waiting room; dominating it was the official presidential portrait.

Then the door opened and I was staring at the man who stood a heartbeat away from having his own portrait in every federal building. With the Vice-President was a diminutive Oriental, a bland-faced man whose chunkiness was accentuated by black rectangular-framed eyeglasses and a European-cut sharkskin suit. The two men were laughing.

"Thanks again for stopping by, and please convey my regards to Tandy."

"I sure will, Ted, and my best to Judy and the kids." The visitor clasped the Vice-President's right hand with both of his, then turned to leave. That's when his eyes fell on me. For some reason we Orientals can usually intuit the ethnicity of fellow Asians on the basis of physiognomy and physique; in the instant it took him to peg me as Chinese, I knew for certain he'd traveled a long and prosperous road since embarking from Korea.

Now Fairleigh stepped forward and cleared his throat. "Mr. Vice-President, this is Hiram F . . . pardon me, this is Raymond Huang."

The Vice-President's good humor suddenly melted and when he glanced from my clothing to his watch his eyes narrowed further until they were slits. "Adam, I want Vic before my eleven o'clock." With that he wheeled, led me across the office, and pointed to a chair. As I sat he continued on around his desk. On it lay a bulky red envelope. He picked it up and inserted it in his inner left breast pocket. Then he unconsciously smoothed the outside of his jacket and, still standing, opened a slim, vinyl-bound briefing book. "Mr. Wang, it is my . . ."

"Excuse me, sir, that's pronounced 'Huang.'"

The Vice-President slowly inspected his manicured fingernails before looking up. His face was tight, as was his voice. "Am I given to understand that you lack respect for the office of the vice-presidency?"

"Sir?"

"Do you consider it proper to keep the Vice-President waiting? Do you think it appropriate to arrive at the Vice-President's office wearing an outfit better suited for a... for a Polack wedding?"

I started to protest that I hadn't known whom I was seeing but his trick of remaining on his feet was properly intimidatory so I stared at his desk.

"I asked you a question, Mr. Wang."

Now I made myself raise my eyes to meet his. "Sir, I have great respect for the *office* of the vice-presidency."

He flushed, then adjusted his collar. "I didn't choose to perform the rather disagreeable task at hand, but I think I'm going to relish it immensely. Let's see how noisome you are when we get through." I winced at his misuse of "noisome" but he missed it because he was taking his seat and turning his attention to the briefing book. "Mr. Raymond T. Wang, it is my duty as the Vice-President of the United States to inform you on this twenty-eighth day of September, 1972, of the following: your President deems the information you recently acquired vital to this nation's security, in that it relates to communications intelligence. Therefore, it must remain confidential. With that on the..."

"What information?"

He looked up with puzzled eyes. "Why... why the information you recently acquired."

"I'm a journalist. I've acquired a lot of information recently."

The Vice-President frowned and dipped his eyes back to the briefing book. Jesus, I thought, he hasn't the foggiest idea of what this is all about—he's just an errand boy. Then he turned the page and relief flooded his face. "The information in question is that information that you recently acquired relevant to the activities of one Dr. Henry Hemsley. Now if I might continue.

"With that on the record, the Justice Department advises

that any attempt by you to communicate this information shall be considered in violation of Title 18 of the United States Codes, specifically Sections 793(e) and 798(a).

"I now quote the pertinent passages of Section 793(e): 'Whoever having unauthorized possession of, access to, or control over any document, writing or photographic negative relating to the national defense, or information relating to the national defense which information the possessor has reason to believe could be used to the injury of the United States or to the advantage of any foreign nation, willfully communicates, delivers or transmits the same to any person not entitled to receive it, or willfully retains the same and fails to deliver it to the officer or employee of the United States entitled to receive it, shall be fined not more than ten thousand dollars or imprisoned not more than ten years, or both.'"

The Vice-President paused for breath. He couldn't resist looking up; the sight of me slumped ashen-faced in the armchair brought a smug smile to his face. "I take it that though you're a layman, you read us loud and clear." Then he glanced at his watch, made a face, and resumed: "I also quote the pertinent passages of Section 798(a): 'Whoever knowingly and willfully communicates, furnishes, transmits or otherwise makes available to an unauthorized person, or publishes, or uses in any manner prejudicial to the safety or interest of the United States or for the benefit of any foreign government to the detriment of the United States any classified information'—I skip now to paragraph 3—'any classified information concerning the communication intelligence activities of the United States shall be fined not more than ten thousand dollars or imprisoned not more than ten years, or both.'

"Therefore, Mr. Wang, should you reveal to others or publish information and/or material concerning the activities of Dr. Harry Hemsley, you shall be subject to prosecution by the United States Government."

Now he picked up an envelope. "A copy of the pertinent Codes, which I'd peruse carefully if I were you. Any questions?" When I mutely shook my head, he allowed himself another thin grin before punching the button on his intercom.

"Yes, Mr. Vice-President."

"Is Victor there? And send in Adam to fetch Mr. Wang." Then the Vice-President busied himself with some papers, dismissing me much like a bank teller closing his window on a conga line of lunch-hour depositors.

29 September 1972: New York

A guest pass awaited me at the security desk, and when I arrived at Mrs. Shipley's door she immediately led me into her boss's office.

As Fanning rose and came around his desk he extended his hand; I took it. "Mr. Huang, you have my apologies... come, join me in some coffee." He ushered me out of the bright late-afternoon sun to the couch in the corner, in front of which the low table was already laid out with chinaware and silver service. Fanning poured with rock-steady hands but I could sense his agitation when he spoke. "I hope, sir, you'll believe me when I tell you I didn't know Mr. Blair's true role."

I nodded.

"Mr. Blair no longer serves as Small's liaison with us."

"Jesus, you mean he's still on their payroll?"

"Stan—Stan Harmer, who heads Small—is frankly unhappy. But because of his own background, and because of Small's history with the CIA... well, he's behaving more charitably toward Mr. Blair than I would."

"So Blair really is CIA."

He dropped his eyes to his coffee cup. "We don't think so."

I slumped back into the sofa. If even Fanning and Harmer didn't know...

Then Fanning fished out a Chesterfield and asked me to recount my travels. As I described the session with Blair his face remained impassive, but when I got to the Vice-President he made no attempt to suppress his scowl. "No disrespect intended, son, but it sounds like they went after a flea with a cannon. And I don't understand why that imbecile saw you, rather than a Justice lawyer, but he's one reason Mr. Stans left my office without a pledge." He stubbed out his cigarette. "Had I been on top of matters when we met at the Dakota, you would have been spared a great deal of anguish. I'm sorry."

"Accepted. And I guess in hindsight I owe you an apology, too, for landing on you so hard."

"Nonsense, Mr. Huang, I'm richly compensated for absorbing pressure."

"Oh, speaking of compensation..." I took out an envelope and passed it over.

Without looking inside he must have known it contained the blank check and the unused cash. "You're sure."

I nodded.

At the door Fanning offered his hand again. "I'll wish you good luck, Mr. Huang, though I doubt you'll need it." Then he smiled.

An hour later, after Martha and I had squeezed onto stools at the bar of the Russian Tea Room, she reached into her Time-Life tote bag and pulled out a package. I removed the gift wrapping. It was a book. I instantly recognized the author, Franklin W. Dixon, but not the title, which had been altered to *The Hardy Boys Get Stonewalled*.

1 October 1972: New York

I peered at my reflection and straightened the knot of my tie. "Hey, I was rereading the Codes that the Veep threw at me."

Martha was applying lipstick so she grunted.

"The law says I have to surrender stuff on demand. Like the microfilm and Datatec's name."

"Shit." She tissued off the botched makeup.

"If the CIA's as hot as Blair says for that stuff, how come nobody's asked for it?"

The lipstick tube hovered near Martha's lip as in the mirror her eyes shifted to meet mine. "Maybe they lost your file, or maybe they never had it—maybe Blair and the White House are running a scam together." I looked away. "Look, Ray, you're carrying stubbornness too far. I can't make you talk about the anger building inside you, but I can say that it's getting pretty damned self-destructive." She started on her lips again and botched it again.

It was 6:20 P.M. by the time we emerged from the Lincoln Center subway station and hiked west to the People's Republic mission. Our invitation admitted us into a good-sized anteroom. As we shuffled forward in the reception queue I recognized the Chinese Ambassador to the United Nations, Huang Hua, from his newspaper photos; his grey tunic was tailored noticeably better than the other greeters'. When Martha and I finally began introducing ourselves, our names failed to elicit either notice or interest.

We proceeded to a large room dominated by a gargantuan portrait of Chairman Mao and walked across to the bar.

"Wine or *mao tai*?" the bartender asked.

I ordered two *mao tais*. Martha began to protest but I cut her short. "The wine's very sweet, sweeter than sauterne. These are good—just go easy on them."

She discreetly sniffed her drink before trying it, but once she got over the shock of its fiery entry she smiled. I sipped mine; compared to this, the expensive *mao tais* I'd had in Hong Kong tasted like moonshine.

We decided to work the room on the off chance we'd see someone we knew. The Chinese hadn't been here long enough to redecorate, though they had managed to camouflage the fact that we were standing in what had until recently been the lobby of a fancy motel. The crowd started to thicken. As we pressed on I noted that the senior mission staff, in simple charcoal or black tunic suits, seemed far more elegant than the spiffily dressed, heavily cologned guests. Eventually Martha and I refilled our glasses and headed for the three white-linened tables bearing food.

Most of the other guests were elbowing each other to get at the trays containing such familiar hors d'oeuvres as egg rolls and chicken wings so I steered her to the more exotic fare. I eagerly picked up a thousand-year-old egg. Martha looked at the greenish yolk and the translucent blackness that had been the white and winced; she never knew what she missed. But she did like the fragrant pieces of fried carp enough to indulge in thirds and fourths, and then I got her to sample a crunchy shredded goody. "Hey, that's not bad." She took another mouthful. "What is it?" I didn't have the heart to tell her.

We were back at the fried carp when I felt a tap on my shoulder. "Huang *hsien-sheng*? *Wo shih* Kuo Yu-tang."

I turned. Kuo Yu-tang, the press attaché who'd sent me the curt note rejecting my request to photograph within the mission, was a square-faced, robust man in his late thirties. When I introduced him to Martha, I found his smile atypical for a Chinese in that it was open, with his whole face animated. "You guys both enjoying the party?"

"It's been interesting," Martha replied. "These *mao tais*—am I saying it correctly?—they're something else. If all the women in China drink them, I can see why your population's exploding."

Kuo laughed.

Then Martha pointed to the plate of crunchy shredded goodies. "What's that? Ray won't tell me."

Kuo looked conspiratorially at me. I shrugged so he told her: "Raw jellyfish."

"Oh."

"Some folks swear it promotes long life."

"Fascinating."

He laughed again and turned to me. "I've got to apologize for that abrupt note last spring. It was pretty hectic then, what with our move and all, so I had an associate write it. His English is awful." Kuo's own English was perfect; could the drawl tinging it be Californian?

"You can cement your apology by turning me loose upstairs with my Nikon."

"Who knows, maybe someday I will." He smiled, took out a pack of Chinese cigarettes and offered them around; they were unfiltered and strong, but not harsh. "Say we let you in. Who do you offer the takes to?"

"My first stop would be *Life*. I've never shot for them, but they know me. If you'd like, I'll sound them out."

Kuo shook his head. "First, I've got some heavy selling to do on my comrades. They don't quite buy the value of showing that, deep down, we're just plain folks too. Anyway, I know *Life*'s interested—there've been overtures already." Then he smiled. "*K'o shih ni shih Chung-kuo jen.*"

But *you* are Chinese: that must mean if Kuo could convince his comrades, I had the inside track. Suddenly the reason for our invitation—PR knows no national boundaries—became clear, leaving only one unanswered question: "This is a cliché, but where'd you study English?"

"A cliché for sure ... would you believe Stanford? Actually, that's where I picked up the Americanisms. I learned English in Hong Kong, where I was born."

"When did you go back to *Ta Lu*?" I asked, using the Chinese term for the Mainland.

"Fifty-eight. Perfect timing—I returned just in time for the 'Great Leap Forward.'" Kuo seemed unabashed by his heresy, but then his face grew serious. "What you really want to know is, 'Why?' I'm not sure. Maybe it was a reaction to the discrimination I felt in Hong Kong and California. Maybe it was because my family had no ties with the Kuomintang, which meant I had no real future on Taiwan."

Just then another mission staffer approached him and rattled off something in a dialect I thought Cantonese. Kuo turned back to us. "If you'll excuse me... we'll talk some more."

A short while later the clink of metal on glass, and the crowd began to swing its attention toward Ambassador Huang Hua, who stood in front of the portrait of the Chairman. When the din subsided he launched a stem-winder. We had trouble following his soft voice, but like all accomplished orators he underlined his key phrases: we "close friends" of the People's Republic were "always welcome" at the mission; the recent Peking-Tokyo treaty was "a meaningful step" between two nations "so closely linked by history"; the People's Republic would shortly "liberate" Taiwan. Finally the Ambassador proposed a toast to the "newfound harmony" between America and China. As most of the guests slugged back the last of their *mao tais* most of the Chinese in the room just touched glass to lip.

It was nearing 7:45 P.M. so we decided to leave. As we filed toward the anteroom, I spotted Kuo some twenty feet away, listening attentively to a distinguished-looking Indian diplomat, and managed to catch his eye. He smiled, mouthed the words "See you again," and returned his attention to the Indian.

7 November 1972: New York

Cronkite, Chancellor and Brinkley, Smith and Reasoner—they were all side by side and gabbing but they looked like five aquarium inmates because the volume controls on the three sets were turned down, the staffers in the lounge on Martha's floor preferring conversation to a play-by-play of one of the grand routs in the history of U.S. politics. Over in one corner the balding writer named Gurney, flushed with bourbon and intoxicated by the success of his team, loudly offered ten to one McGovern and Shriver wouldn't carry a single state west of the Mississippi; nobody was rushing to cover. I sat in a subdued circle whose votes reflected more loathing for Tricky Dick than faith in the Democrat's starry visions.

As I listened to the desultory postmortems I couldn't help but wonder if I'd done right by respecting the Vice-President's command to silence. Granted, it appeared I'd brushed against a CIA operation. But why had Blair acted so irrationally and why had Washington, as Fanning implied, practiced overkill on me? And why hadn't the Feds followed up? Or had I been stifled for reasons other than "national security"? Then I glanced at the numbers flashing on the TV screens; no matter what it had really involved, it couldn't have affected this election. But then why was I still gnawing on this meatless bone instead of concentrating on my free-lancing? In the last month I'd had a grand total of two assignments that together paid $650.

By 9:30 P.M. all three networks had tabbed the winning ticket. Two hours later McGovern's face filled the three screens. Someone turned up the sound so we could hear the concession and then to Washington for the acceptance speeches of the men more than 60 percent of all Americans who'd voted wanted four more years of—Richard Milhous Mixon and Spiro Theodore Agnew.

28 November 1972: New York

"What do you think about this one?" Martha was holding up a conservative grey dress.

"You'll look woebegone, that's for sure."

"Then how about this?" It was a clingy white wool number with a cowl neck.

"You going down there to pick Tim up or to divorce him?"

She blushed, then slipped into the clingy white wool number.

After Martha left for her court data I drew a deep breath

and called Duke. "Hi, it's Ray. Know anyone looking to buy cameras?"

"Yours?" He sounded surprised.

"Yes."

"What's the matter, kid?"

"Oh, I don't know, I..." Hell, I thought, if I can't be honest with Duke, I might as well pack it in. "I'm selling them because they're collecting dust. I'll concentrate on writing for a while, then maybe pick up a new system next year."

"Will you accept a loan?"

"No."

"Then sell them to me."

"What for? You need two more Nikons like you need another Countess Mara."

Duke laughed. "Just shut the fuck up and bring them by this morning."

An hour later I was down two bodies and four lenses but up $750; it was a painful way to make my year-end nut.

24 December 1972: New York

The previous Christmas Martha had given me a Lucite desktop organizer and I'd given her a French omelet pan; both presents had been inexpensive but apt.

Now she was opening the box from me. When she saw the eggshell-colored Jaeger turtleneck she moistened her lips. "Oh Ray, it's beautiful, but it must've... you shouldn't have, you really shouldn't have."

"Well, I did." They were right: money can't buy happiness. Then I unwrapped her package. Our psyches were so similar it was eerie; she must have dropped a bundle on the telephone answering machine. "Hey, thanks, but you're the one who shouldn't have."

"I couldn't resist. Anyway, it was on sale." As I hooked up the machine to the phone in the living room she gave me a hug. "May you wear it out recording new assignments."

"Amen."

1 January 1973: New York

When I awoke, Martha got up from watching the Cotton Bowl and poured me a Bloody Mary. "You had a rotten time last night."

"Not really. It's just that watching instant replays of the ball dropping on Times Square doesn't make me jolly." Which was only part of the truth: we'd gone to a big bash at Duke's, and like their host, most of the guests had been high-powered; playing the wallflower had seemed preferable to listening to deals being wheeled.

"Mind if I nag?"

"No."

"You've got to make a resolution that you'll leave the house more this year." I looked away. "It's very depressing to come home at night and find you still in your bathrobe. So the world isn't beating a path to your door—go out and hustle 'em eyeball-to-eyeball."

"Yes, coach."

"Have you got any queries out?"

"Well, I told you about the textbook contract."

Martha's face suddenly darkened. "Jesus, what a cop-out. It'll turn you into a vegetable, and probably me, too. What are they offering?"

"Ten thou."

"That's fucking great pay for twelve months' work." Then she must have remembered it was the first day of a new year because she backed off. "Come on, anything's better than that. Don't sign."

"I won't if I can wangle some assignments, which I promise I'll start trying for tomorrow, as soon as all the hangovers have melted away."

Martha smiled. "Attaboy, that's the old Raymond whom I allowed to pick me up."

12 February 1973: New York

The jurors' bull pen on the fifteenth floor of 100 Centre Street was a dim, stuffy cavern. I'd reported there for my first day of duty not so much because of civic responsibility but because, with the free-lance hopper still empty and the textbook contract still pending, the twelve dollars a day the city paid looked pretty good. As I looked at the jaundiced walls of the smoking anteroom, I thought ruefully how just one year ago I'd been traveling through Asia. In fact, I'd been in Bangkok, about to fly to Vientiane...

My name was called so I trooped with fifty other peers to a courtroom in which the case involved possession of a controlled substance, to wit, marijuana. During my *voir dire* the prosecutor noted I was a writer. Had I ever written on drug abuse? I had; he excused me.

At lunchtime I slid into my parka and hunched my way a few blocks east. Chinatown had been a Sunday ritual during my childhood, when my parents drove down from Westchester for an hour of marketing and their decent Chinese meal of the week. But now they lived on the West Coast and now I rarely set foot in the area. I used to think it was because Chinatown was too near, that I was blind to it the same way many native New Yorkers have never seen the Statue of Liberty. In light of my trip the previous year, though, I now had to entertain a more uncomfortable possibility: did I avoid Chinatown because of the subtle dissonances it inflicted on my Western-oriented sense of self?

I began searching for a restaurant on Mott. This street had been laid out with a sharp bend in it so clean-living Chinese folks could escape pursuing demons, demons being able to run only in a straight line. It took several minutes but I found it just below the bend. Memory served me well—Hop Kee was warm and as rowdy as a Village tavern and its *lo mein* good and plentiful. Best of all, it was cheap.

When I climbed back onto Mott I still had twenty-five minutes to kill. Down the street I spied a large, vertical sign that read "Port Arthur." Why not, I thought, smiling to myself as

I headed not for the restaurant-bar announced by the sign but the penny arcade just before it; though this grotty pleasure palace must have had a name, to me it was the real Port Arthur, as it was to every Chinese-American kid ever given a dollar to amuse himself while his parents shopped.

I ducked in the nearest plate-glass door. The arcade was quiet. The wizened old Chinese man who doled out change from a news vendor's apron sat reading a paper while the young man behind the counter sorted the coupons with which the Port Arthur rewarded high scores on its gaming machines. A decade of misspent Sundays had left me with some 110 points' worth, which still lay rubber-banded together at the back of my file cabinet; another decade of Sundays and the whoopee cushion was mine.

I hit up the old man for change. When I bowled a Skee-Ball game worth two points I called him. He looked around with annoyance, tried to see my score from his chair, and then asked how many points I'd won. "Three," I shouted. On my way out the old man looked up scornfully when I asked for the coupons.

"For my nephew," I said.

He hawked into the spittoon at his feet and went back to his paper.

I had one thin dime left in my hand as I started for the door. That's when I remembered the poor cluck that was the focus of many an animal lover's ire.

The Port Arthur chicken was a goodly-sized white rooster in a glass cage as big as a two-hundred-gallon fish tank. The cage was partitioned in two: on the right was the roost, on the left a turntable. I dropped in my coin. The bird roused itself and looked sharply about its roost, then pranced through the partition and began hotfooting it around on top of the turntable. After the disk had spun about five seconds, a handful of grain released in the roost. The bird ducked back through the partition to peck its reward; at that moment the machine spat out a 3½ × 5½ card.

Represented on it were eight playing cards. I checked my hand: Club Q, Spade J, Heart 8, Club 8, Spade K, Heart 10, Heart 9, Heart J. Straight, King high. Then I read the fortune at the bottom:

GENTLEMEN'S CARD
You will be invited to a party where two women will entertain, and where you will meet a dark man who is wealthy. If you are wise you will cultivate his friendship. 6 Cards give a complete reading.

I pocketed the card and made a mental note to spend another lunch hour divining the rest of my future; the chicken's version had to be better than mine.

19 February 1973: New York

Martha was still asleep when I climbed out of bed at 7:30 A.M. to get ready for another day of jury duty. The past week had made my army pre-induction physical seem interesting; prosecutors, it turned out, are loath to impanel writers because they fear our imagination and our cynicism will tempt us to give defendants more than a reasonable doubt. As a result I'd yet to sit on a case, though I'd had to undergo *voir dire* at least once a day.

I was padding toward the kitchen to start coffee when I saw on the vestibule floor an envelope that looked as if it had been pushed under our apartment door. The outside of the envelope was blank. Inside was a typewritten note:

Ling How Fun restaurant, 22 Doyers Street, 12:20 P.M. sharp.
Ask for Wellington.

There was no signature.

When my head stopped buzzing I thought instantly of Blair, then just as quickly rejected him. Fanning? No, he wasn't eccentric enough to set up a meet in Chinatown. That was the key, it had to be someone who knew I was stuck downtown on jury duty. Alan or Duke, playing a joke? Then I looked back toward the bedroom—or was Martha subwaying down to cheer me up at lunchtime? Slowly the uneasiness evaporated, if not the curiosity.

Court recessed at 12:12 P.M. I hurried across Centre Street, cut through the playground, and ascended Park Street. Then left on Mott, a quick right onto Pell and right again on Doyers, a street that like Mott had a sharp bend in it.

The Ling How Fun was on the right-hand side, just at the bend. The restaurant was crowded. As I stepped inside a bald Chinese man in his fifties wearing a shapeless navy-blue suit approached. "Taber for one?"

"No, I want to speak to Wellington."

He opened one of the menus in his hand, stared into it, peered at my face, and rechecked his menu. "Okay, you forrow me." I smiled; it had to be either Duke or Martha.

Wellington led me up a staircase near the front door. At the top we turned right, onto a dim corridor. There was a series of curtained doorways to our left; I peeked through a partially open set and saw a private banquet room. Now he ducked through the fourth set and held the curtain open for me.

The room was empty. I wheeled toward Wellington but the protest died in my throat for he had his right hand on a sconce-like lighting fixture and he was twisting it counterclockwise.

"Go there, prease."

I followed his finger and saw the far wall sliding silently to the right to reveal Kuo Yu-tang.

"Huang *hsien-sheng*, thank you for coming . . . please enter, please enter," he said in Chinese.

I glanced around dazedly and then walked across my private banquet room into his private banquet room, which seemed to be part of another building altogether. Kuo pressed a yellow button on the wall. I turned; the movable partition was sliding shut. Now he uncurled a scroll so it covered the yellow button. "*Ch'ing tsuo, ch'ing tsuo*," he said, motioning me to a seat at a long table.

"What the hell is this?"

Still in Chinese, he asked, "You feel more comfortable if we talk in English?"

"Yes."

"Okay, first my message, then your questions. Do you know you're under twenty-four-hour surveillance?"

The blood left my face.

"Now you know."

I finally recovered enough of my voice to croak, "Who?"

"Beats me. Who do you think it is?"

I had several candidates but I wasn't about to share them

with him. Instead I said, "What makes you so sure?"

He poured two cups of tea. "You can see right into your apartment from the commercial building across the street, especially the corner office on the third floor."

The building with the "Space Available" sign... the phone call from Duke's chief assistant Mario... the sign that was gone when I looked again. I began to sweat. "Wait a minute. The only way you'd know that is by staking me out yourself."

"Just because you're one of us, you think we'd let you run around our mission without vetting you first?"

"*Life* folded two months ago."

Kuo smiled. "*Una golondrina no hace verano.*" When I stared dumbly, he translated: "'One swallow never makes a summer.' Cervantes."

"I thought you were supposed to quote Chairman Mao... or are spies exempt?"

"Who's a spy?"

"Where'd you pick up a term like 'vetting,' from Le Carré and Deighton?"

"Sure. Isn't that where you got it?"

Kuo was toying with me; I drank some tea to simmer down. Finally I said, "I suppose when you're not reading Cervantes you like to build walls that slide."

He laughed. "That? Late nineteenth century, put in by one of the big *tongs* for security... some brownnosing merchants told us about it when we first hit New York. Our entire staff's tailed by at least two Feds every time we leave the mission. That makes this wall damned convenient—you come in through Doyers, I come in through Mott, and just so long as nobody's eating in either room, we can hold private meetings like this."

"And just why are we meeting?"

"I told you. To let you know you're being watched."

"Okay, so I know. Now what?"

"Nothing."

"Come off it. You must want something."

Kuo made a wry face. "They told us in Peking that altruism's mistrusted in the West, but I didn't want to buy it. Well, as Cervantes would say, 'Forewarned, forearmed.'" He let me stew for a while longer, then said, "Hey, join me for lunch. The food's not bad here."

"No thanks, you've killed my appetite." I stood and started for the door.

Kuo intercepted me. "That'll take you to Mott. It'd be better if you left the same restaurant you entered." He rolled up the scroll, pressed the yellow button, and the wall began to slide. As I descended the stairs of the Ling How Fun I saw Wellington again. He returned my look but his eyes were blank.

Back out on Doyers I tried to light a cigarette but the thought of hidden eyes on me was so unsettling I had to steady my right hand with my left; I hoped they took the trembling for cold. And then I was inexplicably racked by hunger. But could I afford to walk into another restaurant after just leaving one? I looked at my watch. I'd been inside about ten minutes, not really enough time to eat, so I retraced my steps to a small coffee shop on Pell, instinctively took a table at the rear, and sat with my back to the wall. I shouldn't have. It was damnably hard keeping my eyes off the other patrons as I greedily attacked a *pao-tze*, a steamed dough-wrapped meatball. I must stay casual, I thought, I can't let them know I know until I can confirm who they are. But how the hell do I do that? Phone the CIA and ask? Suddenly the steamy coffee shop turned claustrophobic so I stuffed the last of a second *pao-tze* in my mouth and left.

I began walking down Mott. Which of these restaurants contained the banquet room I'd met Kuo in? And then I reached the Port Arthur and the urge was irresistible so I went in and fumbled a dime into the chicken's box and the bird strutted through the partition—give me a clue, give me some sign, I'll believe, I really will... The turntable turned and the grain shot down and as the white rooster started to peck a card popped out: Club Q, Spade J, Heart 8, Club 8, Spade K, Heart 10, Heart 9, Heart J. Straight, King high.

LADIE'S CARD
You will be invited to a party where two women will entertain, and where you will meet a dark man who is wealthy. If you are wise you will cultivate his friendship. 6 Cards give a complete reading.

The little Chinese grandmother, her hair drawn in a tight bun, almost dropped her shopping bags when I burst from the arcade cackling hysterically.

On returning home that afternoon I wanted to immediately close the shutters on the front windows but I didn't because it would be breaking my pattern. Instead, I started my inspection in the rear of the apartment; by the time I got to the living room it was dark outside and unless they had special night field glasses they'd never be able to see me searching in back of prints and under cushions. When I finished I knew the place was free of any object resembling my conception of a miniaturized microphone/sender. But could our phone be tapped? And had an intruder invaded our space—had I placed a couple of files back slightly askew? Hadn't I tucked the chain of my heirloom pocket watch inside its chamois pouch before returning it to my cache? I just couldn't remember.

I took one last look at the darkened windows of the third-floor office across the street and then turned on the apartment lights. Martha would be home soon. She mustn't know—not yet, anyway.

22 February 1973: New York

I'd earned my penultimate twelve dollars from the tax coffers by being excused from one jury in the morning and another in the afternoon. As boring as this travesty was I was nevertheless reluctant to leave the courthouse, for my trips to and from 100 Centre Street had become exercises in terror: I still had to play dumb because I still didn't know who they were.

When I got home I checked the answering machine—nothing—and shuffled quickly through the mail—no editor had written to say yes, my query was wonderful, go do it. Then I was out of chores and then the tension became unbearable so I called Martha.

"How did it go today?" she asked.

"Enhh. You?"

"Boning up on Watergate." With Judge Sirica leaning on the burglars and the Senate forming a committee chaired by Sam Ervin and Woodward and Bernstein digging ever deeper, Martha's magazine had recently assigned her to its own task force on the shenanigans. "The stuff never quits—like today, Woodstein reported that Howard Hunt was mixed up in the Dita Beard fiasco. Seems that last year he put on some sappy disguise to visit Beard at her sickbed. Get a load of this: Beard's son describes Hunt as, quote, very eerie, he did have a red wig on cockeyed like he put it on in a car..."

Red wig... red wig. Why did that sound familiar? Suddenly I remembered my neighbor, Mrs. Morabito, and her story of some clown hanging around the building...a clown who'd looked like "Rackety-Ann," whose hair was of course...

When I finished blurting out my suspicions we fell silent. Then, referring to her magazine's reigning Watergate expert, Martha said, "Ray, will you come in and talk to Mag?"

"I've got to wrap up jury duty tomorrow—maybe you can sound him out on a meeting early next week?"

When I got off the phone I made myself a drink. Were the people who'd sicced Red Wig onto me a year ago also watching me now? Most likely. Was it Onyxx or Fanning? No. Washington? It had to be. But what part of Washington, and why? I'd held my tongue. And then I remembered the four Hispanics posing as telephone repairmen at my psychiatrist friend's office.

Alan's service said he was gone for the day so I dialed his home. When I got his answering machine I said at the *beep* it was urgent we talk. Evidently he spent the night at his lady friend Kathy's because he never called back.

23 February 1973: New York

I finally reached Alan in the morning and arranged to see him late that afternoon. As soon as I was dismissed from my last day of jury duty I subwayed to his office, not worrying about the tails because they'd know of our relationship.

When I finished he looked up from his notes: "Are you on some GOP shit list?"

"Not that I know of. You?"

"No. I wouldn't give to an AMA fund for Nixon, but I doubt if many psychiatrists did, except maybe the guy who treated him." We kicked the mystery around for half an hour more before Alan said, "What're you up to tonight?"

"Not much. Martha's on closing."

"Let's go up to my club. Maybe something'll come to us."

We were both so psyched up that on the basketball court we played like a couple of demented gorillas. Perhaps the exertion sapped us, for the dinner chitchat that followed was desultory, or perhaps it was because our minds were back grappling with issues impenetrable. Each time I felt on the verge of telling Alan about Harry and Fanning and Blair and the Vice-President, I drew back, for surely "national security" hadn't been a factor in the rifling of his office and my apartment. Finally over coffee we agreed on a course of action. We'd ask our mutual friend Freddie, late of the Democratic National Committee, to determine from his Washington contacts which of the proliferating Watergate investigatory bodies seemed most capable; we'd then approach that body with our suspicions.

Shortly after 11 P.M., as I inserted my door key, the phone began to ring. By the time I got inside the machine had answered. I flipped on a light and hustled to the nearest phone, the one in the kitchen. When I picked it up I heard my own voice: "... leave a message at the beep. Thank you." Had the caller hung up? Only one way to find out: "Hello, hello? This is Ray, I just got back."

Beep.

"Ray? George Blair—glad I caught you. Remember the emergency rendezvous?"

The phone booth on West Street. "Yes."

"Be there midnight sharp."

"Why?"

"Not on an open line."

I hesitated, at once confused and suspicious.

"Ray?"

"I'm not sure I want to do it."

"Harry's uncle says it's vital."

Harry's uncle—Uncle Sam? "Uh, I need time to think."

"Midnight... and don't play tag on the way."

Click.

Tag. I started to shiver: he'd unwittingly confirmed I was under surveillance. And not by the CIA—if the tails were the Company's, Blair wouldn't want me to lose them. In desperation I dialed Martha's office. No answer; she'd be huddling with her writer or her editor at this hour. My clothes were suddenly too tight and itchy to boot. Though I knew it meant I'd have to tell all, I called Alan. He hadn't got home from the club yet. Damn Blair, I couldn't afford not to go. But how to lose the tails? It took me three minutes to improvise a plan;

then I grabbed a magazine and headed back out into the cold night. It was 11:13 P.M.

I walked to Sixth Avenue. The temptation to look back was overwhelming but I didn't. I crossed Sixth and proceeded to the uptown entrance of the Washington Square subway station. On the first underground level of this four-tiered maze are the token booths. Below that are the platforms for the Eighth Avenue line, then a mezzanine, and finally the platforms for the Sixth Avenue line. From the mezzanine I could make a last-second dash for the train I wanted; could I also isolate and identify the person or persons shadowing me?

I descended the steps to the first level, bought three tokens with a five-dollar bill, and meticulously counted my change. As I dawdled I scanned the people who'd followed me down the stairs: a girl with a long peasant dress under her duffel coat, two young blacks shivering in windbreakers, and a bearded guy about my age in a ski parka. Peasant Dress and the Windbreakers got in line behind me.

I shoved through the turnstile and walked down to the uptown Eighth Avenue platform. It was almost empty at that time of night so I had no trouble spotting Ski Parka sitting on a bench ahead of me reading the *Post*.

I continued to the mezzanine and waited. Ski Parka didn't follow; chalk him off. Now boots on the steps behind me, treading slowly—or was it cautiously? I sensed the rumble before I heard it and then it was growing under my feet. Uptown Sixth Avenue, the train I wanted, but should I take it? The brakes hissed. I made my decision and skipped down three steps at a time.

As I tumbled into the front car I heard running boots. It was Peasant Dress, who piled in right on my heels. The doors bucked toward each other. She was the one. Then a shout and Peasant Dress was holding the doors apart as a Hispanic in a finely tailored overcoat edged aboard—followed by the two Windbreakers. Before I could jump off Peasant Dress released the doors and they slammed shut.

My turtleneck was clammy with sweat. Peasant Dress had made holding the doors seem natural, but where'd Tailored Overcoat come from? And why had it taken the Windbreakers so long to get down here—had they been lurking back to see which way I'd go? I looked around the car. The Windbreakers sat by themselves. Tailored Overcoat was across from them. Peasant Dress sat on my side, about twelve feet away. She had long sandy hair drawn back, no makeup, nice lips: a common Village look, but did I think so because I'd frequently seen that very same lady? I buried my face in my magazine.

At 14th Street several people got off and two cleaning women boarded.

At 34th Street the car filled with people carrying programs from a Madison Square Garden track meet.

When we pulled into 42nd Street my face was still deep in the magazine but over the top of the pages I could see the Windbreakers get off. Now there were two and now I was ready for my move. As the train jerked back into motion I looked up, screwed my face in exasperation as if I'd missed my stop, then stood and walked to the doors.

When they opened at 50th Street I stepped onto the platform. Peasant Dress remained seated—but Tailored Overcoat followed me off. I went up the stairs to the mezzanine. So did he. Then with a mighty effort to look straight ahead I crossed the mezzanine and descended the stairs to the downtown platform. Would he break cover? No—I heard his footsteps continue to the exit, but was it my imagination or had his stride faltered for an instant?

11:26 P.M. Come on, train: I was cutting it close for my rendezvous, and every passing minute gave them more time to muster reinforcements.

In two minutes an F arrived. I boarded the rear car and as the subway rumbled downtown began walking forward through the train. Nobody followed. When I reached the front car I took a seat on the right-hand side near a door and surveyed my fellow passengers: a wino slept outside the motorman's compartment, and a young couple avoided each other's eyes, as if the issue of sex would soon rear its ugly head.

The train finally eased into 23rd Street. I drew my legs under me. The doors popped open. One, two, three, four, five... I burst from my seat and through the closing doors; as they clunked shut behind me I knew I'd been the last one off. The exit was at the far end of the platform, which was why I'd walked to the front of the train, and before me now I could see the other passenger who'd got off, a stocky man in a night guard's uniform.

By the time I climbed to the token-booth level the night guard was long gone. Ahead were the stairs to the street, to my left the entrance to PATH, a system running beneath the Hudson to New Jersey. I dropped a quarter into the PATH turnstile. In the distance the screech of an approaching train so I broke into a trot, reaching the platform as a Hoboken-bound train pulled in. I had just enough time to look back up the ramp: it was empty.

I got off at the Christopher Street station in the West Village, just two blocks from my destination, and hurried through the exit gate and up the long tunnel toward the street. When I hit the sidewalk the bitter cold made me gasp. Still, I made myself duck into a darkened doorway and wait, for I had to be dead sure. Within thirty seconds the other deboarding passengers had climbed to the street. Two couples and a trio of gays ready to cruise, and none of them so much as glanced around; I was clear—and feeling very, very proud of myself.

As soon as they moved off I lowered my head and started toward the river. I had the street to myself. As the wind picked up the temperature seemed to drop even more and soon my breath was coming in short, sharp gasps.

I reached West Street, with its ranks of immense girders supporting the elevated highway. To my right, between the looming girders, stood the fleet of parked trucks in which homosexual matings were consummated. I turned left, saw the phone booth, and hurried to it.

The booth stank of urine but I closed the door to shut out the numbing wind. The overhead light was out, so I flicked my lighter to check the time: 11:57. Then I lit a cigarette and started to jiggle my knees. Never the most savory of places at night, West Street was especially depressing in winter. Not only was the area deserted but across the way the streetlights thrusting up from among the concrete planters and wooden benches on the riverside esplanade were all smashed, and would remain so until spring. What illumination there was came from the strong bulbs over the gate guarding the pier a block to my left, at the foot of Morton Street.

Though I'd been expecting it the phone's loud trill startled me. I swallowed smoke as I fumbled in the dark for the receiver. "Hel..." I shuddered as I tried to suppress another cough. "Hello?"

Silence.

"Hello? Blair?"

A sigh. Then *click*, and the line was dead.

Suddenly the glare exploding off the booth's glass and chrome made me flinch. I reflexively glanced up at the overhead bulb: it was still dimmed.

Now an engine stuttered and caught.

I turned toward the sound and found myself squinting into a pair of white-hot dimes. I threw up an arm to shield my eyes. The car whose headlights blinded me was parked under the highway. No, it was moving. Toward me.

I pushed against the door of the booth.

Now the light inside my glass cage flickered like a discothèque's as the car jounced across cobblestones.

The door was still jammed.

The dimes had grown to quarters.

Phone booth doors open in—they open in...

The half-dollars surged forward like surfers riding a wave of pure noise.

I pulled and the door opened and I jumped.

Metal rending metal and the thin tinkle of shattering glass and the squeal of brakes and a heavy, hollow *thummmmppppp*.

I picked myself off the pavement and looked back. The black Chrysler had leveled the booth and hurtled fifteen yards along the sidewalk before skidding broadside into a building. Even as I gawked the car lurched as the driver clunked the transmission into reverse.

Move, move, move your ass... The nearest help was in the gay bar two blocks up West Street. Behind me the engine snarled, then a long scrape as the Chrysler backed off the building and a crunch as it bounced onto the street. I kept running.

And then my path became the Milky Way as the headlights found me. Tires yelped under acceleration. I knew I'd never make the bar so I veered sharply for the nearest highway girder. Dark, light, dark as the Chrysler swerved to find me and then light, light ever brighter as it riveted me in its beams... seven yards to go... the V-8's deadly song jumped yet another octave and the headlights began to broil my back so without breaking stride I made a forty-five degree cut to the left but a split second too late for one foot snagged the base of the girder and pinwheeled me through the cold and suddenly black air.

I was on my side and I hurt. All I could hear was my own dazed panting. I flexed my limbs and arched my back; no major damage so I rolled over and pushed onto my knees. The wind had died. Now another sound over the spooky hush on the waterfront, hissing punctuated by a slow, steady drip. It was the car. The Chrysler was a mess—it had hit the girder dead on and with enough force to stave in its front end. Yet the headlights still shone, though now the beams angled acutely toward each other. In their cross-eyed glare steam billowed from the cracked radiator.

I staggered to my feet and took a step toward the car.

"Come on," a low voice growled from within. "Come on, you're okay."

Jesus.

"Joe. Joe. Get your ass outside... no, put that fucking piece away, I don't want no shooting."

"Aw, shit, Vinnie, what the fuck're we gonna do, tickle him to death?"

"Just shut up and go back across the street," Vinnie commanded.

I looked around wildly: the nearest cover was the planters and benches on the esplanade some fifteen yards away. Joe started grousing again but Vinnie cut him short. As I turned and tiptoed for the esplanade, swinging wide to stay clear of the headlights, the starter motor hacked in vain. Then a car door opened and slammed and I could hear Joe trudge in the opposite direction, cursing all the while.

"See anything, Joe?"

"No, and get off my case, god damn it!"

I darted the last few yards to the esplanade and crouched behind a planter.

Again the starter motor hacked. Just then the passenger-side door of the Chrysler swung open. The man who emerged flicked on a portable searchlight and began to play it quickly and systematically on the surrounding girders and over the pavement between them. Finally he said, "The guy must be by the river, Vin." Now the engine caught. Vinnie gunned it; judging from the squeals and knocks, the collision had wrenched a lot of parts awry.

The planters and benches would only hide me another minute. Behind me was a railing and then a sheer drop to the Hudson, in whose icy waters I doubted I'd last long. I looked left. The pier up West Street was not only enclosed, which meant I'd have to jimmy my way in, but it was 150 yards away. I looked right. The pier at the foot of Morton Street was much closer and it was open-air, which meant I could climb in—but I'd be in the glare of those strong lights over the gate.

Metal groaned as Vinnie peeled the Chrysler off the girder. Then the man with the searchlight started toward the esplanade and Vinnie nosed the car forward. I had no choice, so I scuttled for the pier at the foot of Morton Street.

Two minutes later I was studying the jerry-built barricade guarding Pier 42. In the middle were two twenty-foot-high gates of cyclone fencing. Flanking them was a pair of twelve-foot-high segments of cyclone fencing. Next to these were nine-foot-high panels of corrugated metal; I knew from my summer visits here that a guard shack stood behind the panel nearest me. I looked farther down West Street. The next pier, also enclosed, lay 150 yards away, with no shelter between it and me. I decided to go for the corrugated metal section nearest me: it was partly in shadow, it was relatively low, and the guard shack on the other side should make getting down easier.

The man with the searchlight continued working toward me. I began to breathe slowly but deeply. He was thirty yards away. Inhale. Exhale. Now he turned. Inhale, exhale. He started back to the car. Inhale exhale, inhale and hold and I was on my feet, first the shuffle step to adjust stride and then driving hard and then jumping and stretching for the stars.

The claws that were my hands hooked the top of the fence while my legs bicycled for purchase and as I flailed I wondered why they didn't hear the tattoo my shoes were beating on the metal.

"Hey... hey!" Joe's voice carried crisply through the frigid air. "Hey, the pier, he's at the pier over there!"

Suddenly my back felt like a bull's-eye for the alarm caught me with my leading foot still below the top. I grunted and heaved upward again, and this time I hooked my heel over.

Boom—but it was only a car door.

I hoisted myself up and dove at the guard shack two feet away, hitting the galvanized roof with enough force to bounce, and then I blinked the heat lightning from my eyes and peered back over the fence: Joe raced toward me while behind him the Chrysler lurched away from the esplanade. I crawled to the edge of the roof and vaulted off; as I dropped, one elbow slammed hard off a protrusion from the shack. I struggled to my feet. The Chrysler's tires protested as Vinnie slalomed the car through the girders to set up his run at the gate. The protrusion I'd hit on the way down was a fire-alarm box so I yanked its lever down, pushed it back up, and yanked again before fleeing down the concrete pier.

Another squeal from the street and then the engine's groan became a snarl. The deserted ribbon I raced along stretched endlessly ahead. A terrible sound as the Chrysler rammed the fence. I kept running. Now the crippled V-8 ebbed: Vinnie hadn't broken through. But here it came again, accelerating, still accelerating, still... Metal exploded and the air trembled with the rasp of a thousand fingernails drawing down a blackboard and then silence—and then the stitch in my side struck with such ferocity I doubled over, broke the fall with one arm, and collapsed gasping on the concrete.

The steam-shrouded Chrysler was stopped on this side of the ripped gate, its cockeyed headlights smashed in its jousts with the fence. Joe was edging his way through the gap. Now the passenger-side door swung open and the man with the searchlight flicked it on. As the beam probed toward me I involuntarily flattened myself on the pier but I was well out of his range. And then Joe had a light in his hand too, but it was much weaker, most probably a flashlight. He hurried with it to one edge of the pier while the man with the searchlight marched to the other. What were they doing? Then I remembered the construction of the jetty. Its concrete top was bordered by foot-thick railroad ties which acted as a curb to prevent vehicles from rolling into the river; below these ties was the network of pilings and beams on which the pier rested. The pair, infinitely thorough, was making sure I wasn't hiding in that network, and as they worked my way Vinnie kept the Chrysler in pace down the middle of the jetty. How much pier did I have left to retreat on—enough to avoid them until the fire engines arrived?

It was so dark only the protruding railroad ties which acted as a curb kept me from stumbling off the end. Here, beyond the lee of the adjacent jetties, the wind stabbed through my clothing. The twinkling skyscrapers across the Hudson on the Jersey shore looked warm and inviting and safe, but my finger of concrete was half a mile too short. I squatted my tortured body for warmth and bleakly considered my options. In my exhausted state the frigid and fast-currented river was more suicide than salvation. Sneak back through the briskly approaching cordon? Impossible. I listened for sirens and heard none.

Then I looked down at the weathered railroad ties. These rose a good foot above the pavement, high enough to stop a car. But the wood had been sitting out here for years; had it rotted? Rotted enough so a car moving at speed might... Then I noticed that to my left a section of tie was missing. I hurried over. The gap was about six feet wide; all that remained was a pair of foot-high metal spikes that had once braced wood to concrete.

My pursuers were halfway down the pier and closing.

The river was low, its surface nine feet below me. I tried to reject the plan forming in my mind, but then I realized it was this Chinaman's last chance so I stripped off my parka and set it up. Next I lit a cigarette and laid it on the pier, its glowing end pointed inland. Finally I paced off fifteen yards from the edge and pressed my body to the concrete; my convulsive shivers came less from the cold than from fright.

They'd closed to within fifty yards when I heard faint sirens above the wind whipping off the river. The fire engines would not make it in time.

Now I thought, now... I couldn't but I did: I forced a primal scream that ululated for seconds and then minutes and then hours...

The searchlight beam began to dance around my body. I fought the impulse to squirm from its merciless stare. The beam locked on me; then darkness and fast footsteps and the slam of doors. When the beam found me again I was on my feet and frantically massaging my right knee. I made myself glance up. As I'd hoped, the man holding the searchlight was leaning out the passenger-side window so he could keep an unrefracted beam on me.

Now the Chrysler lurched forward. I spun and faking a hobble started for the end of the pier. The light on my back bobbed eerily in the blackness as the car gained speed. The sirens were coming into full wail but they couldn't drown out the enraged roar of the Chrysler. A millisecond of panic and then my straining eyes finally targeted on the cigarette I'd lit: eight yards.

The jackhammering of the engine was so close my eardrums shrieked when I broke out of my hobble with two long strides and tucked into a classic baseball slide with feet high and left toe pointed directly at the cigarette and now my legs and then my torso rode over the butt and then over slippery nylon and then momentum was carrying my body over the edge of the jetty.

At that instant the still-accelerating Chrysler rocketed past above my head, its freewheeling V-8 whining like a speared tiger.

I was dropping toward the water when my trailing arm finally snagged the parka I'd knotted between the two metal stakes; I pendulumed back into the wooden bulkhead with numbing force. The whine continued to doppler up and now above it a thin death scream and suddenly my body was pitching downward, plunging me shin-deep into the brutally cold water: hold, I prayed, hold...

Out in the river a splash and then the soft liquid laps of the Hudson flowing on as if nothing more momentous than a stick had entered it.

24 February 1973: New York/Boston/New York

They found me barefoot and shivering and gesturing wildly at the river as I babbled about a big car zipping off the pier and then me almost tumbling in after it. Two policemen promptly bundled me to the Sixth Precinct. Coffee helped, as did a change into dry clothing. Yet twenty minutes later I still seemed to be in shock, though now I was feigning it, for my problem was complicated: Blair had set me up, but why? I ruled out Fanning as a likely participant. The CIA? If so, they'd not only deny it but paint me as some paranoid fool. Did Blair do this on his own, as revenge for his firing from the Onyxx account? If so, why wait five months? Even more troubling was the fact that I couldn't prove him responsible. But he'd soon know his thugs had failed, and unless I could implicate him—shake him up—he'd try again. The two patrolmen were debating whether to drive me to St. Vincent's Emergency Room for a checkup when I finally walked over and asked to see the ranking detective on duty.

Detective Aloysius Coady was a stocky, moonfaced man who kept darting his red-rimmed eyes to the wall clock as one of the patrolmen briefed him. When we were at last alone Coady sighed and wearily pulled out a tape recorder.

I gave my name and address and then said, "Shortly after eleven this evening—that'd be Friday night—I received a call at my home from George Blair, who lives at Thirty-four College Lane, Wellesley, Massachusetts. I've met Blair twice in my life. He asked me to be at a phone booth near West and Christopher at midnight sharp for an important call. I went, the phone rang at midnight, but when I picked it up a black Chrysler started to charge the booth. In the chase that followed I found out there were three men in the car, one named Joe, another Vin or Vinnie. I finally escaped by making them drive off the pier into the river."

Coady's eyes had cleared as I talked. "Can you prove this Blair called?"

"No."

"Why did you go?"

"To the booth?" I lit a cigarette: this was delicate. "He said he had important information that he couldn't give me over my home phone because my line's tapped."

Coady stared at me for several seconds. I could guess what must have passed through his mind: was I an informer? A spy? A counterspy? A criminal who'd had a falling out? Or was I a total wacko, the kind who comes in every full moon to confess the latest unsolved crime? Finally he pulled a card from his desk drawer. "This is to inform you that you have the right..."

"I know those rights and I waive them."

Coady returned the card to the drawer and began doodling on his blotter. "Tell me about your relationship with this Blair."

"I can't. I've been ordered by the federal government to keep my dealings with him confidential, under penalty of fine or imprisonment."

As my statement sank in, Coady covered his eyes with his

left hand; I was either mixed up in something he didn't want to know about or I was a fruitcake. He let out his breath heavily. "This Blair, he works for the government?"

"I don't know, and I really don't care—he set me up for murder, and I hope to hell you can pin it on him."

"You've given me diddly-squat to go on, buddy."

Suddenly I thought, Let Washington try to prosecute me for protecting my own life, so I said, "I think Blair's connected with the CIA." Coady stopped doodling. Then I decided the hell with Kuo Yu-tang, so I added, "I also think some people, maybe the men who tried to kill me, have been watching my apartment from an office across the street."

Coady watched the tape spin for a while. Then he told me to wait outside. I went to a pay phone and called Martha's office. No answer. I called the apartment and heard my own voice on tape; she was either in transit or still working.

Forty-five minutes later Coady summoned me back into his office. "I requested the Wellesley police to call this Blair. They asked him if he knew you. Affirmative. Did he call you last night. Negative. Where was he last night between the hours of eleven and midnight. Home. Can he prove it. Affirmative, dinner guests and wife will verify. Did he use the phone between those hours. Affirmative, he received a business call from the Coast at approximately eleven twenty-five P.M. Did he make any outgoing calls. Negative. I've requested his phone records as well as the pay phone's."

"How about the CI . . ."

Coady looked up from his notes. "Do I tell you how to do your job, buddy? Washington's been queried, but I don't expect shit from them. We start fishing the river come morning. And I'll have that office across the street checked out."

"Thanks for taking me seriously."

"Buddy, you tell me Daffy Duck orders a hit on you and I have to look into it."

After a few seconds I said, "Can I get police protection?" Coady studied his pencil. "Or do you think Blair's been scared off?"

"I'd say you've done a fucking good job of putting him on notice."

"Well, can I get an officer to see me to my apartment?"

Coady put his pencil down. "Now, that I can arrange."

When Martha walked into the apartment at 2:45 A.M. she froze. "Just what the hell are you doing?" she asked, pointing to the pie plates balanced on our windows.

"You'd better grab a brandy before I tell you."

She'd polished off a fourth of the bottle by the time I finished, but the liquor was having a converse effect: "You knew someone was spying on us and you didn't tell me? That's fucking unforgivable! What else are you keeping from me?"

"Nothing." I wearily refilled my own snifter. "Look, I didn't go looking for trouble, it came after me. Anyway it's finished now. You were right, I should have gotten it out in the open a long time ago, but now I've done it so you've won, okay?"

"Nobody won, Ray, it's not a game. Can't you see that?" Martha started to light a cigarette but didn't. Finally she said in a soft, sad voice, "I . . . I'm very tired and I'm going to bed. Good night."

We were both still on edge when we got up in late morning. The all-news radio stations were reporting that a car had plunged off a Village pier by accident. Was Coady keeping my involvement hush out of discretion or because he didn't believe me? I longed to go to the river to watch the dredging but realized I'd best keep my profile low, so when Martha went marketing after lunch I turned on the Saturday college basketball game.

Suddenly the willies hit with such force I had to phone the Sixth Precinct. Coady had gone off duty and wouldn't return until evening. The pressure to talk kept mounting. Finally I began rummaging through my files for the scrap of paper with Fanning's home number on it.

The butler said he was with guests. I insisted. Four minutes later Fanning was on the line and as I related what had happened I could visualize him groping for his Chesterfields. "So that's where it stands now, sir. The cops don't know anything about what happened last year, and if I can keep Onyxx out of it, fine."

"Thank you, Mr. Huang, but this matter falls well outside corporate loyalty—if I can help I shall. Now, you say you can't prove Mr. Blair called."

"I'm afraid not. The cops are trying for phone rec . . . Oh my God!"

"Hello. Hello . . . Ray. Ray, are you all right."

I stared at what I'd been fiddling with as I talked. It was my answering machine.

"Ray! Ray, are you there!"

"I, uh...I think I have proof. Hold on."

I flipped the answering machine to "Playback." A couple of screeches and then Blair's voice: "Ray? George Blair—glad I caught you..." Thirty seconds later I said to Fanning, "Did you hear that clearly?"

"Good God yes." I heard the rasp of his cigarette lighter. "You know you must take it to the police. But, uh..."

"But?"

"But I'd like to make a copy first."

"Why?"

"Stan Harmer should hear it."

"I can't hold it until Monday."

"Will you hold it for another ninety minutes."

Learn to trust, Martha had said. I'd come to trust Fanning—was I right? "Okay."

"I'd like Harris Knox to sit in."

"Sure."

"Ninety minutes then."

It was only after I'd hung up that I realized Fanning had called me Ray.

About an hour later I spotted Martha pulling the shopping cart down the street, so I went out to help her; we were still on the stoop when the Mercedes 600 eased up. Its two passengers stepped out before Clarence could get the doors. Fanning's utilitarian down vest seemed out of place over his Ultrasuede safari suit; Knox wore a torn Harvard sweat shirt over a turtleneck, dungarees, and waffle-stompers.

Martha suppressed her confusion admirably as I made the introductions and ushered everyone inside. When I told her about the tape and why Fanning and Knox were here, though, she regarded the two men with indecision. Then she said in a level voice, "Ray, have you thought this thing through?"

"Yes."

Rather than being put off by Martha's pointed question, Fanning and Knox seemed to study her with newfound appreciation. Now she shrugged and said, "Okay, it's your ball game."

Fanning quickly set up his portable Sony. Then as he placed

his hand over the controls of my answering machine Martha let out an involuntary gasp: the "Record" and "Playback" switches were next to each other. Fanning's eyes flicked from her to me and then his finger plunged downward.

Static. Followed by more static.

Fanning stared stone-faced at the answering machine but Knox couldn't hide his distress; Martha looked sick.

I went to the machine. The depressed switch read "Playback" so I dipped into a pocket and offered Fanning the real tape: "I had to be sure."

He held my look for two heartbeats, then calmly switched cassettes and turned on my answering machine again.

When the tape finished Fanning said, "Harris, your opinion, please."

"From what little you've told me, Frew, I'd say it's not enough to convict. Of course I'm not a specialist in criminal law, but defense would be remiss not to raise certain technical challenges—is that in fact Mr. Blair's voice, can prosecution prove the tape has not been spliced together, and so forth. In addition, it's impossible to establish when the call came, or for that matter the location of this so-called 'emergency rendezvous.'"

Fanning massaged the scar on his forehead, then placed a credit-card call to Boston. "Stan, it's Frew. Very good, thank you. Listen, I'd like you and Mr. Blair at our hangar at Logan in two hours. No, I'll explain then. Yes." Next Fanning dialed the mobile phone in the double-parked limousine and told Clarence to have the airport ready the jet. "Ray, I trust you'll join us." Now he turned to Martha. "May we have the pleasure of your company as well."

She surprised me by blushing. "I wouldn't miss it, but I've got... Oh damn, there's ice cream in those grocery bags."

"If it's anything with chocolate in it," Knox interjected, "perhaps we might take it with us. I, uh, haven't lunched yet."

We were still giddy with laughter when we piled into the Mercedes. True to his word, Knox immediately began slurping his way through a quart of Häagen-Dazs. We stopped first at the Sixth Precinct, where I dropped off the tape and an explanatory note for Coady. Then we whizzed up the West Side toward Westchester Airport. My best middle-of-the-night time from the Village to Purchase was forty minutes; Clarence had us at the ramp to the Learjet in twenty-eight.

Once aboard the plane Fanning took a seat by himself and began scribbling on a legal pad. Knox, who still hadn't been filled in on everything, sat with Martha and me; though his conversation was delightful, our hour in the air still seemed like three.

When we landed Logan the pilot taxied to the sector reserved for private craft. Fanning picked up the intercom and instructed him to park far from the other planes. I looked out a window. Blair and an older, silver-haired man with a soldier's bearing strode across the tarmac, their vaporized breath streaming away in the cold wind. After the pilot lowered the steps Fanning told him to go get himself some coffee.

Now the silver-haired man stepped through the door. "What the fuck's going on, Frew?" Then Harmer noticed Martha and added, "Please excuse my language."

"Thanks for coming, Stan... and simmer down."

At that moment Blair ducked through the door. He blinked to adjust to the cabin lights; his eyes continued to dilate and his jaw muscles began knotting when he saw me.

Fanning had us take seats and then without fanfare pointed to the Sony, said, "This recording was made last night," and turned it on.

"Ray? George Blair—glad I caught you." Blair's eyes wavered. "Remember the emergency rendezvous?"

"Yes."

"Be there midnight sharp."

"Why?"

"Not on an open line."

Now Blair's jaw muscles were spasming; he cupped his mouth with his left hand.

"Ray?"

"I'm not sure I want to do it."

"Harry's uncle says it's vital."

"Uh, I need time to think."

"Midnight... and don't play tag on the way."

Click.

Blair's glassy gaze remained on the Sony as Fanning punched off the machine and said, "The rendezvous was a telephone booth. When Mr. Huang arrived, three men in a car tried to kill him. Needless to say, they failed."

Harmer switched his puzzled look to Fanning. "Isn't this Huang fellow...isn't he the one who started that flap last year?"

Fanning nodded.

Harmer turned to Blair. "Well, George?"

Blair slowly took his hand from his mouth. His jaw muscles were under control. "That tape's meaningless as evidence."

"That's not what I asked."

"I've no further comment."

Fanning cleared his throat. "If this is a CIA stunt, you'd better tell us now."

"Why don't you ask them?" Blair sneered, his cockiness returning.

"I intend to."

Harmer tried again: "George, what's this all about?" When he got no response, his voice grew icy. "Very well, I'll expect your resignation Monday morning."

Blair spat on the carpeting.

Harmer's face was crimson as he turned to Fanning. "What are you doing with this tape?"

"The original's with the New York Police Department. I pledge Mr. Huang my full cooperation and I expect the same from you."

Harmer shifted uneasily. "I can't do that, Frew."

"God damn it man, we're talking about murder!"

"Attempted murder. And it pains me to say it, but George is right—this tape is inconclusive."

"Why don't you just come out and say you're scared shitless of the Company, that you're scared of queering your profitable little romance!" Fanning's rage took our collective breath away; he was far angrier than the night I'd grabbed him at the Plaza. "Stan, I expect you to find out if this was one of their jobs. If it wasn't, I expect your cooperation."

"Oh fuck, Frew, you know they never acknowledge an operation, especially if it's domestic." Harmer shifted his weight again. Then he said softly, "Don't get so holy with me...I prize our relationship with Onyxx, but we both sleep around so stop acting like you're the only client I have to service. Give me hard evidence it was attempted murder and

I go along with you. But you don't have it, so here's all I can do."

He wheeled to Blair. "Can that resignation request, you're fired as of right now on grounds of unprofessional conduct. Don't appeal it, don't try to cast me in a bad light... if you do, I not only cooperate with Fanning, I'm in line ahead of him."

Blair didn't bother to cover his quivering mouth.

"Point two: if anything happens to Huang, I don't give a rat's ass who's behind it, you pay. And should that day come, mister, you'll know how it feels to piss through a catheter." Harmer turned back to Fanning and snapped, "Your move."

Just then Blair, his face the color of putty, bolted from the plane.

Fanning flicked a shred of tobacco from his tongue as if nothing had happened. "I think your action should suffice, Stan. Thank you."

Harmer drooped visibly; he looked suddenly old. Then he smiled wanly. "You bastard, you squeezed more out of me than I was willing to give."

"I wouldn't say that, Stan... not to your face, anyway," Fanning replied as he, too, broke into a tired smile.

Harmer pushed himself to his feet. Mine was the last hand he shook, and he held my grip. "Sorry, son, that's really all I could do. I'm glad you made it out of harm's way." Then he stiffened his spine and marched out the door.

When we were airborne Martha asked, "Did he really concede more than he was willing?"

Fanning looked noncommittally at his cigarette so Knox said, "Since Frew won't toot his horn, permit me. General Harmer seemed willing to discharge Mr. Blair, but I suspect he'd have preferred to stop there. So as I see it we won two concessions. One, a cosignatory on Mr. Huang's life—Small has joined forces with Onyxx in warning off Mr. Blair. Second, another lightning rod for Mr. Blair's animosity—in terminating his employment for cause, General Harmer has ensured himself Mr. Blair's eternal enmity." Knox broke into a wide grin. "So the verdict is—yup, Frew sure as hell stampeded the General."

"Damn it, Harris, your silver tongue should have run for office." Now Fanning, no longer able to suppress his own glee, turned to Martha. "Will you join me in a victory margarita."

"Who's bartending?"

"Mr. Huang, just where did you find this creature." Fanning turned back to Martha and said archly, "I think enough of my recipe to use Conmemorativo."

"In that case shake me up a double."

We laughed our way into the sunset.

2 March 1973: New York

As I trudged homeward from the subway station my thoughts were as dark as the soot-speckled slush in the gutters.

The previous Sunday, some eighteen hours after our return from Boston, Coady had called to say my tape was with the District Attorney's office and police divers had located the black Chrysler at the bottom of the Hudson. At that moment I'd felt on the verge of shucking the terrible monkey that had planted itself on my back a year ago in Vientiane.

But on Monday morning a courier had knocked on my door and handed over a letter typed on Oval Office stationery:

February 25, 1973

Mr. Raymond T. Huang:

This is to inform you that:

1) Mr. George F. Blair of Cambridge, Mass., is not now, nor has he ever been, an employee of the United States of America, nor any of its agencies, in particular the Central Intelligence Agency.

2) The strictures placed upon you by my Vice-President on September 28, 1972, still pertain, and should you violate the Codes of the United States, the United States of America will prosecute.

Best wishes

It had been signed by the President's personal secretary; a copy had been addressed to Coady, whose query had triggered it. When I read Fanning the note he commiserated; he also reported with chagrin that Harmer still refused to use his CIA connections to double-check Blair.

On Tuesday Coady had telephoned. New England Bell's

records verified that Blair had placed no long-distance calls between 10 P.M. and 1 A.M. on the night of February 23–24. New York Tel's records showed that neither my home phone nor the pay phone near West and Christopher had received a long-distance call between those hours. The bodies had been recovered from the Hudson; the fingerprints were being processed in Washington. The office across the street had been leased by a firm called D. & D. Coins, which appeared to be a dummy corporation; the letting had been done by mail, the rent was paid by money orders, and the superintendent of the building was an alcoholic with a poor memory for faces.

Then on Thursday Coady had called me down to the precinct house and shown me three mug shots. Had I ever seen those faces or heard the names Vincent DiLorenzo, Joseph Iannucci, or Albert Robilotto? No. He wasn't surprised; the first two were hit men from San Diego and the third a thug from Chicago. Needless to say, there was no evidence linking the trio to Blair. On this day I also gave up trying to reach Kuo Yu-tang; six unreturned messages over two days had been ample enough hint.

I got back to the apartment and fixed myself a drink. The blow that had just fallen was the worst: in a forty-five minute meeting, the District Attorney's office had said they believed there'd been an attempt on my life and Blair had ordered it, but there was no proof.

It seemed the previous Sunday as if all the pieces of the jigsaw were at last on the table. Now the parts not only refused to interlock, it appeared they came from different puzzles.

14 March 1973: New York

Ignore the eyes, they can lie; focus instead on the hips for a man can't go where his hips don't. I looked at his eyes. They flicked left so I shifted left and he dribbled past me on the right, forcing Alan to slide across the foul lane to cover. My man dumped a pass to his now open teammate: lay-up and game.

My psychiatrist friend's invitation to his club had seemed a welcome chance to work out my escalating frustrations. In the two weeks since my last meeting with Coady, I'd of course continued to fume over Blair. Worse, I'd begun to take out my anger on Martha, who'd not only absorbed it silently but had tried to cheer me by signing us for a package tour to the Caribbean. I'd churlishly refused to go, mumbling poor finances—I already owed her two months' rent—and the pending textbook contract; after another non-argument she'd flown to Antigua by herself. All I'd done in her absence was brood. Martha had brought me the closest to the one word missing from my vocabulary—"love"— and yet I seemed to be doing my damnedest to drive her away. Why? And in the hour I'd been at the club, why couldn't I force myself to seek Alan's counsel?

In the sauna he finally broached it: "Want to talk about her?"

"No."

He got up from the redwood bench and ladled water onto the glowing rocks. The steam was unbearable but I craved it.

Finally I said, "I'm destroying the best thing I ever had. I . . . I also can't generate decent story ideas anymore, I behave like an anxious fool when I talk to editors, I can't pay attention to the simplest things. Look what that turkey I was guarding tonight did to me—six baskets."

"How come you remember the number of baskets?" The sweat dripping into my eyes stung but I didn't wipe it away. "You know, Ray, we don't see each other that often, so I'm in a good position to notice changes. Looking back, I'd say something fairly traumatic happened to you last year."

Suddenly I could feel my heartbeat.

"Whatever it was, it stripped you of your self-confidence, that much we agree on. But it's done more. You've become . . . jumpy's not the right word, you've become defensive. And Martha's incredibly bright and sensitive."

"So?" The stinging had grown worse; I toweled my face.

"Have you considered the possibility that your drawing apart isn't a unilateral act? Mustn't she have sensed the changes in you? And couldn't she be preparing herself for a possible breakup?"

The steam was clearing. As I got up to ladle more water on the rocks I said, "She bent over backward to be understanding. I mean, even this Antigua fiasco started as an attempt to cheer me up."

"And what's been the effect of all her efforts?"

"Why, to..." Suddenly I felt crushed by the weight of the wheels-within-wheels insight and vaguely angry at Alan for so professionally prompting me to this flash point. But was I mad because he'd overstepped or because he'd forced me both inward and outward?

"You used to laugh a lot, Ray, and tell awful jokes and puns. And you used to talk my ear off. What happened?"

The sauna was turning into a pressure cooker. God knows I wanted to talk his ear off about Martha and about my other *bête noir*, the one born that night in Vientiane, but for what purpose? I finally said, "When I sort it out, you'll be the first to know. End of topic, okay?"

As we left the sauna Alan said, "Oh, I forgot to tell you, Freddie called today." The last I'd heard, our mutual friend was still using his Washington contacts from his volunteer stint at the DNC to find us an investigatory body to tell our Red Wig-Cubans story to. "One of Dash's aides is willing to see us if we go to Washington. Freddie says, though, the guy made it clear that they weren't terribly interested. Seems our information is at best circumstantial, and they're after much bigger fish. I say fuck it."

"Fuck it," I agreed.

22 March 1973: New York

Our kindness toward each other since Martha's return from Antigua was murderous because it was so formal. Requests were accompanied by unaccustomed "pleases"; sex was solicitous and without abandon; reading and TV watching were replaced by bright but brittle conversation on every topic save our future together.

I met her for dinner at a Japanese restaurant. She surprised me by ordering a saketini, a bastardized martini calling for *sake* in place of vodka or gin.

"They offered me the textbook contract this afternoon," I said. "I took it. It means my nut money plus some; any articles I can squeeze in'll be gravy."

She turned to study the Kyoto rock garden in the photograph hanging above our table. I tasted my plum wine and wished

I'd ordered a saketini. When the waiters brought our *miso* Martha sipped the soup, then finally spoke. "I had a rotten time in Antigua, Ray. All I could think of was why we continue on."

"Things'll get better."

"Will they?"

"They have to."

"Not for the next year, not as long as you're doing that damned textbook."

"Oh, hell, what do you want from me?"

"The *chutzpah* you used to have. I realized in Antigua that I've begun to dread coming home at night. There's no joy, no fun, no laughter anymore—it's like stepping into a grey cloud bank."

"I'm trying."

"Oh, Jesus, I know you are. I hate to find you in your bathrobe so you get dressed for me. But sometimes your hair's still wet from the shower, and that gets me so mad I go out of my way to feel if the TV's still warm."

"You want to run my life for me?"

"No. But I get no thrill seeing you waste it. Ray, I've been putting this moment off because you've been through some incredibly hard times, but now this Helmsley thing's been over for almost a month and I still don't see any silver lining."

My head pounded as the inevitable approached but curiously my adrenaline flow and heartbeat felt normal and my throat uncongested. "Why're you pegging it to me taking on the textbook?"

"It's symbolic, I suppose. You live for challenges. I've met damned few people who need to live on their wits, to bounce off other people, as much as you. When you're up against it you become aggressive, amusing, alive—and that's a turn-on. This book's going to turn you into a cabbage."

Now I needed to clear my throat. "Look, we can make it a point to get back into the social scene, to cop long weekends, things like that. I'll try harder. Promise."

"We've both been busting our chops and it's killing us." Time slowed. Within the restaurant's hubbub a bubble of perfect silence formed around Martha and me. Her lips parted in slow motion. No, I wanted to say, no, but instead I sat transfixed by her mouth, hypnotized as her tongue flicked out on the diphthong and her lips compressed on the plosive and the bilabial. And then, like a badly synced movie, her words came trailing after to rupture the bubble: "I think it best if I move out."

Pulse—none. Visceral churning—none. Words—none.

"I knew it would be like this," she murmured, her eyes shut.

"Like what?"

"That you'd make me do it. And that it'd go well—no blood, no sweat, no tears." She opened her eyes and began to tremble. "How very civilized we are."

As soon as we got home Martha tossed her tote bag onto a chair and went to bed. I was puttering around the living room when something in the bag caught my eye: it was a copy of *f.y.i.*, the Time Inc. house organ. In it Martha had marked with red ink four entries under the classified section titled "Sublets."

1 April 1973: New York

We spent the morning dividing our spoils. Martha had wept in frustration upon seeing how few cartons she needed for her belongings—"Almost thirty years old, and I have less than a goddamn Gypsy." We figured out what I owed her, including her half of the furniture, and I promised to mail it as soon as my textbook advance came; she said no hurry. One last sweep through the apartment during which she found a dispenser of birth-control pills over the headboard, and then I was outside hailing a cab and helping shlepp her suitcases and cartons into its trunk.

"See you around, Ray."

"Yeah. Take care." I watched the cab until it turned the corner.

I was back inside trying to work off the numbness by sorting the pieces of a new jigsaw puzzle when the irony of the date struck me. Who'd written, "April is the cruelest month"? Then I remembered and wished I hadn't.

25 July 1973: New York

I stared at the cubes in my iced coffee. The little window air conditioner in the bedroom struggled vainly against the early-morning heat. More than two months had passed since I last talked to Martha; it was over, I told myself, let it be. But I couldn't, not on this day. At 8:45 A.M., when I knew she'd be up, I dialed. No answer. Maybe she was in the shower. Or maybe... Out of masochism I tried again shortly after nine.

"Hello?" She was panting.

"Hi, uh, it's me." Despite myself I strained to hear noises in the background.

"Oh, hi. How're you doing?"

"Not bad. Yourself?"

"Pooped and sweating like a pig. I just got in from jogging."

"Oh. You're jogging these days."

"Yeah."

The silence stretched four heartbeats before I said, "Well, I just called to wish you happy birthday."

"Hey, thanks." Her voice mirrored the smile I'd raised. "How's your book coming, Ray?"

"On schedule. How about you—Watergate?"

She sighed. "What else? It's fun, but it's also damned hard... hey, what do you make of the tapes?"

"I couldn't believe it when I read about them last week. How come none of those hotshot investigators found out until now?"

"Apparently because nobody thought to ask."

"Wow. Well, it sure looks from here as if the Tricky One was in on it from the start. If he could fuck over Dean's testimony, he'd have sent a limo for Archie Cox instead of refusing to hand the damned tapes over."

"True."

And then we seemed to be out of things to say.

Martha coughed. "Well..."

"Uh, I also called to see if, uh, if we might have brunch this weekend."

Dead silence. Then, "That's a nice offer, Ray, but I've started seeing someone."

"Oh."

"Yeah. Well look, thanks again for calling. You were very sweet to remember."

"Sure. Take care."

Maybe I was making progress, for rather than allow paralysis to set in I marched immediately to my typewriter. My copy that day stank but there was a lot of it.

18 October 1973: New York

I'd worked through the summer like an automaton on the first draft of the textbook—1,500 usable words per day or else—but now my concentration waned before the turmoil growing outside my monastic life. Within the previous eleven days: Egypt and Syria had rabbit-punched Israel to start the Yom Kippur War; the vice-presidency was vacated and Representative Gerald R. Ford (R., Mich.) nominated to replace; Watergate Special Prosecutor Archibald Cox and Richard Nixon crouched eyeball-to-eyeball over the President's tapes; and OPEC, a hitherto ineffectual clutch of oil-producing nations and fiefdoms, had jacked the price of crude seventy percent.

I was gloating my way through the *Time* and *Newsweek* accounts of Agnew's humiliation—he'd plea-bargained a *nolo* on charges of failing to inform the IRS he'd pocketed bribes—when my doorbell rang. I ducked my head into the hallway and looked through the glass door to the lobby.

George Blair grinned when he saw my shocked stare. He was puffing nonchalantly on a Havana, as natty as ever. I finally pressed the buzzer to unlock the glass door. He swung it open, poked his head around, and gestured at my bathrobe. "Get dressed. I'll wait outside."

"What the hell for? I'm not going anywhere with you."

"Curious about what really happened, Huang?"

"I know what happened, and I know it's over."

His eyebrows arched mockingly. "Is it? No questions about Entrepays? Or how I called that night?"

"You're setting me up again."

Blair laughed. "Frisk me. If I don't do it no one else will—can't afford a button anymore. I'll be on the steps." He gently closed the door and strolled out to the stoop.

I wiped my palms on my bathrobe. I should call somebody, but Coady would have closed the files by now. Fanning? What for? And Martha was now part of someone else's life—why intrude at this late date? I waited five minutes and peeked out my front window. Blair sat quietly savoring his cigar. I dressed and then called the Sixth Precinct. Coady was on vacation. I called Fanning. Mrs. Shipley said he was at an emergency meeting in Washington. Of course—he'd be hip-deep in the OPEC quagmire. I called Martha. She was at lunch. Someone had to know so I called Alan. As I'd hoped—for there'd be so much explaining to do—he was with a patient so I told his receptionist, "I'm calling for Ray Huang. Tell him Ray can't keep their date because George Blair of Wellesley just showed up at his apartment."

Now I tapped on the front window and motioned Blair inside. He was passing through the glass door when I showed him the baseball bat in my right hand. He kept coming. From up close I could see his collar was slightly frayed, his suit almost in need of pressing, and his eyes were laced with pink. As soon as Blair entered the apartment I double-locked the door and started to pat his jacket with my free hand.

"Not that way." He spread-eagled himself against a wall with his feet a yard from it. When I'd moved to his inner thighs he added, "Don't be squeamish . . . feel higher and do it right."

Finally I lowered the bat. "Okay, Blair, what do you want?"

"Not here. Outside."

"Why?"

"Because."

I looked out the window. The foot and vehicular traffic in the Village was heavy; was there safety in numbers? Reluctantly I nodded, and went to a closet to pull out my portable tape recorder.

"No tapes."

"No tapes, no talk."

Blair shrugged. "Have it your way."

When we got to the street he headed for a black Chevy double-parked two doors down.

"Unh-unh, not unless I know where we're going," I said.

"An aimless drive. I talk better in cars."

"How do I know it's not booby-trapped?"

He sighed. "Where's the nearest car-rental agency?"

"Fourteenth Street."

"Okay, we'll get a fresh one." Blair flipped the cigar butt into the gutter, unlocked the Chevy, and pulled a briefcase out.

"What's in there?"

He rested the briefcase on the hood and snapped it open. Inside were a few magazines, a gizmo that looked like a pocket calculator, a copy of Erdman's *The Billion Dollar Sure Thing*, and stationery supplies. "Okay?"

We began walking up Christopher.

Suddenly from the corner of my eye I noticed two men emerging from a navy-blue Buick parked down the block. Calm down, I told myself, lots of people come to the Village. As we waited for a light at Greenwich Avenue I pretended to look in the pastry-shop window. The two men were half a block back. The light changed and Blair started across. I hurried after him. "Blair, we're being followed."

"Yup."

"Well look, I'm leaving you now."

"It's too late."

My jugular began to pulse. "Too late for what?"

"For them not to know about you." My eyes darted in search of a cop car. Blair continued striding briskly. "Relax, Huang, they're tailing me, not you. I know something that makes me dangerous. But those goons..."

"Who are they?"

"Stick tight and you'll find out. Those goons only watch, they don't act."

I thought it over and then pulled up at the corner of Sixth Avenue and 10th Street. "Blair, it's been real."

"Go. But they might assume I've passed you the dope that scares their boss."

"So?"

"When the crunch comes, wouldn't you like to know what you're dying for?"

I stood swaying like a drunk. The two men, stopped some twenty yards behind us, made no effort at concealment. One spoke into a walkie-talkie and as I glanced down the avenue I saw the navy-blue Buick idling up Sixth. Blair was on the march again. No, I thought, cut out now, but I found myself breaking into a trot to catch him.

At the rental office Blair charged the orange Mustang on

his American Express card. As I started to open the passenger-side door he said, "You'll be less nervous if you drive."

Damn it, he was right again. I swung behind the wheel.

"Where to?"

"Up the West Side Highway, then the Cross-Bronx to the Triboro and back down the FDR." He seemed true to his word: if nothing, this circumnavigation of Manhattan was aimless. "The Buick'll follow. Everything's fine unless you panic and try to lose them."

"What..."

"No. No talk until we're on the West Side Highway."

I started driving toward the Hudson, setting up my tape recorder with my right hand. When we'd ascended onto the rickety elevated thoroughfare at 22nd Street I punched on the machine: "Okay, now talk."

Instead Blair opened his briefcase, retrieved the gizmo that looked like a calculator, and unsnapped the leatherette case. The black box inside was no calculator. He put his thumb on the box's single red button and suddenly frantic honking from the station wagon behind me as we slewed into its lane; I didn't care, nor could I take my eyes off the bomb.

"Shit, Huang, get your fucking eyes back on the road!" His scream broke my trance; I wrestled the car under control. Now Blair said, with artificial calm, "It's only a jammer. Look in the mirror... see the Buick's spotlight? And how it has no lens?" He depressed the red button. "Now they can't listen in." In the rearview I saw one of the men in the Buick begin to fiddle with the spotlight.

As I dropped the Mustang back down to forty to regain my breath, Blair discreetly touched a handkerchief to his forehead and lit another Havana. Then he said, "It began in the mid-Sixties, with my Saudi petroleum engagement. Didn't take long to figure out that someday the natives sitting on the reserves would grab the spigots." His sudden chuckle carried no humor. "Thought it'd take a decade but it took eight years. Anyway, I figured when Mid-East crude finally went skyhigh, the industry had only one place to look—China. So I took an engagement in Macao."

I looked at my recorder's sound-level needle for Blair's voice was soft, as it had been at Harry's and at the restaurant in Boston. Was this the voice he lied with?

"Learned three things in Macao. One, Peking secretly estimates inland crude reserves of sixty billion-plus barrels, treble what we thought. Add offshore reserves, they've got more oil than anybody except the Saudis. Two, the Chinese face technological problems. Their oil's waxy and needs special refineries, plus which they lack the hardware for offshore drilling. Lesson three: Peking's cash-poor. The potential's so vast that Western aid's no sweat, but they're paranoid about 'foreign devils'—they go the extra mile to deal with people they know.

"After Macao I liquidated my trust fund, remortgaged the house, then capitalized Entrepays through a front."

"De Brouilly," I said, remembering the Datatec dossier.

"Right, de Brouilly. With my contacts, it was a snap to turn a small profit on import-export through Hong Kong and Macao. But Entrepays was really a sleeper—a way to establish dependability in Peking's eyes."

"What for? With your capitalization..."

"The fantasy went like this. I was an oil expert. Small dealt with the Seven Sisters. There wasn't much I couldn't know." Blair fell silent. When I glanced over he was staring out the windshield at the George Washington Bridge, a wistful smile on his face. Then he remembered where he was. "Onyxx retained Small in 1970 to help map its long-range Asian policy. I... Shit, Huang, know how it feels to be privy to every forecast, every plan of the world's biggest oil company? Explorations, refineries, pipelines, deepwater ports—I knew it all, and I knew it was so good Peking had to go with Onyxx. Fantasy had become reality... time to awaken Entrepays."

"But how could Entre..."

"Ever hear of remoras? Fish that attach themselves to sharks; they feed on the host's scraps. Parasitic, but for some reason sharks don't mind. I was going to clamp Entrepays onto Onyxx's game plan and ride it to kingdom come. The Chinese need tankers? We got tankers. Pipeline sections? Sure. Technicians, concrete, oil rigs, expertise—Entrepays was going to subcontract it all."

"But if you were working on a deal with China, why was Harry mucking about Southeast Asia?"

"One of Onyxx's options. The Chinese may have hit a new field off Hainan in the south. When the dominoes topple, which should be before 1976, Peking stands to win a sphere of influence in Southeast Asia. Which means Onyxx needs to know offshore and shale potential down there. If the numbers're high, they pitch a super-refinery to handle Hainan that'll also process oil from farther south."

"Then the cooked report wasn't a CIA job."

"No. My idea, to tease Onyxx into springing for a major exploration. Peking would read that as good faith."

"Thereby weighting negotiations in Onyxx's favor."

"Like I said, Huang, you're a bright boy."

"I still don't get it. If Onyxx and Peking made a deal, you'd have been one of the most important men in the oil industry."

Blair watched me thread the cloverleaf onto the Cross-Bronx. Finally he said, "'I shall wear white flannel trousers, and walk upon the beach. I have heard the mermaids singing, each to each. I do not think that they will sing to me.' Fuck the trappings, Huang, nobody gets rich on someone else's payroll."

"I saw the figures on Entrepays. You weren't getting rich dealing in vacuum cleaners and silk, either."

"By early Seventy-one I'd set up the line of credit I needed."

"How much?"

"Fifty mil."

I laughed. "Two small potatoes like you and de Brouilly?"

"Not de Brouilly, me." Blair glanced out the window. "Where're you going?"

"I'm doubling back to a subway station. I've got something in my typewriter that's more important than this bullshit."

"Huang." He said it softly but the imperative in his voice made me continue past the exit ramp. "My petroleum engagements put me on a fast track. Didn't take long to fill a phone book with high-rollers who put their money where there mouth is, and I could've raised fifty mil without getting past the C's because I was selling the world's most seductive goods: inside knowledge. I throw in with venture capital, though, I have to show a nice return, which means taking the company the good, grey middleman route. Nobody spits on a dollar, but Entrepays could've been more. It could've been the Mafia of the oil industry—you hate it but you can't snuff it out so you keep paying. The men I finally chose understood. They also had the clout to make it happen even faster. All four wanted in, though one dragged in a fifth."

"And then you all ran to Liechtenstein to incorporate."

"Grow up, Huang. As an acid test of sincerity, I asked each to give me a handwritten confession to something carrying no statute of limitation, or something heavy enough to destroy him if it was made public today."

"Come off it, Blair. Even if you could really tap five movers and shakers, why should they trust you with their skeletons?"

"Never saw the confessions, that was part of the deal. They were collected by a middle-echelon British spook I heard was peddling NATO secrets to East Germany. My proposition was simple: stand trial for treason, or run my mission, suicide out at the end, and earn his survivor one mil U.S. He accepted.

"I clamped twenty-four-hour bodyguards on him. The guy was never alone except when he received each signed and sealed confession. In return he'd hand over a notched coin. Soon as he bagged the fifth letter he went to a neutral site, where each of the five sent a rep to redeem his marker for someone else's dirt."

"If this . . . this daisy-chain blackmail was working, why did the five men need you?"

"My access to Onyxx's plans."

The deeper it got, the more consistency Blair's story seemed to gain, but so had Lewis Carroll's fables. Finally I said, "Okay, who are they?"

Blair smiled. "Bourbon, Caviar, Ouzo, and Sake, and the fifth, whom Bourbon forced on me, I called Velveeta. Apologies to Eliot, but collectively they're the Cocktail Party."

"The names, Blair—I might start believing you if you give me the real names."

"Unh-unh, it's the only insurance policy I still carry."

"What do you mean?"

"The courier's dead, leaving me the only person with all five names."

"What?"

"Right, Huang. Each of them only knows about himself and the guy whose letter he's got. Divide and conquer—thought it'd be my trump card."

"What about de Brouilly?"

"That jerk?" He snorted, then handed me a dollar bill for the toll.

As I wound my way through the gate and onto the FDR I

suddenly realized he was dangling the names like catnip, that he'd not reveal them until he was good and ready. Time to change subjects: "Why are you telling me all this?"

"Because the Party's over. Nixon's the only politician gutsy enough and crazy enough to ram through diplomatic relations with Peking in the near future. He won't finish his term... thanks to you." My head snapped toward him. "Watch the road, Huang. You'd seen the fag buy the farm, but after the meet at Helmsley's I guessed you knew shit about his mission, and about Entrepays. Still, I ditched my papers and the typewriter"—so that's why Fanning and Harmer hadn't found the incriminating materials mentioned in the Datatec report—"and I had you vetted by tossing your apartment and your shrink pal's office."

"You trashed Alan's place?"

Blair nodded. "You were writing him the kind of big checks psychiatrists get. We figured if you did know anything, you'd tell him, only he wasn't your shrink—didn't even find a file there. But at your place we found a calendar notation, something like 'FW at Watergate regarding GOP,' and phone records showed you making some calls to DNC at Watergate. To play it safe, to make sure you weren't feeding this 'FW' something he could pass on to O'Brien, we set a tap. We got zilch. Fact is, the bug was being pulled the morning of June seventeenth... aw shit, the rest's history."

I started to laugh.

"What the hell's so funny?"

How could I possibly explain the frivolity of my wall-calendar notation? My pal Freddie'd been so low on the DNC totem Larry O'Brien probably didn't even know his name; I shook my head and wiped my eyes. "Tell me, what was the Vice-President's role in all of this?"

"Poor slob was told to stomp on you—never knew why and never asked."

"And Fanning?"

"He parroted what I told him. Damned impressive front, don't you think?"

I flipped on the parking lights as we entered the tunnel beneath the UN. "Did you tell Fanning the truth about Harry's death?"

"Two secret services fighting over opium?" Now it was Blair's turn to laugh but the sound coming from his throat was bitter. "Talk about the passage never taken, the door never opened—if Helmsley doesn't rape one of Kittikachorn's nephews in Chiang Mai the Thais don't blow the fucking fruitcake away and you never witness a murder. And you don't see the murder, Huang, and I don't see the eternal Footman hold my coat, and snicker."

"What do you mean?"

He gestured at the navy-blue Buick, still five car lengths behind. "My leash's short, or haven't you noticed?"

"If the Party's over, why should they care?"

"I'm the loose end, the only outsider who can possibly bare the bones. One of the five's obviously not happy with that situation, because he's the one paying those goons back there."

"It could be a joint effort."

"They don't know each other, remember?"

"If you think you're going to die, why not strike first? Blow the whistle on all five."

Blair shook his head. "For a bright boy you're awfully fucking dumb. Knowing some guy's private phone's no proof we cut a deal. The confessions—without those confessions I can't touch any of them."

"So why aren't you dead now?"

"Whoever hired the goons is still buying the bluff I'm running."

"Which is?"

"Unh-unh, Huang, then it wouldn't be a bluff, would it?"

"You still haven't explained why you ordered the hit on me. Revenge for triggering Watergate?"

"Don't be an ass. You'd just found out about the man in the red wig. I was..."

"How'd you know that?"

Instead of answering Blair pointed to the 14th Street exit: "Get off here and return the car."

"I said, how did you know that?"

"A tap run from the building across the street, set after you barged in on Fanning. Thought I could still stonewall it and keep Nixon in office—didn't need you roaming around Washington blabbing about your visit from the Plumbers."

"And your call that night?"

"Know what a blue box is? Used one to patch into an automatic relayer in the building across the street. That way the calls log in as locals."

"Who tailed me through the subways that night?"

Blair laughed again; this time he was amused. "No one. Just wanted to make you sweat."

"But why kill me? Other people knew what I knew."

"I didn't give a shit about those documents, Fanning already had a good cover story. Just the girl, because she also knew about the red wig. When my buttons finished you off they were going to your place to wait for her."

I almost rammed a double-parked car near Avenue C. Shock slowly turned to anger and anger into bloodlust; the murder methods I contemplated all involved sadism. But wait, I could nail him legally—what I had on my tape recorder was more than enough to call Coady back from vacation.

As if reading my thoughts Blair said, "Don't take that cassette to the cops without playing it first." Then he waved his black gizmo and smiled. "This is more than a jammer, it's also an electromagnet."

I stared at him as the awful implications registered. Then I fumbled for the "Rewind" switch. The characteristic Donald Duck squawks were missing. Sweating now I hit "Play." The tape was blank; Blair had erased it. I slammed my fist into the steering wheel.

"Come on, Huang—got a plane to catch."

The anger suddenly melted into despair; I'd had him cold and I'd blown it. As I dully swung the car back into traffic, the Buick eased into motion behind us. At the garage I slowly gathered up my recorder and started to open the door.

"Wait, I'll cab you down after I settle up," he said.

"Fuck you."

He shrugged. "Then listen, and listen good. Whoever's after me's getting close, because the tightrope's shaking. If I die, go to the post office near Penn Station exactly twenty-eight days after my death. There'll be a letter care of General Delivery. Twenty-eight days... wait longer and you'll join me."

I pulled myself away and got out. Twenty feet from the Mustang I heard him call out the window, "Goodbye, Huang." I looked from him to the navy-blue Buick parked across the street; its three occupants ignored me, so intent their concentration on Blair. Then I noticed the car's license plates were obscured by mud.

When I got back to my building Blair's black Chevy was gone. I scanned the block: no sign of the Buick, either. Once inside, I turned on the tape recorder again. I listened to the static for a while before pouring myself a stiff drink, twirling two sheets into my typewriter, and beginning my re-creation of the phantasmagorical conversation.

Midway through, the phone rang.

"Hi, Alan. No, not today... oh shit, I know who left the message. I asked a friend to call an editor—he must've dialed you by mistake. Yeah. My life? Enhh."

19 October 1973: New York

When I finally forced my eyes open the late-morning sun glinted through the bedroom window; I had a headache and my body felt bloated by toxins. I made myself coffee, then read the sheets I'd typed the day before.

Blair's Cocktail Party was patent bullshit, my alleged role in Watergate almost as absurd. Onyxx's Asian game plan? That felt closer to the mark, as did his explanation of the attempt on my life. And the tails in the Buick were, of course, indisputable. As I pondered Blair's typical mixture of fact and fiction I again had the nagging feeling I was being set up. But for what? Should I seek help? All I could prove was we'd rented a car, and the mileage on the Mustang's odometer would correspond to our jaunt around Manhattan. Enough to call Coady or Fanning with? No.

By the time I got back from the Empire State Building I'd just about convinced myself Blair had cracked under the strain of losing his job, and that the main purpose of my brief trip uptown had been to get some air, rather than to deposit my notes in the safe-deposit box.

31 December 1973: New York

As a reward for working right through the holidays on the accursed textbook, I'd bought the best shell steak the Jefferson Market had to offer and a bottle of Piper. I'd planned to consume all of both myself, then fall asleep to Guy Lombardo—a fitting purgative for the worst year of my life. I was crushing peppers on the steak when the phone rang.

"Ray, i...rew."

"Hello?"

". . . me now . . . anning . . ."

"I'm sorry, I can't hear you."

There was some more breakup and then the line went dead. I was pretty sure it was Fanning, but what in the world could he want? Three minutes later the phone jangled again. "Ray, it's Frew. Can you hear me this time."

"Yes."

"Happy holidays."

"Thank you, you too. Where're you calling from?"

"Hawaii."

"Nice work if you can get it."

"I wish it were a pleasure trip," he said, laughing. Then his voice grew serious. "I'm sorry to interrupt your evening, but I've just heard from Stan Harmer...Mr. Blair is dead."

I slumped against the sink. "How?"

"He was driving home alone on Route One-twenty-eight last Friday night. He apparently lost control of his car. The state police estimate his speed at sixty miles per hour when he rammed the abutment."

The clicking of the range-top clock seemed suddenly loud. "They're listing it as an accident?"

"Yes. Stan's read the report. An eyewitness, another driver, stated there was no car near Mr. Blair's when he started to skid." Fanning hesitated, then added, "May he rest in peace. And us, too."

"Yeah."

"Have you been all right since we last spoke, son."

"Fine," I lied.

"And Martha."

"Okay, I guess. We...we've split."

There was a pause. "I'm sorry to hear it. It appears 1973 hasn't been a good year for too many of us, has it."

"Except maybe our Arab friends at OPEC."

Fanning laughed. "Then here's to a happier 1974. And Ray—remember, if I can be of assistance, call."

"Thank you, sir."

As soon as Fanning rang off I dialed Duke. Much to my relief the invitation I'd declined to his bash was still open, for I knew if I followed my original plan of spending the evening alone, I'd brood so much over Blair's violent death the new year would start as a continuation of the old. And that would be bad.

24 January 1974: New York

"B: Then listen, and listen good. Whoever's after me's getting close, because the tightrope's shaking. If I die, go to the post office near Penn Station exactly twenty-eight days after my death. There'll be a letter care of General Delivery. Twenty-eight days... wait longer and you'll join me."

I looked up from the Xeroxes of my notes to the large "X" on my wall calendar: it was the twenty-eighth day since Blair's death. Go, I thought, go. But I was reluctant. Was it fear his paranoid ramblings might be true? Or was it because the opening weeks of the new year had been like the shaft of sunlight after the thunderstorm? At Duke's party I'd met a lady; nothing serious yet, but Bonnie was the first with whom I'd felt comfortable in bed since Martha, and that was progress. Plus I'd finally completed the first draft of the textbook. Plus Herb, the editor of the credit-card magazine, had called out of the blue to assign me a piece, and as if some cosmic logjam had been freed by this propitious omen, I was now snaring assignments from other sources as well. It'll only take an hour and two subway tokens to check out Blair's story, I told myself; get it off your mind. But that car ride with him had taken place so long ago, way back last year, back in 1973. I looked out the front window at the lowering winter sky. Then I put the Xeroxes back in my file cabinet and returned the call of an industrial filmmaker interested in my services.

27 January 1974: New York

"Hey—Happy New Year," Bonnie whispered in my ear.

"Mmmmm. You're several days late, but thanks. Ooh, ooh, more..."

"What year is it?" she asked, not stopping.

"Rabbit."

"Is it really?"

"I don't know, I forgot to check the *Times* last Wednesday."

"Some Chink you are."

"Mm. Mmmmm..."

We were in the shower when I said, "What time's your train?"

"Ten-thirtyish. You don't have to leave, you know. I'll be back around eight... there's no way Gramps can stay awake after the party we've planned for him."

"Thanks, but I really should go back to my place to fiddle with a treatment. Let's grab breakfast and I'll drop you at the station."

After seeing Bonnie to her train for Princeton I was cutting across Penn Station toward the subway when I saw the post office across Eighth Avenue. I hesitated: should I?

Inside the gloomy building I stepped to the General Delivery window and gave my name. The clerk returned four minutes later: "Got some ID?" I pulled out my driver's license. He glanced at it and dropped a bulky envelope onto the counter.

"Hey, move it up there!" My trance broke; I looked back at the line growing behind me and shuffled numbly toward a writing counter, the envelope heavy in my hand. It had been mailed from the post office I stood in on January 23, which meant I could have picked it up the next day—the twenty-eighth after Blair's death. Would ignoring his directive prove costly? Minutes ticked by and still I couldn't make myself find out. Finally I stuffed the sealed envelope in my parka and walked outside.

I needed a drink but it was Sunday morning so I ducked into a nearby coffee shop. Why was I afraid of what was inside? Who's afraid of the big, bad wolf? Not me, certainly, not me; after forcing down half a cup of coffee I gingerly drew out the envelope and slit its flap with a spoon handle.

Clipped to a multi-paged dossier was an undated covering note:

Huang:

No matter what you heard it was murder. But vengeance shall be mine, even if posthumously, and you're playing a role in it.

First let me tell you about my bluff. Remember the goons in the Buick? Turned them into unwitting accomplices; their reports of my eavesdrop-proof meets with a dozen people, including you, must've given their boss pause. Then I tightened the screws by warning all five of the Party those meetings were to bare Entrepays's skeleton, and that one of you twelve gets the flesh, too, 28 days after I die. Thus, the man behind the goons wants me out, he's got a hard choice. Does he gamble killing the one who gets the flesh'll end it, or does he also waste everyone I claimed I gave the skeleton to? To prolong his dilemma, I threw in the 28-days crap, because that's how long he'd have to keep tabs on a dozen people scattered across three continents.

Why was it a bluff? You're the only one I discussed Entrepays with. Plus, the "flesh" I have to peddle weighs less than a pound; had I been able to profit from the attached report, I'd still be whole.

Well, my bluff was called. My present to you is meager pickings but you're good at solving puzzles, aren't you? Have fun. Just one catch: to make it sporty I had five other letters posted the day after this one. Addressed to my ex-colleagues, among them my murderer, these finger you as the man who knows too much. Your grace period depends on the vagaries of the mail; better get a coffee spoon to measure out your life.

My revenge? Soon either you, the loose cannon who triggered my downfall, or the members of the Cocktail Party will hit the fan. This certainty doesn't make my own impending death easier, but it is not altogether lacking in solace. Just between you and me, Huang, I hope they get you first. And I hope death comes slowly and painfully.

Cheers,
G.

I tasted bile on the roof of my mouth. Was this one last macabre joke? Then I paged through the attached report. In that peculiarily flat jargon used by policemen, the sheets recounted in meticulous detail the itinerary of a British courier as he traveled around the world in 1970. Airports, hotels, car rentals, meetings—facts and figures and dates danced and spun but I couldn't concentrate. No, I needed to squirrel myself away for a few days while I studied the report and tried to run checks. Dare I go back to my apartment? Too risky if Blair was telling the truth, and anyway I had credit cards on me so shelter and transportation and food and clothing would be no problem. But wait: plastic leaves tracks. In addition, my passport rested right next to my savings passbook in my secret cache. I pondered it some more and calculated if Blair really had my death warrant mailed according to the timetable in his note, those letters would have gone out on Friday, just two days before. No way, I thought; no, with our postal system,

I'd be safe for another day, so I went outside and hailed a cab.

But by the time we got downtown caution was speaking so I ordered the driver to cruise slowly past my building. I peered inside my ground-floor windows: nothing seemed amiss. Still, I had him pull around a double-parked UPS van, continue to Sixth Avenue, and turn the corner.

I got out and started back down the block. The sidewalks were empty, but that was normal for a Sunday morning. As I passed Gay Street I glanced up it. The short, narrow one-way running toward me was also deserted, as usual. Then what was bothering me? I took a few more hesitant steps. Had I not been at nerve's edge I wouldn't have thought twice about the brown United Parcel van but now I realized with a start that I'd never known UPS to deliver on Sunday. From sixty yards away the vehicle appeared unoccupied. I didn't like it. Finally I turned back toward Sixth Avenue; give it fifteen minutes, I thought, so I picked up a Sunday *Times* at the kiosk and began skimming it over another cup of coffee at the bagel joint.

Back to the corner now: the van still stood double-parked. Not sure of what to do, I started forward but when I passed Gay Street again that part of the brain that screams danger screamed once more. I wavered, then decided to retreat.

As I turned I almost ran into a muscular man carrying a batch of take-outs from the coffee shop on the corner. "Excuse me," I said.

He nodded. Then his eyes bulged. "Hey! Hey, hey, it's him!" he roared, shifting to block my way. Behind me a truck engine ground to life. I instinctively clutched my Sunday *Times* with both hands and roundhoused the seven-pound paper into his face; the man's bags dropped but he didn't so with a scream that was a cross between a curse and a moan I swatted him again and this time he went down, hard.

I looked back. The boxy UPS van was accelerating. I'd never make the avenue so I flung aside what remained of the paper and fled up Gay; now the squeal of brakes reverberating along the short street and now I could hear the van starting up it the wrong way—if only there was oncoming traffic... Gay runs into another one-way, Christopher, and on Christopher a bus was slowly approaching so I turned the corner and dashed toward it—that should block off the van. Right again onto Greenwich, now past the pastry and cheese shops, now the "Don't Walk" signs on the next corner beginning to blink. I started my finishing kick and as I hurtled into the crosswalk a visceral awareness of cars and trucks charging in a phalanx up Sixth Avenue and then horns blaring and two taxis skidding as they swerved to avoid me.

Seventy-five yards past the intersection I risked a glance over my shoulder: there were men weaving through the unslackening flow back on the avenue.

I continued east in desperate search of a cop car or a store full of people but at this hour on the Sabbath the Village still slumbered. The church, where the hell was that church? I couldn't remember so I kept running.

My pursuers numbered four; I gained on two but the other two were holding their own.

Across University Place now and still going flat out when suddenly my right leg buckled and I was falling and then bouncing headfirst along the sidewalk and as I fought for breath I saw and smelled the squishy brown pile I'd stepped in.

Then I looked up: the nearest pair was at seventy yards and closing.

I struggled to my feet. My right ankle was on fire. Just ahead the BMT subway station—sanctuary? Now the branding iron was stabbing deeper into my ankle but I made myself run and as I neared the subway entrance I heard the roar of an approaching train so I grabbed the handrails and took the steps five at a time.

The train was easing to a stop. Should I vault the turnstile? The doors sprang open. No, I had a token; it would take longer but I'd attract less attention. Now the passengers were spilling out, now I fumbled out the token, now I spun through the turnstile, now I hobbled across the platform, and now as I piled aboard the doors started to shut.

And froze midway. Open again, closing again, again the doors froze.

Click, and over the public-address system a tinny voice: "Stand back from the doors. Please stand back from the doors so this train can move out."

In the car behind mine two teen-age girls continued to hold the doors as they gigglingly exhorted their pal at the token booth to hurry. Jesus ... Their pal was through the turnstile and nearing the doors when I heard shouts from the token booth. Now their pal was through the doors and the doors were bucking shut when I heard pounding feet. No ... Yes—the doors were less than six inches apart when they froze again.

Click..."Hey, man, get offa those doors!"

For five seconds a standoff; then the conductor gave in and the doors sighed open. My pursuers were aboard.

As the train lurched into motion I hobbled toward the front of the train, testing the conductor's cabins along the way. Two cars up the one on the local side was unlocked and as I tumbled in I brushed eyes with a slack-jawed shopping-bag lady and then I was pulling the door tight behind me. How long would I be safe in this womb? And where was the train heading? Finally the shriek of brakes and the lights of a station and as we slowed I could read the signs: Prince Street. I was headed downtown. Soon the train moaned back into motion and we resumed our raucous plunge through the void.

Metabolism steadying, ankle still throbbing like hell; why was I having so much trouble deciding whether to ride the train all the way to...

Without warning the cabin door banged hard into my side.

"What the fuck...hey, man, why you be in here?" It was the conductor; behind him, the smugly smiling shopping-bag lady. Now he caught a whiff of the dog excrement still on my shoes. The conductor's nose wrinkled: "Aw, shit...you didn't, not in here..." I ducked his wild grab, rammed the door back into him, and dove from the cabin.

As the conductor pulled himself to his feet the passengers in the car quickly turned their attention elsewhere. Now he touched his jaw and grunted and now he pinpointed me in his narrowing eyes and now he started up the aisle after me but then the car's windows began to spangle with the lights of the next station. The conductor hesitated, clenched both fists, and then duty won as he wheeled back into the cabin to tend to his chores.

Around me the passengers preparing to get off were massing at the doors. Should I stay aboard or should I join them? The problem solved itself: at the far end of the car two men, one burly and the other slim, were scanning all faces as they pushed my way.

At the instant their eyes met mine the train lurched to a halt; doors popped open and I began shoving and elbowing onto the platform. Then someone nearby yelling "Get him!" so I burrowed headlong into the crowd waiting to board—odd so many were Chinese—and now the conductor broadcasting "Stationmaster... stationmaster!" and now I was pulling up short at the turnstiles. Come on, lady, come on, but still she couldn't fit token into slot so I grabbed her hand and before her shock could turn to anger I'd spun past. She'd been Chinese, everyone seemed Chinese... of course! The station was Canal Street, the stop for Chinatown...

The exit stairs were clotted. I wedged my way onto them and began to climb.

Suddenly gunfire crackling on the street above but before I could retreat an even worse sound—"There he is!"—and the shout came from so close behind I had no choice but to continue upward. Now a second volley, followed by a third. There seemed to be a firefight raging overhead but then why were the people descending the steps so unpanicked? And suddenly I understood: the explosions were firecrackers, the occasion the weekend Chinese New Year's parade, the one held for tourists. Above the numbers would be there—would safety?

When I finally made it onto Canal I was immediately swept up like a twig in a torrent by the crowd surging eastward toward Mott. Don't look back, I told myself; don't look back...

Approaching Mott now where the dragon was assembling for its ritual dance, and then I was flowing with the mob around the corner and onto the narrow, bending street. Here the very buildings reverberated with the Gatling cracks of ladyfinger skeins and the discordant clangs of marching bands and the concussive booms of cherry bombs. Every sound raised a flinch, every jostle more nape hairs, and yet I kept my face pointed resolutely forward because don't we all have straight black hair, don't we all look alike from the back?

Now a great cheer coursed along Mott: the dragon was astir. Slowly at first, a little jig to unloosen, then curling into a lazy drill to set rhythm, and now the two dozen men beneath the gaily colored rice-paper skin were ready. At that moment the dancer dressed as a monk cavorted past, holding high the smoking orb that symbolized long life and prosperity. Drumbeats quickened and the dragon stretched to full length as it began a serpentine, sidewalk-to-sidewalk weave in chase of the orb.

When I pushed across Bayard the knot of spectators at the curb grew to five deep, compressing us passersby to a trickle along the storefronts. Shuffling with the petty pace of a begowned mandarin strained my nerves, but then my pursuers were mired in this mess too, I told myself; keep going, don't look back...

Drumbeats slackened and out on the street the dragon slowed, winded by its sprint after the long life and prosperity the monk kept dangling just out of reach, just tantalizingly out of reach...

Ahead now the bend in Mott: would that it'd thwart my pursuing demons. I reached it and was edging through it when suddenly I felt my profile opening. Don't look back...

Like Lot's wife, I looked—and turned to salt: they were ten yards behind in the crush and staring directly at me.

I lowered my head and bulled like a fullback into the spectators at curbside. Around me outraged cries but I ignored them as I searched through the welter of bodies for sight of the street. Suddenly a sharp pain lanced my side and from the corner of my eye I glimpsed the umbrella being raised again but I kept plowing forward and the second thwack only grazed my rump. Then softness screaming and falling away under me and then I slammed into a slab of granite: he was Caucasian and he was enormous and when he saw his trampled wife at my feet he roared and drew back a fist the size of a ham. I lunged at him. His roundhouse numbed my left shoulder but now I was wrapping myself around his waist and now my legs were driving and now I was toppling him backward into the street; as I scrambled off him one knee sank into his stomach and the last of his breath whooshed out.

The mounting crowd-shrieks weren't for the approaching dragon. To my left a ripple of activity along the sidewalk; across Mott was the beginning of Pell, along which the crowd seemed thinner. Now the ripple along the sidewalk was turning into a bulge as my pursuing demons fought after me so I hobbled across Mott and onto Pell.

Away from the parade route this street was virtually deserted but someone was blowtorching my ankle so I'd made less than forty yards when I heard "No! No, alive!" I'd never reach the end of Pell but off to my right was Doyers Street—and the restaurant with the sliding wall...

Gimping down Doyers now and as I stumbled through the entrance to the Ling How Fun I thought I'd lost them but before the door swung shut a distant shout—"In there!"—so I bolted past the startled maître d', Wellington, and using the banister for support clambered up the steps. Which room, which room contained the sliding wall?

Downstairs a door banged. "We have no tabers! You wait here prease..." And now a gruff voice was overriding Wellington's: "Shut the fuck up you old fart..."

I knew it wasn't the first banquet room so I whipped through the curtains into the second and now a peripheral awareness of stunned eyes and slack jaws and chopsticks suspended in midair as I wrestled with the lighting fixture near the door. Nothing.

Downstairs Wellington and the gruff voice still screamed at each other.

The third banquet room was empty. I hit the fixture so hard it tore from its mount but the far wall remained stationary.

Downstairs Wellington was threatening to call the porice and now a muffled yelp and now "Upstairs—he must be upstairs!" and now footsteps trembling the treads.

The fourth banquet room was also empty. I yanked the lighting fixture. It pivoted.

Curtains being wrenched from rod and now "The next room, check the next one..."

The far wall was moving so ankle be damned I started to run. And then I saw the people eating in the room I'd met Kuo in but it was too late to stop so I took one more giant stride and folded my arms in front of my head and launched into a racing dive. I landed atop the long table set end-on to the sliding wall and skidded along it, bulldozing before me plates and bowls and glasses and serving platters, my momentum carrying me its entire length and into the lap of the pudgy gentleman at its head.

The yellow button, the yellow button... I picked myself off the floor, lunged for the scroll, ripped it aside, and pressed the button. The sliding wall reversed direction.

Now chairs scraped as the shock of my entry wore off. A young Chinese man sprinkled with food scraps rose with murder in his eyes and a pair of chopsticks in his hands; I grabbed a metal pitcher and flung it at his face. As I fled the room a ruckus behind me followed by the sounds of violence—the diners were venting their anger on the second and third gatecrashers.

When I tumbled down the stairs and out of the restaurant onto Mott the sidewalk groaned under the crowd awaiting the approaching dragon. I tried to squeeze up the street but couldn't. I tried to squeeze down the street but couldn't. With a sob I began hacking my way toward the curb; it was like running the gauntlet through molasses but I suffered the vile curses and the pummels and now I was almost there and now back near the restaurant entrance incoherent yelling—my pursuing demons?—and now the last man before me wouldn't give way so I kidney-punched him and as he doubled over I broke through onto the street.

It was red and green and yellow and white and it had dozens of legs: my way was blocked by the dragon as it gathered itself for its final dash after the Orb of Brightest Future. Should I? Had to... Two strides and dive, and as I slid headfirst across the pavement and under the dragon I clipped one of the dancers, and now his full weight was writhing across my legs. Come on, come on... Drumbeats quickened and now the snap and crackle of rice paper swirling into motion and as I finally squirmed free other dancers, tripping over their still-fallen colleague, began to thud to the ground. I crawled out from under, then turned to look: the dancers at the head, unaware of the trouble at the tail, continued to sprint forward, and now, almost in slow motion, the brightly colored dragon stretched and stretched and then it ripped in two.

On the far curb the stunned crowd parted before me. As I limped through I spotted winking lights: there had to be a back way out of the Port Arthur so I jerked open the nearest glass door and plunged past the chicken into the game room.

It was empty save for the wizened old Chinese changemaker.

"Back door!" I shouted. *"Hou men, hou men!"*

His gaze was blank. I started toward the rear but suddenly the street cacophony swelled so I turned back to the glass doors.

My slim pursuing demon leaned against the jamb, panting and glaring. His clothes were dirty and torn and his face was bruised; most important, the eyes riveted to mine dripped blood.

I began to edge backward. His partner, where was his partner... I glanced behind him; someone or something must have stopped the other man. Could I handle this one alone? How was he armed... Suddenly a hard object rammed into the small of my back and even as I yelled my slim pursuing demon broke into a smile for I'd bumped into a pinball machine. The old changemaker's cough broke the moment; I reached out one trembling hand and began to sidle around the machine.

Now my slim pursuing demon straightened. He was still smiling as he slowly reached one hand into his overcoat and he was still smiling as he slowly withdrew the hand but now his wrist was flicking and suddenly light sparkled off the tip of his switchblade.

Thumps now as the old changemaker dropped to his knees and crawled for safety.

The knife blade's slow figure eight was mesmerizing. Now my slim pursuing demon sprang onto the balls of his feet and casually, effortlessly began to narrow the distance between us: seventy feet, sixty-five...

The more I backpedaled the more he gained but I didn't dare take my eyes off the gleaming metal: sixty feet, fifty-five... I needed something in my hands, anything to give me a chance against the knife. Hurry up, hurry up: fifty feet. To my left stood the bank of Skee-Ball machines and in one I spied several unbowled balls so I spun and scuttled toward it. When I had a ball in each hand—they were wooden and just the size of a baseball—I turned to face my killer.

Fifty feet and closing.

I drew back an arm.

His smile turned into a smirk. He raised his left arm to act as a shield, then ducked into a crouch and resumed his sinuous stalk: forty-five feet, forty...

Under pressure I tend to throw with a three-quarters motion which causes my ball to rise and tail to the right. Aim left of target, I reminded myself as I set up in a pitcher's stance, aim left of target...

His smirk had frozen into a death leer and now he waved his free hand gently, taunting me to throw: thirty-five feet, thirty...

Had he been closer I'd have had to watch his hips but now I could concentrate on his eyes so I lobbed the Skee-Ball in my left hand toward him in a high, lazy parabola and as his eyes flicked automatically upward to an object that could do him no harm I retargeted on his right shoulder and hurled the second Skee-Ball with all my might.

The wooden sphere rose and tailed to the right and cracked

sickeningly off his temple, the impact standing him straight and driving him back a step and then he was crumpling and as the knife clattered harmlessly under a pinball machine his head rebounded off a metal stanchion.

The throw and the fall began to instant-replay in my mind's eye. Finally I tore my gaze from the inert body and searched out the old changemaker. "Where's the back door? *Hou men tsai na li?*" He continued to quaver silently behind the counter so I wheeled and at the rear of the arcade came across a dim passageway that led to a door. It was locked. Three kicks later it wasn't. The dank air shaft boomed with the captured echoes of the parade; I began to hobble down it toward the light at the end.

Book III

28 January 1974: New York

Every so often, usually when schools are in recess, a team of teen-agers armed with maps and timetables will descend into the New York subways to travel each of its two hundred-plus miles as rapidly as possible. Twenty-four hours is considered good time. By Monday morning I'd been underground almost a day and it felt as if I'd traced most of the trackage. Yet I was in no hurry to quit the system: possessing only credit cards I dared not use, less than fifty dollars in cash, and a conspicuous lack of safe harbors, I figured there were worse roles than that of mole ricocheting through the world's most complex maze.

Subways are not for sleeping but they proved passable for washing, eating, and even reclothing. I'd bathed my bruises and scraped myself clean in the squalid men's room of a station in the Bronx. Many platforms held hot-dog and pretzel stands which I no longer regarded as malodorous nuisances. And late the previous afternoon, when crowds were thickest, I'd ventured into the garish arcade of the Times Square station to purchase cut-rate shirt and jeans and a ski cap that pulled down into a balaclava; lacking money for a new coat, I'd completed the disguise by blackening my parka with liquid shoe polish.

I may have appeared the model of cunning resourcefulness those first hours on the lam, but in truth it was my subconscious responding to such drives as survival and hunger, for my mind had been blank: the past hurt and was therefore unthinkable, the present was surreal and therefore unfathomable, the future was death and therefore unimaginable. Seconds, minutes, hours, they were all the same as I hurtled through the eternal subterranean night. And then a heavy hand on my shoulder and I woke up screaming into the friendly but puzzled face of a transit cop. And then a change of trains at track's end and I set off in disoriented flight, managing all of three steps before my ankle buckled. And then the men's room was locked and I didn't have a dime so I threw up in a garbage can.

And then it was daylight. I blinked; my train was atop an elevated portion of the IND. I blinked again; horrendously fitful as my sleep had been, it must have knitted the raveled sleave, for the sour fever had passed. My face was dry, my mouth fresh, my senses of perception frighteningly atuned. I willed my ankle to stop throbbing and it did.

Suddenly I understood why, instead of panic, utter calm: with only one thing left to lose, I was going to make those bastards work like hell to administer the *coup de grâce*. But how could I fight back if I was stuck in the subways? That's when I realized that even if my pursuers had the manpower to stake out my apartment and haunts, the odds of their spotting me at large in the city were slight.

The coffee shop on Queens Boulevard was big and busy. I took a booth and drew out the report from Blair.

The top sheet was dated February 3, 1970. It was a letter in which Blair, seeking to lay the foundation for the Entrepays daisy chain, had asked a man identified only as "Wm." to "devise a sterile routing for an international courier. Mission: the sanitary collection of five documents. Scope of trip: Europe, Asia, North America, South America. Duration of trip: 12/17 days." When the documents were in hand, "courier will proceed to another site to redistribute them among messengers dispatched by parties rendering originals (need marker system to identify messengers)." Evidently Blair had indeed turned a British agent; his courier, named Geoffrey Kenton, "is under coercion . . . will require 24-hour escorting . . . [and] will self-terminate at engagement's end."

The second sheet was dated February 9, 1970. Wm.'s proposal was masterly.

The "escorting" of Kenton—whom he chose to refer to as "GK"—would be by twelve agents working in "three teams of four, each team covering twenty-four hours on two-man shifts, six hours on and six off." To keep the immediate party small, Wm. would leapfrog off-duty teams. Air travel would be first class when possible, ground travel by rented cars; they'd stay at luxury hotels, for Kenton would eat mostly room service.

The "sanitary collection" of each of the five documents would take place at another luxury hotel in the same city: "Require three interconnecting suites—GK and agents in one, subject rendering document in another, rdvz in middle suite." For maximum security Blair would book these suites and have the "subject rendering document" in place before notifying Wm. of the site. Further, Kenton would enter each meeting naked, carrying only the marker for the messenger; for these Wm. would "notch five new U.S. coins of different denominations with a star-shaped punch." Finally, "Security of collected documents: metal-lined courier pouch with tamper-activated acid-release mechanism. GK to carry only key, on neck chain." The cost of the mission, pending itinerary, was $65,000 to $85,000 U.S. plus Wm.'s fee.

The third sheet was dated March 30, 1970:

Wm.
  Plan acceptable. Tentative itinerary:
  22 May: Pick up GK/London, England
  23 May: Rdvz 1/Paris, France
  25 May: Rdvz 2/Shiraz, Iran
  27 May: Rdvz 3/Tokyo, Japan
  29 May: Rdvz 4/Newport Beach, U.S.A.
  31 May: Rdvz 5/Las Vegas, U.S.A.
  3/4 June: Redistribute documents/Rio de Janeiro, Brazil
  4 June: End of engagement
Will notify immediately of any itinerary change. Binder has been paid your account Geneva. Good luck.
                                                G.

The next seven sheets were dated June 7, 1970. They comprised Wm.'s minute-by-minute police-blotter report of the mission, with each day followed by a summary:

22 May 1970. 1630 hours: Kenton was fetched at his London

home in the presence of his daughter. A car to Heathrow, the 1830 Singapore Airlines flight from London to Paris, check-in at the George V, room-service dinner; Kenton asleep shortly before midnight. SUMMARY—GK VERY EMOTIONAL IN FAREWELL TO DAUGHTER—MOODY DURING TRAVEL—ATE ONE-THIRD DINNER.

23 May 1970. 1059 hours: Rendezvous 1—Kenton took a notched penny into Room 421 of the Plaza-Athénée Hotel. 1127: He emerged with a sealed envelope bearing the Plaza-Athénée's return address, which he placed in the special pouch. A car to Orly, the 1400 Iran Air flight from Paris to Tehran, check-in at the Intercontinental Tehran. SUMMARY—GK REMAINS UNCOMMUNICATIVE—SLEPT ENTIRE ORY-THR FLIGHT—AGENT C OBSERVES GK AS DAZED ON EMERGING RM 421, PLAZA-ATHÉNÉE.

24 May 1970. 1430 hours: Iran Air flight from Tehran to Shiraz, check-in at the Park Saadi. 1707: "GK demands stroll—Agents H and I accompany GK to Eram Park—sanitary expedition." SUMMARY—GK EXHIBITING IMPROVED APPETITE—SEEMS TO RESPOND TO AGENT H—NOTICEABLY LESS DESPONDENT POST-STROLL.

25 May 1970. For the first time, Kenton awoke himself. 1000 hours: Rendezvous 2—Kenton took a notched nickel into Room 704 of the Hotel Cyrus. 1016: He emerged with a sealed envelope bearing the Hotel Cyrus's return address, which he placed in the special pouch. 1027: "GK expresses wish to see Persepolis." Accompanied by his on-duty agents and, by special request, Agent H, Kenton driven to the ruins. Back to Shiraz for the 1700 Iran Air flight to Tehran, then onto the 2230 Pan Am flight from Tehran to Tokyo. SUMMARY—GK'S REQUEST FOR PERSEPOLIS OUTING GRANTED VIEWLY 1) SKED NOT JEOPARDIZED, 2) WITH 10 DAYS TO RUN ON MISSION, GK'S DELICATE TEMPERAMENT NEEDS ALL POSSIBLE STROKING—GK'S FRIENDSHIP WITH AGENT H ENCOURAGING AND MAY PROVE USEFUL.

26 May 1970. At Hong Kong stopover, Kenton inspected duty-free binoculars but did not buy. Arrived Tokyo at 1920 hours, check-in at New Otani Hotel; Kenton snacked in the coffee shop on another "sanitary expedition." SUMMARY—GK FATIGUED BUT IN GOOD SPIRITS—PERMISSION TO SNACK TO MINIMIZE "PRISONER" SYNDROME.

27 May 1970. On awaking Kenton caused a row because

he wanted to buy binoculars for his daughter's upcoming birthday; Wm. placated by "promising post-rdvz shopping trip." 1628 hours: Rendezvous 3—Kenton took a notched dime into Room 1071 of the Okura Hotel. 1807: A nervous agent notified Wm. that after more than an hour and a half, the meeting was still in progress. 1842: Wm. arrived at the Okura. 1912: Kenton finally emerged with two letters. One, sealed and bearing the Okura Hotel's return address, he placed in the special pouch; the other, unsealed, he gave Wm. Upon learning the rdvz suite was empty, Wm. entered it and gathered extra typing paper, crumpled typing sheets from the wastebasket, and the carbon ribbon of the IBM Selectric typewriter; these Wm. burned in the bathroom. Back at their own hotel, Wm. packed Kenton off to a non-English-speaking prostitute in Ropongi, then called Blair long distance and read him the courier's unsealed letter:

My dearest Henny,
   I wish you a very, very Happy Birthday. Again my abject regrets for not sharing my little (no, make that "big") girl's Sweet Sixteenth. Enclosed is my present to you. I would dearly love to join you on your birding rambles with it. My thoughts are ever with you, Hen—please think of me, too. You have given me the most joy in all my life. Again, a most Happy, Happy Birthday. Take the very best care of yourself. All the love in the world,
   YOUR DAD

Blair agreed the letter was harmless and could be posted. When Kenton returned from yet another "sanitary expedition," he quickly fell asleep. SUMMARY—DELAY IN RDVZ DUE INABILITY SUBJECT RENDERING DOCUMENT TO SPEAK ENGLISH—TRANSLATOR SLOW—TRANSLATOR'S HANDWRITING JUDGED ILLEGIBLE BY GK SO ELECTRIC TYPEWRITER ORDERED—GK PERSONALLY TYPED DOCUMENT—GK WROTE DAUGHTER WHILE DOCUMENT RETRANSLATED TO CHECK ACCURACY—WM. PERSONALLY DESTROYED TYPING MATERIALS UNSEEN BY ALL EYES—PROSTITUTE ARRANGED TO CALM GK, WHO WAS IRRITABLE FROM LONG RDVZ AND DEPRESSED BY LETTER TO DAUGHTER.

29 May 1970. In the morning Kenton purchased a pair of $10\times$ binoculars at Matsushima in the Ginza. 1522 hours: At Haneda Airport, Kenton allowed to personally airmail his present and letter to his daughter in London. The 1630 Pan Am flight from Tokyo to Los Angeles crossed the International Date Line; check-in at the Beverly Wilshire at 1108 on 28 May, local time. SUMMARY—GK CHEERED BY POSTING OF PACKAGE— ABOARD PLANE GK ASKED TO SIT WITH AGENT H—AGENT H REPORTS GK TALKED AT LENGTH ABOUT MORALITY.

29 May 1970 (cont.). After sleeping seventeen out of twenty-three hours to remedy jet lag, Kenton asked to visit Disneyland. Wm. refused. 1410 hours: Kenton departed the hotel for Newport Beach. 1528: Rendezvous 4—Kenton took a notched quarter into Room 66 of the Newporter Inn. 1557: An agitated Kenton emerged with a sealed envelope bearing the Newporter Inn's return address, which he placed in the special pouch. 1602: "GK demands to be driven north along Coast—Wm. grants permission." 1909: At the Pierpont Inn in Ventura, "GK becomes physically ill—runs to men's room— when Agent K arrives GK is vomiting." Back to the Beverly Wilshire at 2038, where Wm. decided no doctor was needed; Kenton asked for a bottle of Scotch, got it, and drank until he passed out at 2241. SUMMARY—GK SERIOUSLY DISTURBED BY RDVZ—GK HAS NO FEVER—ILLNESS AT RESTAURANT APPARENTLY EMOTIONAL—REQUEST FOR WHISKEY SURPRISING SINCE INTAKE TO DATE ONE DAILY PRE-DINNER DRINK—WM. BELIEVES GK'S BEHAVIOR PARTLY TRAUMA OF RDVZ, PARTLY CUMULATIVE TRIP PRESSURES.

30 May 1970. Kenton allowed to sleep until 1120 hours. 1132: He threw up. 1408: After refusing a trip to Disneyland, he began drinking again. 1945: He vomited again. 2018: Kenton passed out; Wm. immediately called Blair. SUMMARY—G. AND WM. AGREE GK SUCCUMBING CUMULATIVE TRIP PRESSURES—VIEWLY GK'S AFFECTION FOR AGENT H, WM. CHANGING AGENT ROTATION SO AGENT H CAN BABY-SIT GK DURING WAKING HOURS SUPPLEMENTARY TO ON-DUTY TEAMS—G. APPROVES BONUS PAYMENT TO AGENT H.

31 May 1970. 1210 hours: Kenton flown by chartered plane from Los Angeles to Las Vegas. 1532: Rendezvous 5—Kenton took a notched half-dollar into Room 810 of the Desert Inn. 1655: He emerged with a sealed envelope bearing the Desert Inn's return address, which he placed in the special pouch. A chartered plane back to Los Angeles, arrive the Beverly Wilshire at 2005. 2009: Kenton began drinking again. 2115: He asked Agent H, his newfound "friend," to join him in Bible reading. 2235: Agent H raced into the bathroom to wrestle away the razor Kenton had at his wrist. Wm. sedated Kenton to sleep. SUMMARY—DETERIORATION SEEMS IRREVERSIBLE—WM. TO TAKE ALL MEASURES TO HOLD GK (AND MISSION) TOGETHER FOUR MORE DAYS.

1 June 1970. The 1015 Pan Am flight from Los Angeles to Rio de Janeiro; at the Guatemala City stopover Agent H notified Wm. Kenton composing a long letter. SUMMARY—WM. ASKS AGENT H TO ACT AS GK'S CONFESSOR—WM: ALSO ARRANGING TO ISOLATE AGENT H FROM OTHER AGENTS—TACTIC RISKY BUT UNAVOIDABLE IF MISSION IS TO RUN TO END.

2 June 1970. After check-in at the Copacabana Palace Hotel, Kenton refused lunch and continued to write. 1510 hours: Kenton demanded to see Wm., whom he handed a "bulky sealed envelope addressed 'Miss Henrietta Kenton' (see address above)—GK orders it posted or he will abort mission." A frantic call to Blair, then Wm. accompanied Kenton to a post office, where Kenton personally mailed the letter. But even as Kenton returned to the hotel, two of Wm.'s agents hit the post office: "Agent L gives postmaster $50 U.S. to retrieve letter 'inadvertently' mailed by friend—in full view Agent K, Agent L burns sealed envelope." That night Wm. "dismisses all Agents except Agent H—to insure prompt departure Brazil, Wm. promises $1,000 bonus to each Agent telegraphing Wm. from continental U.S. by 2000 hours, 4 June." SUMMARY—TO GUARANTEE GK'S LETTER DESTROYED UNREAD, WM. ASSIGNS AGENTS C AND F TO SURVEIL AGENTS K AND L—GK AT PEACE AFTER POSTING LETTER—PHYSICAL CONDITION OF GK ALARMING VIEWLY MINIMAL FOOD INTAKE SINCE 29 MAY—AGENT H AND WM. TO SHARE GUARD DUTY, WITH GK SEDATED AT NIGHT.

3 June 1970. 0315 hours: Kenton awoke with a high fever; Wm. gave him aspirins and a sedative. 0759: Kenton awakened; he threw up breakfast. 1000: Messenger 1—Kenton exchanged the envelope with the Okura Hotel return address for the notched quarter. Kenton's fever shot to 104 degrees, he threw up lunch—consommé and dry toast—then passed out. 1415: He was reawakened. 1500: Messenger 2—Kenton exchanged the envelope with the Plaza-Athénée return address for the notched dime. 1518: Kenton collapsed. 1915: He was reawakened. 2000: Messenger 3—Kenton exchanged the envelope with the Newporter Inn return address for the notched nickel. 2022: Kenton's fever 105 degrees; he fell asleep without sedation at 2037. SUMMARY—SIX (6) OF 11 DISMISSED AGENTS

RESPONDING FROM U.S. WITH ANSWER-BACK TELEGRAMS—GK'S FEVER UNABATED BY ASPIRIN.

4 June 1970.

0720	GK awakes himself—fever broken
0745	Room-service breakfast—GK devours
1000	Messenger 4 arrives—exchanges envelope with Desert Inn return address for notched penny
1035	GK and Agent H read Bible together
1235	Room-service lunch—GK eats steak, champagne—talks religion with Agent H
1500	Messenger 5 arrives—exchanges envelope with Hotel Cyrus return address for notched half-dollar.
1512	GK requests Wm. leave room—Agent H stays
1608	Wm. readmitted to room—GK chooses O.D. barbiturates—Wm. hands him vial of 12 pills—GK consumes pills with champagne—lies on bed
1642	GK asleep
1644	Wm. terminates Agent H with one (1) bullet to forehead from silencered Walther
1652	Wm. arranges room to scene of struggle—empties $8,000 of industrial-grade diamonds on floor—places Walther in GK's right hand, fires second bullet into Agent H's body—Wm. terminates GK with stab to heart—knife bearing Agent H's fingerprints left sticking in GK
1710	Wm. exits room locked with "Do Not Disturb" tag in place
1955	Wm. rec'd telegram ex-agent B—all 11 agents in U.S.
2300	Wm. departs Rio de Janeiro (Varig—coach) for New York

SUMMARY—AGENT H TERMINATED AS PROBABLE SECURITY RISK—TO SET ROBBERY/DOUBLE MURDER COVER WM. DISPENSES GK ONE (1)BARBITURATE, 11 PLACEBOS—AUTOPSY TO SHOW GK DRUGGED BUT CAPABLE REPELLING ATTACKER—GK LEFT WITH OWN ID, AGENT H LEFT WITH FALSE ID OF FRENCH NATIONAL—MISSSION ENDS WITH DELIVERY THIS REPORT TO G.

The eleventh and final sheet of Blair's bundle was undated:

Huang:

Hopeless, eh? Wm. was a resourceful guy, discreet, could have helped me live—too bad I ordered him terminated 6/8/70, the day after he hand-delivered his report. Cheers,

G.

By now my earlier resolve had vanished. Wm.'s cold-blooded report, replete with nameless men and police-blotter euphemisms and arcane abbreviations, made Graham Greene and Kafka seem optimists: whatever sins courier Kenton had committed, did he deserve such a hellish end? Worse, Blair had had these sheets, and the names of the five participants, for four years: if he'd come up empty, how could I possibly break into the daisy chain?

My options seemed meager. Just pretend there'd never been another hit attempt and return to my apartment? Beg some publication to run my unsubstantiable paranoia? Ask the authorities for protection? As I groped for answers I found myself mapping a two-phased campaign to stay alive.

Phase 1: I had to get clear.

Phase 2: When and if I got clear, I had to find some crack in Wm.'s apparently hermetic operation through which to crash the Cocktail Party.

How to get clear? I needed a temporary hiding place in New York. The Onyxx safe house; would Fanning let me use it? I needed money. Tens of thousands Harry and Pat would never spend moldered in a Swiss bank; could I tap the account? I needed false papers. A college classmate named Carl had put himself through school manufacturing IDs for Vietniks fleeing the country; was he still in business? And finally I needed a way out of the city. My credit card; had my pursuers managed to get an alert issued on it?

I launched Phase 1 by entering an Army-Navy store honoring Master Charge and selecting a surplus overcoat whose low price required no telephoned authorization. The register was near the front door. I placed the coat on the counter and handed over my plastic. Suddenly I felt a slight residual twinge in my ankle—if it came to it, could I bolt past the pudgy rent-a-cop at the door? When the salesgirl pulled out the bulletin listing bad cards I breathed easier for the dog-eared leaflet looked at least two months old; then without missing a chomp on her chewing gum she peered at a fresh sheet taped to the register. I jammed both hands into my parka pockets to hide the shaking. She coughed, glanced up, and then slid my card into the machine: I'd passed.

It took three calls to locate the Philadelphia advertising agency where Carl worked. Hi there good buddy, know of a pay phone I could ring back on? No, but he would in ten minutes. I found a fresh phone, called his office again, jotted down the number, and quickly set off for still another booth; at 11:32 A.M. we were talking safely, coin phone to coin phone. Yes, he'd fix me up with false papers, but did I want American or Canadian? Canadian. A bona fide Canadian passport was $2,000, miscellaneous support papers several hundred more, and since I was a pal his fee was $300. How long would it take? A week to ten days. Could I stay with him while I waited? Sure—the doorman would have his keys.

As soon as we rang off I dropped in another dime and dialed Datatec. I identified myself to Emmett Culver Stahl's secretary as Harry Helmsley; Stahl was on the line in fifteen seconds: "Hello, who's this?"

"Harry Helmsley."

"Who is this, please?"

"I said Harry Helmsley—why don't you believe me?"

"Cut the games, mister."

"Okay, I've got the original of the report you did for Harry."

"So?"

"Seems the CIA'd like a peek at it—they think you pissed on one of their bushes." His silence told me I might have struck a nerve. "Plus, some of your blue-chippers may be amused by the non-corporate types you sleep with, as well as the bag jobs you'll do, like the one for Helmsley. And oh, did I forget to say the press would have a field day?"

The line sounded dead. Shit, I thought, I wouldn't even get the chance to bait the hook. Then Stahl said, "I don't pay blackmail."

"'Blackmail' is such an ugly word—anyway, I don't want money, I only want you to do a simple job for me."

Come on, come on, rise to the bait... Finally, he did: "Depends on what the job may be."

"I want a photostatic copy of a particular Social Security

card. Get it for me by tomorrow morning, I hand you the original report."

Another long pause; good, he was nibbling now, for his only hope of learning my identity was to nail me when I picked up the card. "Why should I trust you?"

"No reason at all."

"Look, uh, even if I wanted to be of help, I couldn't possibly have it tomor..."

"Don't give me any of that bullshit! Yes or no?"

"I, uh... how do I know you have the report?"

"The subject's name was George Frederick Blair of Wellesley, Mass."

Stahl grunted. Patience now, patience... and then the hook was in his mouth and planted. "Okay, what's the name?"

"Patrick W. Ritchie. That's R-i-t-c-h-i-e. Male, date of birth Forty-two or early Forth-three, place of birth unknown. Last known address, as of February 1972, was Fifteen East Sixty-ninth Street, New York."

"That was Helmsley's roommate, wasn't it?" I didn't answer. "All right, where do I deliver?"

"Be at your phone at nine-thirty tomorrow morning." I hung up and left the booth. Would Stahl get the card and bring it? Probably. Would he arrive with something else up his sleeve? Certainly. Would I be able to outwit him? Maybe.

Shortly after 1 P.M. I entered the bowels of the Empire State Building. After withdrawing my material from the Michelle Films, Ltd. safe-deposit box I proceeded to a card shop on Thirty-fourth Street to Xerox Harry's aerogram, the notes of my bizarre car ride with Blair, and the eleven pages that had just arrived. Then I ducked back into the subways. I now had $1.45 left to my name.

At 2:45 P.M., from a pay phone on the uptown platform of the 72nd Street IND station, I dialed Onyxx. I told Mrs. Shipley it was an emergency; Fanning picked up in five seconds. "Yes, Ray."

"It's hit the fan and I need help. Is your line secure?"

"Hold on." I heard him ask somebody to leave his office. Then he gave me another number he said was free of taps. As I dialed it I remembered Onyxx was one of Stahl's clients— did Datatec keep this line clean? Fanning answered on the first ring.

"Sir, Blair may be dead, but whatever he was mixed up in doesn't seem to be, because there was another attempt on me yesterday. I'm okay for the moment, but . . . but I need some favors."

"Name them."

"There's some papers you should see. And I need the safe house for one or two nights."

"Hold on again." After a minute Fanning returned. "It's free through Wednesday afternoon. If you require it past then, we'll work something out."

"Through Wednesday should be fine, thanks."

"I can meet you in thirty minutes."

"When do you usually leave the office?"

"Sixish."

"I'd rather you stuck to your normal schedule—someone with a long memory might throw a tail on you. How's six-forty-five?"

"No problem. Give me a name to leave at the door."

I looked around. Some twenty feet up the subway platform two Hispanic teen-agers were scarfing up a box of Kentucky Fried Chicken so I said, "Arthur, first initial 'P' as in Peter. See you in four hours."

I should have left the booth then but I didn't. Was I tempted to call Martha because with her intimate knowledge of all that had gone before she might be able to offer some telling insights? Perhaps. Or was it because, being plugged into a data bank and an international communications system with few rivals, she might be of long-distance help? Perhaps. Or was it because I not only cared, I cared a hell of a lot? Probably. But what dangers might I be exposing her to? The second hand of my watch crept full circle and still I couldn't act. If the next train into the station is an uptown, I decided, I call; if it is a downtown, I don't. I heard the rumble and then I saw the lights. Downtown—but I dropped in the dime anyway, dialed JU 6-1212, and asked for the researcher who sat in the cubicle next to Martha's.

"Erika? It's Ray Huang. Hey, I know this is kind of off the wall, but could I talk to Martha on your line?"

"Have you been drinking?"

"Yup."

"Thought so. Okay, let me go get her." The receiver clunked against the desk. Then Martha was saying, "Hello?"

"Hi, it's me."

"This isn't amusing, Ray."

"It's not meant to be. They tried to kill me again."

"What!"

"Yeah, yesterday. I..."

"God damn it, can't they nail Blair now?"

"Blair's been dead for over a month. It...it's way too complicated to explain over the phone. Look, I called to say..."

"You need help."

"Yes, but..."

"I can look after myself, thank you, or I wouldn't have offered. Hello, Ray, are you still there?"

"Yeah. Damn it Martha, I want to say thanks, but the risk's too great and I love you too much so goodbye, but I...I guess I need you."

Three beats, and she came back in her tough-cookie drawl: "You do have a way with tender emotions. Now cut the shit, how can I help?"

I gave her Fanning's bug-free number and told her to arrange a ride with him. "Oh, I almost forgot. Do you have any, uh, social engagements tonight?"

"Sure, Joe Namath, but don't worry, he's easy to cancel."

"Look, we haven't seen each other in a long time, but they might remember. I don't want you breaking your patterns."

"Sorry. No, I've got nothing on tonight. Except you."

I unfurled the ski cap into a balaclava and, face covered, pushed through the exit gate and climbed to Central Park West. The sun was a sickly yellow disk in the grey winter sky. Once upon a time not so very long ago, I'd trusted with my mind but not my heart. That had reversed: now I embraced Martha and Fanning with my heart, but part of my mind trusted no one; it was this part that demanded that I watch the Dakota before, during, and after their arrival. I crossed to the east side of the street and found a spot behind the wall that afforded me a clear view of the building's arched entrance.

At 3:30 P.M. children began straggling home from school.

At 5:15 P.M. dusk fell and with it the temperature, but at least I could move around without fear of notice. As lights winked on I checked the ninth-floor windows of the safe house. They remained dark.

At 5:40 P.M. the last of the curbside slots filled so I stumbled from my vantage point to inspect every parked car within four blocks. All were empty. But now cabs swarmed to the building's entrance to deposit the bacon-bringers and now cars started to double-park on the streets. I studied the vehicular confusion and sighed; why didn't thriller writers ever describe the difficulties and frustrations of a real-life stakeout?

At 6:39 P.M. the Mercedes 600 glided up, its rear-window curtains drawn. I scanned the streets: no suspicious cars idled nearby. A minute passed, but neither Clarence nor the Dakota's doorman was helping the passengers out; then another minute and still no movement and now I began shivering from more than the cold. Suddenly the doorman popped through the arched entrance and in his wake a tall, patrician gentleman—what the fuck was Harris Knox doing here? The windows of 9-C were still dark. The lawyer ambled past the two oversized carriage lights on the side of the building; now he was at the limousine, now he was in it, and now the Mercedes was U-turning on 72nd Street and swinging downtown on Central Park West.

My balaclava was wet with sweat. Cars and cabs continued to pull up to the Dakota but none disgorged Fanning or Martha. Perhaps they'd slipped in by a back way? No, the windows were still dark. Finally I pulled out the silver in my pocket: four quarters, a dime, and a nickel, just enough to start me on my escape route, but what if it was a double cross and what if Martha was in danger? A fresh wave of nausea swept me as I realized there was only one way to find out.

At 7:16 P.M. I uncurled from my sanctuary and flapped my arms and stamped my feet to chase the numbness. I hadn't smoked since dusk but there the telltale glow of a cigarette wouldn't matter. There was only one left in my pack... Then, playing the amateur professional to the last, I canvassed the double-parked cars in the area. Nothing suspicious. One last drag, butt into the gutter, and I stepped from the womblike blackness past the two oversized carriage lights and through the archway.

The doorman swung the door open. "Yes, sir."

"My name's Peter Arthur."

He glanced at his clipboard. "Apartment 9-C? This way."

When the elevator door slid shut I peeled off the balaclava. The car clattered upward, its paneled walls pressing in on me like a vise. I hopped out on nine and walked slowly down the hall. Which of these unmarked doors was the fire escape, and would I have time to get to it? And then I reached 9-C; there's still time, I thought, but I knew there wasn't so I gingerly pressed the bell.

Without a sound the door whipped open and Fanning was standing there with startled eyes: "Jesus!" and now he was grabbing at one sleeve and yanking me inside and as I crossed the threshold I spun from his grasp and cocked both fists chest-high—and that's when I saw Martha pressed against a corridor wall, trembling like a stalked doe.

I lowered my hands and began to breathe again. We stood rooted there, Martha and I, everything and nothing passing between us, until finally I found my voice. "Hi."

"Hi yourself."

"We were worried," Fanning said.

"I was outside when Clarence drove up. Then Knox came out, and the windows up here stayed dark, so I figured something had come apart."

"You weren't the one we hoped to deceive."

"Then you are under surveillance."

"No, Clarence called a few minutes ago. We're clean. But we didn't know it then, so we took a cab and entered through the service entrance. Harris was good enough to act the decoy."

The lights were on in the living room but dark velvet had been jerry-rigged as blackout drapes on this side of the shutters. Two cigarettes smoldered in an ashtray already half filled with butts. I withdrew Blair's packet and the transcript of our car conversation from my overcoat: "These'll explain everything better than I can." Fanning took them and walked Martha to a couch; I made for the bar.

Finally Fanning cleared his throat and flexed his neck muscles. As he shook out another Chesterfield Martha put down the last page and wrapped her arms around her chest. I settled into a chair opposite them and said, "Could Blair have gotten away with it?"

"Perhaps." Fanning flicked the tobacco shreds from his tongue. When he began massaging the scar on his right temple he suddenly looked sixty-four. "With a fifty-million-dollar line of credit perhaps it would have worked. Damn it, this mess is all my fault."

"Come on, what could you have done..."

"Mr. Blair's cover-up—it hinges on his cock-and-bull about the reasons behind Dr. Helmsley's death. I should have investigated further, especially after our meeting with General Harmer. I..."

"That's history now," Martha interrupted. When Fanning and I turned she had a no-nonsense look on her face. "Let's stop the *mea culpas* and figure out a way to get Ray off the hook."

Fanning smiled wearily. "You're quite right, my dear. The trouble is we probably lack the evidence a reputable magazine, such as yours, would need to print Ray's story. Yet, I'm afraid the press is our only hope." Martha looked puzzled so he explained, "Mr. Blair never spells out the links between the White House, the CIA, and himself. Judging from this material, though, it would certainly seem foolhardy to ask the federal government for help." He stubbed out his cigarette. "Ray, I'd like to use Onyxx facilities to check some of the points raised in these pages. For instance, was there a Mr. Kenton; did he die in Rio; were the hotel rooms occupied on the dates mentioned, and, if so, by whom." I nodded. "Good, I'll make my calls now. If you two can work a microwave oven, there's food in the freezer."

We'd found steaks in the walk-in freezer and popped them in the commercial-sized oven before Martha said, "Ray, why did you call? I would have killed you if you hadn't, but it's been half a year."

"Because..." I couldn't repeat the magic word. "Because I got the impression the last time we talked that you'd found your prince. And if you didn't, well, telephones work both ways."

"*Touché*." She picked a cuticle. "What happened was my prince turned into a frog, and his warts were bigger than yours."

"I'm flattered you learned one of my tricks." Martha looked up. "A great backhanded compliment—thank you."

She laughed.

By the time we carried the dinners into the living room Fanning had finished his phoning; answers were due by 4 P.M. the next day. Then as we ate we began to sift through my papers for clues to the guest list of the Cocktail Party. It was like a parlor game, except that the prize was life or death— mine. We gradually evolved three assumptions. First, the nationality of each of the five conspirators was foreshadowed by the code name Blair had assigned him. Second, each had the financial resources to gamble ten million dollars. Third, each occupied a high but vulnerable position—why else require a damning confession to seal membership? Finally we formulated some educated guesses.

Bourbon and the man he'd forced Blair to include, Velveeta, were both American. There were more than enough moneyed Americans to choose from, but in scanning the list of courier rendezvous sites Fanning fixed on the Desert Inn; our most bashful billionaire, one whose fortune was founded on oil-drilling rigs, might still have lived there in 1970. "If he's Bourbon, Velveeta's got to be our friend in the White House," I said. "God knows they've been chummy enough in the past. And look at my experiences with Washington—and isn't Newport Beach near San Clemente?" Fanning disagreed. "He doesn't have a million to his name, much less ten million to invest in something like this. And when he's at the compound, he rarely leaves except to golf. It'd be damned hard for him to make a motel rendezvous with his entourage and the press corps." But when I asked for a likelier candidate, he was stumped. Martha broke the logjam by phoning a friend working the lobster shift in Edit Ref and firing off two quick queries.

Caviar could be either Russian or Iranian; we decided Iranian, because of the courier rendezvous in Shiraz. Fanning dryly noted that if we were correct the man's identity posed no mystery, for in that tight monarchy, who would dare such a scheme except the monarch?

Ouzo was Greek. There'd been no courier rendezvous in that country, but surely Blair's choice of the Plaza-Athénée in Paris had been no coincidence. What's more, Fanning said, that hotel was the French base for several leading Greek shippers—who were of course among the world's prime transporters of oil. Which tycoon? Fanning thought it could be any of five.

And Sake was Japanese. But here the Rice Paper Curtain cloaking that country's movers and shakers stumped even Fanning: we came up empty.

Then the phone rang; it was Martha's friend in Edit Ref. The bashful billionaire we suspected was Bourbon had indeed been holed up at the Desert Inn in 1970. My candidate for Velveeta had not only been in California the last weekend in May 1970, but on the twenty-ninth he and his faithful Sancho Panza had taken an unexpected drive up the Coast—and Newport Beach lay north of San Clemente.

Fanning began to massage his scar again. Finally he looked at his watch and saw it was almost 11 P.M. "If you'd like, I'll stay with you tonight."

"Thanks, sir, but I doubt if it'd do either of us any good."

"If we draw blanks tomorrow, I trust you have a plan." I nodded. "Good. I knew you would. There's food here—what about money."

I hadn't planned on borrowing from him, but suppose Stahl didn't come through with the Social Security card? And then I realized even if he did, I needed fast money to pay Carl for the false papers. I asked Fanning for five thousand dollars in small bills.

"You can have more."

"No thanks, but I'll take two more favors." I handed him the envelope containing all my data on Harry. "Would you stick this, and the material you read tonight, in some deep-cover safe-deposit box that Martha can have access to? Great. Now this one's tougher. I've got to pick up a package tomorrow, but I can't let the party sending it learn who I am." Fanning lit a Chesterfield, then rattled off a plan so foolproof I had to grin. "That's absolutely brilliant, sir—how do you know about things like 'dead drops'?"

He chuckled. "You said it yourself the first time we met, son—big business isn't the nicest of all worlds." After we'd hashed out the details Fanning gave me his home and limousine phone numbers as well as a code to let me know it was either him or Martha calling the safe house. Then he turned to her. "May I offer you a ride, dear."

"No, I'll stay a little longer, Frew." Her use of his nickname surprised me, as did her blush.

Not until Martha and I had seen Fanning out the door did I finally understand her blush and her familiarity: "You've gone out with him."

"Yes. He phoned me just after the first of the year. His wife was out on the Coast, he was working late, could he buy me dinner." She smiled ruefully. "His heart wasn't really in it, and anyway I spent most of the evening...I spent most of the evening talking about you."

"Aw, shucks." As I started to loop a platonic arm around her she edged away skittishly and snuggled into a wing chair. I brought over nightcaps and sat opposite her. I'd forgotten how fine Martha looked when she was a touch haggard. And then I found myself musing that if her prince had turned into a frog, why hadn't she been in touch? Or for that matter why hadn't I kept calling? Probably mutual sutbbornness... To break the growing silence I said, "Jesus, I hope there's an alarm clock here."

Martha kept working on her cuticle. "I have to give you the pay phone numbers and the voucher code. I might as well make it a wake-up call."

"Great."

"Ray..."

"What?" I answered, a beat too fast.

"Nothing." She finished the last of her drink, uncurled from the wing chair, and stretched.

I lowered my eyes to my glass. "If I get out of this in one piece, kid, you're going to find me camping on your doorstep again."

Hearing no response I looked up. Martha stood stock-still; a vein pulsed in her parchment-white neck. Now she unconsciously moistened her lips and slowly drew her left hand to her breasts. A tear welled. As it spilled down her cheek she started to tremble so I rose and crossed to her and took her in my arms. "Hey, hey, what is it?"

I could feel her shaking her head into my chest and then sobbing she plastered herself to me and now her fright was so contagious I clutched tighter. Suddenly we were at each other's buttons and zippers and belts and now she was falling half-naked and spread-legged onto the couch and pulling me atop her. The moment was too fraught for any act save one so I rolled my thighs between hers and rocketed along that comfortably familiar route up into her, and as I plunged through to the underbelly so silken and warm and moist I sensed home. Her head snapped back on my thrust and from the beautiful throat now exposed issued sounds I'd almost forgotten. Thrust mated with counterthrust, once more and again and again and now an exquisite quiver; down came the ultimate stroke and now I was exploding and dying and even as the numbness set she flushed and gasped and her thighs became a tourniquet whose fierce pinch hurt but was delicious; then, ever so slowly, she sagged back into the cushions, with me melted on top of her.

Martha began to giggle.

"What's so funny?"

"Congratulations, we've won the refrigerator on *Beat the Clock*." Her laughs turned to shivers as I grazed a fingernail lightly up her thigh. A contented snuffle, and she started caressing my back and nuzzling my neck. Her breath was soft as a kitten's. Finally Martha whispered, "Hey, I think we missed something the last time around."

I undid the last few buttons of her blouse. "Like this?"

"Mmmmm. And this."

Was it better without fear, without urgency, without haste? Maybe.

It was after midnight when we walked to the apartment door. "I know why I can't stay tonight, Ray, but... but at least I'm sending this soldier off in style."

Then we both realized the implications of her jest so we clung to each other a while longer and then Martha gave me a peck on the cheek and was gone.

29 January 1974: New York

At 8:30 A.M. one ring, followed by silence. After the fifth ring of the second series I picked up: it was Martha with the pay phone numbers and the cab company voucher code.

At 9:29 A.M. I dialed Stahl.

"Did you get it?"

"Yes."

"Good. Take this down fast, because I'm not giving you time to trace this call. I'm running you through a simple drill to make sure you don't plant tails on yourself."

"I assure you I wou..."

"Humor me, Stahl, humor me. I want you carrying the goods inside a Bloomingdale's shopping bag, and I want you wearing a red ski cap..."

"I don't have a red ski cap."

"Then get one! Be on the northwest corner of Sixtieth and Lexington at eleven-fifty-five. A cab'll come by looking for a man with a red cap and a bag. Give your name, get in, and then keep your mouth shut. When he says, 'Here we are,' you'll see a phone booth. Leave the shopping bag in the cab so he doesn't think you're beating the fare, then go to the booth. I'll call with the final destination. Got it?"

He read back the instructions.

"Right. A friend's watching the booth, so any tricks, your ass is dead."

Next I phoned Dial-a-Cab, a fleet of radio-dispatched taxis. I identified myself as Mr. Newcomb of 545 Madison Avenue, ensured service with the Time Inc. voucher code, and then spelled out my instructions for the pickup of a red-capped associate named Stahl. "And listen, tell the driver if he makes it to my building by twelve-thirty, there's an extra fifteen bucks in it for him."

The dispatcher laughed. "Mr. Newcomb, for that kinda bread, you be ready at twelve-twenty-five."

At 12:13 P.M., through a barely cracked shutter, I saw the radio-dispatched Checker cruising up Central Park West start to slow. Back down the avenue a black Ford also slowed. When the cab reached 72nd Street it pulled to the curb on the southeast corner. On the northwest corner both pay booths stood vacant. The black Ford had taken station four blocks away; close enough to screw up the plan? No. I lifted the receiver and began to dial. Now the driver turned to speak to his passenger. I dialed the seventh and last digit. As Stahl hopped from the cab, he heard the phone ringing so he slammed the door shut and sprinted into the intersection and now I heard the squeal of the Checker's tires from nine floors up as the cabby peeled a quick right into Central Park—he only had sixteen minutes left to earn that fifteen dollars. And now Stahl was stopped dead in the middle of the street; a honk as a station wagon swerved around him but he kept swiveling his head from the vanishing cab to the black Ford. The indecision cost him his only chance at pursuit, and Stahl must have realized it for he ripped off the red ski cap and dashed it to the pavement. I gently replaced my receiver. Through the leafless trees of the park I could see the Checker already well along the winding drive en route to "Mr. Newcomb," who was being impersonated by Fanning's chauffeur, Clarence.

At 2:20 P.M. the doorbell of the safe house rang. When I got to the vestibule I saw the four envelopes that had been wedged under the door. The three thick envelopes held five thousand dollars in used bills, none larger than a fifty. The thin envelope held a photostatic copy of Pat Ritchie's Social Security card. Stahl must really be scared of his report on Blair, I concluded as I went to fetch my contacts of Harry's microfilm.

There was a typewriter in one conference room. I rolled in two sheets of paper and began:

> January 29, 1974
>
> Herr Adolf Zeiss
> Leclair & Cie
> Geneva, Switzerland
> Dear Herr Zeiss: *In re*: Acct. No. H4–982
>   Please immediately remit to Mr. P. Arthur, c/o American Express, Istanbul, the following: a) the sum of $20,000 U.S.; b) the envelope in our safe-deposit box bearing the return address "Datatec, 666 Fifth Avenue, New York." Kindly instruct Istanbul that *in lieu of presenting his passport*, Mr. Arthur will identify himself by answering this question: "What is in the glass cage?" The answer: "A chicken." I must repeat, Mr. Arthur is *not* to be asked for his passport. Thank you for your attention.
>   Sincerely,
>   PATRICK W. RITCHIE
>   123-34-2421

I twirled the paper out of the machine and took the top sheet to a glass coffee table under which I set a lamp. I laid the Social Security photostat atop the glass, positioned my letter over the card, and traced Pat Ritchie's signature in place. Then I addressed the envelope and, to be safe, stuck on way too many stamps.

Credit card, forger, now the letter to Leclair & Cie: the instruments for Phase 1 were lined up. Would I have to use them?

At 5:20 P.M. Fanning called. "Ray, I'm afraid it looks bad."

He was right. Geoffrey Kenton, a middle-level British Intelligence liaison to NATO, had unexpectedly resigned on Friday, May 22, 1970; by the time MI-5 received his notice the following Monday, he'd vanished without a trace. MI-5 immediately interrogated Kenton's sole surviving relative, a teenage daughter named Henrietta. She stated that her father had taken on a courier assignment, and would be home in June. On June 5, 1970, Interpol notified MI-5 that Kenton had been killed in Rio. The efforts of British Intelligence to reconstruct the missing two weeks were for naught; all they learned was that he'd been in Tokyo on May 28, and that fact only because a grief-stricken Henrietta had shown them her father's last letter, the one accompanying the binoculars. The investigation was currently inactive but technically open: MI-5 believed Henrietta innocent of her father's activities, but no one could explain the mysterious Swiss trust fund, administered by Leclair & Cie, that now supported her studies at Oxford.

In Rio, Fanning continued, his man had ascertained that on June 4, 1970, a British diamond courier named Geoffrey Kenton had died of stabbing in his room at the Copacabana Palace, but not before shooting to death his assailant, a Frenchman named Yves Boisset. Wm.'s trick had worked perfectly; Rio police considered the case open-and-shut.

Finally, from the five rendezvous cities, Onyxx agents had reported that each of the suites mentioned in Wm.'s report had been rented on the dates mentioned, but always under a name that was the local equivalent of "Smith." "So we know the daisy-chain blackmail probably occurred," Fanning concluded. "Unfortunately, we seem no closer to breaking into the chain."

"It does look kind of bleak, doesn't it? Any suggestions?"

"Son, I had a long talk with Harris this morning. We agreed the rot in Washington notwithstanding, most of the Justice bureaucracy is honest as hell. Harris is certain we can arrange protection and a thorough investigation of your material."

Fanning's selflessness stunned me: by going to Justice, much of Onyxx's Asian machinations would be, if not public, then on the record, which was close enough. "Would you take that route, sir?"

"I don't know." He sounded suddenly tired.

"Are you reachable this evening?"

"Chris and I have ballet tickets. I can cancel..."

"No, I'll call you afterward. And... and sir, no matter which way I jump, thank you."

At 6:50 P.M. I dialed Erika's number. Martha answered on the first ring. When I'd briefed her on Fanning's report and outlined his option we fell silent. Finally she said, "Well?"

"I've been sitting here for the last hour thinking that the odds are Justice can protect me, and that perhaps they can crack the case. But suppose they can't. They'd gradually lose heart, someone'd get careless, and that would be that. I know I've been lucky, Martha, but for the last two days I've listened to my instincts, and I'm still alive. Now the instincts say run, run and fight another day." When she didn't respond I pressed: "Don't dummy up on me now, kid, I've got to have your thoughts."

"I think you should trust your instincts," she whispered. Then she blew her nose. "Take care of yourself."

"You too. I'll be in touch when I'm safe. Hey—I must have been a real asshole last year to let you go, because... because I love you."

"Your usual exquisite timing," she said huskily.

"Yeah. See you around, kid," and I broke the connection.

They'd expect me to bolt so all air, rail, and bus terminals would be under surveillance; it'd take an army, though, to cover all roadways connecting Manhattan to the rest of the United States, as well as all car-rental offices. But I couldn't afford to drop a car in Philadelphia, not if Carl wouldn't have my papers for another week... Then I hit upon a solution that might even pay a bonus; by now the travel agencies were closed, so I began searching for the Yellow Pages.

At 10:35 P.M. the Lincoln Center box office said the ballet curtain had fallen. I dialed the mobile operator and had her patch me into Fanning's limousine.

"Yes."

"Hi, it's me. Thanks for presenting the option, but I'll pass."

"I, uh, I didn't speak earlier because I didn't want to influence you. But you've made the decision I would have... stay in touch, son, and Godspeed."

30 January 1974: New York/Washington/Miami/Philadelphia

At 8:10 A.M. I descended to the lobby of the Dakota, mailed the letter to Leclair & Cie, and hailed a cab.

At 8:25 A.M. I entered the Hertz office at 76th Street off York; the Mercury Cougar went on my Master Charge. Four hours and ten minutes later I returned the car—at National Airport in Washington.

At 1:45 P.M. I stepped to the Varig counter; the one-way ticket slugged Washington/Miami/Caracas went on my Master

Charge. Thirty-five minutes later the gate clerk tore the top coupon from my ticket and passed me aboard.

At 5:45 P.M. I crossed from the Miami International transit lounge to the Eastern counter; the one-way ticket north did not go on my Master Charge. Three hours later I stepped from the 727 onto the tarmac at Philadelphia International and smiled. Not only had I worked my way to Carl, but I'd laid one damned fine false scent, one that'd look the work of a panicky oaf.

4 February 1974: Philadelphia

After dinner Carl began unpacking the oversize Korvette's shopping bag he'd brought home. First he pulled out barbering implements; when he handed me a mirror ten minutes later I winced at the scalp shining through the crew cut and the semicircle of white above each ear. Next he produced a pair of absurdly ugly eyeglass frames fitted with plain glass lenses; when I put them on I looked like a just-landed immigrant. Now he dredged up a secondhand polyester sports coat, a cheap dress shirt, and a skinny tie; when I put these on I looked like a just-landed immigrant who'd come steerage. Then Carl snapped a roll of black-and-white head shots, ordering a smile for some, a frown for others, and an impassive stare for the rest. After developing the film in his bathroom lab he selected a frame in which I sported a constipated smile.

"What about a name, Ray?"

"I'm still working on it."

"Using these papers long?"

"I don't know—why?"

"If it's for more than a one-shot, go with your real first name. That way, if somebody calls from across a room, you'll respond automatically."

Jesus, surviving underground wasn't going to be easy, I thought, but I was learning, I was learning.

6 February 1974: Philadelphia

Everyone was staring. That's what it felt like as I made my way through the bitterly cold streets in heed of Carl's suggestion that I lose my self-consciousness over the new haircut and the glasses. He was right: my first half hour downtown would have given a blind security guard pause.

When I had my nerves under control I entered a Market Street men's store to buy a drab but highly serviceable wardrobe, then a pawnshop to redeem a nicely worn suitcase. I cabbed out to Philadelphia International Airport with the packed suitcase, left it in the checkroom, and headed back to Carl's.

At 11:14 P.M., as we were watching the late news for details of the bizarre kidnapping of newspaper heiress Patricia Hearst, the phone rang once, then three times, then once more. Carl took $2,600 from me and disappeared into the night.

He was back in ninety minutes.

Inside the plastic American Express passport billfold he tossed me were: a Toronto library card, blank; a Canadian driver's license, blank; an international driver's license, blank; an American Express card, blank; and a Canadian passport, blank.

7 February 1974: Philadelphia

After calling in sick to his office Carl eased up two parquet flooring squares. Though the recess between the studs was dusty the black leather bag he withdrew wasn't. "What's the name going to be, Ray?" When I didn't answer he glanced up. "Come on, write it down so I get the spelling right."

I felt so guilty I had to look away. "I'd rather keep it to myself."

"Jesus H. Christ," he said softly. "I put you up, I keep my old lady out of the house for a week, I put heat on to get the shit fast, and now you won't give me the fucking name."

I made myself meet his glare. "It's not a matter of trust, Carl—right now you're the only one who knows where I am. But there's a contract out on me, and when I cut out, I prefer to leave the snow unbroken."

He stood and walked to a window. Two minutes later he sighed and began. Carl worked partly on an IBM Selectric, changing typing balls to suit the document, and partly with an impressive array of rubber validation stamps. It was late afternoon before he finally called me over to review his masterpieces. "Use this ball to type your name on this." He passed me the Toronto library card. Then came the Canadian driver's license. "And this ball's for this. Carry the license in your trouser pockets until it ages some; it's supposed to be eighteen months old."

"Is this Toronto address real?"

"It's a flophouse near the station." He handed me the international driver's license. "This is for if you really have to drive. Get in a hairy accident, though, and it'll do you diddly—stall with it, but get ready to call the American Embassy."

"You mean the Canadians."

"I mean our guys. The Canucks see these papers, they'll bail you out just so they can toss you into their own slammer." Carl pointed to the American Express card and then to an embossing machine. "Set your name into that groove and stamp the card. Again, for extreme emergencies only—if you use it, chuck it immediately. AmEx's damned good at nailing bad cards." Finally he handed me the passport in which he'd forged a departure frank from Toronto and an arrival frank at Kennedy Airport to show I'd entered the States legally. "The number on here's live. There's a slim chance it's been declared bad, or that the real one'll show up at the same airport the same day, but it's safer than me making one up. Now, I wouldn't go into Canada or any Canadian Embassy waving these pieces around, but elsewhere they'll pass so long as nobody's suspicious. Fuck up, though, and you are real naked."

After we'd double-checked which typing ball I'd use on which document I said, "Let me stand dinner out tonight."

"Fuck you, Huang." He drew on his coat and stomped to the door. "I'm spending the night at my old lady's. I'll want to stash this gear—can you be out of here by eight in the morning?" I nodded. "The passport negs're still in the bathroom—don't forget to destroy them. And don't forget to sign all the papers." And then he was gone.

For the same camouflaging reasons I'd chosen the name "Ozu Kurosawa" to cosign Duke's safe-deposit box, I now selected another Japanese *nom de guerre*: Tetsuo R. Sasaki. When I completed the documents I destroyed the carbon-ribbon cartridge from the typewriter and the strip of passport negatives. Then I went from room to room with a dustcloth; by the time I finished wiping, there was no proof I'd ever been in Carl's apartment. Finally I left three hundred dollars in an envelope on Carl's bed and cabbed it to the combat zone. Just before entering a five-dollar-a-night hotel, I bought a pint of brandy in the hope it would keep me from calling Martha one last time. It did.

8 February 1974: Philadelphia/Bermuda/En route to London

When the midmorning Eastern Airlines flight through Baltimore landed Bermuda I lingered until a queue had formed at the immigration station before joining it. My passport felt like a Cracker Jack premium but the bored inspector behind the counter never even looked up as he stamped it. Inside the terminal I squeezed into a pay phone from which I could see the British Airways clerk answering my call: yes, seats were available on their 10:25 flight that evening. Rather than hang around the lobby for half a day I bused into Hamilton and sat through *Five Fingers of Death* twice. At 9:10 P.M. I was back at the airport counting out the money for my ticket. An hour and a half later the British Airways VC-10 roared aloft and banked eastward over the Atlantic on its way to London.

18 February 1974: Istanbul

The mug of sweet, silted coffee and the hard roll were set on my table as soon as I entered, for Rauf, the proprietor of the blue-collar café near my flophouse, had come to accept me as a morning regular.

Why Istanbul? First, none of the Cocktail Party appeared to be Turkish. Second, from Yesilkoy Airport I could bolt to virtually any part of the world on any given day. Third, the city's shopping bargains attracted jumbo jetloads of Japanese, and to Western eyes there was little difference between their kind and mine. This had been driven home a week ago on my first visit to Rauf's—after I'd declined his offer of a string of amber beads, he'd shrugged and given me my change with a hearty *"Arrigato."* To be sure there were other cities in which I could have enjoyed equal anonymity, but I'd chosen Istanbul.

And what had I done since arriving from London? Pored over Wm.'s report, rehashing courier Kenton's last fortnight until my dreams had become a hellish montage of his life and mine: as my body slept my mind's eye saw airports and Martha and typewriters and notched coins; Fanning and courier pouches and birding binoculars and Blair; hotel suites and naked men and subway stations and penny-arcade chickens. Slowly I'd developed two long-shot leads. Before I could pursue them, though, I needed to replenish my all but exhausted coffers.

At 9:15 A.M. I again phoned American Express. The room tilted: Harry's Swiss account was still active—the remittance from Leclair had just arrived. I hurried back to my flophouse to fetch my suitcase but I told the clerk to hold me a room, I'd be returning in the late afternoon. The bus trundled through the narrow streets of the Old City down to the Golden Horn, then across the Galata Bridge and up the hill to Taksim Square. There I booked into the Park, the dowager of the city's first-class hotels.

The Istanbul American Express office was a half mile away, in the lobby of the Hilton. I located the manager, gave my name as "Peter Arthur," and I said I was expecting a remittance. When he found the correspondence from Leclair he frowned. I didn't blame him; the instructions were most irregular. But then it wasn't his money.

"Ahem. What is it that is in the glass cage?"

"A chicken."

"How do you wish the money?"

"In cash—dollars U.S."

His frown deepened. "Do you think this is advisable?"

"I'd like it in cash, please." Of course I didn't, but I had to launder the money, and if he glimpsed my passport as I purchased traveler's checks, the Leclair-to-P. Arthur-to-Tetsuo R. Sasaki connection would be there for the finding.

It took him several seconds to overcome his banker's instincts. Then he passed me the envelope containing the original Datatec report and led me to the teller's window; as I watched the twenty thousand dollars being counted out I could feel his eyes X-raying my back.

I made myself stroll through the Hilton lobby and out the long, curving driveway before looking over my shoulder. Nobody had followed; now to unload the cash. I knew I'd raise suspicions by buying all the traveler's checks at one place, so I went first to the Barclay's down the block. There, under the name Sasaki, I purchased five thousand dollars' worth. And then, because it's a Chinese custom to go out with a clean slate,

I bought a five-thousand-dollar money order payable to Franklin R. Fanning. Next to a bank selling First National City checks for another five thousand dollars' worth; I also changed five hundred dollars into Turkish liras, giving as my local address not the flophouse in the Old City but the Park. Finally I dawdled among the fancy shops on Istiklal until 12:15 P.M., when I phoned American Express and asked for the manager. As I'd hoped, he was out to lunch, so I went back to the Hilton and converted the remaining forty-five hundred dollars.

The remittance was now safe, liquid, and clean, and my false papers had passed the acid test of acceptability: end of Phase 1, I was clear.

I immediately launched Phase 2 by persuading an agent in the American Express travel bureau to sell me a back copy of the *Official Airline Guide*, the two-inch-thick directory listing worldwide airline schedules.

The deskman at the Park commiserated when I told him I had to check out because of new marching orders from my company. In fact I craved the urbanity of the Park, but it and its entire ritzy neighborhood were the logical haunts of those I sought to avoid.

Back at the flophouse, as it was the first time, registration was waived for cash up front. The clerk gave me the same room as before. I plopped onto the sagging mattress and looked around. The grimy cubicle measured seven feet by eight and its one cracked window overlooked a dismal alleyway, but, I thought, it didn't matter as long as I didn't have to die in it.

19 February 1974: Istanbul/Munich/Istanbul

The Lufthansa 727 landed Reim Airport at 10:12 A.M. I had a call to make and two letters to post that I couldn't afford traced; I'd come to Munich because I could fly in and back to Istanbul the same day.

At the postal window in the sterile terminal I purchased two airmail envelopes. In one I placed the money order for five thousand dollars that would square me with Fanning and "Onyxx Account E." I addressed the second to Stahl. After wiping the original Datatec report sent by Leclair clean of fingerprints I slipped it inside, wiped the envelope, and, holding it by its edges, dropped it into the slot.

The Turk Havla counter attendant said yes, there were seats on the next Istanbul flight and yes, I had time for a quick call. I took the change from the ticket in deutsche marks and hurried to the row of booths reserved for international calls. It was 11:02 A.M. in Munich, so it was 5:02 A.M. on the East Coast; I'd have to phone Rye, but was that line secure?

Seven minutes later Fanning's sleep-fogged voice said, "Hello."

"Frew, it's me... the Dakota Kid himself."

It took him ten seconds to link but when he spoke his voice was suddenly wide-awake. "Excuse me, son, I had something in my throat. You're well, I trust."

"Not bad, thanks. Is it, uh, convenient for you to talk?"

"I wish I were in my office—I left your draft of the contract next to my private phone. But I think I remember enough to discuss it. Just don't overwhelm me with fine points."

So he wasn't positive his line was secure, but thought we could talk, preferably in legal metaphors. "I've been reconstructing the case, Frew. I'm afraid my client's actions weren't as consistent as George would have liked. For instance, that boner in Rio—that wasn't part of the game plan."

"No, it wasn't." Was Fanning just keeping the dialogue alive, or had he caught my reference to the letter by Kenton which Wm.'s agents had burned? Then I knew we were on the same wavelength, because he added, "Geoff's indiscretion could have been a real Party-pooper."

"Well then, it seems to me that if he had the inclination once, he might have had it on other occasions. Query one: would he have tried verbal or written communication? My guess is written—it'd be too hard the other way."

Fanning grunted agreement.

"Query two: when could he have, uh, when could he have dropped it off? Assuming our friend Wm. was his usual thorough self, I see only two possibilities. In that Tokyo hotel room, during the long wait for retranslation, or in Ventura, at the restaurant where my client had, uh, indigestion."

Fanning thought it through, then said, "You're making sense, son."

"I know these are long shots, and that my client probably kept his word, but better safe than sorry, eh?"

"Absolutely. I'll move on it right away. By the way, have you found yourself an apartment yet."

I laughed. "That's kind of you to ask, but I wish you hadn't. No, we're still checking the international *Trib*'s classifieds every day."

"Well, happy hunting. You'll hear from me soon."

It was 11:13 A.M. when I hung up; plenty of time to catch the return flight to Istanbul.

24 February 1974: Istanbul

For the fourth consecutive morning I started my day walking from the flophouse to the news kiosk by the university, buying the *Herald Tribune* and turning to the classifieds. Now my eye caught on the second of three "Personal Notices":

> ARTHUR. Test results negative. All not forgiven at home but offer to arrange interview stands. Keep in touch. Love from everyone, Fru

So Fanning's agents had come up dry in Room 1071 of the Okura in Tokyo and in the men's room of the Pierpont Inn in Ventura. I should have expected it—after all, four years had passed—but I'd been so damned sure Kenton, facing his own coerced suicide, would have tried to get a message out...

I walked numbly to Rauf's and over coffee skimmed the rest of the paper. Patty Hearst, it seemed, had been snatched by an obscure terrorist group demanding as ransom a $230 million food giveaway to the poor; her dad had just counter-offered $2 million in groceries. To prove craziness wasn't exclusively Californian, an even more obscure group had kidnapped an Atlanta newspaperman. Their terms: $700,000 and the resignation of elected officials, starting with Nixon. Too bad the President didn't assent, I thought, for he'd save everyone a lot of trouble—now he was stonewalling not only Jaworski, the special prosecutor succeeding the fired Cox, but also the House Judiciary Committee, which had been galvanized by the disclosure of an eighteen-and-a-half-minute gap on a key Oval Office tape. And on the Continent the newly exiled Solzhenitsyn was in Zurich trying to duck his fellow writers of the West, and in the Middle East Iranians and Iraqis were killing each other over Kurds, and in Asia the Khmer

Rouge was wasting Phnom Penh—surely Cambodia would be the first domino. Here it was 1974 A.D., I brooded, and much of the world, including my little piece of it, was a nightmare.

As I pulled out Wm.'s fraying report I reread the *Trib* classified. Maybe Fanning was right, maybe I should take a flier with Justice. What other options did I have left?

28 February 1974: Istanbul

I must have been in a shallow dream phase because when I bolted upright in the pitch-blackness my eyes were wide open. What had stirred me? The old part of Istanbul was never still and the flophouse creaked with night sounds but I was an urban creature so those shouldn't have been enough. Had two bodies been thrashing and moaning on some nearby bed? I sank back into the pillow and suddenly remembered the dream: a table; a typewriter; twirling in two sheets; keys compressing the paper; words forming. But what had those words been? And then the luminous dials of my watch read 4:12. I didn't think I'd get back to sleep but I was wrong.

The day broke raw. I'd been woodenly tramping the streets under the white sky all morning; now, across the Golden Horn, the noon ferry was boarding. I knew its route well. The boat would ply slowly up the Bosporus, alternating landfalls on Asia Minor and Europe, until it reached the Black Sea; the return voyage in late afternoon was, if the sun peeked through, incandescent. I had nothing better to do so I crossed the Galata and paid my fare.

Shortly after we'd glided under the spidery new bridge linking two continents the jitters struck with such intensity I had to get off at the next stop.

The café by the ferry slip of the town in Asia Minor named Vanikoy was cozy and the view from it unspoiled but I was too preoccupied to notice: why couldn't I face the fact that Wm.'s report, though tantalizing, was a dead end? As I mechanically shoveled down a stuffed pepper I heard a commotion at the door. It was a tour guide ushering in an American couple and their two teen-age daughters; here were folks with few worries, I thought bitterly as I tried to block out the girls' excited natterings. I pushed aside my *dolma* and ordered yogurt and coffee. Now the younger girl was running back from the jukebox to ask her father for a coin. He reached into his pocket, then made her promise to play no more than one American song—they were, after all, in Turkey.

> *A long, long time ago,*
> *I can still remember how that music*
> *used to make me smile...*

Don McLean, *American Pie*, the fight with Donny at the engagement party—what had I told Martha afterward? That I preferred running to fighting. Well, I was a man of my word. The two girls began to sing along, unerringly mimicking every inflection and every pause. The tart yogurt was delicious but I left half of it; in the past three weeks I'd eaten simpler and less, and the ten pounds or so I'd shucked had left me the fittest in years. This irony, too, did not pass unnoticed. As the beat on the jukebox accelerated the parents began to sway in time, and the family's joy soon proved infectious, for the café proprietor and his stout wife, though they probably didn't understand a single lyric, started to grin and bob.

And now the tempo faded:

> *...the Holy Ghost,*
> *They caught the last train to the Coast*
> *The day the music died.*

And now the grinning girls were matching McLean's hoarsening voice:

> *And they were singin',*
> *Bye, bye Miss American Pie,*
> *Drove my Chevy to the levee but the levee was dry...*

And now something touched me deep inside: suddenly I yearned to rush to this family out of a Kellogg's ad and ask did the girls have beaus who came calling on Saturday night with hair freshly slicked, was Mary Tyler Moore still chaste, had meat prices fallen, how about the Celtics—in short, how was America? My eyes began to sting so I lowered my head.

And now the final refrain, a dirge really, and they were all singing so I silently joined:

> *Bye, bye Miss American Pie,*
> *Drove my Chevy to the levee but the levee was dry,*
> *Them good ol' boys drinkin' whiskey and rye,*
> *Singin' "That'll be the day that I die."*

The incongruously gleeful applause made me look up. Mine was the only unsmiling face in the café so I awkwardly plunked down some liras and lurched outside.

The cobblestone road led uphill past old wooden houses overlooking the strait and then through the village outskirts. Ten minutes later I was atop the ridge greedily inhaling the cold and incredibly clean air. Behind, across the Bosporus, the wooded hills of easternmost Europe and ahead the flat fields, now fallow under frost, of westernmost Asia Minor.

My eyes followed the fields to the horizon, where they merged with the bleached winter sky. I knew my future could be equally open: the world was indeed a great big place with infinite doors that Carl's papers and Harry's money could open. Perhaps I wouldn't thrive, but I'd survive—and that seemed far preferable to praying Justice could break the vicious circle. If going home was out of the question, though, why was I hanging about Istanbul instead of searching for a bolt-hole?

I stamped out the butt and sat back on the large rock. I wasn't searching because of my past—the words to *American Pie* that had triggered my melancholia were facile to a fault, but then it takes one to know one. At thirty-three half my natural days were now spent, and they had been spent enjoyably if not terribly constructively in America, in cities, and most of all in the company of intelligent and ambitious people. Of course I had the resiliency to start anew—hadn't my parents? But unlike them, for they had no roving goon squads to flee, I'd have to throttle back into a low-pressure, low-profile style of life. And as I rusticated, my lover and my friends and my peers would in time forget me. But could I forget them? And could I ever forget the improbable, implacable men and machinations that had so shattered my life?

The brownish lump fell faster and faster out of the sky and as it neared earth a half mile away wings spread to brake; a violent cough of snow and soil and then the hawk was laboring upward, the hare spindled on its talons. I crumpled the empty cigarette pack and looked down at the semicircle of butts at my feet. The ferry would be returning soon.

And then descending the ridge to Vanikoy I made my decision: I'd go back. Spitting in the wind? Maybe—but suddenly I felt, if not great, then good, for during the past weeks I'd learned that worse than fear is limbo. Should I use this last respite to see more of the great big world? No; what pleasures the solitary voyager, what good was traveling except to share? Just then I passed a rambling grey house with a dazzling view of the Bosporus. Here, I found myself fervently vowing, here's where I'll return someday—with Martha.

As I stepped from the ferry onto the quay in Istanbul I glimpsed myself in a mirror; my pants were laughably baggy and my head a mass of spiky tendrils that had sprouted from Carl's amateur haircut. To Taksim Square it would be, then, for a drink or three, a haircut, new clothes, and finally the call to alert Fanning.

From my seat in the Hilton cocktail lounge I could look down the steep hillside carpeted with red-tiled roofs to the Bosporus. I ordered a Gibson, my first in almost a month—bars in the Old City served drinks neat and straight. Four tables away a tanned, elegant man pecked furiously on a battered Olivetti 22. I eyed the Italian trench coat slung casually over an adjacent chair and the Gucci overnight bag and pegged him for a glamour-puss foreign correspondent. Now he was ripping the paper from the typewriter, peeling the two sheets apart, and loudly snapping his fingers. A bellhop hurried over to take the page of prose to the telegraph desk. The journalist placed fresh paper over his backing sheet, tamped the corners square, rolled them into his carriage, and began his next take. My Gibson was marvelous. Now one last burst of typing and the correspondent slumped back into his chair with a sigh: finished. He snapped his fingers once more and, as he balled up the backing sheet, held out his last take to the approaching bellboy.

The man had packed his Olivetti and been gone for five minutes when my blood suddenly congealed: *twirling in two sheets*, yes, that's how my dream had gone, *keys compressing paper*... The correspondent, like many practiced typists, had automatically used a backing sheet, a second page to protect the rubberized roller from the impact of the keys. Kenton had used a typewriter at the Tokyo rendezvous to bat out Sake's confession. Had he used a backing sheet? If so, did an IBM

Selectric, the typewriter he'd used, make indentations on the backing sheet distinct enough to read? If so, could Kenton have deliberately written the birthday letter to his daughter Henny on the backing sheet?

There was an electric typewriter behind the front desk of the Hilton, not an IBM but it would do. The deskman's automatic protest died when he spied the folded five-dollar bill in my sweaty palm.

Three minutes later, out on the curving driveway, I examined the backing sheet I'd just used. The machine had compressed the paper with enough force to form subtle indentations. Could they have escaped Wm.'s notice? Yes, if he hadn't been looking for them. Then I held the sheet to the light: totally indecipherable. Suddenly I remembered all those B movies in which hero finds message on convenient scratch pad so I fumbled out a pencil and rubbed it lightly over the dimpled area:

The quick brown fox jumped over the lazy dog

Sweet Jesus, I thought, let Henny be the sentimental kind who saves missives from dear old dad, and let dear old dad have written his last missive on the backing sheet, because this was absolutely the last chip I had to play.

1 March 1974: London/Oxford/London

The only "Kenton, H." in the Oxford directory lived at 52 Southmoor Road. I got directions at the information kiosk across from Carfax Tower and pointed the hired Vauxhall north. The quaint streets I threaded were flanked by weathered stone buildings that on this overcast day seemed to loom straight from a medieval history textbook; fittingly so, for the oldest of Oxford's colleges celebrated bicentennials long before Columbus hit his first New World landfall.

Southmoor Road was just over a mile away but its nineteenth-century houses had not aged nearly as gracefully as the ancient academic buildings at the city's center. I pulled into a space in front of No. 47. Along the street students toting bulky book bags flowed in and out of the tattier dwellings; these, I guessed, belonged to pensioners supplementing meager incomes with boarders. No. 53 seemed such a house: not even the thick ivy creeping up the walls could disguise its disrepair.

I lit a cigarette. My only lifeline might lie inside that shaby brick Victorian, but how to get it? Tell Henny Kenton her late father had been a traitorous spy blackmailed into a suicide mission? Pull a second-story job? I shifted in the car seat to wait for inspiration.

Ninety minutes later rays of pale sunlight darted through a rift in the clouds and tempered the pall blanketing Southmoor. Now the door to No. 52 swung open. The matron was stout and white-haired; she wore a red-and-yellow knit cap, a shapeless black woolen overcoat, and galoshes. The leash cinched around her right wrist stretched tautly back into the house. She tugged on it. "Come on, Crispin. Come on, come to Mummy." When Crispin didn't come she yanked harder. Finally a corgi bundled in a red-and-yellow knit jacket, the kind with "sleeves" for its legs, reluctantly emerged.

At the bottom of the steps the dog lunged for a bush near the house but the matron dragged it along the walk to the street. Just then two young men strolled past. The dog growled; obviously it was a one-owner pet. At curbside it sniffed and as it squatted the matron turned to admire the leaves that had yet to bloom on the barren trees. When she finally felt the dog shake itself, the matron praised it effusively. Then she lifted the corgi to check beneath the tail; satisfied her precious was clean, she ignored its obvious yearnings for a good romp and dragged it directly into the house.

There'll always be an England, I thought, an England in which matrons smother dumb animals with anthropomorphic follies. And suddenly inspiration came. Jesus, did I have the nerve? But on the other hand, did I have the nerve to confront Henny? As I started the Vauxhall I noted the time: 11:47. It took five minutes in downtown Oxford to locate a pub catering to students; then I headed back to London.

Shortly before midnight, from the pay phone of my Sussex Garden bed-and-breakfast, I dialed the number of "Kenton, H." in Oxford.

On the fifth ring a sleepy voice answered, "Hello."

"Hi, is this Miss Henrietta Kenton?"

"Yes."

"Great! I'm selling tickets to a lecture by Guru Maharaj Ji..."

"Get stuffed, creep!" The slammed phone didn't offend, for now I had the first half of my confirmation.

2 March 1974: London/Oxford/London

At 9:15 A.M. a pretty brunette and a tall, broad-faced girl emerged from 52 Southmoor Road and set off on foot for campus. When the matron finally dragged the corgi out the door I checked my watch: 11:36. Now I had the second half of my confirmation so I started the car and headed back to London.

I spent the afternoon running errands, which included booking a room at the Ritz in the name of a representative of the Swiss bank Henny and I shared, and sending a telegram:

> MISS HENRIETTA KENTON
> 52 SOUTHMOOR ROAD/OXFORD, ENGLAND
> AM NEWLY ASSIGNED ESTATE GEOFFREY KENTON. URGENT WE CONFER. PRESENTLY EN ROUTE LONDON. SUGGEST WE MEET RITZ HOTEL 1000 HOURS MONDAY 4 MARCH. APOLOGIZE SHORT NOTICE BUT LOOK FORWARD MEETING YOU.
> ADOLF ZEISS, LECLAIR & CIE/GENEVA

4 March 1974: London/Oxford/London

On reaching Oxford shortly after 10 A.M., I dialed Henny's number. Ten rings later I hung up; she wasn't home, but was she in class or had she taken my bait?

There was a parking space in front of No. 52. Sheer insanity, I thought, still time to return the goods and get a refund... Don't think, act: I stubbed out the cigarette and got out of the car.

The mailbox bore an engraved plate reading "Cavendish," under which was taped a handwritten card reading "Jolly/Kenton/Paechter." I rang the bell. The dog began growling, then footsteps, then "Shush, Crispin, do be quiet," and then the front door cracked open; upon seeing my Oriental face, the matron rearranged her rubbery features into a frown: "Yes?"

"Good morning, ma'am. Is, uh, is Henny in?"

"No."

"Oh. I see. Uh, uh, you must be Mrs. Cavendish."

"Yes, that's right, that's right."

I forced myself to smile. "Henny's often mentioned you, ma'am—she thinks the world of you." The flicker of surprise told me this was a palpable lie but her frown dissolved. "She, uh, she asked me to come by today to hook up her stereo."

"Stereo?"

"Yup, it's out in the car. She didn't tell you? Henny won a raffle down at the, uh, the Turl."

"Oh my, oh my! No, she never mentioned a word, the lucky gel!"

"She sure is. I was suppos... Oh gee, Mrs. Cavendish, I'm sorry, my name's Johnny Nakamura, I'm a Rhodes from Hawaii."

I'd guessed right on the magic word that would in this town lift me above racial prejudice because suddenly Mrs. Cavendish beamed "Good heavens, good heavens, a Rhodes? Why didn't you say so? Come in, come in while we chat, you'll catch cold out there."

The dog growled again but when I stepped into the dim, musty vestibule it stopped, sniffed, and began to stare at one of my jacket pockets. I withdrew my hand and dangled it within the corgi's reach. "You see, ma'am, Henny asked me to hook up the stereo for her, because it comes in parts."

"It does?"

"Yup. And you know how she is about wires and things like that."

"Oh, I do, I do. Deathly afraid of the beastly things m'self."

"Well, that's why I promised to hook it up." I made my face fall. "Gee, she said she'd be here this morning. Do you know when she'll be back?"

"Oh my, oh my, she shan't be returning until much, much..." Mrs. Cavendish broke off when she noticed her dog licking my fingers; she seemed surprised. "Where were we? Oh yes, Miss Kenton shan't be returning soon, some unexpected business in London, I should think."

So Henny'd taken the bait. But the rest of the plan could never work... Don't think, act: "Gee, ma'am, that puts me in a bind. The car outside's borrowed, and I have to return it soon." The dog's tail wagged like a beserk metronome; I leaned down to pet it and to avoid having to look at its owner. "I, uh, I don't suppose you'd permit me to leave the components outside Henny's door? It sure would save me a lot of trouble."

The request was perfectly reasonable; then, as I'd prayed, so was Mrs. Cavendish: "Certainly, young man, certainly you may."

Before she could change her mind I fetched the first carton from the car. She led me up the broad staircase to the second floor and pointed to Henny's door. Carton deposited, now offer the dog a hand, now start downstairs again; then, as I prayed, the corgi trailed. Hitting the vestibule, pulling goody from pocket, if not this act then violence or no letter but I couldn't, not under the trusty gaze of those liquid brown eyes... Don't think, don't feel, act: I flipped the meat patty to the floor. It was gone when I returned with another carton so I fed the dog the second patty, too.

Five minutes later Mrs. Cavendish was nervously eyeing the four bulky cartons, which I'd arranged to all but barricade the hallway. "Uh, young man, couldn't you, couldn't you just set the boxes one atop the other?"

"Well, I could ma'am, but, uh, this electronic stuff's very very delicate, and if I did that, we might break something."

"Oh."

"Yes. Well, Mrs. Cavendish, I thank you for helping me out so graciously."

"Uh..." Her rubbery face quivered with indecision, my knees with desperation; then, as I'd prayed, expediency bested propriety. "Uh, young man, if I opened Miss Kenton's room, would you be so kind as to move these boxes inside?"

"Uh, uh, gee, be glad to..."

Henny's room was large, high-ceilinged, and furnished mostly in thrift-shop eclectic. To the left of the door stood an armoire and next to it in the corner a metal steamship trunk surmounted by a neat obelisk of cardboard packing boxes. The madras-covered daybed ran along the left wall beneath reproduction Audubon prints and a poster from a Budapest String Quartet concert. A thicket of plants hid the windows across from me; there were even pots atop the desk. In the far right corner stood the only furniture in the room that betrayed Henny's trust fund, an Eames chair and ottoman. The right-hand wall was taken up by a cinder-block-and-pine-board bookcase crammed with textbooks and record albums and a cheap phonograph. An inexpensive Indian rug covered the painted floor.

When all four cartons were on the rug there was nothing

left to think about because the die was cast. "Mrs. Cavendish, might I presume upon you for one last favor? If you'd spare me another, oh, twenty-five minutes, we can give Henny a big surprise—that's all the time it'd take me to hook up these components."

"Oh, well, oh, dear me..."

Jesus, it wasn't going to work... And then I flashed on a trick so cheap and tacky that bile rose. But I made myself squat: "What say, Crispin, wouldn't it be swell if Miss Kenton came home and it was done?"

The dog responded by licking the last of the meat juices from my hand.

Finally Mrs. Cavendish's paralysis wore off. "Uh, uh, of course I'd have to chaperon..."

"Gee, I wouldn't have it any other way, ma'am."

"I shouldn't be doing this, young man. But do you know why I am? Because of Crispin—he adores you. I only take young gels in this house, you know, and Crispin never likes their gentlemen callers, do you, Crispin? No, you don't. In fact, he hasn't liked any man since the late Mr. Cavendish passed away."

"Ma'am, I don't know what to say..."

Mrs. Cavendish walked to the Eames and lowered herself into the leather chair. Then, as I began unpacking the cartons as slowly as I could, she said, "Young man, will it disturb your work to tell me about your native country? I never miss *Hawaii Five-O* on the telly."

Anything was better than being asked for my impressions of Oxford, so I quickly started in about surfing and Diamond Head and hula girls. While I filibustered I also cased the room. Where the hell would Henny keep letters? The desk first, I finally decided, then the armoire, and finally, God forbid and if time allowed, I'd try the cartons and steamship trunk in the corner.

Twenty minutes later I was sprawled on the floor with wires in both hands and my frowning face deep in the instruction manual. My consternation stemmed not from the schematic diagrams, though, but from the corgi, which nestled contentedly by my side: if one super-strength laxative could speedily unloosen a 165-pound man, how long should it take a triple dose to unplug a 20-pound dog just about due to go?

"Johnny?"

"Ma'am?"

"Tell me more about Queen What's-er-name, the one with the museum."

Just then I felt the dog stir. "Well, uh, Queen Sacajewa was a very wise queen who ruled our island in the, uh, the twelfth century..."

Now a little whine of distress.

"...and, uh, she was most warlike, but she fought in the name of peace..."

The corgi uncurled itself, stood, and began to whimper.

Mrs. Cavendish looked down. "What is it, darling, what is it? It's not time for you to go out yet, no, Mummy's watch says it's only ten-thirty-three, and you know Mummy never takes you out until after elevenses..."

The corgi dashed from the room and skipped howling down the stairs.

"Oh dear, oh dear!" Mrs. Cavendish fought her way out of the deep Eames and tottered to the landing. "No, Crispin, no-no, wait, let Mummy open... NO! WAIT... DON'T..." And then heavy brogans clumping down the stairs...

As I jerked open the long horizontal drawer of the desk I glanced at the silver-framed photograph atop the writing surface: a mousy-faced middle-aged man held one arm awkwardly around a tall, broad-faced teen-age girl. The drawer contained stationery and so did the top right-hand drawer—come on, come on... The middle drawer housed a hot tray, now I was fumbling open the double-depth bottom drawer, now I was riffling through the upright manila file folders—"Estate," "Taxes," "Tuition/Somerville College," "1st Year Essays," "Donald"—and behind the last folder a letter box bound in marbled paper.

I yanked it out, ripped off the red velvet ribbon, and lifted the top. Amidst fading snapshots and ticket stubs and theater programs lay several neat packets of letters, each fastened by a length of yarn, each identified by a little card tucked under the bow, and one card read "From Dad" and at that instant I spotted the engraved return address on the topmost envelope: Okura Hotel, Tokyo.

Quickly I slipped the envelope from the bundle. Quickly I withdrew the single sheet from the envelope. Quickly I unfolded the sheet. The message was scrawled in felt-tip:

My dearest Henny,
   I wish you a very, very Happy Birthday. Again my...

Not daring to breathe, I raised the paper to the light. Indentations!

The front door was wide open but Mrs. Cavendish was in the vestibule on hands and knees, scooping dog shit off the throw rug. When she rose and hurried off in full mutter, I dashed down the stairs, out the door, and past the corgi, which was dragging itself across the yard in a sitting position.

The Vauxhall laid rubber all the way down Southmoor.

Ten minutes later I pulled into an expressway lay-by and retrieved the letter. As I carefully worked a soft black pencil over the indentations the words emerged:

27 May 1970
   In early June, 1945, my agents in Imperial Household learn cowardly Hirahito, he lose stomach for War, because Corigedoor, and because barbaric US firebombs on Our Homeland. I also learn Suzuki and Kido, they want peace, news give me lots distress. Hirahito, he plan secret trip, to Kyoto, want beg forgiveness from nobel ancestor spirits. I pretend I leave Shanghai, go on business trip to Peking, but I go really back to Japan, I hide in bouillion boat. On 18 June, maybe 17 kms east of Otsu, there is prepared, for me, dynamite on train tracks. Hirahito is late. He not come before 2300 hours. I push #1 trigger, it not work, and when I push #2 trigger, last 3 cars explode. I learn later, cowardly Hirahito in another car, he consult spinless advisers. Exploding not mentioned, so I escape to Shanghai. Before I try again, My Homeland disgraces by Cowardly Surrender. I die 1,000 deaths because my shamefull failure.

Kenton had skipped down several lines to allow for the signature and then typed in Sake's name. It was one I'd never heard.

As soon as I got back to London I called the Time Inc. bureau for the New York telex number of Martha's magazine. Then I sent a telegram through that number direct to her office:

ALIVE AND WELL IN OLD WORLD, WISH YOU WERE HERE. RAN
ACROSS SPLENDID SAKE AT INTRIGUING RESTAURANT NAMED

K—— Y—— RPT K—— Y——. YOU MUST LOOK IT UP. LOVE TO FREW, WHO WE'LL CALL 1300 RPT 1300 YOURTIME TOMORROW. HAVE FUN IN EDIT REF HAHA.

             LOVE CLAY AND TOBY J.

5 March 1974: London

The day passed interminably; not only was New York six time zones behind, which meant waiting until early evening to call, but the only topic of conversation in the city was the resignation of Prime Minister Heath and the dramatic political resurrection of Harold Wilson.

Finally at 6:50 P.M. I booked a transatlantic call to Fanning's tap-free office phone. It was answered on the first ring.

"Hi, it's me."

"Oh God," Martha said, while at the same time Fanning was asking, "Are you okay, son."

"Everything's fine here. I didn't know you had an extension on this line."

"You're on a conference-call box," he replied. "What've you come up with?"

I quickly filled them in on the backing sheet and on Sake's confession.

"Good Christ!" Fanning said. "If this gets out they'll string him by his balls! The Emperor's person is holy—most Japanese never even heard his voice until the surrender broadcast of Forty-five. Even we Americans respected Hirohito—when LeMay firebombed Tokyo to the ground, our pilots had orders to drop well clear of the imperial palace grounds." Now I could hear Fanning's smile in his voice. "Ray, you've done it. We've got enough to squeeze this character."

"We would if my piece of paper had a signature on it," I said softly. The silence deepened. Finally I said, "Martha, did you dig up anything?"

"A really bad number, Ray. He's a combination of Boss Tweed and Vito Corleone—a political kingmaker and one of the godfathers of the *yakuza*, the Japanese Mafia."

"Jesus, Blair had good taste. What the hell's Sake's power base?"

"Dirty money. In the early Forties he held the Japanese

franchise on looting China. He operated out of Shanghai, just like he said in his confession, and his company sent gems and precious metals home to the war machine. A *Times* clip from Forty-five claims he fled Shanghai just after V-J Day on a ship loaded with gold bars. By the way, he may have used some to buy his freedom—the occupation authorities tossed him in prison for three years, but for some reason no one's ever explained, he never stood trial."

"How did he parlay the money into power?"

"By bankrolling the Liberal Democrats, which is really a conservative party that's dominated Japan since the end of occupation. At least one of his protégés made prime minister, back in the mid-Fifties. That's about it from me, Ray."

"Frew?"

"Just rumors. I'm told his palm is often greased by multinationals seeking business in Japan. We've never tangled with him because he seems to specialize in industrial and aviation deals. Remember when Lockheed was on the brink a couple of years ago."

"Vaguely."

"Two things got them over the hump. One, the White House squeaked a quarter billion bailout pool through Congress. Two, a domestic Japanese airline mysteriously canceled its options with McDonnell to buy planes from Lockheed. Sake is said to have engineered the switch."

"Wow. I..."

"There's more, son. Again speculation, but the switch occurred shortly after the Hawaiian summit between Nixon and Tanaka. Tanaka is of course a Liberal Democrat."

"Shit, that's another good reason why I'm not going to Justice."

Fanning didn't bother to reply.

"Listen, this paper I have is virtually worthless, but I'm sending it over. Martha, what if I pouched through Time Inc.—think it'd be safe?"

"Hmmmm. You may have trouble getting a field bureau to packet personal mail. I know, slug the envelope 'World Economic Survey Data.' That's a long-range cover story everybody prays never runs."

"Got it. Just add it to the stuff in the safe-deposit box, okay?"

"Will do," Fanning said. "By the way, your remittance arrived. You're sure you don't need the money."

"Positive. I've got more than enough for what I plan to do."

"Which is?" Martha asked.

"Does either of you have an address for Sake?"

"Why," Fanning said, sounding suddenly apprehensive.

"Because I'm going to pay him a call."

"Ray..."

"It's an idea I'm dying to be talked out of, no pun intended. Go ahead, suggest something better—I'm all ears."

7 March 1974: London/Anchorage/En route to Tokyo

The top of the world was beautiful but barren. From the transit lounge of Anchorage International Airport I watched the fuel trucks disgorging the last of their high-octane cargo into the JAL 747. It was time, I thought, so I walked to the Western Union desk. "How long for a night letter to reach Tokyo?"

The clerk glanced at a chart. "Thursday here, so it's already Friday morning there—it'd get there first thing Saturday."

"Great. Make this a night letter." I handed him my message to Sake:

IMPERATIVE WE MEET RE YOUR CONTRACT OF 27 MAY 1970, SIGNED AT HOTEL OKURA, TOKYO, CONCERNING TRANSACTION NEAR OTSU ON 18 JUNE 1945. MY ASSOCIATES, WHO POSSESS CONTRACT, BELIEVE RENEGOTIATION VITAL. CONTACT ME SOONEST VIA "JAPAN TIMES" PERSONAL NOTICE WITH MESSAGE UTILIZING WORD "DIME," AS IN DIME WITH STAR-SHAPED NOTCH. P. ARTHUR

On my way back to the plane I picked up a copy of the Anchorage *News*. A Washington grand jury had indicted a viper's nest of Watergaters, including John Ehrlichman, for the break-in on the office of Daniel Ellsberg's psychiatrist. So my pal Alan wasn't the only shrink the Plumbers had trashed; and even had Blair's goons silenced me on the waterfront, the stonewall would still be crumbling.

As we lifted off and circled the wilderness that pinches

Anchorage I lowered the plastic window shade to shut out the early-afternoon sun. My own body clock, still set on London time, said it was past midnight, and there'd be little to study for the next eight hours except the frigid waters separating Alaska from Japan.

13 March 1974: Tokyo

I double-checked to see that I had all my papers and then locked the door to my spartan hotel room. No city's fun when you're waiting, and Tokyo was no exception. Upon landing five days earlier I'd searched for a hotel far off the path beaten by journalists, the last thing I needed being recognition by somebody I'd met in Southeast Asia. I ended up at the Ginza Capitol, a small businessman's hotel that despite its name lay in Tsukiji, a dull section on the "wrong" side of the Ginza but ideally situated for my timid sorties into the city.

When I left the Capitol I took the subway to the Ginza to purchase that morning's *Japan Times*, the country's premier English-language newspaper, and quickly flipped to the classifieds. At last, contact:

MR. ARTHUR. Tel. 571-0617 and ask Minoku for dime.

How fast can they trace calls in Japan? There was no way of finding out so opting for safety in numbers I took another subway to Tokyo Station and settled into one of the pay booths that march endlessly across the lobby.

"*Hai,*" the female voice lilted. "*Jesaku desu.*"

"I'd like to speak to Minoku, please."

"Yes? I am Minoku, please."

"My name's Mr. Arthur."

"Ah so. I have message for you . . . what is your real name, please?"

"I'm sorry, I don't understand."

"Your real name, Arthur-*san*, I give message only if you know your real name, please."

I wiped fresh sweat from my forehead—what kind of trick was this?

"Hello, hello," she said.

"I'm still here." And then I realized that if Blair had indeed sent those five letters—and how else to explain the chase in Chinatown—then Sake would know my identity. "My real name is Raymond Huang."

"That is correct. You will telephone 583-4224, please."

"*Arrigato*," I said.

"*Doomo*."

I slumped back into the booth to rehearse my heart. How much else did Sake know about me—enough to hunt me down with? Or was my telegram with its mention of associates holding the confession enough to check his *yakuza* dogs? I fumbled out another ten-yen coin and dialed the second number.

"*Moshi-moshi*." It was a man.

"This is Mr. Arthur calling."

"Ah... Mr. Huang, is it not? You are most prompt. What may we do for you?"

"Are you Y——?"

The man laughed. "No. My employer does not speak English. I am empowered by him to assist you."

"Then arrange for me to meet him."

He laughed again. "Impossible—he is a very busy man."

"Listen, unless I get a meeting *moshi-moshi*, and a safe-conduct pass to and from it, my associates make the contract public."

When he spoke again there was no levity in his voice: "This is a decision I cannot make. I must consult, so I place you on hold."

"No!" I said quickly; prolonging our connection could be dangerous. "I'll call you back."

I waited twenty minutes, took another booth, and dialed again.

"*Moshi-moshi*."

"Huang here."

"The meeting is approved for this afternoon."

"Unacceptable. I want it the day after tomorrow, on Friday."

"But..."

"Friday," I repeated. "If you have to confirm that, I'll call back again."

He sighed. "Friday is possible. Now, about a rendezvous..."

"Pick me up at the Imperial Hotel, let's say eleven A.M. I'll answer a page under the name 'Arthur.'" I took his grunt for assent. "Two other things. To guarantee myself safe-conduct at least one way, I've got a little stunt worked up, so warn your man to follow my instructions. Don't worry, it won't be anything illegal." His second grunt sounded suspicious. "Two, I want to tape-record the meeting."

"Out of the question."

"Your boss doesn't speak English and I don't speak Japanese. I want to be damned sure his translator doesn't fuck up."

"No."

"The demand's non-negotiable."

A long silence, then "Very well, Friday the fifteenth, eleven A.M. at the Imperial," and I broke the connection.

14 March 1974: Tokyo

I'd set back the meeting to give myself time to prepare. Capturing the session on tape would at best nail Sake's coffin, but to stay alive I needed the confession of the next man in the daisy chain, who from Wm.'s report I had deduced to be Ouzo. Unless I was mistaken, Sake would never surrender the Greek's document, for without it he lacked any leverage whatsoever. Perhaps, though, I could twist him into letting me photograph it, so in addition to buying a Sony tape recorder I picked up a Polaroid 195 and several packs of Type 105 film; this specialized stock not only produced a 3½ × 4½ print in thirty seconds, but at the same time a permanent negative. Then, because Sake would certainly have me followed from our meeting, I spent the afternoon mapping an escape route through Shinjuku, a bustling theater and restaurant district not unlike London's West End. I found myself drawn to a *pachinko*, or pinball, parlor with entrances on three streets. The establishment's business card featured a map so I took one. Finally I spent the evening poring over the *Official Airline Guide* in search of a way to leave Japan undetected.

15 March 1974: Tokyo/Osaka

The wake-up call came at 6:30 A.M. My bed was a shambles; it must have been a night of tense dreams. By the time the overseas operator patched me through to Fanning's safe line the Thursday-afternoon rush hour had already started in New York.

"Fanning."

"Hi, it's me. I see Sake in about four hours."

"How do you feel."

"Scared shitless. Look, I'm calling because we're coming up on a weekend, which means Martha won't get telexes and you won't be at this line. I need a code word so I can telegraph as soon as I get clear."

"My wife's name."

"Okay."

"Son, what precautions are you taking?"

"Damned few, because I'm on Sake's turf. The only things I came up with can't save me, but they might nail him if... if I don't get clear. One, I'm mailing you hard evidence fingering whoever picks me up. Two, I'm leaving all my papers here at the hotel, plus a letter incriminating Sake. They'll be in the safe of the Ginza Capitol in Tsukiji District."

When I'd spelled it out Fanning said, "Got it. Ray..."

"Give my love to Martha," I blurted as I hung up.

At 9 A.M. I began calling airlines. Fifteen minutes later I held three reservations: as "P. Arthur" on that day's 6 P.M. Tokyo-to-Tehran Pan Am flight; as "R. Huang" on that day's 6 P.M. Tokyo-to-Los Angeles Varig flight; and as "T. Sasaki" on the JAL flight to Kuala Lumpur departing at 1 P.M. the next day from Osaka.

Down at the front desk I settled my bill and gave the receptionist my suitcase and a sealed envelope to hold until later that afternoon. Then, hitching up the camera case containing the Polaroid and the Sony recorder, I started for the Imperial.

They were punctual: the page for "Mr. Arthur" came at 11 A.M. sharp. From my carefully chosen seat in the Imperial's lobby I studied the people waiting at the front desk, then scanned the vast room. No suspicious men lurked, nor did I expect a hit in so public a place—but then why was my back crawling? I shouldered the camera case and walked to the front desk.

When I gave my name the receptionist gestured to a thin, sallow young Japanese man with a small Band-Aid high up on his right jaw, near the ear. He looked bored. Band-Aid motioned me to follow and started across the lobby.

A long black Toyota limousine with curtained rear windows idled at the entrance. As we neared it its chauffeur jumped out to open the door.

"Hey," I said. Band-Aid turned. "Do you speak English?" He looked at me blankly so I held up my hand in the universal "Stop" gesture. Then I quickly dug out the Polaroid, set it up, and beckoned the uniformed doorman; handing over the camera and a thousand-yen note, I pantomimed for him to take a shot of me and my two friends. Band-Aid and the chauffeur glanced at each other apprehensively but they complied as I posed us in front of the car. The doorman made the exposure. I counted to thirty and peeled off the backing paper: the photograph was in focus and, best of all, the Toyota's license plate showed clearly. I put fixer on the print, dropped it into a stamped airmail envelope, addressed the envelope to Fanning, and slid it into a mailbox. Suddenly my two escorts realized what I'd done for they began barking at each other. I ignored them as I retrieved the Polaroid and climbed into the back.

The driver was skilled and most of the journey was by expressway but it still took an hour before the Toyota glided up to a high-walled compound in an ostentatiously affluent suburb. Manning the gates were two lean men in razor-creased khakis. Though they obviously knew the driver and Band-Aid the guards inspected their papers before opening the gates.

The compound was dominated by a sprawling Western-style house. As Band-Aid and I crunched across the white-pebbled driveway I noticed that the air here was cleaner by far than Tokyo's.

Then the front door was swinging abruptly open to reveal a bekhakied side of beef the size of a sumo wrestler; the white silk scarf knotted jauntily around his thick neck did little to soften the image of the man blocking our path. "Arthur-*san*," Band-Aid mumbled. White Scarf looked me over with contempt. Then he signaled "Hands up," gave me a heavy-handed frisk, and rummaged through my camera case. As he wheeled and clomped back into the house Band-Aid nudged me to follow.

The three of us trooped down a marble corridor, past a Western-style living room furnished in leather and chrome modular units, to a hall running at right angles. We turned left onto it.

Along this passageway were several traditional Japanese rice-papered sliding doors. White Scarf stopped at the third panel. As Band-Aid slipped off his shoes White Scarf swung a hundred-pound elbow into my ribs; I quickly kicked off my loafers. Now White Scarf pressed a button and the door—which I noted with surprise was a good four inches thick—slid back with a soft whir. Band-Aid motioned me in and entered after.

The room was large and light because the wall to my right was glass. Through it I could see an immaculate Zen garden. *Click*, and the door shut behind us. On the wall to my left were mounted three exquisite Chinese scrolls of the *shan-shui*, or mountain-and-water, school and a shelf holding a stunning Buddha; on the far wall two more scrolls, these calligraphic, flanked a second door to the room. Band-Aid led me to one of the cushions on the tatami mats.

Now the stillness was broken by the entrance of a young male servant bearing a tray on which sat a porcelain teapot and two cups. The leaves in the cup he served me were green and fragrant. I caught Band-Aid's eye and pointed to the other cup. He quickly shook his head so I again savored the steam rising from my tea and then set it untouched on a low lacquered table.

Two minutes later I spotted a lens hidden in a ceiling recess near one corner. I had no doubt but the TV camera was on and its focus was me. Hands steady, metabolism only slightly high. It was the middle of the night in New York; what must Martha and Fanning be thinking? And then I sensed Band-Aid's movements and when I looked he had rolled onto his knees to face the door humming open in the far wall, and as the two men in charcoal-grey kimonos stepped through he pressed his forehead to the tatami.

The older man, in his sixties, was short and chunky but he swaggered lightly on stockinged feet. His scowl seemed congenital. The younger man had the slightly bulgy eyes of one who wore contact lenses.

"This is my employer," the younger man said; he'd been the one on the telephone. "I am here to interpret."

Now Band-Aid, who had scrambled to his feet, deferentially approached Sake and whispered in the old man's ear. As Sake listened he gazed out at the rock garden. Finally he grunted and Band-Aid, stooped and with his head cocked obsequiously, backed his way to the door we'd entered and vanished through it.

Sake was so short I could look down and see scalp glinting through his crew cut. His size, his bantamy posturing, his paunch, everything about him was comical except his eyes: through their rheuminess glowed the feral cruelty of a killer. The aide started to plump a cushion for his boss. Sake cut him short with a gutteral "*Iran!*" and then, never taking his eyes from me, sank to the tatami in the lotus position. I eased onto a cushion across from him and the interpreter seated himself to Sake's right.

I cleared my throat. "I wish..." Sake didn't blink but the younger man's head jerked toward me, his astonished expression a sign that I was grievously breaching protocol by speaking first. I didn't care: "I wish to set up my tape recorder now." The aide frowned but translated. The old man's glare was so mesmerizing I almost missed his slight nod.

When I turned on the Sony, Sake said, in a soft but arrogant voice, *"Anata o wagaya ni omaneki shita ga, anata wa watashi no kooi o muni nasutta."*

"I invite you to my home," the aide said, "and you insult my hospitality."

When I looked baffled Sake added, *"Anato no yunomi wa ippai-dakedo, moo hiete masu na."*

"Your teacup is full and it is cold."

"I was waiting for my host," I replied.

Upon hearing the translation Sake snorted and signaled for the second cup. *"Anata wa watashi no kooi o muni-shita-dake-de-naku, watashi nimo burei o hatarakareta."*

"Then you insult not only my hospitality but me."

Sake tossed back the scalding tea and banged the empty cup down. *"Waga ya dewa ranbo suru koto wa yurushite oran!"*

"I do not permit violence in my home," the aide said blandly.

Sake withdrew a handkerchief from the sleeve of his kimono and touched it to his lips. He was looking at the handkerchief when he said, in a voice I thought vaguely appreciative, *"Washi no miuchi-no-mono ga iiyotta-ga, omae-san wa hoteru dewa nakanaka umaku yari-otta soodesu na."*

"My man tells me you were most clever at the hotel."

I didn't respond.

"Ittai zentai omae ga hoshii-nowa nanjai. Kane-kane?"

"What the, uh, what the hell do you want, money?"

"No, I want to know if your boss ordered me killed in New York."

Sake's face rearranged itself into a sneer. *"Moshi washi-ga omae-san no usugitanei inochi-ga hoshikattara anata wa ima kooshite oran-noja!"*

"If I wanted you dead you would not be here now."

"Why did Mr. . . . ." Suddenly I realized that, while he spoke directly to me, I'd been speaking to the aide and referring to Sake in the third person, so I turned to the old man and said, "Why did you do it?"

He ran a meaty paw over his bristly scalp. *"Tenno wa okubyo de orareta. Kore ijyo no gisei o harau-koto o osorerareta noda."*

"The Emperor was a coward. He was afraid of, uh, of making sacrifices."

I shook my head. "No, I mean Entrepays."

"Omae-san wa mikake yorimo orokana kataja-naa," Sake snorted. *"Washi wa Nippon ne hairu Shina karano sekiyu wa subete nigireru-no-ja."*

"You must be more stupid than you look. I would have controlled all Chinese oil coming into Japan." The aide's voice was robotic; hearing the old man's snarl leached through it was proving hallucinatory.

"Aren't you powerful enough already?"

Sake smiled thinly. *"Omae wa ikura hoshiin-da-ne?"*

"How much do you want?"

"I'm not here for money, I came for the Greek's confession."

When the aide translated "Greek" Sake couldn't disguise his chagrin: any lingering hope I'd just strung together a few lucky guesses was now smashed. He looked at his handkerchief and said, *"Naze-dane?"*

"Why?"

"One of the f . . ." I coughed and sipped my tepid tea; I'd almost revealed the number of conspirators. "One of your colleagues is trying to have me killed. I want to live."

He chuckled. *"Omae-san, otoko-ja-neeika! Dare ga washi no himitsu o nigitte-iruka o omae-san ga hanasu-yooni sasete miseru wa."*

"You have balls. I permit you to see it if you tell me who has my confession."

I refilled my teacup to stall until my heart stopped racing. He was smart enough to know I didn't have his confession, but he feared I had a copy of it, and that fear was strong enough to make him bargain. But swapping information would be suicide: if I snitched on someone else, wouldn't I later snitch on him? I looked up and shook my head.

"Ittai doyatte omae-san ga washi no himitsu o nigitte-iruka washi ga wakaruno-kane. Sore wa omae-san no burafu ja naino-kane."

"How do I know you see my confession, that this is not a bluff?"

Careful now, I thought, don't overplay the bluff. "You don't."

Sake sneered again and launched into an explosive little monologue.

"You are Chinese," the aide said. "The big man who steers you to this room, the man with a white scarf—he does not talk. A Kuomintang pig ties him on a rack and slices his throat. It is thirty years now, but he still enjoys slicing a Chinese throat."

I couldn't hide my fright so I didn't try. "If I go down so do you—my associates will act unless they hear from me by four P.M. Tokyo time."

Sake studied me as a stallion studies a horsefly and spoke again; his contempt needed no translation.

"Brave talk," the aide said. "You do not tell me who has my confession because you do not know. Which means you do not see my confession at all."

"The dynamite was planted seventeen kilometers east of Otsu. The first trigger failed. By the time..."

Sake waved me to stop—he didn't have to speak English to understand "dynamite" and "Otsu" and "trigger." Slowly he folded the hankerchief. *"Naiyoo o shitte-iru to iukoto wa, bunsho o motte-iru to iukotoo onaji dewa nai-ja naika. Denka no nootoo o nuku hodo no koto mo nai. Totto to kiesero!"*

"Knowing the contents is not the same as to have a copy. You are not worth making my sword rusty—go to hell."

So now we were both bluffing, and he was calling. I shrugged and stood. I was within three feet of the door when Sake said, *"Mate."* I wanted desperately to turn but I didn't.

The shattering bang and the tearing paper and the shout *"Chikusho, mate!"* came at the same time.

Finally I forced my eyes open. The bang had been Sake's teacup shattering on the door; through the torn rice-paper I could see the plate glass that accounted for the door's thickness. I turned slowly. Sake was dabbing his upper lip with the handkerchief. The interpreter was ashen. *"Mate."* I stood my ground. *"Dare ga washi no himitsu o nigitte iruka itte kuretara motto odoroku yoona himitsu o oshiete yaroo."*

"I, uh, I permit you to see the Greek's confession if you tell me who has mine."

"I want to photograph it."

Sake refolded his handkerchief. *"Yoroshii. Shasin o saki ni tore. Sorekara ore ni hanashi o shiro."*

"Okay, you photograph it, then you tell me."

"No."

Sake's left eye began to twitch. *"Kono himitsu de omae-san wa nani-ga kaeru-to-iu-nokane. Ore wa omae ni kane o kurete-yaruja naika."*

"What can a confession buy? Look, I give you money."

"Money can't buy back my life. I want to live." I softened my voice. "If I can stop whoever's trying to kill me, you will have my undying gratitude."

Sake gazed at the rock garden as he mulled over the implications of my promise. Then a little shooing motion of his right hand and as the interpreter walked shakily past me to the corridor door Sake closed his eyes in meditation.

Outside a sparrow fluttered down and perched on one of the rocks jutting from the meticulously raked garden.

When he opened his eyes he looked different. And then I had it: his bull-like shoulders had jellied in resignation. He rose with a sigh and gestured; I grabbed my camera case and followed him through the door in the far wall.

At the end of a wide hallway fronting the garden rose a flight of wooden stairs that sang melodiously under our tread. The chirps were no accident, I thought; he doesn't even trust his own staff. The door at the top opened into a resolutely Western-style office. As the old man walked to a safe I looked around. A polished collection of long swords hung behind a desk heaped with papers. The bookcases overflowed. Two walls were covered with photographs of Sake posed with various associates; most had been taken when he was young, during the war.

He padded back with an envelope, fought with himself for several more seconds, then said, "Yo hab mine?" I frowned, then realized he was speaking English. "Yo hab mine?" he repeated. I nodded. He abruptly thrust the envelope into my hand and crossed to the window.

The seal on the upper left-hand corner read "Plaza-Athénée."

I opened the envelope, withdrew the single handwritten sheet, and smoothed it out:

To Who It May Concern,
   During the Second World War, I alone of Greek Ship Owners am not molested by the Nazi U-Boats. The reason why is that I am secretly transporting personnel and materiel between Germany and Argentina. My last mission for the Third Reich commences on 27 May 1945. I order my freighter *Penelope* to make the rendezvous with a U-Boat off the Canaries. Nine German officials transfer aboard, including Martin Bormann and Josef Mengele. The *Penelope* follows a Southern route across the Atlantic, and reaches Buenos Aires on 2 July 1945. For this service I accept from Bormann *La Bella* by Tiziano.

I studied the signature. The fleet of ships and the opera diva and the private Ionian island and the glamorous widow I knew about, of course; I'd not known Ouzo had been a collaborator, or that he had a sweet tooth for fine paintings.

I dug out the Polaroid, unfolded it, and carried it and the letter to the window. Sake continued to stare unblinkingly at the garden while I made three exposures. I peeled the developed films apart: the images were sharp. After fixing the positives and plunging the negatives into a plastic container of sodium sulfite solution I slid the confession back into its envelope.

"*Arrigato,*" I said. Sake didn't turn so I placed the envelope on the windowsill. Then I picked up my camera case and walked back down the stairs that sang to the deserted meeting room. The teacup fragments here had been swept away, the gashed panel on the rice-paper and plate-glass door replaced. White Scarf awaited me in the corridor; I slipped into my shoes and followed him to the limousine.

Band-Aid was nowhere to be seen. That worried me—as a knee-jerk response Sake would have me tailed. As we sped along the expressway back to Tokyo I peeked out the rear window several times. Nothing suspicious. I fished the negatives from the sodium sulfite solution, rinsed them in a container of fresh water, and laid them on the back seat to dry. Damn it, I thought, they must be keeping tabs on me—Sake would never just let me walk away. Could they have planted a minitransmitter on me? What had they had access to? My shoes... Making sure the chauffeur couldn't see my movements, I inspected my soles. The nails securing the left heel seemed fractionally shinier than the ones on the right heel.

When we neared the city I saw that the negatives were dry so I pocketed one and divided the other pair between two envelopes already containing one print each. Then I said to the driver, "Shinjuku." He looked at me in the rearview mirror. "Shinjuku, okay?" He frowned so I passed forward the business card of the *pachinko* parlor. He glanced at it and nodded.

It was almost 2 P.M. by the time the elevated Shinjuku subway station loomed through the smog. Soon our limousine was contributing to the pollution, for traffic here moved in yards, not miles, per hour. Good, I thought; if I was really under sophisticated visual surveillance, this should throw them. Then I spotted the *pachinko* parlor a couple of blocks ahead on Shinjuku-Dori Avenue. Now? No, not yet.

Four minutes later we were almost abreast and stuck at another red light. Now? The traffic signal governing the cross street flicked to amber... now. I threw open the door and bolted and the startled driver began yelling but I was already entering the *pachinko* parlor, and now out the far door onto another street and then sprinting through the crowd to a narrow lane which I followed until it intersected with another alley. I skittered around the corner and pressed myself to the wall: the only sounds I heard were the drumbeats of my own heart.

The shoe store had trouble fitting me so I purchased a pair of sneakers. When the clerk started to wrap them I handed him my old shoes instead.

The Shinjuku subway platform was crowded so I had a wide choice of marks. When a train bound for Ogukibo started to slide in I joined the riders surging forward and eased the package with my old shoes into the half-filled shopping bag carried by a burly man. Then I crossed the platform and hopped a train going the other way.

I got off at Otemachi and walked the few blocks to the building in which Time Inc. maintained its Tokyo bureau. In the lobby I took out the two envelopes containing the sets of Ouzo's confession. I addressed the one with airmail postage affixed to Fanning and dropped it into a mailbox. I addressed the other to Martha, wrote "By Packet: World Economic Survey Data" on it, rode to the eleventh floor, and handed it to the Time Inc. receptionist.

Now a cab to the Ginza Capitol to collect suitcase and papers and then to Tokyo station; I made the 4 P.M. *shinkansen* with five minutes to spare. At 6 P.M., when I hoped Sake's men would either be chasing my shoes in Ogukibo or haring frantically around Haneda Airport checking the Tehran- and Los Angeles-bound flights, I was speeding at 125 mph on the "bullet train" to Osaka.

18 March 1974: Bangkok/Athens/Nicosia

The Swissair DC-10 from Bangkok wheeled over Athens and began its descent. As soon as I cleared entry at Central Airport I checked the flights to Cyprus: convenience had routed me to the Greek capital, but I wasn't lingering in Ouzo's lair while awaiting contact. Then I looked up his shipping company in the telephone directory and sent a telegram to that address:

> PER DISCUSSIONS WITH MY ASSOCIATES, WHO KNOW ALL, WILL EXCHANGE TITIAN FOR SHIP "PENELOPE." SUGGEST WE MEET SOONEST, PERHAPS IN CANARIES ON 27 MAY OR BUENOS AIRES ON 2 JULY. CONTACT ME VIA "HERALD TRIBUNE" PERSONAL NOTICE WITH MESSAGE UTILIZING PHRASE "PENNY," AS IN PENNY WITH A STAR-SHAPED NOTCH.
>
> P. ARTHUR

Five minutes later I boarded a flight to Nicosia.

I booked into a second-class hotel just inside the walled city of the Cypriot capital and slept off the jet lag until midnight. By the time the local operator found a way to connect me with Fanning it was almost 5 P.M. in New York.

"Hi, it's me."

"Good to hear your voice, son. I received your telegram from Kuala Lumpur Saturday, and Martha received the packet this morning."

"Good, that means I can move as soon as I make contact with Ouzo. You..."

"Ray, I think you should come home. You've broken the daisy chain—let the professionals finish the job."

I'd anticipated this. "Who? The UN? Interpol? What professionals have the jurisdiction to ring all the bells that have to be rung? And by the time some goddamn bureaucracy moves on it, we'll all be dead...from natural causes."

"I'm thinking of the danger you face. Suppose Sake warns Ouzo you're coming."

"No. I've spent a lot of time analyzing this, Frew, and he won't, because each confession's a double-edged sword. Sake may have Ouzo by the short hairs, but if he sounded the alarm he'd reveal himself, and that might mean popping up in the wrong end of a Greek shooting gallery. By the same token, he'll keep his mitts off me because he's afraid of my unnamed associates. That's one of my imperatives, keeping you two anonymous. That's why I ran that complicated escape number, to get away temporarily so I could contact you without one of his goons watching me dial."

"You say 'temporarily.'"

"If Sake wants to find me again all he has to do is run a simple stakeout—he knows exactly where I'm headed. That's neither here nor there; I'll just have to ditch them again. My other imperative's staying below the radar of the men I'm still stalking, although only one of them really scares me."

"Caviar."

"Right. From what I hear he's a little squirrelly."

"Megalomaniac's a better word," Fanning said dryly.

"Back to Ouzo. You must know him—what can I expect?"

"So you're going through with it. Well, when I knew him he was very charming but very volatile. Since his son's death last year..."

"A plane crash, wasn't it?"

"Yes. Ouzo swears it was sabotage—I understand he's offering one million dollars for information. Oh...Martha asks if you need a dossier."

"No, he's in the news enough, what with his deals and his marriage and his health."

"Martha also checked with a couple of art experts. The Titian in question is reliably thought to hang in the Pitti, in Florence."

"Really. I'll have to mention that when we meet."

"It might be a while, son. Ouzo's been in the States lobbying for the construction of a refinery in New England."

"Somehow, Frew, I don't think I'll have long to wait."

22 March 1974: Nicosia

Durrell was right: Cyprus was indeed a very special island, though with my preoccupation three days of exploring it seemed two days too many. After breakfast I strolled down to the news kiosk on Metaxas Square. The day's *Trib*s had just arrived. I turned to the ads:

> P. Arthur. Will page you Central Airport, Athens, 10 a.m. Monday, 25 March. Penny

25 March 1974: Nicosia/Athens/An Ionian Island/ Brindisi/Rome

The earliest plane out of Nicosia—ironically on Olympic Airways—landed Athens just after 10 a.m., but I'd deemed it preferable to flying in the night before. As I cleared Customs I was intercepted by a tanned, well-preened young Greek man wearing a body-hugging electric-blue suit and sunglasses. "Mr. Huang? I am Yanni—you will follow me, please?"

"How did you know I'd be on the Cyprus flight?"

"You are not here at ten, so I think you maybe fly here, and all arriving passengers, they come through this door." Even as he broke into a self-satisfied grin he signaled a confederate watching the main entrance. "If you will follow?"

"Where are we going?" I said as I reached into my camera case for the Polaroid.

"Plane ride."

"Where?"

He shrugged.

"Are you going with me?"

He shook his head.

"Then how about a picture, Yanni?"

"Why?" he asked warily.

"You're a very handsome guy."

He beamed, whipped off his sunglasses, and struck a peacock pose. As we waited for the film to develop I suggested we pose for another one together. He instantly summoned his buddy over to act as photographer. When both prints were ready I handed Yanni his portrait and dropped the other one into a stamped envelope.

"What you do?" Yanni said, suddenly nervous.

"In case I never return... My friends will want to know who was the last person to see me alive." He blanched and lunged for the photograph. I fended him off and growled, "If you've got problems, go call your boss. If not, wait here." He stared sullenly as I crossed the lobby, wrote Fanning's name on the envelope, and posted it.

An Olympic Airways Jeep ferried us to the section of the field reserved for private craft. By the time we reached the DC-6 its four engines had already been fired, and as soon as I hopped aboard the pilot began taxiing.

When I saw the Gulf of Corinth through the blurred circles described by the propellers I knew we were flying west, and that I was most likely meeting Ouzo on his private island in the Ionian Sea. I unfolded my list of contingency escape routes and rechecked the getaway from that island against the timetable in the *Official Airline Guide*. Then I looked up the cruising speed of the DC-6. Working backward, I figured I'd have to leave Ouzo's island at 5 P.M. latest. When I looked out the window again we were back over land, passing still westward above the green, wrinkled foothills of the Pindus range.

At 11:15 A.M. we began our descent.

The airfield bristled with military planes and as I stepped from the DC-6 I could make out the big block letters over the terminal: AKTION. A Jeep was waiting at the foot of the ramp. I climbed in and was sped not to the terminal but to a helicopter; now overhead rotors quickened, now lift-off and now we were tilting south over the Ionian. For a man of uncertain health, I thought, Ouzo still ran a damned tight ship.

Twenty-five minutes later I sighted our destination.

Ouzo's domain consisted of two heavily wooded hillocks joined by a low-lying isthmus; it looked like a green mole growing on the pale-blue sea. There were two mini-islands off its coast, one to the south and one to the east. As the pilot throttled back we swooped toward the isthmus, hovered over two villas overlooking the cove, and settled onto a concrete pad.

It was hot and the sun was blinding. Just beyond the rotor's swath stood a young, white-jacketed male servant; he took my suitcase, turned, and led me toward the villas. When we passed a stone quay I felt a flash of *déjà vu*. Then I recognized the quay as the backdrop for those nude shots that had titillated several continents—this was where Ouzo's wife sunbathed on her infrequent visits to the island. We continued past several flourishing flower beds and entered the larger villa through a side door.

It was dark inside and the conditioned air uncomfortably cold. The boy started down a flight of stone stairs. By the time we reached the bottom my eyes had adjusted to the dimness but I was still shivering.

Ahead was a glistening stainless-steel door; when we were three feet from it, it began to open.

Ouzo's underground office was a communication freak's ultimate dream. On the right-hand wall were implanted a dozen TV screens to serve as surrogate windows. Along the left-hand wall stood a bank of six teletype and wire-service machines, their characteristic chatter muted. Straight ahead was a desk the size of a conference table flanked by a multi-line telephone console that could have serviced a brokerage house. Behind the desk the wall was bedecked with dozens of photographs. I turned to ask the boy where Ouzo was but all I saw was my suitcase on the floor. Then my eyes traveled to the two life-size, backlit, living-color transparencies on either side of the stainless-steel door. They were of Ouzo's wife and obviously from the infamous nude takes.

As I turned back toward the desk at the far end of the room I caught movement on one TV screen. It was the servant boy climbing the stairs we'd just descended. Now in the upper right-hand corner I saw the helicopter sitting on its pad, and across four screens the deserted stone quay; these were apparently monitors for an elaborate closed-circuit system.

What was Ouzo trying to prove with this exhibitionism? And where the hell was he? Then with a start I realized that the high-backed swivel chair behind the desk was turned away from me, and over the chair hung a thin gauze of smoke.

"Be seated, Mr. Huang." The voice was gruff and aged.

I walked across the room and sat.

Slowly his chair swung around. I had to suppress a gasp: Ouzo looked like death itself. His leonine head drooped to one side. One lens of his heavy-rimmed glasses was smoked, the other jet black, but even these couldn't hide the puffy and bruised bags under his eyes. His cotton T-shirt was smudged with grey ash streaks. Slumped in his oversize swivel chair, Ouzo looked disconcertingly like a wizened child.

Keeping the one eye I could see on me, he stubbed out his cigarette and sipped from a tumbler of milky fluid. I caught a faint whiff of licorice: he was drinking the beverage Blair had code-named after him. Finally he whispered, "What do you know?"

I placed the Polaroid print I'd kept on the desk.

He picked it up with trembling hands and held it close to his face; as he peered at it his expression became if possible even more mournful. Then he wiped his mouth and said, "You come to sell me the name of the man who possesses this. Okay, I pay one mil..."

"I'm not in this for money. You or one of your colleagues ordered me killed."

"It is not I. But you help me, I help you, eh?"

"I'll look after myself, thanks. What I came here for..."

"Look at me." Ouzo's plaintive voice was as tired as his face. "I am still strong, because I can be of service to you, but I am also broken, broken in the heart. Have you no pity?"

"No."

Suddenly he straightened in his chair, a hard smile animating his features. "Good. Very, very good! I do not think you are soft to come this far, but I must test. No, you are an individualist, a bastard after my own heart. Good!" Ouzo took another sip. "So now we talk business, eh?"

"No."

"But you do not hear my offer."

"I..."

"Blair says you are writer. All writers, they need money, we decide how much later. Now, I am in the commerce, but I understand you artists—you need more than money, you need raw materials, am I correct? No no, do me the courtesy and hear me. First I must explain to you why I must know this man's name. The reason why is that I must defend what I build. You have children?"

"I'm not married."

"Children, there is so much to teach them." Ouzo gestured at the photos on the wall behind him; almost all were of his late son. "I had two. My son, he can defend what I build, but they assassinate him, eh? It is done so we will not talk of it again. Now my daughter, she inherits all. A bright girl, a lovely girl, her smile melts your heart, but she is not tough yet, she needs time. When I am alive I defend her, but when I am gone? Many many people want her harm. And what do they use, eh?" He brandished the Polaroid. "They use this, they harm her with her daddy's mistake! Yes, I make a mistake. I admit it to you right now, I am wrong to help the Nazis. Thirty years before I am wrong, but now I repair the mistake, and also I help you, and also I help myself, eh?"

Ouzo drained his tumbler and leaned forward again. "Here is what I propose. I show you the American's confession, maybe he is the one who tries to kill you. I pay you tax-free money in Switzerland. And I give you biggest damn story of your life, eh? I tell you where Mengele lives in Paraguay, I tell you how Bormann dies in Brazil, I tell you who smuggles back to Germany his body to fool the government. I do all this to help you, you only must tell me who has my confession."

"Tempting, but no deal."

"You refuse this?" His puzzlement seemed genuine.

"If I tell you, you'll have him killed. And then your next logical targets are me and my associates, because we've got your signature on film. I'm sorry, but the only chance I've got is maintaining the balance of terror."

Ouzo scowled. "Then you do not see the American's confession."

"Then my associates make yours public."

He spat out three Greek words and angrily refilled his tumbler.

"Look, I'll be straight with you," I said. "I don't give a shit about your good name or your empire. All I want is the American's confession. Show it to me and I promise I'll sit on yours unless there's another attempt on my life—or unless I die an unnatural death, in which case my associates tell all."

"But then you make me answerable for the actions of others! This is not right!"

"You made the bed, I didn't."

"What if I give you . . ."

"The confession—no more, no less."

Ouzo slowly removed his dark glasses and massaged his eyes. The left lid, which he kept hidden behind the blackened lens, drooped grotesquely. Then he replaced his glasses, pulled himself to his feet, and made his way around the desk, stopping so close to me I found myself uneasily studying his baggy shorts and tattered sneakers. Ouzo remained standing but his voice was a kneeling man's: "You must tell me, I beg your mercy you must tell me. All that I build, all that I have...I must defend this, I cannot permit it to be placed in danger." The soft taps of the muffled teletypes were the loudest sounds in the room. Finally he sighed. "Okay, okay..."

A gentle chime and Ouzo was turning toward the wall of TV screens. I followed his gaze.

On four monitors, from four angles, a vision of serene grace wrapped in a white terry-cloth bathrobe stepped from the shadows onto the stone quay. She paused to adjust her sunglasses. Then, trailed by a white-uniformed servant, a stocky, teen-age Greek girl, she crossed to a lounge chair. A quick tug on the terry-cloth tie string and the robe fell away to reveal her naked torso. She languidly plumped the cushions of the lounge chair and then melted stomach down into them. The servant set her tray on an adjacent table, selected a plastic jar from among its magazines and beverage glasses, scooped out a handful of unguent, and began to slather it over her mistress's backside. When that backside sparkled from nape to ankle with sunscreen, the lady rolled over. I was surprised that she no longer seemed relaxed. Then I noticed her nipples starting to stand to dusky attention, and then I noticed that the Greek girl's touch had grown light as a soufflé as she worked downward from the throat. I couldn't help but glance at Ouzo, who stood beside me. His breathing was rapid, the front of his shorts stiffened. The servant ladled out more glop. *A party where two women will entertain,* I suddenly remembered, *and you will meet a dark man who is wealthy...6 Cards give a complete reading.* The servant had disappeared from the four monitors and her mistress was wiping her sweaty upper lip with the back of one hand and reaching for a pack of Kents when I heard a noise in the room and finally blinked.

Ouzo was shutting a wall safe; in his free hand he clutched a black plastic box with buttons on it that resembled a remote-control TV wand. While his back was turned I remembered to look at his telephone console and memorize one of the numbers. He began walking calmly back toward me. He saw my dazed expression, chuckled and gestured at the two life-size transparencies beside the stainless-steel door. "You are surprised I possess these?"

"No, I heard you purchased the negatives from the frogmen who took them."

Ouzo's laugh was mirthless. "Why do I buy what is mine? You think they come into my waters without my knowledge, without my permission?"

"Then the rumors are true. Why?"

Now his one visible eye gleamed. "I want to make Stavros jealous. That bastard, he likes expensive women who are skinny. Mine is the most expensive, the most skinny—I want him to see, I want whole world to see!" His coughs exploded with such fury he had to clutch the desk. When the spasm passed and he finally straightened the fire was gone. "Come, we go get the American's confession, eh?"

Stepping from the villa was like plunging into a klieg-lit oven; the shimmering whiteness scorched my eyes and sapped my knee marrow. Ouzo, though, seemed to gain strength from the sun and the heat. I followed him away from the stone quay to a wooden jetty to which a speedboat was moored. As I scrambled aboard and stowed my suitcase and camera case he fired up the inboard engine.

"The lines," Ouzo commanded.

I threw off the ropes and we burbled away from the jetty. Then he rammed home the throttle; the engine snarled and the prow rose and we launched into a skittering arc past the stone quay on which the lady now read a magazine and out toward the Ionian. On clearing the cove we swerved to starboard and began skipping over the glassy blue waters, our course paralleling the curving shoreline with its dense stands of young trees marching up the steep hillside.

It took five minutes to round half the island. As we approached the isthmus on the side opposite the cove Ouzo steered away from shore and straight for the tallest tree on one of the outlying islands I'd seen from the air. Then he surveyed the main island, found his triangulating landmark, and cut throttle: "Stand by with anchor." I hoisted the spiked metal hook. "Now." I heaved the anchor overboard, and when the line slackened I snubbed the rope around a cleat.

Ouzo rose from the pilot's seat, the black plastic box in his hand. "If you are not harmed you will defend my secret?" I nodded. He studied me with his one visible eye for several seconds more before punching the box's buttons in a sequence.

The cylindrical aluminum canister broke water off the port bow. I climbed over the windshield onto the prow and used the gaffing hook Ouzo passed forward to fish it alongside. It was coupled to a line that disappeared into the depths. I unhooked the line, secured it to a cleat, and hefted the canister from the water. It had the size and weight of a fire extinguisher.

Ouzo wiped it dry with a towel, then unscrewed its tip. In the recess was a locked compartment. Shielding the canister with his body, Ouzo dialed the combination, swung open the compartment, and withdrew a packet wrapped in heavy-gauge plastic.

Inside the waterproofing was an envelope from the Desert Inn. Inside the envelope was a two-page letter written in a spidery longhand:

Dear George,
    Back in 1937 I met a girl by the name of Francine D——, she was from the little town of Brogan, Oregon, and she had come to Hollywood for the purpose of becoming a Motion Picture star. Now as you know I was not at that time making Motion Pictures, but we hit it off anyway. In August of that year I did agree to establish her with a residence and with household expenses on the express condition that she would employ precautions. You see, I did not want issue forthcoming. Well, George, she deceived me, because in February of 1938, I think it was, she did inform me that she was carrying my issue. I was disbelieving at first, but my men who surveiled her did report that she had not been with another man, so when she resisted a trip to Dr. H——, I did the honorable thing, to wit, I advised Francine I would support the child and her too. I became a father on June 12, 1938, when a baby named Catherine D—— was born in Mexico City. I thereupon instructed my aide to remit to mother and daughter the tax-free stipend of $2,000 per month, which you know was a lot of money in those days. On the evening of March 14, 1939, Francine called at my residence on Muirfield Road to express her pique at seeing another Motion Picture actress. She did then inform me that I should increase her stipend to $5,000 per

month. When I allowed as to how this was blackmail an argument did ensue and I did with my own hands kill Francine D——, a tragedy my aide did disguise by making it look like an automobile accident on the road. I feel much remorse for taking another's life, and to make amends I did anonymously contribute to the welfare of child Catherine, who was raised by her maternal grandparents. I am happy to be able to say, George, that the last reports to reach me indicate that child Catherine is presently a mother and a happy homemaker in the city of San Francisco.

The signature was the bashful billionaire's.

After I snapped my Polaroids of Bourbon's confession I coupled the resealed canister to its line and Ouzo tapped another sequence on his black box. We were watching the canister descend rapidly toward the seafloor when he said, "That paper, it is worth maybe one billion dollars U.S."

I looked up with surprise. "Oh? I mean he confesses a murder, and I guess there's no statute of limitations on that, but he's an old man living in another country. Would my government bother to extrad..."

"It is worth maybe one billion dollars," Ouzo repeated. Then he took a last drag from his cigarette, flipped the butt overboard, and ignited the speedboat's engine.

Back at the cove his wife still lay on the stone quay, stomach down to brown her backside. As Ouzo and I moored the boat to the jetty I said, "If it's worth a billion, why don't you sell it to him?"

"Because his corporation buys it, then they kill me."

"What could be worth..." And then I understood: Bourbon had no known heirs and was too old to produce one. The explosive section of the confession was thus not the murder but the acknowledgment of paternity—if Catherine were alive, she was entitled to the entire estate, will or no will.

Ouzo chuckled at my sudden comprehension. "So now you know, eh?"

When we arrived at the pathway to the villas he said, "I tell my pilot to fly you back to Athens."

"Thanks, but I'm not going there."

"Eh? Where you go?"

"Be at the phone in your office at six P.M. sharp and I'll tell you."

"You do not trust me."

"No."

"Good, very good! I am right—you are a bastard! Is that why you do not ask to see the Tiziano, because you wish to hurt my feelings?"

"I'm told the real *La Bella* hangs in the Pitti."

Ouzo smiled wryly and wiped his mouth. "Pleasant journey, eh? And you defend my secret or I be very very angry, eh?" He turned abruptly toward the larger villa. Perhaps his brave front cost him the last of his energies, for he had trouble dragging open the heavy oak door.

As I walked to the helicopter pad the lady heard me passing the stone quay and looked up. I returned her Delphic gaze, glanced appraisingly at her glistening flesh, and resumed my trek.

The helicopter landed at Aktion at 1:30 P.M.; lots of time, so I told the pilot of Ouzo's DC-6 I'd give him our destination at six sharp, then cabbed into the town of Preveza to pass the afternoon at a taverna.

Back at the air base I beckoned the pilot to a pay phone. Then I placed a call to the number I'd memorized. "Hello? Huang here. Your pilot's flying me to Brindisi. If I don't get there by seven-thirty P.M., your time, to call my associates, they go to the media. That's seven-thirty, about ninety minutes from now, so here's your man—tell him not to dawdle."

The message must have got through because the pilot rammed through flight plans, lifted off from Aktion at 6:22 P.M., and landed Brindisi, an Italian port city some 195 miles north-by-northwest across the Adriatic, just fifty-six minutes later. When I cleared Customs it was already 6:38 P.M., local time, but I hurried not to a phone booth but to the Aero Transporti Italiani counter.

I was the final passenger to board the 6:55 P.M. jet, the last of the day from Brindisi. Even if Ouzo had scrambled an agent to intercept me, I thought, and even if the agent could get his counterpart in Rome to Fiumicino Airport in the next sixty minutes—highly unlikely—I could still shake that tail in the madness that is the Eternal City.

26 March 1974: Rome

"We guessed right," Fanning said.

"Yup. Listen, I swung by the Time Inc. office this morning, so Martha should have her copy tomorrow. Yours might take longer, the postal system here's a mess."

"Have you contacted Bourbon."

"No, and I need a favor before I do. It seems to me that unless this daughter's alive, I don't have a whole lot of leverage. And I've got a sinking feeling that she may not be, that somewhere along the way one of Bourbon's people decided to clean up his boss's act."

Fanning took down Catherine's family name and the town in Oregon. "For speed, I'll call in an agency we keep on retainer."

"Oh?"

"Don't worry, Datatec is reliable and discreet."

I decided to remain silent.

27 March 1974: Florence

The frescoed ceiling was superb and the two major Rubenses magnificent but the star of the Venus Room at the Pitti Palace was unquestionably the canvas titled *Portrait of a Gentlewoman*. The creaminess of *la signorina*'s skin was accentuated by her slightly flushed cheeks, by her titian tresses, and by the warm amber chain spilling from her neck onto the brocaded dress of dark-blue-and-russet silk.

Footsteps clacked across the marble floor. It was a guard. "La Bella *si bella, eh?*"

Yes, she was truly beautiful. But was she truly a Titian?

28 March 1974: Rome

At 11:37 P.M. the all-night telephone-and-telegraph office off Piazza San Silvestro stood virtually deserted. My line to New

York was staticky but Fanning came through loud and clear: "The girl's alive."

"Wow. How do you explain that?"

"I can only speculate Bourbon's people out in Encino haven't read the confession."

"The hell with the confession. Things like murder and paternity just can't be hushed up, at least not within his empire."

Fanning snorted. "You don't know much about his empire. Only a handful of trusted aides has ever been privy to Bourbon's personal life. The current palace guard may seem omnipotent—for instance, they control all access to him—but they simply weren't around back in the thirties, at least not in trusted positions. And the men who ran the show back then, the ones who probably knew, they're all gone."

"But Bourbon knows."

"He seems to be keeping it to himself, doesn't he."

Fanning gave me the name of the man I'd have to negotiate with to see Bourbon, the organization's telex number, and the Las Vegas telephone through which for some reason all calls to Encino were routed. When we rang off I shredded the telegram I'd composed and under the sleepy eye of a telegraph clerk began anew.

To contact Bourbon I had to approach Encino. Did Encino know about Entrepays? Probably. Did Encino know that their boss, in order to gain entry to Entrepays, had to confess to criminality? Probably. Did Encino know the substance of that confession? Evidently not. To protect Catherine, therefore, I had to bluff Encino into relaying my message without hinting of her existence. I soon realized that my only hope was that Encino had 1) collected Caviar's confession in Rio; 2) peeked at Caviar's confession; 3) surmised from that peek the magnitude of Bourbon's confession. Shortly after 1 A.M. I dispatched a redrafted telegram to Bourbon, c/o the Xanadu Princess Hotel in Freeport, the Bahamas, with a copy to Encino:

YOUR ENTREPAYS AGREEMENT OF 31 MAY 1970, SIGNED AT DESERT INN, PAYING BELATED AND UNEXPECTED DIVIDENDS. MY ASSOCIATES, WHO POSSESS COPY, THINK IT TIME FOR PUBLIC OFFERING. SUGGEST MEETING SOONEST TO AVOID SERIOUS EMBARRASSMENT. WILL CALL ENCINO FOR INSTRUCTIONS 1600 RPT 1600 HOURS PACIFIC TIME 29 MARCH. P. ARTHUR

30 March 1974: Rome/Frankfurt/Nassau/Freeport

The deskman at my *pensione* was surprised that anyone would want a wake-up call at such an ungodly hour but he dutifully complied. I answered on the fifth ring and asked for an overseas operator. By the time he roused her and she called back with Las Vegas on the line and Vegas connected me to Encino and Encino plugged me into my party my watch read 1:07, which meant it was 4:07 P.M. in California.

"Hello?" The voice was male and wary.

"This is P. Arthur calling. Wh..."

"Is your line secure?" So Encino did know about Entrepays—and that the subject was sensitive.

"No, it isn't."

After a lengthy silence he said in a soft, raspy voice, "We don't understand your telegram. It's too cryptic."

"Then show your boss the copy I sent to Freeport. He'll understand."

"He's a very, very busy man."

"You're his adviser. Advise him to make the time."

"I'll be happy to consider it, once you explain yourself."

"Okay. Your boss signed a piece of paper on May thirty-first, 1970, at the Desert Inn..."

"He signs documents every day."

"Listen, I'm being euphemistic because we're on an open line. Want a taste of the nitty-gritty?" There was no response. "Your boss's paper was collected by a British courier who handed over a half-dollar. It had a star-shaped notch in it. It was redeemed four days later, in Rio, for a letter written on the stationery of the Cyrus Hotel in Shiraz, Iran. Convinced?"

When he finally spoke his voice was still urbane: "It seems you're familiar with the logistics of the, ah, the transaction. Now convince me you know the contents of the document."

"Your boss'll be the sole judge of that."

"I told you I will not waste his time until I've investigated the matter further. I see from your telegram you're in Italy. I'll have one of my repre..."

"No."

"Now be reasonable. How can we make an offer without examining the goods?"

"Because I'm not selling."

"Oh?" He couldn't completely mask his surprise.

"That's right. All I want is a meeting with your boss."

"Preposterous!"

"Would your boss rather see me or see the Entrepays agreement in print? His handwriting's a little shaky, but I'm sure the experts'll have no problem identifying it."

The line crackled with static for a full ten seconds before he said, "Let's assume I'll waive inspection of the merchandise. What would be the purpose of an audience?"

"One, I want to ask him if he's put out a contract on me."

"What!"

"There've been two attempts so far. The first time it was Mafia hit men—a species I believe you're acquainted with from your Vegas holdings."

"Good lord, I assure you..."

"I want it from your boss's lips, not yours. And two, I want to see the Persian's document."

"I see. I, ah, I'll do my best, but I'm not sure..."

"I want more than your best," I snapped.

"Don't lean, young man! I, ah, I need time to get authorization. Give me twenty-four hours."

"No, but I'll be a sport and give you eight."

"Impossible."

"Then you're shit out of luck, mister. If I don't get a 'Yes' when I call back, I run straight to the media."

"Washington would stop you," he replied with sudden confidence.

Washington—did he think Bourbon's confession implicated someone in Washington? If so, I'd further the misconception: "Maybe, but that still leaves my associates, who I've got on fail-safe. Unless I stop them the whole thing blows. And remember—it'll be more than your boss's ass in the wringer, it'll be Washington's, too." A brief pause for effect, then "Mister, you've got exactly eight hours," and I hung up.

My bravado notwithstanding, I quickly packed my bags and settled my bill; if the answer came back "No," or if despite my threat Washington was alerted, I wasn't about to loiter in Rome. It was after 1:30 A.M. but I found a cabby a few blocks away at the Stazione Termini. As I piled in I said, "Fiumicino, *per favore*."

Deserted airports are lousy places to hide; I spent the night in a men's room stall studying the *Official Airline Guide*. I needed to enter and exit Freeport without touching American soil, a precaution that seemed suddenly mandatory. In addition, my escape route had to give me a chance to shed the tails Bourbon would surely plant. It was almost dawn by the time I'd drawn up a list of contingency plans.

Shortly after 9 A.M. I wove on tired legs through the now crowded terminal to the bank of overseas phone booths.

"It's been approved," the man with the raspy voice said.

My fatigue suddenly lifted. "Good. I want a Bahamasair charter to meet the Frankfurt flight arriving Nassau at 5:55 P.M."

"Which day?"

"Today."

"That's not..."

"Remember—double-cross me and you're up shit's creek." I hung up and started to call Fanning when I remembered it was Saturday. Quickly I composed a cable to his Rye address in which I explained my haste at flying to the Bahamas in one phrase: "PROJECT 'SOURMASH' POSSIBLY LIAISING WASHINGTON." Then I hurried to the gate where the Alitalia flight to Frankfurt was boarding.

As we winged north across the Continent I brooded over my Polaroid prints of Bourbon's confession: if I was searched in Freeport, Catherine would be a secret no more. Finally I pulled them out and began to memorize, and when we landed Rhein-Main Airport I shredded them and flushed the bits down a toilet. Then I boarded the Nassau-bound Lufthansa DC-10.

We began to chase the sun. Try as I might, I could not fall asleep; by staying awake through the long and chilly night in the Fiumicino men's room I'd kicked myself into third wind, the state in which the body passes beyond fatigue and the mind floats free-associatively. Long-distance runners know the phenomenon well, as do doctors on thirty-six-hour call and journalists on breaking stories and students on No-Doz crams and snow-removal men during fifteen-inch blizzards. I ordered champagne in the hope it would act as a soporific. Instead it made the in-flight movie very comical indeed, even without the headset. And then I conjured up a goony insight, the kind third wind inspires: my thus far successful brinksmanship with the Cocktail Party conspirators was the result of neither luck nor a long-hidden talent for turning screws. Rather, it was the payoff for meticulous preparation. Not a step had been taken without doping the odds and then trying to improve them; given time, I reasoned, there wasn't a vulnerability the moderately intelligent person couldn't exploit. Maybe this was the secret of spies and criminals and even bill collectors and harassing landlords—time, the time to scheme. And then the physiological traits of third wind struck. As I stood to go pee I began to giggle at the thought that my growing experience would make me one damned fine dunner.

We continued to drone westward. The worst part of third wind is the fluid and mineral depletion of the body as it starts to consume its reserves so, finally deciding to go with the flow, I drifted back to the plane's galley and chatted up the Wagnerian stews as I cadged sodas and instant-energy sweets. Hours later, when the pilot decided the sun was uncatchable and started his descent, I felt bloated but still reasonably alert.

Nassau shimmered in the heat; the humidity was thick as phlegm. I hurried down the metal steps and crossed the softened tarmac to the terminal. On the other side of Customs I spotted a cardboard sign that read "Mr. P. Arthur." The man holding it was a jaunty middle-aged black wearing a shirt monogrammed "Bahamasair."

"I'm P. Arthur."

"Den let's go, mon, we wantsta land 'fore the sun go down."

The sea below was like opaque glass as the twin-engined Beechcraft winged straight for the right rim of the lowering sun. By the time we landed Freeport the orange orb hovered a finger's width above the horizon.

Waiting for me at the Bahamasair counter inside the terminal was a sandy-haired man in his early fifties. "Mr. Arthur?" I nodded. He scowled as he pushed his glasses up with one pudgy finger. Then he slapped a hotel key into my hand, pointed to a Bahamian chauffeur, and grunted, "Go with my driver. We'll call."

"Am I..."

He wheeled and without a word began waddling toward the airport's waiting room.

The key unlocked Room 714 of the Xanadu Princess. I drew the drapes and searched the room. The microphone was in the ceiling light fixture, and unlike the other hanging decorations, which could be removed, a small convex mirror was bolted to the wall—to conceal a camera? Finally I switched off the lights and flopped fully dressed onto the double bed.

31 March 1974: Freeport/Nassau/En route to Frankfurt

Every time I started to nod off, something—a raucous laugh down by the pool, the wall thumps of screwing in the next room, a toilet flush upstairs—something would joggle me awake. Then at 1 A.M., when night sounds died and lassitude lapped darkly at my feverish brain, my left calf seized in a cramp of excruciating intensity: my body had run perilously low on minerals. A hot shower loosened the knotted muscles but when they contracted again I called room service. The hamburger and fries I doused with a half shaker of salt helped and the milk shake soothed but they also made sleep impossible. That's why I heard them before the knocks, and when the knocks came I immediately yelled, "Coming." As I crossed the room I checked my watch: it was 3:08.

The wedge of bronzed chest, when I finally stopped blinking, belonged to a sun-kissed surfer who looked like nothing less than a six-foot-eight Redford with muscles. Behind him in the corridor stood the fat man from the airport and a hatchet-faced man who was also in his fifties. When the hatchet-face man spoke—"May I come in?"—I instantly recognized his raspy voice from our telephone conversations.

"Sure, it's your hotel."

He stepped in. So did the surfer, who without a glance shut the door in the fat man's face. Hatchet Face flicked his eyes around the room. "Listen, let's not beat around the bush. Show me your copy of the document, tell me who has it, and we'll make it worth your while."

"I came to meet your boss."

Hatchet Face lowered himself primly onto a chair arm. "I'll be frank, Mr. Huang, he doesn't wish to see you. Not only is he averse to visitors, a trait you must surely be familiar with, but he makes darn few mistakes. When he does, the last thing he wants is to be reminded of them."

"Look, I don't care if..."

He stayed me with his hand. "However, my employer recognizes the, ah, the gravity of your knowledge, and he's asked me to satisfy you. Joshua?"

The surfer withdrew an envelope from his polyester leisure suit, held it so I could read the return address—Cyrus Hotel, Shiraz—and then tucked it back into his pocket.

"In addition, Mr. Huang, this is yours." The check Hatchet Face passed me was for $250,000. "That's good-faith money, to prove my employer wishes you no harm. Further, we are prepared to, ah, to preserve your discretion with a monthly stipend of fifteen thousand dollars, paid from an unbreakable trust, for as long as you live. Or, you may elect a lump-sum payment which I assure you would be quite generous. Needless to say, all monies are tax-free."

He was coming on too strong; to hide my confusion I fetched a cigarette. And then I realized what smelled: Bourbon, by sending his top aide to verify the confession, was willing to sacrifice his daughter—so why the major-league blackmail? Unless the blizzard of money was a snow job and Caviar's confession the icing... I glanced uneasily at Joshua, who was intently gnawing a karate callus on his palm; perhaps I'd not be allowed to enjoy even the good-faith check. I decided to call the bluff: "I don't expect to be around come Social Security time. What're the mechanics of a lump-sum payment?"

"We pay it into your bank first thing Monday morning."

"Before or after you verify the confession?"

"Before."

"What kind of money are we talking about?"

"Make me a proposal."

What were they willing to sacrifice as sucker bait? I began to pace. "Let's see, fifteen thou a month is one-eighty a year... how about six million?"

"That's high." But Hatchet Face's perfect poker face told me it wasn't, that he didn't consider my preposterous figure preposterous. Jesus... "I, ah, I don't see how we can go over four million ourselves, but I'll make overtures to the, ah, the other party. Perhaps they'll chip in toward a good cause."

Now the alarm bells came full wail. I walked to the window and gazed at the empty pool. This "other party" again—Washington? If so, what the hell did Bourbon think he'd signed? And would even a maniac squander four million as sucker bait?

"Look, uh, you say your boss didn't order the hit. But if I tell you who has his confession, that man's going to order one on me."

Hatchet Face began to stroke his upper lip. Joshua kept scowling at the recalcitrant callus. Finally Hatchet Face nodded. "Very well. We'll waive the holder's identity, but our offer drops by one million. Now if I might verify my employer's document..."

I turned back to the window. What was I missing in my terminal fatigue? I'd come to see Bourbon and to photograph Caviar's confession. Here I was being offered the confession but in lieu of seeing Bourbon, three million in hush money. Why? If I could only get to the root of my suspicions...

"Mr. Huang, do we have a deal or not?"

"No." I turned from the window. "Any deal I cut will be with your boss himself."

"Out of the question. Be reasonable—here's a man who would rather lose an airline than appear in court. Why should he see you?"

"Then circle your wagons, mister. Today's Sunday. Unless I call off my associates..."

"Show me the document right now, or Joshua searches the room!"

"Be my guest." His eyes widened. "I destroyed my own copy. It's all in my head—and the only person who verifies it is your boss."

Hatchet Face waved Joshua back, shifted on the chair arm, and kneaded his upper lip. Then a sad little shake of his head. "It appears you give me no choice, Mr. Huang. I... I'll waive verification, and Monday we'll transfer three mil..."

"No!" With this last stunning capitulation the pieces suddenly clicked together. Hatchet Face's erratic actions weren't in Bourbon's best interests because Bourbon didn't know his aide was meeting me... "No, I don't want your money because then you'd have a hold on me. But I do want a five-minute meeting with your boss."

"You don't seem to understand..."

"What I don't understand is why five minutes is going to fuck up his schedule. Listen, you say you've been straight with me, so I'll be straight with you. I'm starting to think your boss doesn't know anything about the contract on me..."

"Well, there you are..."

"But I'm also starting to think that someone else in your organization's behind it, and that you're denying me access to preserve the cover-up."

Hatchet Face almost fell off the chair arm. "I, ah, I assure you..."

"Sorry, mister, I've just changed the ground rules. Unless I see the boss man, and unless he puts a stop to it, my associates start calling reporters Monday morning."

He took out a handkerchief and patted his forehead; was this what a cancer patient looks like on being read the verdict? Finally he pulled himself to his feet. Joshua, his face still vacant as a surfboard, opened the door. As Hatchet Face stumbled through it he whispered, "I'll see what can be done."

At 4:25 A.M. urgent pounding woke me from a fitful doze. Hatchet Face was alone but still ashen. "Come on."

"Now?"

"Right now."

As I quickly rinsed face and mouth I remembered those stories of Bourbon overseeing his empire while mere mortals slept; evidently they weren't apocryphal. Then I unlocked my luggage—why have it needlessly slashed—and picked up the Polaroid.

"What's that for?"

"The Persian's confession."

"No! No camera upstairs. You, ah, you can photograph it down here, after the meeting."

I tossed the Polaroid back on the bed and followed him out of the room. An elevator was waiting, its control panel exposed. He flipped a switch to close the doors, then inserted a key into a red-bordered slot and pressed the "Penthouse" button.

When the doors parted I found myself staring into the muzzle of an automatic rifle. Unlike me, Hatchet Face didn't freeze: "He's okay." Reluctantly, I thought, the hulking Bahamian lowered his weapon.

We skirted a second guard perched behind a console containing a half-dozen closed-circuit TV monitors and walked down the corridor to the door marked "C." Hatchet Face waved back up the corridor. Presently a buzz, then the snicks of locks releasing.

The anteroom was small and lined with steel plates; augmenting the recessed ceiling fixtures were two banks of fluorescents emitting a peculiar bluish light, like the kind doctors use to sterilize instruments. Hatchet Face depressed the intercom switch. "Hello, is everything set?"

A metallic squawk: "Right, chief. Jay's in with The Man."

A knock, four quick raps, then two more raps, and Hatchet Face was turning the doorknob.

The large, blandly furnished suite was hot as a greenhouse. On the far side a gaunt, sallow man with snowy hair and neatly trimmed Vandyke sat upright in a tan Barcalounger. Under a flannel bathrobe, Bourbon wore blue pajamas and sandals. Next to him stood a weak-chinned meat loaf of a man; Jay was motioning us in.

As I followed Hatchet Face across the room Bourbon's flashing eyes remained riveted on me. Some eighteen feet from the billionaire was a chair whose cushions and arms were draped with fresh sheets of paper toweling. Hatchet Face motioned me to it, then turned to his boss. "Sir, this is Mr. Raymond Huang."

Bourbon's eyes snaked from me to Hatchet Face to Jay. As Jay leaned to whisper in the old man's ear I began planning how to get rid of these flunkies when it came time to broach the issue named Catherine. Now the billionaire's gaze swung back to Hatchet Face, who repeated in a loud rasp, "Sir, this is Mr. Raymond Huang. He knows about Entrepays."

Suddenly Bourbon's penetrating eyes were boring through mine. With his right hand he began to twirl a lock of lank hair; I was surprised to see an angry polyp on his forehead. Then he cleared his throat—but still he did not speak.

Hatchet Face coughed politely. "Sir, Mr. Huang thinks someone in our organization ordered him killed because of his familiarity with Entrepays. I've assured him that's not the way we operate, but, ah, but he'd like it confirmed by you."

The brooding stare was remorseless. Did he want me to speak first? Finally the silence pressured me to blurt, "Uh, that's right, sir, I'll be happy to go if you'll give me your personal assur..."

Now Bourbon was scowling and turning to Jay. "Call Romaine, Jay, and be quick about it." His voice was like thunder. "I want to get to the bottom of this right here and right now, I want answers! That's right, I want to know where they sent that cock-sucking Reel Six!" Both aides wilted in despair. "Shit, Jay, we ordered it, what was it, we ordered that reel a week ago, and they got flights here to London all the time, don't they, so tell 'em to shake a leg!" He turned back to me. "Goddamn nincompoops, how do they expect me to finish the motion picture without Reel Six? Do you spit?"

I closed my slack jaw and managed to say, "Sir?"

"Spit. You know, sonny, spit—do you spit? All Chinamen spit, that's why you're sick all the time. Do you spit?"

"Uh, no sir, I don't spit."

"Louder!"

"No, I don't spit!"

"Aha!" Bourbon's smile turned cagey. "Then you're a fucking Commie, ain't ya? I know all about it, I heard how this Mousey character won't let you spit, and a good thing, too. You spit now and they chop out your tongue, am I right?"

"Uh, I..."

"Jay, why did you let this Commie in my house? You know how I... Look! Look!" Bourbon pointed frantically at the sheet of paper toweling that had fallen from my chair. "He's not insulated! He's not insulated! Quick, Jay, quick quick..." Now the billionaire's eyes bulged and drool glistened on his Vandyke; I snatched up the paper and threw it back in place. Bourbon's body sagged in relief. "Thank you, thank you, sonny. Have to watch the germs, don't we? Oh dear me, what a scare, eh, Jay?" He snuffled once and then his voice grew preternaturally calm. "I think I'll have my medication now."

Jay glanced uneasily at his watch. "Uh, not quite yet, sir. Soon."

"Right," Hatchet Face said. "And Mr. Huang and I have to be going now..."

"Speak up, Noah!"

Hatchet Face flushed; his name wasn't Noah. "I, ah, I said we have to be going..."

"No, not until we're through here," Bourbon commanded. He drew a breath so deep it trembled his frail frame. "All right now, where were we?"

"Entrepays," I said. "I wanted to know if..."

"How do I look, sonny?"

"Uh, fine, sir."

Suddenly Bourbon grinned. "Yessirree, I sure as hell do.

Got a wonderful barber, best in the world, don't see him enough. Jay, we should have more guests because when we have guests you make me look so fine, and when I look so fine I feel fine, just so long as they don't come around too damned often." He made a funny humming sound deep in his throat. "Now, where were we?"

Hatchet Face cut in quickly. "Sir, I've assured Mr. Huang that neither you nor any of your associates want him dead, so I think we'll be go..."

"Dead? Of course not, of course not—why I don't even know this joker, do I, sonny? We ever meet before? Jesus no, you don't even look like your old man. Horace, now there was one white Chinaman, your dad was..." Bourbon's eyes glazed again. When he returned from wherever he'd gone he asked Hatchet Face, "How's Horace? Haven't seen him in...in years. And why do we want his kid dead?"

Hatchet Face gritted his teeth. "We don't, sir. It's just that he knows about Entrepays, and..."

"So you know, eh?" Bourbon regarded me shrewdly. "Hell's bells, the Company'll shit on your Stetson if you fink about the Glomar to your Commie..."

"No no!" Hatchet face blurted. "Entrepays, that's, ah, that's George Blair's company—you know, the one you signed the confession for?"

"Ahhhh! Well sonny-boy, why didn't you say so in the first place? Could've saved a lot of time, and time is money, yes-sirree. The confession—you have it, do you?"

Sweat sprang to my face—goodbye, Catherine. Finally I whispered, "Yes sir."

"What?" he bellowed.

"Yes sir!"

"Well shit, if you have the confession you know all about it, don't you?" He turned and glared triumphantly at Hatchet Face. "See, I told you, Mr. Smarty-Pants, I told you!" I looked away in anguish but then Bourbon was shouting, "I told you never trust a fucking greaser! You hand him a hundred thou, no problem, what the hell would a Cuban do with it 'cept buy a shitload of tacos, but you hand him half a m..."

"Sir!" Hatchet Face screamed.

"We got no secrets from sonny-boy, he knows! You know, don't you? Course you do. He knows, this wily Oriental son of a bitch knows! Hey-ba-ba-re-bop!" Bourbon's cackle was cut short by whooping spasms of coughing. As Jay tried to comfort his boss I sought desperately to make sense of the reference to the Cuban. Did this old man really believe he'd confessed to political bribery? That's certainly what Hatchet Face had seemed afraid of all along. Or had the veil of madness lifted—was Bourbon lying to protect some all but forgotten daughter? Or was he just out-and-out bonkers? When the painful coughs subsided the billionaire looked up at Jay with a pitiful expression; had he a tail, it would have been wagging. "My medication, please...please give me the box. Just one. Just one blue bomber, promise. Don't make me beg...give me the box...for the love of God, Jay, give me the fucking box!"

"I'm sorry, sir, it's too soon."

"Ooooohhhh..." Bourbon shut his eyes. Once more his body convulsed, this time with sobs. 'Ooooohhhh . . . you're so cruel . . . so, so cruel...how can you all be so cruel to me?" But then his breath miraculously steadied and he pulled himself upright and when he spoke again his voice was whine-free if loud: "Time's a-wastin', time's a-wastin,' let's wrap this up. Now, what's the problem? Where were we?"

Neither Hatchet Face nor Jay would return my look so I turned to Bourbon and said, "I guess there is no problem, sir."

"Good. Good! Hey Jay, I like sonny-boy, he makes me feel real fine. Tell him he can come back, hear? That's right, sonny, you come back so long as you wash your hands and you don't spit." The billionaire suddenly squinched his eyes, grimaced, and turned his face up toward the ceiling.

The whisper of a fart trembled the hushed room like a howitzer.

"Hey! Hey, hey-ba-ba-re-bop! Hear that? It's a-comin', it's a-comin'! My man! Where the hell's my man?"

Jay darted to a door and tapped twice. A muscular man with wavy hair emerged.

"Aha, there's my man! Hear that one?"

"Aye sir, I did, a good one it was."

"Well come on then, shake a leg, shake a leg, it's a-comin'!"

The muscular man could have been lifting a rag doll as he tenderly cradled his master from the Barcalounger. Jay swung open another door and the muscular man carried Bourbon through it. Now a faint stench of Lysol and now Jay banged the door shut.

Hatchet Face was clutching a chair, his pasty face hung down in the resuscitation position. Finally he looked up at Jay. "Jesus, I never thought... Hey, where're you going?"

"To my room," I said; I'd suffocate if I didn't escape this asylum soon. "I'll wait for the Persian's confession down there."

Hatchet Face caught up with me in the steel-jacketed anteroom and grabbed my arm. "I can't prove one of us didn't order the hit on you, but you know what I've just done, don't you?" I nodded: he'd handed me a loaded gun aimed right at the heart of Bourbon's empire—provided I could make someone believe what I'd just witnessed. "That's right, it was an act of good faith, the kind money can't buy. You breach it and I'll use every last dollar at my disposal to bury you."

Down in Room 714 the contents of my two cases were strewn about but Hatchet Face didn't say a word so neither did I. He passed over the envelope containing Caviar's confession. I unfolded the single handwritten sheet:

> History records that on 16 September 1941 our beloved Father, the Shahinshah of Iran, abdicated his Throne, owing to the entreaties of the Governments of His Majesty, King George VI of Great Britain, and the Union of Soviet Socialist Republics. History does not record that it was we, through covert meetings with Ambassadors Bullard and Smirnov, who arranged for our Allies to suggest our Father abdicate. Our pledge was rapid signing of the Tripartite Treaty, permitting British and Soviet Allies on the soil of our sacred Homeland, which our Father opposed; our price was our own ascension to the Throne, plus payment of £2 million to our private account with the Union of Swiss Banks. To prevent our beloved Father from learning of this painful but vital agreement, our loyal subject Nematollah N——, upon our command, successfully introduced strychnine to a repast taken on 16 August 1945 by our Father in Rabat. We deeply regret that the untimely death of our valiant Father occasioned itself three days later, but we are consoled by the fact that it was Allah's will.

Patricide that was also figurative regicide; that should shake them up in Iran. I snapped the Polaroids and handed the document back to Hatchet Face: "As long as I remain safe, so'll your boss's confession. As for his, uh, his condition, I can only promise that I won't be the first to break it."

"Fair enough," he said wearily.

"One last thing—I need another Bahamasair charter."

"What time and where to?"

How much leeway to allow—two hours? "Let's make it for two-thirty this afternoon."

"Your destination?"

"I'll tell the pilot."

Hatchet Face stared at me, finally nodded, and left. I quickly repacked my suitcase, transferring several essentials and one change of underwear to my camera case. Then I double-locked and chained the door, requested a 1 P.M. wake-up call, and collapsed into bed. Now sleep came.

I was still logy when I arrived at the airport. My pilot, the same man who'd flown me into Freeport, giggled upon seeing me. "Hey mon, you break de bank so soon?"

"Sure."

"Den we best get outta here. Where you want to fly this gorgeous day?"

We landed Nassau at 3:36 P.M. Sixty-four minutes later I was aloft aboard the Lufthansa jet returning to Frankfurt, through which I was ticketed back to Rome. Had Hatchet Face scrambled an agent aboard the DC-10? It really didn't matter, I thought, as I passed out again.

1 April 1974: Frankfurt/Paris

The transit lounge at Rhein-Main Airport was congested with early Monday travelers. I squeezed up to the telegraph counter and wired Caviar at his Tehran palace:

HAVE MIRACULOUSLY UNEARTHED INTACT TABULA AT BULLARD-SMIRNOV DIGS. IMPERATIVE WE REVIEW CONTRACT OF 25 MAY 1970, SIGNED AT HOTEL CYRUS, SHIRAZ. MY FULLY BRIEFED ASSOCIATES URGE RENOGIATION VIEWLY FATALITY INCURRED RABAT FIELDWORK. CONTACT ME SOONEST VIA LONDON "TIMES" PERSONAL NOTICE WITH MESSAGE UTILIZING WORD "NICKEL," AS IN NICKEL WITH STAR-SHAPED NOTCH.

P. ARTHUR

It was now 7:57 A.M. I scanned the departure board: the Alitalia flight to which my checked-through suitcase was being transferred took off at 10:20.

At 8:15 A.M. the transit lounge dissolved into chaos as a transatlantic charter was called. I shouldered my camera case, sifted through the crowd to Immigration, and presented my passport. Two minutes later I was standing in the main terminal.

At 9 A.M. I boarded a Lufthansa 747 for Paris. Seventy minutes later we were into our landing pattern over Orly; back at Rhein-Main the final page for Passenger Sasaki on the Frankfurt-to-Rome flight would go unanswered, which meant anyone waiting at Fiumicino would come up empty. But then wasn't today April Fools' Day?

2 April 1974: Paris

When the cinema let out shortly before 9 P.M. the Parisians in the street were still abuzz over the death that day of President Pompidou: whither the Fifth Republic suddenly bereft, after sixteen prosperous years, of a staunch Gaullist at its helm? As soon as I got back to my genteelly shabby hotel in Montparnasse I headed up to my room. My routes into and out of Tehran were complicated, and I wanted to get them right before contacting New York.

I hadn't spoken idly to Fanning a couple of weeks before when I'd mentioned my fear of Caviar, or, more precisely, SAVAK. These imperial bullyboys spanned the globe; look closely behind any overseas Iranian, especially a liberal or a student, and a SAVAK agent was sure to lurk nearby. I'd never seen it rated among the world's most efficient intelligence forces, but rumors abounded that SAVAK was among the most brutal, a trait no doubt honed by its open license on any who dared think ill of His Majesty. Which, as of now, included me.

The "Do Not Disturb" sign was still on my door. Something in the room, though, had been disturbed: the *Official Airline Guide* which I'd left open on the "Baghdad" entries was now turned to "Bahrain." Had the maid ignored the sign? Or had it been a breeze through the slightly ajar window... I dropped my gaze to the floor and spotted the fifty centime piece I'd balanced on the sash when I'd locked the window and now my jugular began to throb. Don't be silly, I told myself. I was on the fourth floor so it couldn't have been a burglar, it must have been the maid airing the room. And then my eyes locked on the ashtray next to the bed: in it, amidst my crushed Benson & Hedges filters, lay the fat black stub of a cheap cigar.

Ring-ring.

I was automatically reaching for the room phone when I suddenly remembered nobody knew I was here...

Ring-ring. Ring-ring. Ring-ring. Ring-ring.

Come on, pick it up, a phone can't bite...

Ring-ring. Ring-ring. Ring-ring. Ring-ring.

Jesus, were they going to ring all night?

Ring-ring. Ring-ring. Ring...

I screwed up my courage and lifted the receiver.

"Monsieur Sasaki?"

"Uh, uh, yes?"

"This is the desk. You have the long-distance call. Please hold..."

"Wait a minute! Where's it fr..."

But I was too late because now a mellifluous male voice was on the line: "Have I the pleasure of conversing with Mr. Raymond Huang?"

My dinner shot halfway up my throat.

"Do not be afraid, do not be afraid, sir! I am Omar, and I call from Tehran on behalf of His Majesty. His Majesty has received your telegram and will most enjoy a..."

"How? How the hell did you trace me?"

Omar laughed. "In good time, sir, in good time. As I am saying, His Majesty will most enjoy a meeting with you. Alas, His Majesty is most busy this week. Will Monday next, that is the eighth, will that be convenient?"

Of course it wasn't, but I knew they could as easily blow me away where I stood as in Tehran. "I, uh, I guess so."

"Splendid, splendid. Say about half past noon?"

"Sure, why not."

"Now for transport. You will of course come via Iran Air... let me see, let me see, yes, our flight schedules are favorable. Perhaps you will like to come tomorrow, and enjoy some of our country's sights?"

"Well, uh..."

"I fully understand, sir! To be frank with you, I too find

Paris more entertaining than Tehran... let me see, yes, we have a deadhead flight to Mehrabad from Orly Sunday night next. Shall I book you on it?"

"That'd be fine."

"Splendid, splendid! Then please present yourself at Orly at twenty-two-thirty hours Sunday. Mr. Huang, I truly love Paris, and I envy you your stay—do enjoy it. Ta!"

Little atoms darted across my eyeballs, leaving contrails. How had they found me? It didn't matter. Should I run? Not as Tetsuo R. Sasaki, that would be futile. Did I have the resources to buy decent papers in a strange city? Probably not. I did have the resources to get drunk, though, so I hung up the dead receiver and headed for the bistro down the street.

4 April 1974: Paris

The spring day was bright and the boulevardiers on the Champs Élysées *très* gay but not even a heavy scarf could stay the chill from my nape: the role of stalkee was infinitely more taxing than that of stalker. Still, I'd made no moves to shake my tails. Perhaps Caviar had put off meeting me because of a heavy schedule. Perhaps, though, he wanted to give me time to bolt— and thereby point him to my associates. Had SAVAK trailed me to the Time Inc. bureau on Rue Honoré when I'd dropped off the packet to Martha? Had agents seen me post the letter to Fanning, and if so, had they the ability to retrieve it from the French postal system? Martha and Fanning must be warned, but on the prayer their identities were still a secret, I wasn't phoning until I could get clear. The problem was that my evasion gambit had to be perfect, because even dimwits wouldn't be caught off guard twice.

On the way to a café I stopped at a kiosk and bought a *Trib*. Two of my fellow citizens dominated the news: Citizen Richard Nixon had just fessed up to tax delinquency, a situation he pledged to rectify with $465,000, and Citizen Patricia Hearst had just made her debut into anti-society, coming out as SLA Comrade Tania. I was idly staring at the travel advertisements when I suddenly conceived a gambit that seemed foolproof. To run it I'd have to use the fake American Express card, but Carl the forger had said to save it for a pinch, and things couldn't get much tighter.

I went inside the café, purchased a *jeton*, the French payphone token, and walked to a booth. A weasel-faced man at the bar was staring at me intently so I shielded my hand with my body as I dialed Hertz. Did they have a Citroën available tomorrow? Certainly. Fine, I said, I'll pick it up at 4 P.M. sharp. Then, so they could prepare the paperwork in advance, I read off my international driver's license, as well as the American Express card to which I was charging the deposit.

Upon leaving the café I went into a bookstore down the block and bought the little red *Guide Général de Paris* and a detailed road map of northern France. Then, because it augured to be a fine spring afternoon, I walked to the Étoile and hopped a Métro for the Bois de Boulogne.

5 April 1974: Paris/Mantes/Paris

For my gambit to work they had to be on foot so when I left the hotel I rode the Métro to the Louvre, where I passed the morning observing that my SAVAK tails had little appreciation for art—and, more important, that they numbered three.

At 12:15 P.M. I emerged from a *charcuterie* with a picnic lunch in a brown bag. I bought a handful of magazines at a kiosk, descended into the Métro, and again rode out to the Bois de Boulogne.

At 3 P.M. I looked up from my perch under a shady oak. Two of the agents appeared to be dozing while the third tugged desultorily on a beer: tired and bored, I hoped, and looking forward to the imminent end of their shift. I got up, dusted myself off, and moseyed back to the Métro.

At the Picquet-Grenelle station I changed lines, making no attempt to elude my tails though the platforms were jamming with workers stealing a march on *le weekend*.

The fourth stop was Concorde: were they sufficiently lulled? As the doors closed, I suddenly darted through them onto the platform. The train began to roll. I turned.

One down but two to go—they were better than they looked. It was 3:34 P.M., not enough time for another subway game, and judging by the glares from this suddenly aroused pair, it wouldn't work anyway. Indeed, they stuck tighter than a corn plaster as I threaded my way through the cavernous Concorde station to the Neuilly/Vincennes line, and once I was aboard a Neuilly-bound train the SAVAK agents surrounded me like bookends.

At 3:50 P.M. we pulled into the Pointe-Maillot station. One man lingered lest I jump back onto the train at the last moment, but when I reached the exit he fell in step with his partner. They remained ten yards behind me the four blocks to Hertz. As I passed the garage I noticed a navy-blue Citroën parked just inside the open doors.

I entered the office and identified myself. The clerk handed over the prefilled rental agreement. Outside, the two Iranians began talking excitedly. Signature on the agreement, card in the embossing machine, *cha-chunk*, signature on the charge slip—"The keys, monsieur, have a nice trip"—and I was out the door and ambling back toward the two men. They stared at me suspiciously; I'd been inside less than a minute. Suddenly I bolted into the garage. Qucikly now into the driver's seat and as I fired the engine one SAVAK man started for the office, fumbling out his wallet as he ran. But now the Citroën was in gear and gliding out onto Rue St. Ferdinand and as I tromped on the gas I spotted the second man; he was wildly—and vainly—waving for a taxi.

To pay their expertise full respect I wove south through the rush-hour traffic to the A-6 Autoroute. *Tout* Paris seemed Riviera-bound so I waited until I approached the N-186 cloverleaf before checking for a backup surveillance unit. A batch of possibles, I decided; I turned west. Fifteen miles later, when I swung north just past Versailles, the possibles had dwindled to a Peugeot, a Mercedes, and two Simcas. Now west again on the A-13 and it was down to the Mercedes.

At 6:20 P.M. I nosed the Citroën onto the exit ramp for Mantes-la-Ville and glued my eyes to the rearview. The Mercedes continued past at speed: I was clear.

There were no underground car parks in Mantes so I stuck the Citroën in the crowded railroad station lot. At 6:55 P.M.— it was five minutes before one in the afternoon on the East Coast—I heard the phone being picked up: "Hello."

"Frew, it's me."

Fanning played it casual. "Hi. I thought the deal had fallen apart when we didn't hear from you."

"Well, there've been some complications. Caviar got wind of my plans."

"Good God!"

"Yeah. His janissaries have been velvet-gloved but persistent. I should've called earlier but uh, but we've been going around the clock, and they didn't want a recess."

"Son, break off negotiations right now. Come on home."

"Don't think I haven't thought of it, Frew. But he'd still know my identity, and besides, he's had more than enough chances to, uh, to enter a take out bid. Instead, I've been offered a meeting with Caviar himself."

Fanning lit a Chesterfield. "What do you make of it?"

"Something's sure as hell screwy. Maybe they want a fix on you and Ms. M., but I've got the feeling that can't be all."

"I still feel you should come home."

"No, the bait's too tantalizing, and I'm too damned close to nailing the last piece. By the way, did you receive the, uh, the material from the distillery?"

"Yes, both of us did. How was Bourbon."

"His brain's a box of Fruit-Loops."

"So the rumors are true." Fanning took another drag. "Any ideas how Caviar tagged you."

"None. And Frew—even though I'm clean right now, tell Clarence to keep a protective eye on you, okay?"

"Of course. And I'll figure out a way to watch over Ms. M."

"Thanks. Look, my appointment's midday Monday—call you afterward. Take care."

I found a pleasant little *auberge* in Mantes called the Chant'Reine, where I took my first enjoyable meal since Omar's call. Back in Paris, I paid Hertz cash; retrieving my charge-slipped deposit meant the American Express card was valid for another emergency. The only blemish on the perfect day came when I finally arrived back at the hotel: across the street, the glowering thugs eyeing me now numbered six.

7 April 1974: Paris/En route to Tehran

Deadheading, I learned at Orly, is the ferrying of an empty plane to a city from which it would be pressed back into scheduled service. I'd been on underbooked flights in my life, but never one with almost 140 seats vacant out of 150. My few fellow passengers were off-duty crew members of both sexes hitching a ride home; they seemed miffed by my presence, as if I was raining on a planned six-mile-high group grope. Shortly after our 11:30 P.M. takeoff I fell self-protectively into a fitful doze.

8 April 1974: Tehran

We began our approach to Mehrabad Airport at midmorning. Smog hung over Tehran like a shroud and as we descended into it the Elburz Range to the north grew fuzzy, like an out-of-focus photograph. The 707 braked to a halt some two hundred yards from the terminal. It was 10:42 A.M., local time.

I stepped from the cabin and squinted from the harsh sunlight peculiar to high altitudes. At the foot of the ramp stood a muscular young man wearing silvered sunglasses and a taut black suit. As I neared him he grabbed my suitcase in one meaty paw, about-faced, and clumped to a khaki-colored Jeep. The soldier at the wheel threw the vehicle in gear and raced us across the bleached apron to a large grey helicopter whose rotors were idling by the time we clambered aboard. I hadn't even buckled my seat belt when the *whack-whack* overhead quickened and we tilted skyward. Such niceties as Immigration and Customs are a snap, I thought, if you happen to own your own country.

We flew at three thousand feet across the northwestern suburbs toward the Elburz foothills. Twelve minutes later we were hovering over a large walled compound dominated by a cube-shaped building that showed a Bauhaus influence; toy soldiers in dark greatcoats patrolled the grounds. The helicopter lowered onto a concrete pad within the walls.

Instantly two soldiers, stooped to avoid the rotors, rushed up. My escort tossed my one suitcase and then vaulted off the craft. The larger soldier, on whom the portable metal detector looked like a child's plaything, helped me down and beyond the slowing rotors' perimeter. He was unbuckling his sensing loop when my escort stopped him; it appeared Caviar was extending me VIP treatment. My escort reclaimed my suitcase and led me across the grounds to an old but well-preserved stone palace catercorner the Bauhaus cube.

As we entered the palace a trim, dapper man in his fifties strode down the wide hallway toward us. He was smiling and as he neared he extended his hand: "Mr. Huang, it is so good to meet you." Omar's handshake was surprisingly limp. "And how is your flight?"

"Okay."

"Jolly good!"

"How..."

He held up his hand and grinned conspiratorially. "His Majesty prefers to answer your questions himself. I fear, however, His Majesty cannot be with you for another hour. Perhaps you will like to freshen up?" Then Omar cast a discreet eye over my rumpled clothes. "And perhaps you have a jacket and tie? Reza here will show you to the convenience, and I will rejoin you when you are changed. Reza understands a little English, so if you require anything..."

Reza hefted my suitcase again and set off down the hallway past a series of intimidatingly large rooms with rococo furnishings to a flight of stairs at the back of the palace. Despite myself my anxieties grew as he started down them; our destination, however, was not the dungeon but the modern locker room that stood in its stead. From the chaste pinups on the wall I guessed the guards changed here.

It was 11:45 A.M. by the time Reza knocked on the door of a small waiting room back upstairs. As we entered Omar put down his briefing book and waved to a silver tray set up with a coffee service and a plate of croissants. "Forgive me, Mr. Huang, I do not warn you deadhead flights carry no food. You must be famished, what?" Then as I attacked my belated breakfast he wittily drew me into a conversation that seemed to range over every topic save two—why I was here, and how they had found me.

At 12:15 P.M. the sullen beats of another helicopter dropping into the compound.

Omar rose. "Two articles of protocol, Mr. Huang. First, His Majesty will determine the course of conversation. Second, in our country, it is bad form to turn one's back on His Majesty. For instance, if His Majesty chooses to pace, do contrive to turn accordingly." With that, he led me across the hallway toward another door.

Outside, the vibrations of the rotors suddenly ceased; the chopper was down.

The room we entered was immense and redolent with the sense of history: surely the imams and viziers of yore had reserved their treaty signings for within these mirrored walls. Caviar had turned the chamber into his office. The furnishings were eclectic—mixed with armor and armaments from long-forgotten wars and ponderous furniture from the nineteenth century and a priceless Persian rug were such modern appurtenances as a map clock displaying all twenty-four of the world's time zones and a quietly glowing gold telephone to the left of the massive desk.

Omar stopped near the desk and turned to face a side door. Then that door swung open and Omar was dipping his head in fealty and Caviar was striding briskly across the vast room toward us.

He wore a thick oatmeal turtleneck under a navy-blue blazer, pearl-grey riding breeches, and supple black boots that glistened like onyx. Caviar seemed a big man but as he approached I noticed that he was actually shorter than me; the illusion stemmed from his slimness and his ramrod bearing. He paused to say a few words in Farsi to Omar, then turned to me. His lean face was that of a landed eagle: the beaklike nose whose line was accentuated by flaring eyebrows, the high forehead surmounted by swept-back hair now greying noticeably at the tips. His appraisal concluded, Caviar turned wordlessly and continued to his desk, leaving in his wake a rough, masculine scent of sweat and horse and leather.

Now he took a pair of heavy black-rimmed glasses from the desk top and donned them. "Mr. Huang, thank you ever so much for coming." His voice was soft and carried a subtle French inflection. "And my appreciation for winning me my wager with Omar."

"Sir?"

He chuckled, then sat. "I bet that you're a man of action, that we will hear from you within twenty-four hours of your leaving the Bahamas. Do sit, do sit—will you take some coffee?"

"No thank you," I mumbled as I groped for the chair. "Your Majesty, how did you find me?"

"Bloody simple, my dear chap. As soon as I receive Mr. Blair's posthumous letter, I order twenty-four-hour surveillance on the Xanadu Princess."

"You know who has your original?" I gasped.

"Of course. Several years ago—1971, Omar?—yes, that's right, when we entertain bids on equipment for our Abadan refineries. You really must see them, Mr. Huang, they're quite splendid. Yes, well, don't you know, one of this chappie's leftenants thinks he can steal a wicket by alluding to a passage from my letter." Caviar suddenly scowled. "If that bloody fool serves me I'll order him quartered."

"But sir, when it all fell apart—why didn't you move to recover the document?"

He looked at me closely, then leaned back. "There's a true story which those in the West laugh at but do not understand. Perhaps you, my dear chap, since you come from the East, perhaps you can grasp the subtlety. In the early 1960s, Sukarno of Indonesia's invited to Moscow. Each night he's given the finest Comrade whores. Well, don't you know, each in and each out is most carefully recorded on film by the KGB. Then the Kremlin seeks Sukarno's cooperation, and in return they will suppress the film." Caviar suddenly grinned and rubbed his hands together briskly. "Can you guess what does the Bung do, Mr. Huang? He not only requests a reel for his own collection, he offers to place Indonesian television at Moscow's disposal. That's right—he wants all his countrymen to see it! Why? Because in their eyes he's the world's number-one cocksman, and what better proof than film of him shagging very beautiful Caucasian women?"

When Caviar stopped cackling he shook out a Gauloise and lit it. "In the eyes of my subjects, I'm a stern father who's merciless if the matter involves the good of my country. Correct me if I'm wrong, old man, but you believe me to be ashamed of my letter. Nothing can be further from the truth—if you wish to publish it, please do." He paused to savor my shock. "That's right, my dear fellow, publish it! Who should care? My allies and my enemies? No. My subjects? Most assuredly not. They know that without me there's no White Revolution, no social progress—that without me they still live in the eighteenth century. You must understand, it's Allah's will that my beloved father founded our empire—and the fact that I must succeed him, to make Iran a world power, that's also Allah's will!"

Slowly Caviar's pupils contracted to normal size. "So you

see, my dear chap, we have precious little to negotiate."

"Then why did you consent to see me, Your Majesty?"

"Very few dare to demand an audience with me, particularly in such . . . such disrespectful tones. I'm frankly curious to comprehend your motivation."

"I, uh, I wanted to ask two questions, sir." He arched one of his bushy brows and waved me to continue. "First, I'd like to know if you ordered me killed in New York."

"I grant a man in your position's entitled to paranoia, but in whose presence are you this very moment?"

"Well, sir, it occurred to me that you might want me alive until you learned the identity of my associates."

He opened a folder on his desk. "On the afternoon of April the first, you go to the Time Inc. bureau in Paris. Then, on April the fifth, you elude my men for seven hours, most probably to effect a telephonic rendezvous." He sighed and turned to Omar. "I know SAVAK does not recruit mental giants, but really, old sport . . . one bloody amateur slipping three agents?" Caviar swiveled back to me. "From previous information Mr. Blair supplies, I'll venture your associate is your ex-mistress, a lady by the name of . . . by the name of Martha."

I felt like throwing up.

He saw my distress and clicked on his 150-watt smile. "Don't look so worried, my dear chap—she's bloody safe from me, and will remain so! And so will you! Now, does that answer your first question? Good. I believe your second question concerns this." Caviar casually reached into the folder with his left hand, picked up an envelope, and flipped it across the desk.

Though the envelope landed facing him, I had no trouble reading the upside-down return address: Newporter Inn. I reached for it. That's when I noticed Caviar's right hand. The .357 Magnum pistol in it was aimed at my heart.

"Mr. Huang, our check shows you're not CIA, nor do we believe you otherwise employed by the American. Of course, we all make mistakes. But if we are in error, you will only compound it if you attempt to destroy that document."

I sat as still as the gun barrel.

"Go ahead, pick it up."

With excruciating slowness I reached out and opened the envelope. The single sheet rattled noisily as I unfolded it.

An explosion of schoolboyish glee, and as I stared dumbly

at the blank paper Caviar said, "What do you think, Omar, shall we trust him?" Then with his left hand he passed over another sheet. Despite his lingering amusement Caviar's pistol still yawned at me so I set the letter carefully on his desk and placed both hands on the table's edge before I began to read:

To Whom It May Concern:

It became known to me, in the summer of 1963, that a nucleus of Free Cubans, that is to say staunch anti-Communists, were forming in the state of Florida. It further became known to me that these men, and there were some women, too, were devising a game plan to avenge the operation known to many as "The Bay of Pigs." In retrospect, and looking at the facts with the wisdom of hindsight, it was my duty as a citizen to inform my government. I didn't, and I freely admit that I was wrong not to. Speaking as a lawyer, however, I would be remiss not to point out that at that point in time, what little knowledge as was known to me was, evidentially speaking, hearsay; that is to say, there was a clear-cut lack of prosecutable evidence. In any event, it further became known to me, on or about November 17, 1963, that the Free Cubans had duped a Marxist stooge for the purpose of stalking the man who ordered air support withheld during "The Bay of Pigs" operation. Now, I'll be frank, the man was no friend of mine, not since 1960, when he allowed it to become known to me that he knew that the Woodstock typewriter was fabricated, *ex post facto*, and that proof existed. It was in fact this bare-knuckled threat, an underhanded manipulation that had no place in American politics, that dissuaded me from petitioning for a recount in the states of Illinois and Texas. But though I could not pardon the man, I wrestled for several dark and agonizing nights of the soul with my thorny problem, for I wanted to do what was right. Finally, I put aside and rose above personal bitterness and rancor, and firmly resolved to discharge my civic responsibility. After all, the man was the President. Pursuant to this decision, I forthwith revised the itinerary of a transcontinental trip, on which I had embarked at that point in time, so as to intercept him when he arrived in Texas to conduct a political tour. I waited in Dallas for the purpose of delivering my warning until the morning of November 22, 1963, at which time the press of critical business affairs caused me to return to New York. Upon landing in New York, I learned the tragic news that my good intentions notwithstanding, the President was dead. Yes, I cried for his soul.

A fresh wave of nausea swept me: so this was what had driven courier Kenton around the bend and into the bottle back in California, this mealymouthed confession by Velveeta to the twentieth century's ultimate misprision of felony. When I finally looked up Caviar had returned both letter and pistol to his drawer.

"How many copies do you wish, Mr. Huang?"

"Sir?"

"How many copies? Will four do?" When I nodded woodenly he slid me four 8 × 10 glossies. "I take it you return now to America to contact this man?" He tossed over a blue-green U.S. passport. I picked it up; it was my own. "You will forgive the liberties I take, old man, but you have enough problems without fraudulent travel papers. By the bye, your bookcase with the false bottom, it's most ingenious for an amateur."

I wiped my mouth. "Why, Your Majesty? Why are you doing all this?"

"Is it not Milton who writes, 'The truth will out'? Yes, I believe so. My dear fellow, I'm bloody serious when I say you must publish your information. All of it! I'm rather curious myself about Entrepays—I of course know of three participants, and I hope your book will enlighten me as to the others." Caviar glanced at his watch and rose.

"Please, Your Majesty, one more question. I can understand why the others joined Entrepays, but I just don't understand your motives."

"I believe you are of the middle class? Yes. Well, my good chap, I'm afraid you can never understand. Now I really must be getting along, my family awaits me at lunch ... pleasant journey and good hunting, what?" Caviar flashed me an imperial smile, strode across the room with a buoyant stride, and disappeared through the door.

I massaged my face and then turned to Omar. "Can you ..."

He held up his hand. "I know nothing His Majesty does not. Now, about your return home. I fear there are precious few westward-bound flights that remain today, so I suggest you enjoy His Majesty's hospitality at the Royal Tehran tonight? Good." As I started to follow him from the room Omar added,

"Please do not forget the photographs and your passport, Mr. Huang."

By the time the Mercedes limousine drove me from the Elburz foothills down to the Royal Tehran I'd concluded Caviar was either a gift horse, which I always insisted on looking in the mouth, or he was playing a loonier tune than Bourbon, which would make him most dangerous. Up in the suite reserved in my name I opened the liquor cabinet and found a bottle of Stolichnaya 100-proof. I was pouring a tumblerful when I suddenly thought to praise Allah for making Caviar the fourth—and not the first—of my encounters.

9 April 1974: Tehran/New York/Rye

"Fanning."

"Hi, it's me."

"You're safe."

"Yeah. And I shook Caviar's tails, so I'm clean, too." I dug out the print of Velveeta's confession. "You're not going to believe this, but..."

I was right; Fanning didn't want to believe it. Finally he refound his voice. "Whatever's on those subpoenaed tapes . . . whatever the man's hiding now . . . it's nothing. My God, I feel sick."

"Frew..."

"Where are you, son."

"Frew, the news I've been getting is spotty, but it looks like Velveeta's about ready to barricade himself in the bunker. I doubt he'll even read any telegram I send, much less make a coherent response. Can you... can you arrange a meeting for me?"

His lighter rasped, and then I heard him inhale. "Perhaps. How do I contact you—where are you now."

"Are you going to the theater tonight?"

"No, Chris is slightly under the weather."

"Then maybe we can meet for dinner."

"What! Where the hell are you!"

I started to laugh. "I'm in a pay phone at Bloomingdale's—I flew in this afternoon."

"Son of a bitch."

"Yeah, ain't it though. Listen, you mustn't tell Martha."

"I wouldn't think of spoiling your surprise."

"No, that's not why. Caviar doesn't know about you, but he found out about her. Martha shouldn't be in any immediate danger. She may be under surveillance, though, and I wouldn't want them to pick me up again through her, not before I get to Velveeta."

"I see. All right, what time shall we meet."

"I was kidding about tonight..."

"Nonsense. We'll go up to Rye, where you'll play the man who came to dinner...at least until I see how much clout I have left with Velveeta."

"Thanks, but..."

"It's settled. Give me a time and a place."

"I think I'll stay at Bloomie's. Jesus, Frew, I never thought I'd miss this place, and its hordes of Upper East Side swells vacuuming up the goodies, but then men've walked on the moon and Aaron's finally hit number seven-fifteen."

I was roaming this pinnacle of conspicuous consumption, drinking it all in, when I decided to buy Mrs. Fanning a small house gift. As the clerk gave me a pen to endorse the traveler's check I suddenly realized I no longer had to answer to Tetsuo R. Sasaki, that my name—the one I'd just entered the country under—was once more Raymond Huang.

At 3:42 P.M. the Mercedes 600 drew up to the northwest curb of Third Avenue and 59th Street. I spun through the revolving doors, crossed the sidewalk, and piled into the back.

Fanning peered over his newspaper. "You know, you look better thin." And then he was beaming and then he was tossing the paper aside and then he was folding me into an enormous bear hug.

11 April 1974: Rye

Shortly before noon Fanning phoned the news: the staff in Washington had chosen to interpret the request, by the chairman of Onyxx, for an immediate and private audience as a most auspicious sign for their beleaguered boss. Velveeta, therefore, eagerly awaited Mr. Franklin Renfrew Fanning—and an aide—at Key Biscayne, Florida, at 11:30 A.M. on Sunday the 14th.

14 April 1974: Rye/Key Biscayne/Washington/Rye

"Unless Caviar's as bent as Bourbon, it's got to be considered," I said over the whine of the Learjet's twin engines.

Fanning kept gazing at the South Carolina coast rushing by some eighteen thousand feet below.

"I can't buy it, Ray. The implications are too incredible."

"More incredible than Caviar's actions? He doesn't seem to give a damn about his confession. One, he could have blown me away in the Bahamas, just after I'd seen it—and before I could pass copies to any associates. Two, the inepts he put on me in New York couldn't follow a tortoise across the street. And the clincher's the fact that Datatec, this agency you respect, they swear there hasn't been a stitch of surveillance on Martha since the day I got back, not even after I shook SAVAK."

Fanning looked drawn and distracted. Because we'd arisen before the sun to begin our journey south by Onyxx jet? Because we'd already argued the same point five nights running? Because he still flinched from the conclusion I was again about to make? Or could it be on this day he was feeling the full weight of his sixty-four years...

"The meeting in Tehran could only have had one purpose, Frew: to sic me onto Velveeta. Shit, Caviar gave it to me on a platter. High-quality photographs, even my own passport so I couldn't be busted when I re-entered. No, he wants me to be the last straw that breaks Velveeta's back, and he wants it bad enough to let me wash his own dirty linen in public."

Now Fanning roused himself. "It's probably a personal grudge."

"Perhaps, but I say it could be that Caviar hopes to get someone he wants high up in the next administration."

"I scarcely see Marion Javits as secretary of state."

"No, I'm serious. When he was back in the House, what was the Vice-President's voting record on aid to Iran? If he's elevated, who stands to join his cabinet? Does he keep Henry around, or for that matter, who'll be the new Veep? I tell you, Caviar's got to think he'll come out ahead if there's a change in the Oval Office."

When Fanning chose not to respond I began feeling guilty about hammering so hard so I joined him in brooding silence. The farther south we flew the more restless he grew. Then the pilot was intercomming back that we were ten minutes out of Miami International and at last Fanning started exposing the roots of his morning-long anxiety: "Son, you've yet to ask me why I'm on this jet."

"Why... why to help me nail Velveeta."

His smile was tired. "You know, until I met you I'd forgotten what it is to be young." He carefully prepared a Chesterfield for lighting. "When I was your age, I swore I would never become part of the rot I saw at the top, I swore as soon as I was up the ladder I'd change things. Now there's no more ladder, Ray, and I've changed damn few things... in fact, it's sometimes hard to remember what used to appall me."

"Frew, I..."

"No, please, this is important to me. It's a moment I've long put off, but now there's no time left so I'd best say my piece." He nervously stubbed out the freshly lit cigarette. "I frankly don't know why I'm sitting here right now, and I'm scared to death I am. We... we may drive Velveeta off the deep end today. If he fights back by slinging it with a pitchfork, there are things you should know."

Fanning turned to stare at the landscape rising to meet us. "I... I wanted to leave Onyxx having presided over its greatest years. I wanted to leave a prosperous, vigorous, responsive company—but most of all a *clean* company, not an ITT or a Gulf or a Lockheed. But I won't. You once thought me the... the all-time establishment bastard, a man who moved bodies and bribed cops, who countenanced any immorality to help the bottom line. Son, your perceptions may have changed, but I did do those things, and I'm still the same man."

"Why are you telling me this, Frew?"

"Because Onyxx is right down in the muck. I don't approve of little white envelopes stuffed with laundered money, so in deference to me ours go to politicians in places like Italy instead of to Congress. Immaterial. What does matter is, I've never dared try to end the practice... I'm afraid over the years I really have convinced myself it's just part of the cost of doing business."

"Why now? Why are you telling me this now?"

Fanning spotted the seat-belt light flashing on and strapped himself in. "Velveeta's been stalling a Justice probe of several multinationals, including us. First it was in hopes we'd chip in on the Seventy-two campaign, now because he desperately needs our political support. When Velveeta's cornered, the man fights dirty. I expect him to use this on us today... and now I've said my piece."

"You still haven't explained why you're doing this to yourself."

Fanning dropped his eyes and cleared his throat. "Son, you've just come back from seeing the darkest side of the world. You have every right to be disillusioned, yet you still count me a friend. I'm deeply flattered, but I also fear your disillusionment might one day spread to include me, so... so I wanted to be the one to tell you. I owe it to myself, and, more important, I owe it to you, Ray."

"No. No you don't, because... because I believe Fitzgerald when he said 'Action is character.' You didn't have to call Washington, you didn't have to get on the plane this morning. You did."

Fanning slowly let out his breath. Then he looked up and smiled.

Three minutes later a *squirp* from the tires and we'd landed Miami.

As soon as the Secret Service men manning the entrance on Bay Lane saw our limousine they waved us past a gaggle of reporters and cameramen and through the gates. The compound was open and bright, the low-pressure eye within a hurricane of impeachment cries—but then calm had also prevailed at Berchtesgaden three decades earlier. We were met at the door by Velveeta's chief of staff, a soldier learning a new kind of warfare the hard way. He greeted Fanning warmly and me cordially, my name inducing not the slightest flicker of recognition.

In sharp contrast to the sunny grounds, the main house seethed with the palpitating tensions that arise from a siege mentality: a judiciary subcommittee subpoena deadline loomed two weeks ahead. Knit-browed men rushed about toting thick legal briefs; harried secretaries scurried after them with chin-high bundles of mimeographing; even servants trod lightly through the halls, as if in fear of tripping claymores.

At 11:30 A.M. sharp Velveeta's chief of staff knocked lightly on a door, then opened it.

The den could have been any affluent man's save for the aquiline emblem presiding ubiquitously from flags and wall samplers and bookends and ashtrays. A fire crackled in the hearth but it was uncomfortably cool in the room; the air conditioning could have shivered a penguin. Velveeta sat crosskneed in an easy chair working on a sheaf of manuscript pages crammed into the clipboard on his lap. From a distance he looked remarkably composed for a man whose ears were being cuffed by the fragments of his exploding world.

He suddenly looked up, saw us, smiled, and said in that familiar bass, "Be with you in a moment, Frank. And thanks, soldier, I'll buzz when I'm done." His chief of staff compressed his lips but spun and marched from the room. Velveeta boldly drew a final slash across a page, then tossed the clipboard onto an end table and started toward us.

"Golly, it was good of you to come, Frank!" Up close the face was haggard, the pouches under bloodshot eyes darkened, the razor nick on his left cheek fresh; beneath the Scope, the stench of soured whiskey. Now Velveeta clumsily tossed an arm around the taller Fanning. "I know how busy you are, Frank, but the minute I was advised you called, I said—and you can verify this with my staff—I said, that's exactly what we need, the staunch support of men like my old and dear friend, Frank Fan..."

Fanning finally twisted from the effusive embrace. "I'm sorry, sir, I'm not here to tender support...I came to introduce a friend." Velveeta glanced at me blankly. "Mr. President, meet Mr. Raymond Huang."

Eyes dilating, lips disappearing, neck veins throbbing: fury and fear spewed from Velveeta like heat from a furnace. The room grew suddenly airless. Out in the garden, laughter and a dog barking. Inside, dead silence. At last I could no longer hold his glare; I dropped my eyes.

Abruptly he wheeled, strode stiffly to the nearest intercom, and in an incongruously flat voice said, "No calls." As Velveeta turned from the end table he brushed the precariously poised clipboard, tumbling it to the floor. He reflexively kicked at it: papers fluttered like snow. Without thinking I stooped to retrieve several sheets that had landed near me. "NO! Get . . .

your . . . god . . . damned . . . hands . . . AWAY!" When I unfroze and straightened he stalked to the window and began to inspect the grounds. Finally, back still turned, voice still choked, Velveeta said, "What the hell do you want, Fanning?"

"Nothing. It's Mr. Huang's show."

I let ten seconds pass, then said, "Sir, did you order a hit on me?"

"Why the hell should I want to, uh, to harm a person, a person who I don't even know? Fanning, I don't know this man . . . that is to say, and correct me if I'm wrong, to the best of my recollection we've never met."

In chagrin I glanced at the floor. One of the pages at my feet read:

P & H—00—3/14/73—cont'd.
H (cont'd): convinced that they have no interest in Strachan at all—and they have all this stuff. And I can see how they feel—Strachan is like a secretary—he is useful as a witness.
P: Now correct me if I'm wrong, Bob, but didn't I always say this Strachan—he's—you know—he's like a leaky cunt.
H: Yeah—well he implies—or has in earlier stuff—he doesn't . . .

The passage attributed to "P" had been scratched out with a blue felt-tipped pen.

I looked up when Fanning said, "Sir, Mr. Huang knows all about Entrepays."

Velveeta remained facing the window. "Entrepays? What's that? To the best of my recollection I've never heard of any company by that name."

My eyes locked with Fanning's. Then I said, "Sir, I have copies of the confession you signed at the Newporter Inn on the . . ."

"That dirty cock-sucking Persian son of a bitch!" As Velveeta wheeled we finally saw on his face the awful grimace of quarry at bay. "He said he'd never tell! What did that prick confess to, god damn it, what's in his confession?" I remained silent. "All right, Fanning, what's the squeeze? What do you want—some dip-shit ambassadorship? Oh no, not you, you're the selfless kind, am I right? No, you probably want some new tax laws for your fucking company. Come on, I know your kind, you wouldn't be in this if there wasn't something in it for you. Out with it, give it to me straight, I can take it, but before you do, mister, you better think about something! You use this to hound me out of office and you won't have me around anymore... that's right, I won't be around to hold off Justice—think about that, my friend, you think about that long and hard!"

If possible, Fanning's glare was even more defiant than Velveeta's, yet his voice was as soft as a child's: "We'll take our chances, sir."

"Good, you do that. I promise you I will personally persecute your company, and your own tax records better be fucking perfect, mister, or..."

"Like yours?" Fanning almost whispered the two words but they throttled Velveeta's rage more effectively than a slap.

Velveeta collapsed sweating against the windowsill. "I, uh, I'm sorry... I'm very sorry, it's just that this, uh, this comes as a hell of a shock. I thought it all ended with Blair's death..." Now he looked plaintively at Fanning. "You've got to tell me how you're going to handle my, uh, how you plan to handle my letter."

"If it were up to me, Mr. President, I'd plaster it across every front page in the country." I'd never seen Fanning vindictive, but now he smiled thinly as he watched Velveeta twisting slowly, slowly... Finally Fanning added, "However, I regret to say it's not my decision, it's Mr. Huang's."

As my power over him dawned Velveeta turned to me like a two-termer facing his parole board. "You can't, young man, you can't... you're too young, too inexperienced to fully understand my achievements, to fully appreciate them... this current thing, this flap, it'll blow away, you mark my words..." He wiped his mouth with the back of a hand. "I, uh, I stand on the, uh, uh, I myself am the key, the key to a new era of world peace, a peace I'll achieve with honor once we set this mess behind it. Oh, I know that you're young and that you hate me, all young people do, but don't you see that to give in to this hate, you only destroy yourself? That's right, you can't win because you destroy yourself and... and you destroy all those poor helpless people in the Middle East, in Asia—and certainly you of all people should be vitally concerned about our friends in Asia—and Africa and South America too, people there have so much to gain by the peace I'll bring with honor once, uh, once I put this current tempest back in the teapot dome. Is that worth it, young man, is it really worth it to publish my, uh, my letter—is giving in to hate worth all those shattered lives?"

When I kept staring at my shoes Velveeta said, in a spent voice, "You... you should know we all make mistakes in our lives, sometimes big ones, you'll come to understand that with the wisdom of a few more years... Entrepays was a mistake. Yes sir, I admit it, it was wrong. But... but do you know the facts? Did you know I was born in the house my father built? That's right, the old man built it himself, he didn't have the money to hire a carpenter. Oh, you'd call him a loser, young people would, but that's because, that's because... Many's the time that we boys ate bread and water for supper, and oh how my mother wept when they found oil on that orchard that would bear no fruit..." He blew his nose. "So when this, uh, this Entrepays thing came along, I looked at my assets, and you know you can't ever get rich in public service, and believe me, I didn't, and I... and I joined... Christ, it was only human."

Fanning finally broke the gruesome silence: "Where did you raise the ten million?"

Velveeta hung his head and shook it. Then he walked to the bar, poured himself three fingers of Ballantine's, and took a sip. The Scotch rekindled his defiance. "Go ahead, publish it, that's the easy way out. Topple the poor bastard, he's had his day in the sun. No, it doesn't take much of a man to give in to petty vindictiveness, to..."

I interrupted. "Sir, I don't hate you, and I'm not out to topple you... Shit, Mr. President, all I want is my life and some peace! Look, uh, you just go on not knowing me, and I won't use the confession to give you the final nudge."

"Why the hell should I trust you?"

"For the same reason I have to believe you when you say you didn't order the attempt on me. Plus, you have little choice. It's been arranged so if anything happens to me, the whole Entrepays plot—including your confession—hits the fan."

He thought it over, then said warily, "You must want something else."

"Yes. The Japanese's confession, to photograph."

"That's all?" Velveeta's eyes shifted between Fanning and me. "No, that can't be all."

"You're right, it's not all." We turned to Fanning, who continued, "There is to be no retaliation, no harassment whatsoever of Mr. Huang. Should there be, you answer to me."

"Now, now, wait a minute, do you know who you're tal..."

"You may have me outgunned . . . sir! . . . but I trust only temporarily."

Velveeta quickly dropped his eyes and studied his shoes. Finally he said to me, "Is that really all you want?"

"All? Yes sir, that's all."

He pushed himself from the sill and walked on rubbery knees to his desk, but when he picked up the phone his voice was again steady, if tight: "Who's on up in Washington? Okay, he'll do. Hello? Yes...listen, uh, there's an envelope in my private safe, it's eyes-only and it's from the Okura Hotel, in Tokyo. Get it and take it to, to..." He looked at Fanning.

Fanning glanced at his watch. "National at three-thirty."

"Listen, take it to National at three-thirty this afternoon and hand-deliver to Frank Fanning—he's the chairman of Onyxx. Yes. When he's done he'll return the, uh, the envelope, then put it back in the safe. Remember, it's eyes-only, so I want you to do it yourself. That's right." Velveeta replaced the receiver and pondered his desk top. Finally, after mustering his remaining dignity, he looked up. "There, I've kept my end of the bargain."

Three beats of silence, then Fanning turned and started for the door. I followed.

We had to be awakened when we landed National Airport at 3:38 P.M. As soon as the ramp was down a courteous young man in civilian clothing but with a soldier's bearing boarded. At 3:51 P.M., the last link of the daisy chain firmly in hand, we were airborne again and banking north.

The Mercedes 600 was parked on the field when we landed Westchester Airport. As Clarence swung the rear door open I deferred to Fanning so when I hopped in I found two faces grinning at me. "Hi, kid," Martha said.

Late that night, in the Fannings' guest bedroom, Martha put her lips to my ear and gasped, "Hey...that refrigerator we won last time? I think we just copped a station wagon."

"Shut up and fuck."

15 April 1974: Rye/New York

Dinner the previous night had been a victory celebration: lunch today was to dispose of the spoils.

Martha and Chris Fanning argued for publication. Fanning ignored our pleas and threats and abstained. The votes were thus there for full and immediate disclosure, but then this wasn't a democracy.

"No, not now, if ever," I said. "Martha, remember when you accused me of wanting everything wired beforehand? I no longer feel that way about a lot of things, but I do about this. Entrepays and the Cocktail Party, that story has to be told right. I probably have enough to expose Entrepays, but Blair's dead, and anyway, was the plot itself illegal, or was it just business? The Cocktail Party's another matter. How the hell can I prove what I've just been through? Four of the men could easily say, 'Raymond who? What meeting?' And we all know Velveeta's running hard this very minute writing his own version of yesterday, even as he tries for smear material on Frew and me. No, unless I want to cop this year's Clifford Irving award, I need hard proof—and all I've got is one tape and a bunch of Polaroids.

"The only consolation's that the Party's over. If Frew's right about Lockheed's bribes surfacing soon, Sake's power is coming to an end. Ouzo and Bourbon are two very sick old men. Caviar's still going strong, but nothing I can do or write'll ever affect him. Velveeta? They'll nail him any day now, without any help from me... and while I'm not saying let's bury the assassination conspiracy, is this really the time to pick that scab, with Watergate running wild?

"What it boils down to is we've bought a kind of peace that's really a balance of terror. It sucks, but right now, in lieu of nailing those bastards, I'll take it."

There was no joy around the table, but neither was there a rebuttal.

16 April 1974: New York

Yes, it was still true: no matter how long you've been traveling and no matter how many hotel rooms you've awakened in, you're never disoriented—not even for an instant—when you open your eyes that first time back in your own bedroom. It was late morning, which meant Martha had gone to work. I swung my feet to the floor and headed into the living room.

The side table was piled with eleven weeks of unpaid bills and anguished dunning threats; there was also a drop-dead note from Bonnie, who waited two hours in a restaurant that January day I'd been running for my life.

I was padding toward the kitchen to start coffee when I saw on the vestibule floor an envelope that looked as if it had been pushed under the apartment door. The envelope was addressed "Sasaki-*san*." Inside was a typewritten note:

Ling How Fun, 2:30 P.M.

Three hours later I stepped into the restaurant on Doyers Street. Wellington, the old Chinese maitre d', never glanced up as I mounted the stairs, turned right onto the corridor, ducked through the fourth set of curtains, and twisted the sconcelike lighting fixture counterclockwise.

Kuo Yu-tang had put on weight in the last year.

I walked past the sliding wall.

"Tetsuo R. Sasaki, you've been one busy little Jap. Here, have some tea and tell me about your adventures."

"Still using this place, eh?"

"Why not? It's secure, no thanks to you."

I sat and sipped the tea; it wasn't that insipid restaurant crap. "Why the hospitality, Kuo?"

"Call it a welcome-home party."

"Gee, thanks."

"*Pu k'e ch'i.* Now it's your turn."

"My turn to what?"

"*Li mao, li mao,*" Kuo said, using the Chinese term for etiquette. "Guests're supposed to bring the host a little something."

"You've got my thanks, and I'll pay for the tea, too."

"I'd rather hear about your trip."

"Hawaii was fine, the weather great, and I got to play Pebble Beach on the way home."

"This is important, Huang *hsien-sheng*."

"To who?"

"My government."

"Why? You guys looking to buy a pineapple plantation?"

He scratched his head. "You've changed since our last meet, for sure, but lay off the Bogey movies, hunh? You hard-boil a dick too long, it cracks. Look, I can't tell you more because I don't know more. Peking wired: debrief Ray Huang. It came Code Blue—that's moderate urgency."

"Why should I let you debrief me?"

"Good faith?"

I remembered the good faith Kuo had shown by refusing to take my calls a year ago but decided to keep my anger to myself.

"Hey, is it really going to cost you to talk about your trip?"

"It was a charter deal I couldn't pass up..."

Kuo sighed and unfolded a sheet of paper. "On January twenty-seventh, you left one hell of a mess down here. We cleaned it up. The..."

"I didn't ask you to."

"Call it charity. The two guys were buttons from the Coast."

"Where are they now?"

Kuo ignored my question and continued. "We set a watch on your apartment. You never show, but Master Charge slips do. They point like a road map to Caracas, but we can't tell what you did after Miami—by the way, that was nice work. Then nothing until... March thirteenth, when one of our Tokyo agents spots you on the Ginza. Traveling name, Tetsuo R. Sasaki; papers, Canadian; local address, the Ginza Capitol. On March fifteenth, you're driven from the Imperial to the suburb called Setagaya, where you meet a real bad number. We lose you again in Shinjuku."

Kuo looked up and gained no clues from my stoic face. Once not very long ago I'd have been trying to disguise the paranoia of being stalked, but having emerged from the crucible intact, what I now hid was a growing rage.

"March seventeenth, you're spotted in Kuala Lumpur. We

stay with you through Bangkok until you vanish in Athens. Then nothing for almost three weeks. On April sixth, there you are in Paris, tagged by half the local SAVAK bureau. Next day, you fly a deadhead to Tehran. Funny thing is, there's no trace of entry or departure from Iran. And then yesterday, eleven weeks after you go screaming down some Chinatown alley, there you are back at your apartment, and you're not running anymore."

"Except back down to Chinatown to meet old friends."

Kuo leaned back. "The Code Blue's from our economic ministry. That bunch doesn't usually truck with Intelligence. Yet here I am, on their orders, trying like hell to debrief you."

So they were on the scent. But what did I owe them? Nothing. How badly did they want it? Only one way to find out: "What's in this for me?"

"In terms of money..."

"Shit, I wouldn't dream of taking payment from the proletariat. I mean, what do I get for cooperating? A medal? A free trip to *Ta Lu*? The promise that you'll answer the phone the next time I call?" When Kuo looked away I stuck it deeper and twisted. "Favors work both ways, friend, you can look that up in Cervantes. Where were you a year ago when I needed you?"

"I couldn't have helped."

"We'll never know, will we?"

"So there's no middle ground?" he asked softly.

"Sure, set up a meet for me with the Chairman. His place or mine, I don't care." I stood and walked to the scroll and then decided the hell with the sliding wall; instead of crossing back into the Ling How Fun I started for the stairs of the restaurant fronting on Mott. Kuo didn't protest.

The chicken looked up as I approached its cage. Dime in the slot and now through the partition and onto the turntable; as I watched the small brown rooster dance I realized they'd changed fowls—what about the fortune? Then the slip of cardboard popped up, its eight playing cards at the top. I read 'em and wept—from laughter. Heart J, Spade A, Heart K, Diamond 9, Diamond 10, Heart Q, Spade 8, Heart A. Royal Flush, Hearts.

GENTLEMEN'S CARD
You will be invited to a party where two women will entertain, and where you will meet a dark man who is wealthy. If you are wise...

21 April 1974: New York

I ran down the list of editors and decided to start with my friend on the credit-card magazine. "Herb? It's Ray Huang. Good, thanks... yeah, I've been out of town for almost three months. No, nowhere special, I was just trying to solve some personal problems. Hey listen, how about a piece on Cyprus? I see. Istanbul? Well, I was thinking about the Old City... yes, that's where the bazaar is, and Topkapi..."

1 June 1974: New York

Martha was sleeping late on this Saturday morning—Watergate stories defied smooth closings—so shortly after 11 A.M. I set off alone for her sublet. When I reached it the new tenants were already unloading their rental van; the only items of hers still there were a carton of pots and pans and a table lamp, which I carried down the three flights of stairs. A taxi was cruising the street. Why not, I thought as I hailed it, I was flush with money—$2,300 in May billings alone—and since a cab had taken Martha away fourteen months ago, it seemed fitting one should bring the last of her gear home now.

9 August 1974: New York

"...Always remember, others may hate you—but those who hate you don't win unless you hate them, and then you destroy yourself..." The strained syntax and quavery voice were familiar, as was the flushed face so tightly framed on the TV screen. Those of us crammed cheek-by-jowl into the lounge on Martha's floor wanted to look away but we couldn't: it was like watching a three-year-old fingering a Zippo. "...And so we leave with high hopes, in good spirits and with deep humility, and with very much gratefulness in our hearts..." At last the cortege from the East room across the red-carpeted South Lawn to the helicopter, the band striking one last "Hail to the Chief," close-up of Julie clutching David, cut to the helicopter steps, the awkward lip-gnawing wave spreading into the final V-salute, and finally, self-immolation complete, he was gone.

And now there were four, I thought.

At 12:03 P.M. Chief Justice Burger proffered the Bible and soon the thirty-eighth President of the United States of America was fixing us with his open gaze: "... our long national nightmare is over..."

At that instant Martha and I turned to each other and winked.

25 September 1974: New York

"Ray?"
"Mmmmm?"
"How do you get a Jewish girl to stop sleeping with you?"
"Mmmmm?"
"Marry her."
"Hmmph."

13 January 1975: New York

Luckily she was an important civil-court judge with commensurately large chambers or we might not all have fitted. It took six minutes; then back out into the cold to the pair of idling limousines for the drive uptown. When we were seated in a private room at Lutece our host rose and looked to each of the guests—both sets of parents, Duke and wife, my friend Alan and Kathy, and, of course, his own wife, Chris. Then Fanning lifted his champagne glass: "If the world is indeed an oyster, may Martha and Ray find the irritants of the past turning into the pearl of the future."

15 March 1975: New York

It was reported on the eleven o'clock news that Ouzo's wife was once more a widow. The Greek had succumbed in Paris to complications following gall bladder removal—or was it the heart broken by the death of his only son two years earlier?

Whichever, now there were three.

14 April 1975: Siena/Rome/En route to New Delhi

"What's so funny?" Martha asked.

"I just realized where I was a year ago today." When she cocked her head I decided to tease so I scanned the five-centuries-old buildings ringing the Piazza del Campo; Siena couldn't have been lovelier or Italy more tourist-free, which meant we'd won our gamble on a delayed honeymoon. Better yet, no one in the world knew where we were, for we'd just begun a two-week jaunt that would lead us wherever our rented Fiat pointed.

"Come on, come on, where were you one year ago today?"

"How quickly they forget... Key Biscayne."

"Well, fuck me!"

"Here?"

We finished our midmorning *espressos* and began strolling from the outdoor café back to the car. On Via del Terme Martha spotted an enticing display of fresh fruit in a grocery window and hesitated. "What time do you think we'll make Florence?"

I checked my watch. "Oh, about..."

"Ray! Martha! Quick!"

Our heads snapped. A car was charging across traffic, a black Bentley, and it was almost atop us... Instinctively I grabbed Martha and pulled her down the narrow street but suddenly up ahead two figures, one armed with a walkie-talkie, deployed to cut off our flight so we pivoted but by now the Bentley had angled to the curb to cut off retreat. I stumbled, regained my balance, and tugged Martha toward the nearest store—too late, damn it, because now the car's rear door was swinging open and now the coiled shadow within was raising an arm but instead of a shot, a shout: "Get in! Come on, come on, get in here, quick!"

Kuo Yu-tang's face glistened with sweat.

Why could I hear nothing but roiling surf? Why were all colors bleached, all motion slowed? At last the cacophony of angry horns broke my trance and at last I let go of Martha and at last I could attach words to Kuo's still-moving lips... "It's okay, it's okay, I'm not going to hurt you, but you've got to come!"

My eyes locked with Martha's. Then, since there seemed little choice, we wobbled across the sidewalk and climbed warily into the back; as soon as the door shut the chauffeur eased the Bentley into gear and continued down Via del Terme.

"How the hell did you find us?"

"I had a bitch of a time, but a mixed couple in Italy's pretty high visibility." Kuo leaned forward to close the glass partition to the driving compartment. "Look, I know I scared the shit out of you, but it's worse in New York—your place has been blown away."

"Oh, my God." Martha's voice was a whisper but she clutched my hand so hard she almost drew blood.

"Late Saturday night, a total gut job...here." He tossed over an envelope.

Inside were five 8 × 10s. The first two were exteriors; the force of the explosion had hurled charred bits of chairs and sofa and tables into the street. The remaining three photos were interiors; the intensity of the fire had even melted my metal-lined bookshelf safe. The work of a professional, but on whose commission? Which of the four surviving Cocktail Party conspirators had reneged on his bargain with me? Finally I looked up at Kuo. "Who did it?"

"You tell me. The cops know squat, which is why Peking ordered me to track you. I've been hauling..."

"Wait a minute, wait a minute. Why should Peking give a fuck about our welfare?"

"We're sure this number's tied to your little disappearing act last year."

"So?"

"Cut the crap, Huang. We don't know what that was all about, but we do know it involves China."

"'We'? You been bumped up from press attaché?"

Kuo leaned back and sighed. "Next time I'll wear my 'Chicom Intelligence' T-shirt, okay?"

"You still haven't answered me. Why did you track us?"

"To arrange the debriefing you wouldn't give last year. Talk now, we protect both your asses from here on in."

"Bullshit."

"This is the third time someone's tried to ring your bell, friend. The first time you cry cop and buy yourself a year. Then you flit around the world under deep cover and buy another year. Now what—who's to help, where do you run, how much time can you possibly buy? And don't forget, you're not alone this go-around. How's the missus at hide-and-seek?"

The Bentley was almost out of town; ahead, the tranquil hills of Tuscany rolled lush and green. Who'd commissioned the hit? Jesus, if I could only figure out whether it had been Bourbon's top aide, Caviar, Sake, or Velveeta...

"Time to shit or get off the pot, Huang."

"Stop leaning, god damn it!"

"Look friend, I assure you the next welcome wagon's already on its way. Peking said make contact, not stand in the line of fire... this here boat sails at one-thirty, with or without you."

I looked at my watch: 11:13. False papers: none. Money: enough for two weeks. The Polaroids that could save: back in New York, back where killers stalked. Finally I said, "Okay, okay. Hop in front, I have to talk to Martha."

At 1:18 P.M. I dashed into a phone booth; I owed Fanning the call because, despite the post-Nixon stalling of an American-Chinese rapprochement, Onyxx was still negotiating with Peking.

At 1:27 P.M. I finally got through to Rye.

At 1:32 P.M. Kuo stopped pacing and twirled his hand in a hurry-up gesture.

At 1:34 P.M. Fanning finally spoke; his voice was uncharacteristically shaky. "We, uh, we may have acted naïvely in our dealings with China, but never dishonorably. Onyxx has nothing to apologize for... just, just tell the truth, son, like it happened."

At 1:35 P.M. I hung up and sprinted after Kuo.

At 1:39 P.M. Martha turned to me. "Was... was it like this on your trip?"

"Every minute of every day."

"Jesus." She looked down at the white-tipped fingernails of her clenched hands.

A snarl now from the mighty jet engines, and we were thrust deep into our seats as the JAL 747 careered down the runway on takeoff from Fiumicino for points east.

16 April 1975: Peking

The Red Flag limousine left the guesthouse and sped Martha and me through the late-afternoon chill across Peking. Though still tired, we pressed our faces to its windows, for this was our first daylight glimpse of *Ta Lu*. Soon I turned away, puzzled. I knew the capital to be neither exotic nor romantic, but still, shouldn't finally setting foot on ancestral soil trigger some reaction? Perhaps it was the jet lag... The sun was lowering when we pulled up before the heavy iron gate guarding a redwalled compound. A pair of greatcoated soldiers marched out; when I noticed their submachine guns cocked and at the ready, a surge of adrenaline chased the last of my fatigue. The soldiers peered cautiously into the limousine, then drew the gate and waved us through.

We were met at the front door of the villa by Kuo Yu-tang. Inside, the furnishings were proletarian but the scrolls and statues Mandarin. Yet it felt as if few eyes had recently appreciated the artwork; the completely odor-free air, the too polished parquet floor, the dusky-pink flowers in the Ming vase so newly cut they hadn't finished opening, these all contributed to an atmosphere of doleful inoccupancy. Martha and I followed Kuo across the vestibule and up the broad staircase. He hesitated in front of a door on the second floor to adjust his collar. Then a knock, and he turned the knob.

The large room was crypt-silent though half a dozen men in grey tunic suits hovered over a bed against the far wall. A faint tang of medicine, an impression of dimness—heavy drapes cloaked the windows—and Kuo was shepherding us into the room, and as the men in the grey tunic suits fell back we finally saw the wasted figure propped by pillows into a sitting position atop the bed.

The Premier of China had, I knew, seen more than seventy

summers. He'd not see many more. Suddenly, irrationally, I remembered my parents relating how back in school he'd been comely enough to portray females in class plays. Now above the twiglike body those delicate features were warped not so much by age as by disease and drugs.

But as we approached the bedside, twin oases leapt from the pasty desert of his face: the Premier's eyes still mirrored the terrible energy and guile that had carried him through China's most tumultuous half century, they still defiantly announced pain be damned, death could never linger long enough. Now those luminous brown eyes turned to Martha and softened and now they focused on me. The hand he extended was as light and brittle and cold as porcelain, his voice soft as snowfall. "Huang *hsien-sheng*, Yu-tang tells me you seldom have the opportunity to practice *kuo-yu*. You would prefer we converse in English?"

"Yes sir, I would."

"Very well, but then I beg your allowance for my lack of fluency. Yu-tang also tells me it was your desire to meet first with the Chairman...alas, he is occupied. I hope I shall suffice."

I blushed. The Premier grinned and gently smoothed one of his distinctive bushy eyebrows; then his eyes wandered my face. "Yes, there is a resemblance...I must again beg your allowance, but an old man retreats ever more into memory. I knew your grandfather from across the table. I believe he passed on before your birth?"

"Yes, sir."

"A pity. You would have profited from knowing him, he was an honest man. Your family is currently in *Mei-kuo*?"

"Yes, sir."

"They are well?"

"Yes, thank you."

"Good, good." The Premier gazed into the distance for several heartbeats, then gestured Martha and me to chairs at the right of the bed. As we sat he picked up a water glass from the night table and took a sparrowlike sip. "Huang *hsien-sheng*, Huang *t'ai-t'ai*, I should like to relate a tale of two beekeepers. The men had but one desire, to produce the finest honey. Alas, they lived at the edge of a great forest and, alas, within the forest lurked a marauding bear which periodically smashed their hives in search of sweets. What to do? In desperation, the beekeepers decided to construct, at great effort and great cost, a fortification that might protect the hives. One day, with the fortification partially built, word came of a man on the other side of the forest who had learned how to keep the bear at bay. 'I shall immediately undertake to journey through the great forest,' one beekeeper proposed, 'for if the secret can be gained, would not our costly fortification be rendered unnecessary?' 'But surely the marauding bear shall eat you,' the other beekeeper protested, 'and then in rage turn on me.' The two men bickered and bickered... and still bicker to this day." The Premier looked up at us. "My parable is not too oblique? Good, good."

He waved toward the six men in grey tunic suits who had taken seats across from us. The youngest seemed my age, the oldest in his late fifties; they sat with the impassive mien of perfect jurymen. "These gentlemen come from various sectors of our government. Because the bickering continues, it would be well if you not learn their names. It would also be well if you not speak of our meeting today, for it is commonly understood I am living out my days in a hospital. True. But though my room there is most attractive and the staff most attentive, the security is lamentable."

He took another sip of water. "Huang *hsien-sheng*, Yu-tang tells me you agree to the terms he proposed—you shall describe the events last year which caused you to flee New York, in return for which we shall guarantee you both future safety."

"Yes sir, that's our understanding. Would, uh, would you mind if we smoked? I'm afraid it's a hell of a complicated story."

The Premier smiled. "Perhaps I shall join you. My doctor assures me it is not medically possible to contract terminal cancer more than once."

As I reached for my pack the six men in grey tunic suits reached for notebooks and pens. Do I tell everything? Everything. What repercussions would my information have? It was far, far too late to worry. One last glance at Martha, then I began: "Sir, the big oil companies of the West are sure China's about to discover a massive new field in Hainan..."

Blair, Onyxx, Entrepays, Harry's shale survey; the six men in grey tunic suits scribbled like courtroom stenographers. The more I revealed, the more the Premier's pallor worsened until finally his eyes closed, though of course he wasn't sleeping. I'd been talking for better than thirty minutes, and was just starting on Ouzo, when the Premier's eyes suddenly shot open and flicked to one of the men in grey tunic suits. I hesitated. Now all note-taking ceased. Unable to decipher the electric silence and unsure of whether to continue, I busied myself with lighting another cigarette.

Finally the Premier cleared his throat. "Huang *hsien-sheng*, you remember the sinking of the ship *Queen Elizabeth* in Hong Kong harbor three years ago?"

I nodded; I'd dined with "Cousin" K. H. shortly after the fire.

"It was widely reported the sabotage was the work of eight members of an electrical union. True. It was reported the leadership of the union was Communist. Again, true. It was reported the sabotage was ordered by Peking. Not true. During the course of our inquiries, we learned that all eight men, as well as their families, had fled Hong Kong the day after the fire. It took us nine months to locate a man who could be persuaded to talk... the sabotage was commissioned by the Greek. Frankly, we were at a loss as to the man's motivation. Now it is clear."

Of course: K. H. had linked the act to the supertanker order the consortium of Chinese shipowners had canceled; read in light of Entrepays, Ouzo had scuttled the *Queen Elizabeth* as the shot across the bow that would clear the China Seas of competitors, so his own fleet could haul the oil Onyxx would help the Chinese extract and refine.

"Mr. Premier?"

He turned to Martha.

"If your government knew this, why didn't you make it known, why didn't you remove the blame from yourself?"

"Huang *t'ai-t'ai*, upon verifying the saboteur's assertion, it was decided it would be well to respond. I believe you are employed by a news magazine? Then you will remember that in 1972 pronouncements from Peking were viewed with considerably more suspicion. So how best to punish an old man? I think the Irish writer Synge phrased it nicely: 'What is the price of a thousand horses against a son where there is only one son?'"

Martha blanched.

The Premier turned back to me. "Your story is most interesting. Please continue."

It took another twenty-five minutes to wrap up the Cocktail Party. Then we broke for tea; as Martha and I tried to relax, Kuo and the six men in grey tunic suits huddled around the bed.

Round 2 consisted of the Premier's questions. Some were to clairfy, some to amplify—and some were attempts to catch me in a lie. Toward the end he was running on will power alone; when the Premier finally collapsed back into the pillows, I had to lean forward to catch his last whispered words. "Huang *hsien-sheng*, if you and Huang *t'ai-t'ai* shall care to dine with Yu-tang, perhaps we may speak again briefly in ninety minutes?"

It was 7:25 P.M. when Kuo reluctantly led Martha and me from the room. Behind us the six men in grey tunic suits were drawing their chairs tightly around the bed. Downstairs in the dining room he headed for a cabinet. "You guys want drinks?"

"Got vodka?"

"No, but how about some *mao-tais*?"

I looked to Martha. "Sure, why not."

Kuo made a valiant attempt at sociability by answering as many of our questions as he could, especially about "the PM," as he affectionately called the Premier, but clearly his mind—and heart—were elsewhere. The three of us toyed with the magnificent dinner as if it were gruel.

At 9:20 P.M. we were finally summoned back upstairs. The Premier appeared to be dozing and the six men in grey tunic suits had gone but the room was still sour with the juices of tension. As we approached the bed I suddenly understood Eliot: I too could see the skull beneath the skin.

When the Premier opened his eyes they were dull, the fires within banked dangerously low. He beckoned me nearer. "Huang *hsien-sheng*, it was decided it would be well to corroborate your information. This shall take time. Yu-tang tells me you and Huang *t'ai-t'ai* appear to be in jeopardy. I believe you to be safe within our borders—you shall accept our hospitality until we speak again? Good, good." The eyelids began to flutter. "If you wish, Yu-tang shall arrange for you to see the land of your grandfather. Your grandfather, he...he would, he would approve." Now the lids were still; merciful unconsciousness had come.

20 April 1975: Shanghai/Yu Tsun/Mu Kan Shan/Shanghai

The bus sighing from Shanghai across the verdant plains toward the distant foothills was packed with five dozen communards, one *hoa chiao*, and one white woman. My haircut and Western clothing alone would have commanded the full if covert attention of our fellow passengers; Martha's presence in the next seat guaranteed it.

To spare us the bus Kuo had offered his limousine and his companionship. I'd refused both, for on this leg of the trip it mattered a great deal that my grandfather had been, in the Premier's conceit, "across the table." Kuo had not been happy, but then we'd consistently sidestepped the China he wished us to admire. Back in Peking, after the obligatory trek to the Great Wall, I had insisted he postpone the factories and model villages and steel mills; instead, we'd headed south.

Is there a racial memory? If so, I was on pilgrimage into an unexperienced past. Or was it mere curiosity driving me to flesh out my family's oral history and sepiaed photographs? If so, I was a tourist.

Shanghai was the city in which my parents had been raised, met, and married. They'd not borne me there because my father was studying in America at the time, nor had they returned because after the Revolution our kind—with grand homes within the cosmopolitan French Concession—we were the outcasts, the reviled "running dogs" and "capitalist roaders."

It had taken Kuo two calls to learn my parents' last address. As we'd set out from the Peace Hotel for it, I'd had a sequence of sepiaed images firmly in mind: a street lined with stately shade trees and high, neat walls; an elegant wrought-iron gate at the entrance to our compound; a two-story stucco building surrounded by lush lawn; and on the second story, the balcony from which my parents, flanked by their parents, had beamed on their wedding day.

But bourgeois materialism had departed the French Concession as surely as the capitalist roaders: the stately shade trees along the streets were dead or dying, the high walls cracked and besloganed. Kuo, consulting his notebook, had led us to a gap in one wall; all that remained of the wrought-iron gate was several rusted hinge bolts. Three families now occupied my ancestral home. They must have been poor, or glass scarce, for many of the windows had cardboard panes. And the weed-ridden vegetable garden, could it ever have been lush lawn? Up on the balcony drying wash hung over a snaggletoothed railing.

What might this decaying hulk be had history been different? My father would have come back and, with an American degree and his social contacts, surely have prospered. Would I have followed him into engineering and expanded the privilege of the Huangs? Probably. Nepotism, a cloistered compound, money and all its perks—I knew these to be the emblems of the rot that had sped the Mainland's fall, yet suddenly I'd been overwhelmed by the enormity of our family's loss. Then a heartbeat later I'd realized our family really lost little: enough privilege and enough money had been retained to begin a new life, one that had allowed me to grow up a product of a cushioned American suburb.

When Kuo had finally led us from the compound I'd turned to study the house one last time. Even through squinted eyes its grandeur was beyond recall—except in oral history and sepiaed photographs.

Now the bus from Shanghai, having crossed the verdant plains, was slowing. Through the windshield one hill loomed higher than the rest; atop it lay my final destination.

The village at the base was named Yu Tsun. In the main square our eyes fell immediately on the giant mural of gaily dressed, toothsomely smiling pastoral workers but this propagandist art aside, the Revolution seemed to have skipped the drab village and its lethargic citizenry. Enough of my Chinese had returned for me to inquire directions. The peak? Ten minutes by motor vehicles, I was told, an hour by foot. Martha was game so we began walking up Mu Kan Shan.

It wasn't much of a hill but, being the highest elevation for hundreds of square miles, it had once served the affluent of Shanghai and Hangchow as a natural summer retreat from the sweltering plains below. On those plains now water buffaloes raised puffs of dust and in the absence of internal-combustion echoes, bird chirps and insect buzzes resounded and the roadside stands of bamboo whispered before the gentle wind. The scene was timeless but it was also pan-Asiatic; had I not known I stood on *Ta Lu*, I could just as easily have guessed Thailand or the Philippines.

The macadam ribbon began to hairpin, for if Mu Kan Shan wasn't high it was steep. Halfway up we paused for rest.

As I'd expected, Martha sat several arm's lengths away. Our blind panic in Rome had mutated into a more invidious dread, for though temporarily safe, the specter of what awaited us beyond China's borders had throttled first desire, then emotion, and finally speech. I lit a cigarette. "Want to talk about it?"

Martha continued picking her cuticle. "I ... I can't believe it's only been nine days since we left our apartment. Or that our apartment's gone. Or that instead of Villa Borghese and the Grand Canal we're sitting on some goddamn hill that might not even appear on a map." She looked up. "You're good at options. What are ours?"

"Not many. I don't see the PM being able to protect us against those guys, but an exposé might. I have to figure out a way to sneak back to New York for the files. Then we go underground until the book's done."

"Where do you plan to go?"

"I was thinking about ... Hey, what do you mean, 'you'? We're both going."

She looked back at her hand. "No, you have to do it alone."

"What?"

"Look how easily Kuo found us. There isn't a place in the world we wouldn't attract attention together."

"That's not true, there's Hawaii, there's ..."

"And what am I supposed to do while you write, Ray, learn a second language? Reread the classics? Remember how back in Istanbul you decided you couldn't opt for a safe but stagnant backwater? How do you think I'd feel counting the minutes until you finished the manuscript?"

"No. Last time they were after me. Now they're after you, too."

"What makes you think I can't take care of myself? Or that you can protect me? If we'd been home a week ago Saturday we'd both be dead."

"At least we would've gone out at the same time, which is

only right, seeing as how we're a couple. Hey, kid, I'm not just worried about your safety, I want us together because ... because I love you."

Martha cleared her throat huskily. "Why do you only say the magic word when you're up against it?"

"That's when words count."

Just as our bodies melted into one for the first time in a week, the calm was shattered by the growl of an approaching truck. We grinned at each other; had the driver come upon us maybe two mintues later, he might have caught an act that would have been the talk of Yu Tsun for years to come. Martha and I broke our embrace and resumed the ascent.

Soon the road crested on a ridge. If the Revolution had changed the village at the base of Mu Kan Shan little, it seemed to have left the hill's two peaks altogether untouched. I knew from oral history and sepiaed photographs that my grandfather had constructed upon the lower peak a summer villa, and to the right of the building, beneath simple headstones, would be his and my grandmother's final resting place. We pressed on.

Unlike the house in Shanghai the villa was in perfect repair, but instead of a family of three it now sheltered the headquarters of the local commune. Curious faces appeared at the windows as I led Martha to the right of the building. If my grandparents' graves remained they were now under the foundation of the new office wing.

The headstones, what had happened to the simple headstones in the sepiaed photographs?

Suddenly I realized it didn't matter, for I couldn't have read the ideograms anyway.

And now I swayed under the sledgehammer impact of *déjà vu*: a café, *American Pie*, another hill half the world away atop which had also come irrevocable insights. Just as quickly, the moment passed. Public displays of affection were discouraged by the People's Republic of China but I wrapped an arm around Martha and squeezed her tightly to me: "Hey ... thanks for coming up here, it wouldn't have meant nearly as much alone."

Then, still holding hands, we started back down Mu Kan Shan.

25 April 1975: Peking/En route to Karachi

Peking's wide boulevards, unlike those of China's other cities, were thick with both bicycles and cars, though like our imperiously beeping Red Flag limousine almost all the cars were government-issue. Soon we turned into an immense complex whose brooding buildings, Kuo said, had been built as a mandarin's palace; now it served as a people's hospital.

The armed guards in front of Room 406 saluted as we entered.

Sunlight streamed through the windows. In nine days the Premier had seemed to shed nine years; the body within the silk dressing gown was still a twig but his face was no longer a pasty desert. As we approached the bed he peered over the tops of his reading glasses, then lowered the briefing book onto his lap.

"Huang *hsien-sheng*, Huang *t'ai-t'ai*, welcome to what has alas become my true home." The Premier's voice, too, had regained strength. "You had an interesting trip? Good, good. While you traveled, the information you so generously provided was checked and proved accurate. We shall never be able to properly show our gratitude, but it is yours."

"How will the infor..."

He stayed me with his hand. "Until the beekeepers cease their bickering, it would be well not to speak of the matter further. Impatience is an American trait with many virtues. I fear, however, it is inappropriate at this time." Then his face softened. "You and Huang *t'ai-t'ai* shall now do what?"

"I'm going back to New York to pick up my files. Then I start my book on the Cocktail Party."

"You shall write because you believe your agreement with these men broken?"

"Yes, sir."

"You have not written earlier for what reason?"

"I lacked hard evidence."

"You have since acquired such evidence?"

"No sir. But, no disrespect intended, we feel we need to take our own measures to protect ourselves."

A strange look—could it be abashedness?—played across the Premier's face. He looked to Kuo, who handed him a slim jewelry box. From it the Premier withdrew a small chamois pouch: "I believe this to be yours?" I stared numbly at the gold heirloom pocket watch, passed down from my grandfather, which should have melted along with the secret bookshelf cache in our apartment. "Huang *hsien-sheng*, Yu-tang removed all that could not be replaced before he set the bomb. We shall of course reimburse you for those things that we destroyed."

"But... but why?"

"Santayana wrote, 'The young man who has not wept is a savage, and the old man who will not laugh is a fool.' Have you wept?"

Almost, I thought, but I shook my head. "No, sir, no lately."

"Nor I laughed, so perilous is the future. It is that future I hope your information shall influence, and in such a fashion that I may not die a humorless fool. But time was so short... Huang *hsien-sheng*, your grandfather was across the table. Yet at the risk of sounding presumptuous I believe tha had he not approved my shameful deed, he would have under stood it, for he, too, loved China." The Premier shifted towarc Martha. "Huang *t'ai-t'ai*, it has been my privilege to mee you." Now he turned his luminous eyes back to mine anc extended a hand still as light and brittle and cold as porcelain *"Chen hsieh, chen hsieh... wo hsi-wang ni men t'sai lai"*— many thanks, and may you both return.

As Kuo led us from the room the Premier adjusted his reading glasses and reopened the briefing book.

26 April 1975: Karachi/En route to New York

The Pakistan International 747 was hopscotching its way around half the world—Dubai, Cairo at dawn, Frankfurt, anc then Paris—but though grueling, it was the quickest way home Now as we chased the lowering sun across the Atlantic Marth dozed. I rearranged the blanket around her and sank back int my seat. My body clock was also sprung but all I could d was stare at the dust motes dancing in the waning light. Wha was thwarting sleep?

Finally I picked up the handful of English-language paper I'd bought during our Orly stopover. On April 16 the Khme Rouge had taken Cambodia; now south Vietnam was on th brink. The front-page wirephotos spoke as no words could: the South China Sea was carpeted with gunwale-jammed boats and the bloated corpses of those who'd fallen, or been tossed, overboard, while back in Saigon panicky mobs bayed at the gates of the American Embassy in search of life-sustaining visas and tickets.

One paper also carried a map of Southeast Asia. As I studied it I realized with a start that the Annamese Cordillera, the range Harry Helmsley had been sent to explore, would soon lie almost totally in Communist hands.

Had I been anywhere except Vientiane on February 16, 1972, might history be different? Three years had passed since I'd seen Harry's body cartwheeling through the dark night. Time enough for Blair to dispatch another compromised geologist? Time enough for that geologist to cook a report? Time enough for Onyxx to be gulled into testing for shale convertibility? Time enough for Peking to read the testing as a sign of good faith? Time enough—with Nixon unsullied by a Watergate that would never have occurred—time enough for Onyxx and Peking to conclude a deal?

But history is alterable only at the instant of its occurrence, and that instant had come when I'd peered around the building back on Rue du Boun. And now, three years later, the shock waves I'd inadvertently triggered had spread beyond Entrepays and beyond the Cocktail Party to a deathbed in Peking; not that we'd ever know, but how could our information possibly affect the future of China?

China—something had happened within the past ten days, something had touched me deep inside. But what?

Suddenly time compressed and continents merged and images intermingled:

The apartment in the Village, the house in the French Concession I never grew up in...

New York, Istanbul, London, Paris, Peking, faces and streets and buildings so different and yet so much the same...

Swaying on a ridgetop in Turkey, swaying on a hilltop in China...

Royalist Laotian troops gawking at me alone, farmers on a sighing bus on *Ta Lu* gawking at me and the white woman by my side...

The articles I wrote, the headstones I could never read...

The spinning stopped. What it was, was that my identity

crisis had been resolved on my ancestral side of the world. I'd gone back two generations before mine and learned a hard, unromantic truth: oral history and sepiaed photographs complete the man, but whatever happened in the past, we are what we are—right now. And right now I was with my wife and going home. And then my cheeks were wet with the first tears of adulthood; by discovering after thirty-five years who I wasn't, I'd discovered who I was.

Postscript

I know that on October 17, 1975, Franklin Renfrew Fanning, upon reaching age sixty-five, retired as chairman and president of Onyxx.

On January 8, 1976, the Premier succumbed in Peking to cancer.

On February 6, 1976, it was announced that Velveeta had accepted an invitation relayed by his younger daughter and her husband and would shortly be the personal guest of the Chairman. The White House was not amused; at the start of an election year, surely the trip would be a red flag in front of those who'd never pardoned the pardon.
"Ray, could this be connected to our trip to the Mainland?"
"I doubt it. Hell, it's been almost a year. What can they possibly want from him at this date?"

On March 24, 1976, a young Japanese right-winger executed his nation's first *kamikaze* flight in three decades; his target was Sake, whose role as a Lockheed bagman had been revealed in testimony before the U.S. Senate Subcommittee on

Multinational Companies. Sake emerged physically unscathed but politically dead.

On May 5, 1976, Bourbon died en route from Acapulco to Houston for emergency medical treatment on a body wasted to ninety pounds by his diet of "blue bombers."

On September 9, 1976, 800 million mourned: already staggered by a string of monstrous earthquakes, China now had to cope with the megashock of the Chairman's death—and the savage infighting that would certainly attend the struggle for his fallen mantle.

On February 19, 1977, the Chinese Chief of Intelligence/ North America dialed the number of an apartment on Manhattan's Upper West Side.
Martha and I were in the midst of Sunday brunch when the phone rang.
"Huang *hsien-sheng*, let's skip the sliding wall and take a meet *chez moi*."
"What's the occasion?"
"The beekeepers've stopped bickering."
"How about making it downtown? *T'ai-t'ai*'s never seen the sliding wall."
Kuo Yu-tang laughed. "Then she's missed the boat—the restaurant in back of the Ling How Fun, the one you had such a good time in, it's been sold. And guess who's the new tenant."
"The Company."
"Nope. The penny arcade from across the street."
"Jesus, the Port Arthur chicken is no more."
"What?"
"Nothing."
When we arrived at the People's Republic mission on West 67th Street Kuo awaited us in the lobby. On each of the several times we'd seen him since Peking his grey tunic suit had been slightly better tailored; now it looked a perfect fit. He took our arms and began guiding us into the mission. "Come on, we need a quiet place."
We stepped off the elevator on the fifth floor, where Kuo unlocked the door to a windowless room whose walls were lined with exotic electronic gear. In the middle of the room

stood a large, square ebony table on top of which lay three videotape cassettes and three bulky manila envelopes.

As we took seats around the table Kuo poured tea. "I trust you guys are clear on who the PM's 'marauding bear' is? Well, in a way our neighbor to the north's just an overhyped bogeyman created to rationalize domestic policies..." With great economy, Kuo proceeded to relate how for more than a decade Peking had been riven into two camps. The "radicals," nominally led by the Chairman's wife, Chiang Ching, feared not only attack by Russia—and hence their beloved fortifications—but all things Western. Their xenophobia, however, was really an outgrowth of their desire to fuel continual chaos and upheaval within China's borders, to keep the fever of the Great Revolution burning hot and pure. The other faction argued that continual chaos and upheaval could only spark a counterrevolution in which they, the leaders, would burn. No, said the "moderates," it was time to placate the masses with such bourgeois goals as prosperity and stability, even if it meant venturing into the great forest of international diplomacy.

In the aftermath of the disastrous Cultural Revolution of the late 1960s, the Premier had wrestled China onto the moderate path. But as his and the Chairman's death neared and as he'd sadly realized that Peking's bureaucratic infra-structure would bend before the strongest post-Mao wind, he'd become haunted by visions of national apocalypse.

Kuo refilled our cups. "The PM really put his neck on the block to invite Nixon back in Seventy-two, but it was a positive step toward the future. He did it again to open negotiations with Big Oil to get the expertise we needed. Well, Onyxx and Entrepays, that's just the kind of ammunition the radicals were looking for, proof the 'foreign devils' were fucking China over again. That's why I had to blow out your apartment—the PM needed to know, and he needed to know first."

"Forewarned, forearmed."

"Ray, there's hope for you yet. Anyway, three months after your visit, the PM summoned sixteen biggies from both factions and told them everything. As soon as the radicals got over the shock, Comrade Chiang Ching just about ODed on her own bile. But the PM shut her up, and fast. He threw the Little Red Book at her by quoting the Chairman on eternal vigilance. Then he said the economic ministry'd been alert enough to spot the plot and squash it, and if the radicals would spend less time playing power games and more time on matters of state, future conspiracies would be stopped even sooner.

"Things got dicey when the PM died, and then the Chairman bought the farm. I got to be straight with you—the Central Committee elected Comrade Hua to be our new chairman, but we were all expecting a radical *putsch* from Comrade Chiang Ching and her 'Gang of Four.' Last October, however, we arrested the bitch and instead of riots, the people celebrated. So the good guys won. Now we'd like to show our appreciation for your help... Martha, would you give me one of those tapes?"

She picked the one that happened to be atop the stack and passed it across the table. Kuo took it over to a Betamax deck, broke the seal on the cassette, and popped it in. Then he depressed the "Play" button.

Long shot: Velveeta in a daze. Now several blinks and he was lurching like a robot to a figure seated in a high-backed armchair. Velveeta drawing himself to attention and performing three stiff kowtows to the Chairman...

Pan: Velveeta making his way across the room to a platform...

Long shot: One last plaintive look at the camera, and Velveeta was fumbling with his belt...

Medium shot: Velveeta supine on a metal table, a long acupuncture needle protruding from two inches below his navel...

Close-up: Light glinting off the scalpel pricking the operative area...

Pan and zoom: The Chairman's moist lips coming together and curling slightly upward at the corners...

Medium shot: The surgical team stepping from the platform...

Tracking shot: Velveeta wobbling toward a nearby desk on which were a sheet of paper, an envelope, a pen, and a red ink pad...

Close-up: An envelope, back and front...

Pan: Past Velveeta, staring glassily into the camera...

Zoom: Drool sliding down the Chairman's meaty chin...

To black.

It was several minutes before we could look at each other.

Finally Kuo broke the silence: "We started out too late to nail Ouzo, but two of the other guys are sitting in those cassettes over there. Want them racked up?"

Martha and I both quickly shook our heads. Then I said, "Which two?"

"Bourbon, who we got to five months before he croaked, and Sake."

"What about Caviar?"

Kuo studied his fingernails, made a wry face and snorted. "His confession's phony."

"What!"

"Yup. Oh, he wrote it, all right. But according to that confession, Caviar had his old man poisoned in Rabat on August sixteenth, 1945. The first Shahinshah actually died in Johannesburg—on July twenty-third that year."

"You mean it wasn't patricide?"

Kuo shook his head. "Nope, just a bluff to get himself into the Cocktail Party. Caviar figured no one would ever check it out, and he was right. When the son of a bitch told us to take our tape rig and stuff it, he was laughing his ass off."

"Jesus. No wonder he didn't care if I published his letter." I looked down at the three bulky manila envelopes Kuo was picking up. He slid one over. I unwound its string clasp. The first sheet inside was a report, written in Chinese by a high CCP cabinet official; attached to it was a translation describing in English the operation on Velveeta we'd just witnessed on videotape. Next was the envelope Velveeta'd held up to the camera. On the back was his signature and, across the sealed flap like a poor man's *t'u chang*, his thumbprint in red ink; on the front, his signature again, beneath a brief passage typed in English which began: "For behaving dishonorably toward all the comrades of the People's Republic of China..." Finally there was a three-paragraph carbon of the letter within this envelope. In the first paragraph Velveeta re-confessed his misprision of felony; in the second he admitted joining four other men to form "a company named Entrepays, for the purpose of criminally exploiting China's oil"; in the third he acknowledged having "discussed my participation in Entrepays with Mr. Raymond T. Huang at Key Biscayne, Florida, on April 14, 1974."

Kuo cleared his throat. "Hard enough evidence, Ray?"

I nodded.

On March 8, 1977, the day broke sunny on the westernmost coast of Asia Minor.

From New York Martha, using false papers courtesy the People's Republic, had flown east. I'd stashed the three confessions, still under seal, and the three videotape cassettes, two still unseen, and then picked up my files and as Tetsuo R. Sasaki boarded a plane headed west. It had taken us two weeks to rendezvous in Istanbul; then a short ferry ride up the strait and we were at a town on the Asia Minor coast named Vanikoy. The cobblestone road starting at the café next to the ferry slip led uphill to a group of old wooden houses. One was a rambling grey structure with a dazzling view of the Bosporus. Yes, it could be rented; we took it.

Now Martha was curled in another wing of the house, rereading *Jane Eyre*. In my den the new typewriter sat on the desk, the translation of the Peking report spread beside it. Bourbon and Ouzo were dead, Sake and Velveeta disgraced, Caviar untouchable; why were we here, hunkering down for a hard and lonely year? I looked up at the slip taped above the desk:

You will have to live with these memories and make them
Into something new. Only by acceptance
Of the past will you alter its meaning.
—T. S. Eliot, *The Cocktail Party*

I studied the boats plying the Bosporus for several minutes. Then I twirled two sheets of paper into the Olivetti and began to tap the keys:

PORT ARTHUR CHICKEN/Introduction
I know that on November 26, 1975, a Red Flag limousine left a government building off T'ien An Men Square in Peking and sped through the morning chill to Capital Airport...

RAYMOND HUANG

Vanikoy, Turkey
May 1978

High Powered Adventure Charged with Relentless Suspense... Impossible to Put Down!

__THE ALEPH SOLUTION Sandor Frankel and Webster Mews	04654-0/$2.50
__JERICHO MAN John Lutz	05003-3/$2.50
__LAZARUS MAN John Lutz	04544-7/$2.50
__THE MAN WHO LOST THE WAR W. T. Tyler	04852-7/$2.95
__THE MASTER SNIPER Stephen Hunter	04800-4/$2.95
__MAYDAY Thomas Block	04729-6/$2.95
__SUSPICIONS Barbara Betcherman	04839-X/$2.75

Available at your local bookstore or return this form to:

Berkley Book Mailing Service
P.O. Box 690
Rockville Centre, NY 11570

Please send me the above titles. I am enclosing $_____
(Please add 50¢ per copy to cover postage and handling). Send check or money order—no cash or C.O.D.'s. Allow six weeks for delivery.

NAME_____
ADDRESS_____
CITY_____STATE/ZIP_____

The ultimate masterpiece of modern horror

Shadowland

Peter Straub

*author of the 2-million copy bestseller **GHOST STORY***

Come to SHADOWLAND. Discover the chilling magic of a world where every truth is a dream... and every dream is a nightmare. SHADOWLAND—the book that millions of *Ghost Story* fans have been waiting for. SHADOWLAND—you have been there if you have *ever* been afraid...

"I loved it...there is an even deeper satisfaction in SHADOWLAND for me than there was in GHOST STORY ...creepy from page one!"

—Stephen King

Coming in November from Berkley Books!

05056-4/$3.50